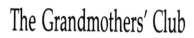

The Grandmothers' Club

Also by Alan Cheuse
Candace & Other Stories
The Bohemians

THE GRANDMOTHERS' CLUB

ALAN CHEUSE

GIBBS M. SMITH, INC.
PEREGRINE SMITH BOOKS
SALT LAKE CITY

This is a Peregrine Smith Book
Copyright © 1986 by Gibbs M. Smith, Inc.

No part of this book may be reproduced
without written permission from the
publisher, with the exception of short
passages for review purposes

Published by Gibbs M. Smith, Inc.
P.O. Box 667, Layton, Utah 84041

Cover illustration by Armen Kojoyian
Cover and book design by J. Scott Knudsen

The author would like to acknowledge
Gregory Rabassa from whose translation of
M. A. Asturias's *The Green Pope* (New York:
Delacorte, 1971) he has adapted several
paragraphs on p. 297 and 298

All characters in this work are purely
fictional and any resemblance to any
person, living or dead is purely coincidental

Grateful acknowledgment is made for
permission to use lyrics from the song
"Mood Indigo" by Duke Ellington, Irving
Mills, and Albany Bigard, copyright © 1931
by Mills Music, Inc. Copyright renewed. All
rights reserved.

Acknowledgment is also made of the usage
of lyrics from "Light My Fire" by The Doors,
words and music copyright © by The
Doors, copyright © Nipper Music ASCAP.

Printed and bound in the United States
of America

90 89 88 87 86   5 4 3 2

FIRST EDITION

**Library of Congress Cataloging-in-
Publication Data**
Cheuse, Alan.
     The grandmother's club.
     I. Title.
PS3553.H436G7 1986 813'.54 86-9522
ISBN 0-87905-253-8

To T.D.C.,
and the memory of her mother,
and her mother's mother,
and for P.Z., with thanks

In your name, Mothers, who in boundless space
dwell enthroned in eternal solitude,
though still gregarious. About your heads there hover,
moving but lifeless, images of living things.
Resplendent glories, now no more,
are stirring still, for they would be eternal.
And you, in your omnipotence, assign them
to light's pavilion or the vault of darkness.

Goethe
Faust, Act I

Some of the old people of the Yucatan say that they have heard from
their ancestors that this land was occupied by a race of people who came
from the East and whom God had delivered by opening twelve paths
through the sea. If this were true, it necessarily follows that all the
inhabitants of the Indies are descendants of the Jews; since having once
passed the Straits of Magellan, they must have extended over more than
two thousand leagues of land which Spain now governs.

Fr. Diego de Landa
Relación de las Cosas de Yucatan

Here is the root of the former word.
Here is Quiche by name.
Here we shall write then,
Here we shall set out the former words,
The beginnings
And the taproots
Of everything . . .
The decipherment,
The clarification,
And the explanation
Of the mysteries . . .
We shall save it
Because there is no longer
A sight of the book of Counsel,
A sight of the bright things to come
From beside the sea,
The description of our shadows,
A sight of the bright life . . .

Popol-Vuh

The Grandmothers' Club

Book One
Afternoon

I t's an old story, darling, so don't get offended.
I'm not offended.
I'm sorry I brought it up.
Don't be so sorry. Mrs. Bloch touched a hand to her auburn hair, a surface so carefully crafted that it appeared to be an object made of stone or dark-stained wood that had been constructed elsewhere and then placed atop her wrinkled forehead.

Now I've hurt your feelings. I'm sorry, Mrs. Bloch.

Why should it hurt my feelings to hear someone's name mentioned, Mrs. Pinsker? I want the best for my son and if that arrangement makes him happy . . .

Mrs. Bloch, I was only bringing up the example of . . .

Of what?

Of a mother-child . . .

A mother-child what?

Mrs. Pinsker looked up from her coffee cup and gave a sign with her large, red-rimmed eyes that it was not safe to speak.

Girls? said the same black, gray-haired stick-thin waitress in white uniform who attended them each week.

It's the unofficial member.

The *ex-ofisho*, Mrs. Bloch said, trying to remember a phrase that she had heard her son Manny use when speaking about temple activities.

More coffee? the thin black woman asked, her voice as much of a mask as her face.

Girls, she calls us, Mrs. Pinsker said. If she wasn't as old as us I'd get insulted.

How are you, sweetheart? Mrs. Bloch asked.

Same. Same as ever. More coffee then?

And a doughnut, Mrs. Bloch said. Don't you think I ought to have a doughnut?

I vote you should have a doughnut, Mrs. Pinsker said.

Something sweet always cheers me up, Mrs. Bloch said.

I didn't know you were depressed, Mrs. Pinsker said.

You think talking about my son's mistress makes me happy?

You said if it made *him* happy you didn't care.

I don't, Mrs. Bloch said.

Girls? the waitress insisted.

Sweetheart, a doughnut please, Mrs. Bloch said. A doughnut to make me happy.

He doesn't make you happy?

Not when he's sick.

You said Doctor Mickey said he wasn't sick.

Not physically sick. He's confused, darling. Why else would he fall? Why else would the world go dark for him? Dark, he said it all went dark. And on top of this he has a mistress, a married woman . . .

A widow. So she's excused.

So she's excused. But he's got her. But if you think of it . . .

Think what?

It's almost part of his job.

Florette?

Because of her . . . you know?

Because of the Holocaust, you mean?

That's what I mean. Because she was in the concentrating camp, because she came to him for help.

You know all this?

I know more than you think, more than Manny thinks, and what I don't know I imagine.

You make it up?

What I make up usually turns out to be very close to what's true. Very close.

Then make up, make up, said Mrs. Pinsker. He's my rabbi, so I'm entitled to know what's going on with him.

You're entitled. For you, darling, I'll talk, Mrs. Bloch said. For the leading lady in the grandmothers' club, for one of the founding members that you are, I'll talk. Talking will help me, I'm sure. Talk, Doctor Mickey always says, talk away.

What a darling man, Mrs. Pinsker said.

His mother Mrs. Stellberg is very proud of him, and so would his grandmother be proud if she was still alive.

Do you know if she's alive?

How could she be alive? Is your mother at our age? Is mine? But I'll ask Sally. I'll ask him. I'll get personal from my side of it for a change. He knows more about me, about my family, than anyone else—because I talk to him—but I don't want nobody else should know.

But you're telling me now.

Grandmother to grandmother I'm telling you.

You're upset. I can tell.

How can you tell?

Your hand trembles when you lift your cup. Ten times a minute you wipe your lipstick with a napkin. Normally you don't do this.

So I'm upset.

So you'll talk.

I'll talk.

Your food, said the waitress from over Mrs. Bloch's shoulder, and with a birdlike quickness set the dish on the table and stepped away.

Who does she think she is? A princess? If I was a waitress I would be more polite.

Maybe she is better than us, Mrs. Bloch said, her viscous upper lip curling back in a smile.

Don't get funny. So tell me the story.

Mrs. Bloch held the pastry up in front of her.

What are you doing? You're studying it?

I'm thinking.

Thinking what?

You were right. It's an old story and I'm remembering it, darling. You want to hear it from the beginning?

From the beginning? From the creation of Adam and Eve? No, thank you, that part I've heard.

No, from Minnie and Jacob, that's what I was thinking. From the creation of Minnie and Jacob.

For that you need to study the doughnut? Better you should get one with a hole in it, so you can look through the hole to the other side.

The other side? I'm seeing the other side without closing my
eyes, without a magical hole in a magical doughnut. Mrs. Bloch
took a bite out of the pastry. She chewed for a moment, and then
said through a mouthful of dough, Don't look so impatient, it's
a long story, I need my nourishment.

I said old story, not long.

Well, what's old? what's long? as long as it's good.

Well, said Mrs. Pinsker, how could it not be good? You're
sitting here, you lived, that's it. A happy ending. I can tell.
You're smiling again, darling.

And I shouldn't smile when I'm thinking about the
beginning?

But so tell me what was going on with his accident.

With Manny's fall?

No, with the President of the United States. Of course, with
your Manny.

With my Manny it was an accident.

I was there, I could see, a man trips, a man stumbles, but
I mean he's all right? He's not sick? A man just doesn't all of a
sudden tumble down after all these years for no reason. Look,
everybody has reasons but not everybody falls down. So tell me
his reasons? What's the matter? he's got a disease? he's got
troubles with you know who?

I told you, nothing. He's got nothing. Nothing is wrong. He
told me earlier in the day he had a little headache.

Headache? It's a tumor, maybe?

Please darling, I told you, it was nothing. He had a little
headache. In the hospital, after his accident, lying there, he told
me everything. Ever since his father died we've been very close,
you know . . .

I've heard, I've noticed.

So you've noticed. So I've been like his *concudante*, do you
know what I mean?

Do I know? Do I know? Don't I have children of my own?
Don't I hear all the stories, all the troubles?

If they talk to you, you're lucky. If they don't, you're happy.

I couldn't agree more, Mrs. Bloch. So tell.

What what?

You're telling me about his accident.

His fall.

His fall. And later his summer and his winter and his spring? Keep talking.

Very funny. Summer, winter, whatever. I'm telling you he had his summer later in life than most boys, with this business he and the brother-in-law are making. And times were rough for him when he was a little boy, when my Jacob passed away . . .

That's the beginning you were talking about?

That's it.

So you'll tell me that later. But now I want to hear the middle. The part I saw. Because even though I saw it I didn't know what I was seeing.

Typical.

What do you mean, darling, typical? You think I'm blind or something? I was there, I was looking down from the upstairs . . .

From up there we get a good view, don't we, Mrs. Pinsker?

The grandmothers see everything, sure. So I was up in the balcony watching, like in the old days, when I'm up there watching the stage show at the Roxy . . .

Looking down at the stage show, of course. So you don't think I remember those things? And let me tell you what I remember . . .

I'll let you.

Thank you, darling. And I'll tell you. What I remember is looking down from the balcony of the old *shul* on my street in the city, peeking from behind the curtain they put up around us to keep the ladies from looking down.

They put up a curtain?

And in some places I hear, of course I never saw, a wall. And you could make eye holes and peep through. They had their old ways. And some were not so bad and some were not so good. I'm telling you, my Manny banged his nose against it when it came time to go to school. But that comes later and you were asking about his accident.

His fall.

It was an accident.

But it comes first, not later.

First I'm telling, but in his life it comes later.

Don't confuse me, just tell me.

I'm telling you. Just the way he told me.

His *concudante*. Like the confessor.

You mean like the Catholics? God forbid.

If He forbid we wouldn't have the Catholics.

Don't joke when I'm thinking about this.

Thinking to you is like praying? I shouldn't disturb you?

I'm just trying to get it right.

Look, darling, sip a coffee, calm a little, and tell me what it was.

When he fell? It was awful. Remember, it was the High Holidays, Yom Kippur, the very last day of the ten days of penitence, when it comes time for God to decide which book he wants to write us in for the coming year—the *Book of Life* or the *Book of Death*.

Stop with the Sunday school lecture already and tell me what happened.

So I'll tell. So Manny woke up that morning, he told me later in the hospital . . .

He tells you everything?

Now your turn to stop.

So I'll stop.

You better stop or I can't tell you.

So go on.

I'll go on. Please. Let me clear my throat. Aherm. Aherm.

So he woke up that morning feeling, he said, very very strange, not in the usual way as though something is going to happen—because you know when you feel that way it never does—but strange because he had the idea that something already had taken place, that something in his life had been decided for him. Do you know? As though God had written in the book already, and he didn't know which one. Except he didn't think of it that way except to explain it to himself, the feeling that something had already gone past him. Or something had been lost.

He went looking, first for his good soft-soled shoes because this was another day of standing all morning and afternoon and he wanted to be as comfortable as he could make himself, and these appeared to be misplaced. He went up to the top of the house, and down to the study, his library, even to the basement, and he couldn't find the shoes. It got so he was cursing, because who wants to stand all day in uncomfortable shoes on top of

everything else—the fasting, the hard work of leading the service, the looking down into the faces of the congregation and
feeling his fatigue rise in him like water crawling up to the brim
of a glass—and then of course he felt terrible because he was
cursing over nothing but a stupid pair of shoes. When he had
so many other more important things to worry about, I don't
have to tell you, he was worrying about *her*, about both *hers*, the
mother with the problem in the store—you didn't hear? I can tell
by your look you never heard, well, so later I'll tell you, but not
now because I don't want to be distracted—and the other *her*,
the daughter with the problem with the boy—both *hers*, *her* and
her. To think, women give him such trouble when all his life
while growing he didn't have no problem with me . . . don't
laugh, don't laugh or I'll close my mouth!

So . . . down the stairs, up—he can't find the shoes, and
then he feels a headache coming on, from the fasting probably,
he figures, an ache so big it's like one of those dark summer
thunderstorm clouds you see blowing in over the beach at Bradley, and he shudders when he thinks what he's doing with his
life, with his congregation, with his business, because after all
what is he? Can he stand every weekend in front of the temple
crowd and make his sermons and still go in twice a week to the
city to work with his brother-in-law in the holding company?
He's wandering around the house, thinking to himself, I've lost
more than my shoes . . . and if I find them how do I find what
else I've lost?

He's in the kitchen, he's looking behind the desk in his
study, he's on his hands and knees snooping behind the couch
and you know what he finds there? He finds a pair of panties
the size the same as *both* hers wear because the daughter has
now reached the point where she has the same hips as the
mother, *and* the same hair, as you know, but God forbid the
same disposition, there it's maybe too early to tell, and so anyway, he says to himself, on top of everything else, What's this?
what's this? and he stuffs the panties in his pocket and keeps
on looking, the panties in the pocket along with a piece of glass
he carries with him all the time, a souvenir, a piece of glass
shaped like a Jewish star, and about this don't ask a question,
because I'll explain in a while if you want me to, or maybe even

if you don't, because it's a story from the beginning, and this
I'm telling you now comes from the middle—and God forbid we
should see the end.

So he's on his hands and knees and feeling the first
drummings of the headache and the first winds of the dizziness,
and then he's up again, shouting for Maby, and where is she?
Who knows, taking a bath? She takes so many baths you'd think
she got herself dirty like a baby when the truth is ever since the
business in the store—and I'll tell you, I'll tell you—she doesn't
go out at all except when he says you absolutely have to, only
to services, not even to temple affairs—so she doesn't answer,
and he calls for Sarah. *Sarah!* he calls, and where is she? Outside on the back porch playing, would you believe this? her guitar! and singing, on the Holidays! He can't believe this either!

>   *Sometimes I feel,*
>   *Like a motherless child,*

Not a bad voice, and on other days he might have stopped
and thought to himself, My daughter, with such a good voice,
but the song, *oi,* the song it gives me heartache.

>   *Sometimes I feel*
>   *Like a motherless child*

A nice song, an American song, because in the old country
we had our mamas, we knew our mamas, and if we sang we
sang to celebrate our mamas, not to tell the world we got lost,
except, of course, for later, for the ones that got lost in the
Holocaust, but that's another story. Here she is, singing the song
of the lost child, she's strumming good, she's singing strong and
loud, and he goes charging off after her, not knowing exactly
where she is, following the music, the song.

>   *Sometimes I feel*
>   *Like I'm almost gone*

How can you do it to me on a day like this? he growls at her
when he bursts out onto the back porch.

I'm playing my guitar, she says. I'm not out in public. I'm
on the porch.

The porch is public, he says, trying his best to keep his voice down. The porch is outside. The porch is the world. Go inside, young lady, and get ready for temple.

I *am* ready, she says, poking a finger at one of the guitar strings.

Are you? And he yanks out of his pocket the panties he found under the sofa and says, Put these on if you're so ready! And throws them in her face.

That's . . . disgusting! she says to him, her face covered over as if with a veil. And she snatches them up in her hand and flings them over her shoulder into the garden.

Pick those up, her father says.

Pick them up yourself, *Rabbi*, she says. And she plucks a loud *chirrum* with both fingers on the guitar.

Maybe if she had only been insolent, just mean, nothing else would have happened. But she added that title, *Rabbi*, and it did something to his temper, to his mind. Fathers and daughters! what a story, an old story, *ach*, and a bitter one, bitter, bitter, bitter. So. She called him what he was, and that changed it all. Why? Even now I'm still finding out, after he's telling me all, after *she's* talking to me, this poor old grandma with the bad eyes, and they're talking to her, but to each other do you think they're talking? You can imagine. Look! He reaches over, and she cringes, like a dog fearing a smack, but he doesn't want her, no, he grabs the guitar and even as she's screaming, No! No! up he hurls it, and it sails end over end, making a strange shape in the air as it spins, and it comes down, like a filmy piece of silk or nylon but also like the thing of wood it is and *smash!* onto the walk beyond the porch steps, and it splinters, breaks into pieces.

What a way to start the holiest of holy days! Everyone already feeling tired and irritated, because of the fasting, because of the heat—always in Jersey it's hot like summer in India when the High Holidays come around—and his breath stinks to his own nose, and now he's got this to contend with! As if everything else weren't enough, as if the life he's made hasn't been enough, as if he doesn't want to pick it up like that guitar and throw it into the air without caring where it comes down in pieces! He can barely stand up to it, and he says, holding down his voice as best he can, but you can hear it trembling—I heard

it trembling because this was when I opened the door and came
onto the back porch . . .

Little girl, he is saying, little girl . . .

And you can imagine what this did to *her*, this girl growing
up so quick, her life like a merry-go-round ride, growing around
in circles at the moment but moving, quickly, quickly—don't I
know what it was like? But she had stung him with that word,
the piercing word, *Rabbi*, though how could she know? Maybe
her instincts told her? Was that how she stabbed right through?
He was thinking about his life, on this holy day, on the day
when God's moving finger or pen or whatever He writes with,
maybe even now a typewriter or a computer, when He—or She
or whatever God is these days—marks in the *Book of Life* or the
Book of Death, he's been thinking, wondering, pondering, sweating in his brain, milking his thoughts, should I go on with this
farce—wait, all this will come to you—should I go on with it? or
should I get out? All week long, all day long the day before, and
all night lying there in a sweat, alongside his sleeping beauty,
the woman dead to the world from all the pills she takes so she
can sleep, should I? shouldn't I? What could the daughter know
of the father? She couldn't know, the children never know until
it's too late. Even now do you think he knows about me? his own
mother? and did I know mine?

I'm telling you, the whole world works backward in reverse,
that the parents should know of the children all the time and
be unable to do anything and the children know only when it's
too late! And even more than the parents of the children it is the
grandmother who knows triple trouble, because she knows the
children and the children's children, and thinking about it,
talking about it, gives me such a headache I'm telling you that
if there is a God in heaven—and don't be shocked that I say
something like this, because today you hear a lot worse from
smarter people than me—but if there is, He must have the biggest headache of all from knowing everything backward, forward, past and future, but then if He's so great I suppose He
can make for Himself the biggest headache powder, no? Poor
little girl turning big girl who I rocked in my arms when she was
a newborn, how could she know what she had said?

You are going to pay for this, my Manny shouts, you are
going to *pay!*

And he turns and goes back inside, walking around me to do it, like I'm a stranger, excuse me, he says, and goes upstairs to his dressing room—because by this time it's separate bedrooms for them, which, Sarah told me, is very troubling to her for not so obvious reasons, and he reaches into his pocket and takes out his favorite piece of glass and sees his finger all slashed from it, and he goes into the bathroom to wash off the blood and put on a little bandage, and there he finds *her*, Maby, throwing up into the bowl. I'm telling you, it's early morning and this man has already had quite a day.

He didn't say: You're not sick, are you? poor dear.

He said: You're sick again and today of all days?

It's the heat, she said, in that voice like a sound trying to shrink back into itself, the voice that came out to shrink only when she was in one of her states. I was taking a bath and the heat got to me, Manny. It made me ill. And this was a big difference between them, my son and my daughter-in-law, him saying sick and her saying ill, a difference in upbringing, her from the fancy Cincinnati school, him from where we came from, from Second Street, from the old rabbi's school, some finishing school that was! When I first saw her, with her red hair, the pale pink face, I asked myself, this is one of us? But then I learned . . . too much I learned, if you ask me.

You know what just got to me? he said to her. And he launches into a tirade against the daughter, telling about the guitar, about her curse—he took it that way—upon him.

I don't want to hear! Maby says, spitting up more into the bowl. Just leave me out of it, do you hear? Leave me out.

She's your daughter as much as mine, he says, and she's insolent and cruel and . . .

She spits up more into the bowl.

And with his bleeding finger, he grabs from the medicine chest a little bandage, and he walks out into his own room.

This was how he started that day. If you think it got any better, guess again, darling, guess again. You were there. You saw the moment. And there were other moments behind the big moment, I'll tell you. Here is what it was. First he's dressed quicker than you can say Jack Ribicoff and then he's standing at the front door calling back to me.

Ma, he's calling, Mama, tell Maby to get after Sarah to get ready because I'm on my way.

I had been standing at the sink, feeling a little bit lost since on a fast day I couldn't cook, I couldn't eat, I couldn't help nobody else do neither.

Don't put it all on the mama, I called to him. The mama has her troubles, too, you know.

He walked back up to the entrance to the kitchen and stuck in his head, just for a change like he was my little boy again.

I wasn't yelling at you, Mama, just calling.

And at the others you were yelling, not calling?

You heard what she said, you heard the way that she said it.

Which one?

Sarah.

Oh, I said to him, you think this is a special event? You should hear how she talks to her grandmother.

She's sarcastic with you, too? he says. Oh, Mama. And he throws up his hands, a man with three women who he understands as much as he understands about cars. Business he understands, the accounting, deals, what he calls them, that he understands, and it goes without saying he understands the business of being a rabbi. Who else could have led the temple through all these years since he arrived in a time when congregations—look, I know, I have ears, I have eyes—where they change rabbis the way countries down south of the border change presidents? My Manny, that's who! So what if he don't understand the women he lives with? I'm helping him, I'm trying. He knows that. He comes to me, he always has. Like this. Poking his head in through the entrance to the kitchen when already he's almost late for the start of services on the biggest holiday of the year.

Look, I say, don't worry, I'll talk to her. I'll help.

You always do, Ma, he says, and the good boy comes and gives me a hug, and a kiss on my cheek, and even a wink he manages, and off he goes to the temple, walking by himself, and I stand at the door watching him walk away, looking at the rabbi, walking, thinking, getting himself ready for the big morning and the bigger afternoon. To see him people would say, There he goes, our faithful rabbi, pondering the day.

And he was. Pondering. Later he told me. Worrying about his life. His future. What it would do for him. For the family. Past cars he walked, past street corners, streetlamps, red lights, green lights. And before he even got to the temple he had decided that he was no good for them anymore, that he had to get out—isn't that terrible? such a good rabbi, such a good leader, such a fine advisor to men, women, children, even on the building committee he's wonderful I hear from reports—and either that or he has to give up the business arrangements with *her* brother in the city because not that the time is too demanding, because no, he goes in there only once, twice a week, just like if he was going to school there as some rabbis do, or to teach, but no, it's not the time, but the feeling he has of living like two people when he is only one man, living mostly for others, living for me, living for her, for the wife, the daughter, living—this he told me and you see how much he sees—living for my poor, dear, all-these-years-departed Jacob.

You know, you have one of those situations, your late husband, years it's been, yes? or if not him, someone? Living for the dead, I told him. How can you live for the dead? And he said to me, Mama, this is what I told myself, because I have always tried to be the best advisor to myself, to counsel myself—notice how dignified he talks even to his own mother?—even as I would have myself counsel others. And he said this to himself as he was walking to temple, he said, Manny, you fool, you stupid holy fool, for whom are you living? For whom do you put in these long hours, this double life? If not for yourself, then for whom? Did he want to live a life dedicated to study? Or did he want to live a life in which he could use the talents he inherited from his father? Which did he want? One? Or the other? He heard a voice in his head telling him. Both! Choose both! Take both! You can have both! You've been living now for the last few years with both! And why should one cancel out the other? Is there a law saying somewhere a rabbi can't know the world and the world can't know a rabbi. Walking, walking, walking, thinking. Past hedges, cars, houses, now a little grocery just opened.

Walking, thinking. Stomach growling, churning. A fast day. And a day for thinking, walking. All too quickly the time passes. He looks up out of his trance, sees a familiar house, a familiar arrangement of tree and bush. And up there in our New Jersey sky, a cloud, and way high up, a bird, swooping. And he knows he will become again a public person, talking and thinking out loud, doing a job, making a performance. Was that how he saw it? Was that what he wanted? Playacting? Making a public display, a mockery even of his inner thoughts? Unable to say all that he felt about what he was doing, what he read about, thought about? Walking, thinking, stomach growling. Feeling a little tingling on the soles of his feet. A big day ahead, standing, standing all day.

And what about his other life? Across the river. The company. A holding corporation, he called it to me. The father-in-law died, left it to the brother, who was absent and then appeared as if by magic, and asked Manny to come in with him, advise him. The brother was a sailor, a shipper-outer, not a man of the city. He had left home early, run away, never really knew the little sister, feuded with the father—and when you know why, you'll know a good reason, and of course I'll tell you, but wait, later, first, this—the brother worked on the ships because the father had been a boat man, first a man who owned boats on a river and then bought containers for shipping—and what?

You're smiling, you're smiling, because you think the old grandmother can't know from the business? So I don't know much. But you think a rabbi can't know? Old dogs, new tricks, you're thinking? New dogs, old tricks, is more like it, but listen—so—walking, thinking, remembering, past hedge, car, tree, driveway, corner, and now the cloud has gone and up above it is a beautiful high holy day blue sky, as if God in heaven had blessed New Jersey with something, the gift of never having had a rainy Yom Kippur ever in a lifetime as far as I remember, and he's thinking, Sporen—this was her father, the man who, well, later I'll explain because first let's concentrate on the walking, thinking—Sporen dying, the prodigal son working on one of his ships hearing the news, returning to the country, feeling helpless, hopeless, calling the sister, the brother-in-law after not having seen them in a long, long time, that too, you'll hear about, just wait, so thinking Sporen, and the business, and what it meant to the sister, wife, to the daughter, then a little little girl, and what it meant to him working in both professions, but could he handle both?

He's thinking the kind of thinking that was right for the holiday, a holiday of thinking, of pondering, of wondering about the writing of God, which book, which book? And wondering if one way, rabbi or holding company man, was life, was death, or could he have both? past hedge, path, bush, tree, stone— thinking one was good for the other, the deep inner life, the thought, the pondering, the study, the wondering also good for the business life, because who else in business could look at things from such a point of view as his? And the sharp, keen, razor-edge practice helped him at the head of the congregation, because he did not lead them astray, he led them straight to where they needed to go, no nonsense, they wanted a building fund, he showed them how, they wanted fund raising, an aging program, that too he showed them, showed them the other side of things, the way he showed the box and bag people, the bottle cap people in the city how they should feel better about decisions about workers, about selling, and while he's walking, thinking, he's thinking how he's been living two lives at once, and not living for himself, and the quarrel with the daughter, the wife sick again (and not just in body, he's worrying,' because he knows her face, the look, the special glow like cinders from a bonfire in the eyes, knows that it's not just in body). This at home makes him worry to the point where he feels his heart beating like a garbage can lid some child in the alley is smacking with a stick, and his legs get cold, and now he stops, takes out his handkerchief and dabbles at his brow, runs a hand through his beautiful white hair and the one dark streak that flows through it, and he looks up and he sees a car passing and inside he sees *her*, and he knows in his bones that his life is not his own.

Which her? *She?*

Yes, the *other* her, Florette.

But does he think, She's riding to the temple on the holiest of days? Breaking the most serious of rules for worship? And, worse, flaunting it in front of the eyes of all who will see her pass by in her car? Yes, he thinks this and then in a flash he forgives her, as he is sure anyone from the congregation who sees her will forgive her, because of all she has been through. Oh, yes, many men have forgiven women many things because they are who they are, and in this case he had only to think of her early life, in the camps, the number he sees on her upper wrist each time they meet. The number, the number, her souvenir of her childhood. Like the star was his remembrance, the number was hers. And so he will defend her should anyone dare to raise an eyebrow, let alone say a word. And so he will say to them as he has said before, each of us has a mark put upon us as an individual, and as a people we have had a mark put upon us together, and let him or her without a mark cast the first stone.

Her. It was *her.* *She.* It made him stumble—like he had caught his toe in a crack in the sidewalk and went pitching over, forward.

Whoa, Rabbi! Doctor Mickey, hurrying up, catches him by the arm. You tripped?

I tripped, Manny said, shaking off his surprise. I was looking at a car, Florette Glass was driving and I lost all of my balance. A funny thing. Looking up, I wasn't looking down. But now I'm okay.

One person in the congregation rides to services on Yom Kippur, and the rabbi is so sensitive he nearly loses control?

He smiled at Manny from behind his large owl-eye glasses. A few years older than his rabbi, he gave the impression that he was always willing to hear advice from the younger man.

She's the sensitive one, Manny said. Her nightmares—has she ever told you about her nightmares?

No, but I can imagine, Doctor Mickey said. They started to walk now again in the direction of the temple. Or, Doctor Mickey said, I don't want to imagine.

She comes in to talk now and then, said Manny, realizing he had said too much already about her. But he could not help himself, explaining more and more as they continued on their way.

Sam, her husband, he said, he always helped her, but now she's alone.

And you and Florette? No, he didn't ask that. Manny was already hearing him ask that, but Doctor Mickey didn't say a word. He made noises, ahem, ahum, the kind of sounds he makes when you're in his office telling him about this pain, that. He's a good listener, that Mickey, like his mother, Mrs. Stellberg. You have to be a good listener to be a good doctor—and to be a good grandmother, too, I think. Because how else could I be telling you all this if I didn't listen?

What he said was: How's Maby doing? Not *feeling.* He said *doing.* If he had said *feeling,* then Manny wouldn't have had to worry about the question. *Feeling*— just politeness. *Doing*—this meant that Doctor Mickey was aware of things, noticing things. But he had sent Maby to the doctor in New York precisely because he didn't want anyone in the congregation to talk. Was he worrying too much about what they would say? The rabbi's crazy wife? Why should he worry? He was thinking about giving it up, the congregation, so why should he care if they talked of his ailing wife? No, here is where the truth comes out. He could do that, and it might be what he wanted, but he would not have anyone else drive him to do it. Stubborn from the day he was born. Look at that star-shaped piece of glass, for instance. You know he's carried it around with him ever since the morning his father died? He never lets it out of his pocket, never for a minute! Stubborn!

Did I mention her to you? he asked Doctor Mickey. Wondering to himself, did I say things that I don't remember saying? Am I losing control? I stumbled—I looked up and stumbled—and what if I gave up the whole thing with my brother-in-law Mordecai? What if I say, Buy me out, and leave me out? A rabbi with a box factory? A rabbi with a bag factory? A rabbi who owns boats, barges, docks? Whoever heard? Sporen, he was thinking. The old man, his late father-in-law. What a legacy he had left him. His own father, my Jacob, left him nothing, if you don't count a piece of broken milk bottle shaped like a star. The man who had something to do with Jacob's accident, Sporen, he gives Manny everything, in life and after life.

So, Doctor Mickey says, You look confused, Manny. Do you feel all right yourself? Fasting doesn't agree with everybody, and sometimes even the rabbi can be affected, you know.

Doctor Mickey, Manny says, catching the man's arm as they cross the next street. I can fast and it's not a problem. My problem is, if you want to hear it, I need to slow down.

Doctor Mickey laughs. They can't talk anymore now because other people from the congregation are coming up to them, saying *Good Shabbos*, good morning and comparing their hungers. One feels like he could eat a horse, another a cow. Manny doesn't like to hear all this joking about something they're supposed to take seriously, if not respect, remembering his own daughter on the back porch playing her guitar. Respect—that's the problem. But the problem is doubled and tripled because he wonders, given his other life, if he can respect himself. What should I do? he wonders, ponders, walking, nodding, listening, talking a little as he makes his way up to the temple, walks to the side entrance, his office entrance. What am I going to do? he's asking himself, noticing almost without seeing the cars in the parking lot, one belonging to the janitor, another that's been there for days, and the Sunday school van, and behind them,

Florette's, and this suddenly annoys him, that she should flaunt her special relationship with him, it annoys him as he walks inside—and then at the sound of another engine, turns and sees Maby, Sarah, and me also driving up.

I told her it was crazy, that he would get not just annoyed but angry. But she wouldn't listen. If you'd like to walk, Mama, then you can. But we're driving, aren't we, Sarah? And the little one, now not so little, pinched her lips up the way she does in imitation—unconscious, I think—of her mother, and nodded her head. I'm certainly not getting left behind, I told them, because I want to be there when Manny sees you pull up in the car. He won't see, my daughter-in-law says. I hope he does, says the granddaughter. Sarah, her mother says, you needn't be mean. I wasn't being mean, just truthful, she says. I think we all ought to say that for the new year we should tell the truth. And you know the truth, sweetheart? I ask her. Mama, Maby says to me, I can't go otherwise. All right, darling, I say to soothe her, we'll do what we have to do. Better you should be there than not. The truth is, Sarah says, I ate breakfast and I think the holiday is dumb, and I don't want to go. Sarah, her mother says. Just her name, nothing else.

As we drove up, Manny averted his eyes. He ducked in the door and went downstairs to his office where he would change into his robes for the beginning of the last day of the ten days of penitence. He felt the headache from the fasting, from his empty stomach—that could do it, it had done it in the past. It stuck with him, his dilemma, boiling in his mind. What, what should he do? or, even, *could* he do about his life? Nearly two decades he had been here, it felt comfortable, like home, and he had the congregation loving him and admiring him and—better yet—needing him. But he couldn't squash the feeling that he wanted to break away—or else he might die. Unheard of—two decades in this place. The very hall he walked along wasn't even built when he first arrived . . . and there was no Sarah then, and no big congregation. He had helped them build and build it up, the building and the crowds. These he could hear, by the way, faintly, like from another room, where they were gathering in the auditorium above him, like the same storm clouds over the beach at Bradley he felt building in his skull.

Into the office he walks to change his clothes. *She*'s sitting there on his sofa, her face in her hands.

Florette, he says, what are you doing?

You mean what am I doing here?

Are you all right? he says.

No, I am not all right, she says. But I am never all right, as you know, so that doesn't matter. Her voice, with that slight Old World accent, the Austrian frosting on her American cake, always intrigued him because it reminded him, he confessed to me once, of mine, but it wasn't mine—not my thick country-flavored way of speaking, not at all, but just a foreignness, do you know? Something out of the ordinary. I need to speak with you, Manny, she says.

This morning? he says. On this day of all days? I have to go up . . .

Precisely because it is this particular morning I must speak to you, she says.

Speak then, he says, going to his closet to fetch his special robes for the service.

To your face, not your back, she says, and he turns to see her sitting up on the sofa, her face all red with the crying she has done.

Florette, I must get dressed. The cantor is waiting, the congregation is waiting.

They'll wait, they have patience. I, however, lost my patience last night, Manny. I had my dreams again. She runs her hand nervously across her tear-smeared face, a pale face, but her hair dark like no one else's in his life, so that she always appears to him more fragile than the rest of us, because our red complexions make us seem healthy, like survivors, when the joke is that she is the only actual survivor he knows.

I'm sorry, so sorry, he says, laying his robes aside on the sofa and sitting down next to her, rubbing her hands.

I can't go on, she says.

You must take the medication, Florette. Doctor Mickey knows what he's doing. You said it helped you before, so you must have stopped.

I did, she says . . . oh, you're so smart, aren't you?

But just how smart—he hears my voice in his head—we'll find out, won't we? Then he says out loud, It's not a matter of smart or dumb. It's what's necessary.

And you know that, of course.

In his head, running beneath the gathering storm clouds, words and sentences rush around like picnickers about to be scattered by the crash of thunder, the threat of the lightning bolts. Words, sentences—she's saying things Maby has also said over and over. Why doesn't she say something different? Why aren't any of them ever different? And with his mouth he says, I have never tried to put anything over on you, I have never pretended to know more than you, I have only tried to use the little I know and feel is right to help you through your troubles. And I would ask, Isn't that the truth? except you might take it as my way of trying to make you bend too much and admit that I know more than you. You, Florette, know more in your bones than anyone here—and he jerked his head up to the ceiling—more than I'll ever know in my life, no, let me change that, more than I hope ever to learn the way you learned it. I have some skills, I have managerial skills, but you have knowledge, which is a lot more than skill ever will be. I stand in awe of your knowledge, my darling, but you could pick up a few skills to manage what you know.

You don't think Mrs. Pinsker, maybe, a man and a woman talk in such a way, sitting there on the couch, he holding her hands, she touching her cheek to his shoulder, resting it there a minute, then looking up, around, and then back again goes the cheek? You don't think this is the way it happened? But so how can we know anything except what we're either there to see for ourselves or what somebody tells us? You think I'd make something like this up about my own son? No, he told me all, as I told you, and so maybe he changes a little bit here, a little there, but then who doesn't? We all change things even as they're happening to us, and the changes get changed, and here we are, and somebody is telling somebody else about us sitting here—the colored waitress, maybe, my Spanish driver—they could change things too, you know, and would we still be ourselves? I don't know, darling, and I don't want to know, because all I am doing is telling you and that's enough for me.

So I'm telling you more, and they're sitting on the couch. I wish, Florette is saying, I wish I could manage. And her eyes explode into tears, like water from the desert stone, wetting his cheek, his shoulder, his shirt front—and he reaches over and dabs at the water with his robes.

You will handle it, he says. You will. You are a . . .

Call me a survivor and I'll scream, Manny, she says.

Don't scream, please, he said. I'm getting a headache.

And he gives her a little pinch on her side.

Very funny, she says. Even on a day like this, with a person like me, you can make a joke?

That's how I get by sometimes, he says. But I want you to know I'm sorry the dreams came back, that you couldn't sleep. Me, you know, I sleep only on special occasions myself. Soundly that is.

I do know, she says. And she's calmed down all of a sudden, thinking, of course, of what he's referring to.

We should meet again soon, he says. After the holidays.

I want to if you do, she says.

Of course I do, he says. It's a . . . special thing for me, Florette. No matter what anyone else would say, it's something I must do. For myself, and, I hope, for you.

For me, of course. She's sitting up now, touching her cheek to his, quick once like a bird, and then she's holding out his robes for him, helping him to dress for the service.

Rabbi? Manny?

A knock at the door and a voice calling from the other side.

It's the cantor, he says to Florette. He's been wondering.

I'm coming now, Manny calls through the door. Go on up.

He waits a good minute or two, his eyes fixed on Florette, and then he reaches for her hand, and plants a kiss on her wrist just beside the faded numbers tattooed there so long ago, and then he opens the door and urges her to go up ahead of him.

Happy new year, he says.

Turning back she asks, You're joking again?

I'm not joking. I want us to have a good new year.

Then we'll have one, she says.

It's not always in our power, he says.

She blows him a little kiss. Save your wisdom for the people upstairs, she says, save your kisses for me.

And she dashes up the hall toward the stairs.

Picture now the rabbi and what do you see? He's as helpless as a little boy who's just gotten his first kiss and the little girl has run off into the park, and the glow of it is spreading, spreading across his face, down his neck, his chest, down below, and he's glowing all over and amazed, amazed, that anything could ever make him feel such a way. And he, this rabbi you're looking at, he's also a man of experience, a husband, a father, the counselor of I don't count anymore how many troubled people from the congregation—and if you don't think I don't hear sometimes about those, then how did I find out about Florette in the first place?—and as he walks slowly toward the other end of the hall from where Florette has now vanished, up the stairs, walking toward the door that will lead him up to the dais where he will conduct the holy day service, he is counseling himself, saying, Get a hold, Manny, take it easy, man, you may be feeling for a moment like a young boy, but young you are not, and if you make a fool of yourself what will that do to your power?

This, finally, was the thing lying most heavy on his mind: the power, the people he could move and the money he could make and the feelings he could drape over himself like the robe he wore as heavily as the thought of losing control. If that went, what could he do for me, the grandmother, the wife, the daughter, himself? Not to mention all the people upstairs who depended on him to remain nothing but what he was supposed to be. To them he was "the rabbi," not a man finally but a function. Did he breathe? laugh? eat? drink? sleep? Like a doctor or a lawyer he had to be there when they had certain kinds of trouble, certain varieties of happiness. But because they expected more from him, they allowed him—as a man—less.

But a man *needs*, he said to himself as he reached the top of the hidden staircase built into the wall behind the dais and pushed open the door that allowed him to step out onto the raised platform just to the left of the Ark of the Covenant. *He needs.* Not more than that, needs not x, y, z, wine, women, song, although of course he had on his mind women, mainly Florette, at this point, and me and Maby and Sarah. But he needs. He needs.

This was how he described it to me, his mental state, physical state, as he walked out into the bright lights. He had, all the time, one hand in his pocket fingering his famous star-shaped souvenir and the other adjusting the fringes on his heavy prayer shawl. One time, when he had a sense of humor, he said to me, You know, Mama, when I do the High Holiday service, I feel like a floor, and I asked, Why? and he said, Because the robes

hang as heavy on me as a rug. And he looks the cantor in the
eye, and gives a nod, and Manny moves to the front of the dais,
and suddenly looks down and sees me—no longer upstairs, of
course, for years no longer upstairs, not since the old days, the
old old days, now I'm down below in the front row, where there
is mixed seating, men and women, boys and girls—and I smile
at him a good smile, my best smile, and this, he told me later,
released something in him—some latch unlatched, some hook
unhooked, lock unlocked, lid pried open, trap sprung free—do
you see what I'm getting at? And he smiled back, and all at once
this feeling rose in his chest like steam from a hole in the ground,
like a volcano erupting, a pressure out of the middle of the earth,
although it was a lightness, a tugging, and even as he felt his
body carry him forward, he looked next to me and saw Maby,
and she turned quickly away, as though suddenly ashamed to
stare her own husband in the eye, and he noticed his daughter, the third of the redheads in a row, and you know what Sarah
does? Does she turn away? No, no, she wets her lips with her
tongue, and with her hands in front of her—the demon!—strums
for him an invisible guitar. This was at least what he *thought* he
saw, like a drowning man whose seemingly endless days suddenly come to an end with a running backward of the life like
on a movie projector in reverse, and at the last second, he caught
a flurry of motion toward the rear of the auditorium, and he saw
the doors open and in walked Mordecai, the brother-in-law, the
partner, bald man, thin, with a beak like a hunting bird, and this
may be—if you want to explain things in some way—why he
says he saw the birds at the top of the ceiling. Two birds, the
pigeon and the parrot.

Mrs. Pinsker, look up next time you're in temple. Look for
birds. Will you see birds? You'll see beautiful designs, stars, rec-
tangles, flowers, lines, columns, but birds? No. Not a pigeon,
let alone a parrot. A pigeon he could imagine, a window open,
in flies a bird. But a parrot? A jungle bird in Jersey? And in the
temple of all places? First thing he thought was, Sarah, that little wretch! Ah, his own daughter, at this high holy time, and
he thinks such a thing, but on this morning his anger etched the
word in for the breaking of the guitar.

Maybe he thought other things. He thought he thought
other things. But how much time did he have to think? He had
no time. Florette! He caught a glimpse of *her* standing up.

Standing out wasn't enough? He might have thought—if he
were thinking—she's got now to stand up? And if he were thinking he might have been thinking about—if the seconds he had
up there, like a kite on a string about to take off in a gust of thunderstorm, could have been stopped and cut into slices thin
enough to give him time to think—thinking about her numbers.
No? Why not? Now and then he thought about her numbers,
because he is a man who loves, among other things, *his* numbers, whether in his business or in his Torah . . .

But if one hand held a kite string and was tugging, pulling
him forward, the other hand held a scissors and quick like that
cut the tie, and my Manny pitches forward off the dais, landing at our feet like the kite crumpling, except there was a thud,
a skid and a thud, like a crate of vegetables or fruit that some
dockworker with muscles thick as rope drops on the ground.

What's all this? Mrs. Pinsker asked. Birds? Kites? Workers? Boxes
of fruit? He fell. I was there. I saw. He walked up to the edge
of the what-do-you-call-it and he tipped over. He wasn't drunk.
He didn't trip. But I didn't see no birds either, darling. No birds.

He saw the birds, Mrs. Pinsker.

Now I believe you that he needs a vacation.

Please don't joke. This is serious.

So who's joking? I'm telling you, I believe you. And I hope
he comes back refreshed. Doctor Mickey said he had no tumor?
No problem like that?

You think to see birds you have to have a tumor? He saw
birds when he was a boy and he didn't have a tumor then and
he doesn't have one now. In any case, he didn't tell Doctor
Mickey about the birds. He told me. His mother.

I'm glad he told somebody.

Don't be sarcastic. You think people don't have visions?
They have visions, let me tell you. His father had visions, and
so I'm not so surprised the son has them too.

A vision? He saw things? Or just he believed in them?
Which?

Both, maybe.

So tell me.

I'll tell you but in order to hear about Manny's first time
seeing things . . .

Oh, so now it's not a *vision* but just *seeing things*?
You know what I'm talking about, darling? My Jacob . . .
All right. So go 'head, talk . . . I'm all ears.
And all earrings, too. Where did you get those?
Oi, don't change the subject. Begin at the beginning. Your Jacob, you were going to tell me.
I'll tell you only because it's important for understanding where the birds came from.
That's not all. Look at your face. Such a smile. Such memories it gives you, no?
It's true. That I can't deny. It makes me feel warm . . . it makes me remember.
Remembering makes you remember?
And forgetting.
Forgetting could make you remember. It could make you want to remember.
But it can't bring these things back. Remembering brings them back.
So remember.
I'm remembering . . . I'm remembering . . .

The waving wands of wheat, the sun baking my Mama's babushka blacker than burnt toast, wavy lines of heat rising from her head, the fields, the sun. Holding Mama's hand walking through the wheat. I feel the smooth and gnarled stalks, the pricking of the stalks, the rough husks. And I am about to tell my Mama all about what I feel when along comes the large dark-bearded person of my papa. He takes me up in rough hands dried from the sun and around his mouth, like winds from a cave, come odors of bread, grass, beer, tobacco, fire, fish.
Fish?
Fish! Don't ask me how in the middle of the fields there's fish for us to eat but sometimes we ate it. Sea of wheat they swim in? Who knows? Papa he grew things, he traded them, so sometimes he must have traded wheat for fish. Or maybe we lived closer to the sea than I remember? Or is the fish part of the dreaming? I don't know. But the odor of it, and the taste stays with me. Except now that I remember it I can't say whether it was Mama was fish and Papa was bread or Mama was bread and Papa was fish, and tobacco, and the smell of wind on his clothes,

and the smell of horse on his rough hands. It all flows together in my nostrils. I remember my papa leaning down—he was a tall man, to me as tall as a tree—and Mama raising her cheek for him to kiss it.

Your Jacob, you were going to tell me.

I'm getting to that. Hold your horses, it's coming. I had begun to bleed. And they had me pledged to a chubby, pimply-faced rabbinical student who had come out to our settlement as part of a group of Torah-crazy boys who wanted to save all of us in the countryside from the forces of the Other Side. It made me sick just to think of him. His smell, it was like dead things we threw away behind our barn. But did that stop Mama? It wasn't her nose, or her life. She explained to me that it was because she felt so close to me that she wanted for me nothing but the best. Mama, I said to her, I want someone who smells like Papa, not a dead dog. Look, in those days, I was direct. I said what I thought. Who knows why? The wheat? The country makes you more direct. You feel things firsthand, you yank on the cow teat in the way you're taught and out comes the milk. No moping about, no big talk. That was what the city boy didn't like. To consider a subject was what he wanted to do. Consider the cow teat? I asked him the one and only time he ever got me alone. He raised a hand to slap me and I pushed him up against the side of a wagon. He went to Mama and complained and that was when she came to me and told me that she wanted for me nothing but the best.

You will learn to like it there, she said.

But I like it here, I said in reply.

You're going, she said. He's a scholar. He'll have a living from a shul his uncle helps pay for.

Let him marry his uncle, I said.

She slapped me.

I don't like this life with all this hitting, all these threats, I told myself, told in my feelings, of course, because back then I didn't know how to talk to myself in my mind.

And my father came to me with his rough hands and his wonderful smell, lifted me by the hips and sat me down on top of a hay bale. Like I was a slave and he was my owner, he explained how I'm going to do what they tell me. My wonderful father! If he smelled like you, Papa, I said, I wouldn't mind. But he's got the stink of a dying animal.

You've got a smart lip, my father says to me. For a girl, real smart.

And for a father, I wanted to say to him, you're very quick to give away your daughter. But I didn't. Daughters didn't say much. I already said enough with my talk about the boy smelling like a dying dog.

You'll keep quiet, he says to me, smiling through his thick black beard. You'll go to the city. You'll marry a scholar, a rich scholar. And you'll invite us to your house in the city. And we'll bring bread and milk and cheese and you'll put us up in a room of our own overlooking the street. And it will be so noisy, the city (I was there, once, so I know), we won't be able to sleep, your mother and I, and we'll leave the next day, return to our farm, and think to ourselves the whole way home, She's got such a life as we never imagined in a million years one of our own could live.

I nodded, nodded, and when he was through with me and went back out to the barn, I hurried off into the fields ready to throw myself into a ditch. But then the ditch didn't look deep enough and so I ran further, toward a stream that ran on the western edge of the big wheat field. This was the end of me, and the end for me, my father giving me away! like I was a cow or a cart or a jar of honey! or less! a length of cloth, a milking stool! a handrag, a handful of grain! *Oi, oi, oi!* For a young girl, I had a lot to moan about! And I rushed to the stream where I hoped to lay myself down and drown . . .

Here, at this point, if you were standing, Mrs. Pinsker, I would say sit. Because if until then my life was just the story of a country girl, here it becomes poetry. A miracle takes place! At least to me it was a miracle. Imagine—this is how the world changed for me. A wooden pin worked loose in an ox cart axle. This pin had been carved by a husky, handsome ox handler from a good strong oak limb, whittled down and down further, until it fit snugly into the hole he had punched with the crosspiece of the axle. The oak was not so strong—it had flaws in the grain, whatever it is that holds the oak together or makes the wood wood. The pin from the strain split into splinters—and the axle rubbed itself against it until it sheared off. *Shup!* Like a wart sliced from the wrist, it went spinning off into the air! And the wheel fell, and the axle dropped and splintered itself. *Oi,* these accidents that made my life so infirm and yet so steady! And here was the carter's son, a bulky-bodied, hairy-chested, strong-armed man with a wide grin and most of his teeth to show off, sitting with his bare feet in the streambed whittling a new pin.

Did you ever imagine, he said to me when I stepped up to the edge of the water, that this little stream flows to the river that flows to the sea? And we could sail along from here over the lost city of Atlantis until we reached America?

You could say, Who was this crazy boy talking like this?

I knew right away it wasn't just a boy but some greater chance talking—the oak that grew the branch that lent itself to the splintered pin that stopped the cart that brought the boy to rest here at the side of the stream where I had decided I would end my life.

Instead, my life began . . . cockeyed—you're looking at me cockeyed. But don't deny it, behind every old lady with her hair dyed my color there's a story like this. Maybe not exactly as much an adventure as this, but some story, a real story. Somewhere a chance comes along—and she either takes it or she doesn't. In my story, I took. Because what else did I have to hold on to? It was a choice between nothing and something. So what do you choose? Nothing? Don't kid yourself—you reach out for what saves your life if you have a feeling that you have a life to save.

So what you're telling me, darling, is that you eloped?

Yes, we eloped. It took a while, it was a slow elopement, but we eloped. Eventually, we eloped. We fought with my parents—they didn't want no ox carter—they wanted a rabbi. But we got married, we had our child, after that we eloped.

How romantic! My own life is much less romantic. Sometime I'll tell you.

I'd love to hear, Mrs. Pinsker, but not now. Now I'm remembering my own. *Oi*, I remember so well. How I left a whole world behind, how I saved my life. Because of an oak branch splitting. Because of an axle. Because of a crack in a wheel. God looked away at something when that particular oak was growing, and it made all the difference in my life, in Manny's, and in the lives of three other women, the daughter-in-law's, my grandchild's, and *hers*.

Pheeww . . .

Don't make a face. My heart weighs a ton. It feels like it's going to lay a big sad egg. It hurts my eyes to talk about it. The sun is going down . . . it's getting late. At times like this I wonder about my parents, about the old country, and, worst of all, or best, I can feel Jacob like they say you miss an arm you've lost, a missing limb you miss. I can feel him sitting at this table. His aura, the granddaughter calls such things. She tells me. We talk something about it sometimes. Why should he be gone? And I'm still here? Because, remember what the story was I was just telling you, if I had listened to my parents, obeyed them like a good girl, and gone off to the city with the student who smelled like a dog, nobody would have been here. Darling, you would have been drinking coffee alone. We would have been caught by the Nazis and melted like wax for candles. They all went— Mama, Papa, the students of Torah, not so many escaped. So maybe all of that time is like Jacob's Atlantis, a lost city, a lost continent, and who knows what the world would have been if it had lasted? But it wasn't supposed to, was it? Like that oak pin, it splintered. God looked the other way. But with what was He so busy that he could blink and lose so many of His Chosen People? You think He was like me and was having trouble with His eyes?

Crazy, I suppose. You think I'm talking crazy. But it's just talk, and I'm just talking.

I'm telling you, Mrs. Pinsker, I can still smell the woods, the stream where we met, the way the wood, that oak, lay on my nostrils. And the boat, the salty sea, the waves, spray, sea birds calling, the boat swaying under my feet—from the cart to here took so many years, a long ride. Oh, if we could only remember the good things and not the bad! The odor of water and horses and not the stink of boys who smell like dogs!

I never imagined when I asked about all this that you'd remember so much with your nose.

I remember with my nose, I remember with my feet. I remember the walking, walking, when we first arrived in the city.

Just off the boat?

Just off the boat and walking. And how we could have used the horse, then, I'm telling you. With our bags, a trunk, I nearly walked off my feet.

They didn't have taxis then it was so far back in the past?

They had taxis, but we didn't have money. We had a little money, but we didn't want to spend it all on taxis. First we needed a place to live. Once we got a place things went well. Well. As well as well could be when a man works every waking hour and sometimes on into his sleep.

He worked in his sleep? That's a new one.

An old one, Mrs. Pinsker, if in your sleep you're so tired you can't sleep.

He had no pleasures? I was poor, too, Minnie, and I had pleasures. A little piece of candy now and then, a trip to the market.

Eventually we had those pleasures. More and more pleasures, sure. And we had the pleasures of our neighbors, the whole building was a little village, one house on top of another. We had friends, we had the Tabatchniks, with a little boy Arnie my Manny used to play with, a wonderful clarinet he played, he was a music student, until the war . . .

I didn't live in a building? I didn't know those pleasures as a girl and as an adult? Maybe it was the Bronx instead of Manhattan, but it was the same place, the same time.

The same station. Sure. It could have been other towns, other cities. All of us lived the same. In the old country it was one way the same, over here another.

Better of course.

Of course better. You can even suggest that it wasn't better? Here we lived, there we died. And if we didn't die, we came here. So what is better? Living or dying?

Living, living, of course. But I got to laugh, Minnie, because a few minutes ago you were telling me it was better to die in a stream than live with a boy who smelled like a dog.

You got to laugh? So laugh.

I'm laughing, darling, I'm laughing.

With your face straight you laugh?

I'm laughing inside.

Who could tell? Darling, who could tell?

More coffee, ladies?

Saved by the bell.

Saved from what, I'll ask.

Ladies?

.   .   .

My poor Jacob, strong-backed son of a country hostler, he felt weighed down by the city at first, like the whole of New York was a wagon tipped over in a ditch and he had to crawl under it and lift it on his back. He worked days, he worked nights. And he worked Saturday, on the Sabbath, and this changed everything.

This, you cannot do, the hump-shouldered little rabbi from our street came all the way up to our floor to say. It must have been important to him—he never climbed stairs, except down and up into his study on the basement of the little shul down the block.

And what is that? Jacob asked, a man who was not used to taking guff from either oxen or horses or men.

You cannot work on the Sabbath.

I am a poor Jew . . . and the Irishmen work Union Square on Saturdays and the working girls eat apples and oranges and bananas, and if I am not there they buy from the Irishmen.

The goyim don't work on Sunday. From you they'll buy on Sunday. Theirs Saturday. Yours Sunday. And it all works out. It works.

Except that all the gentile working girls are not working on Sunday, Rabbi. I'm there and there's no one to buy.

So sell to the Jews around here. You need Union Square only like a hole in the head.

There are too many peddlers already on Rivington Street, Rabbi. And I'm the only one who works the square both Saturday and Sunday.

You work too much. Even the One Most High rested one day a week.

He maybe had another income, Rabbi. I've only got what I make with my hands.

You mock? the little rabbi said, waggling a finger at Jacob. Me, Minnie, I was over in the corner, pretending to fold clothes, but I was so upset by what I was hearing I couldn't even find a seam. Little Manny stood at the window watching the birds. But he was listening. I could tell by the way he held his head that he was listening.

You mock the Most High?

Jacob turned his head aside, not wanting to quarrel. He was a good man, understood fruits and vegetables much better than the Torah, and knew what he had to do.

We were punished for living modern, said the rabbi. We destroyed the Tablets of the Commandments and wandered across the face of the earth. Break the Commandments, Jacob, and you, too, will wander. And your sons will wander.

Rabbi, Jacob said, as close to pleading as I ever heard him. Don't say such things to a working man. I'm going to wander up to Union Square, that's where I'll wander, so I can sell enough bananas to buy this boy a winter coat.

Blasphemy, the humped-over rabbi said with a snort like an old horse in freezing weather.

Well, that autumn Jacob went to work on the Sabbath, and the rabbi was wrong. He didn't wander. He didn't have time left enough to wander. He went out that next Sabbath, Manny trailing behind, and never came back—not the same way. But whether because of God or a taxi cab, I can't figure. It was a cold day. They were both snorting and huffing like horses, and the horses they noticed here and there among the motorcars and trucks, these animals stood like statues with steam rising from them after a sun-melting morning. Except that the sun did not shine so strong. It rose over the tenements on the east side of First Avenue like a little light bulb from which some clumsy woman in cleaning had torn off the shade. It glowed, but it didn't give heat.

And it was a windy day. Winds splashed back and forth across the street, snatching sounds from here and there along with newspapers and box tops, bloody scraps of butcher paper, old tin cans, pieces of clothing, cloth. It was our, his, first autumn in the city—all of us, even little Manny who didn't remember nothing except the sea voyage, we missed the way the earth smelled in the various seasons, the turning leaves, the pleasures that come after a harvest, the rest before the bitter winter, the way the clods frozen after the first frost crumble underfoot, and the color of the sky itself, a thin layer of white fleecy undercoating that it appeared to have slipped on overnight to guard against the cold. Here was the city, bloody butcher paper curling around their ankle tops.

Can he hurt you? Manny told me later he had asked his father as they trudged up the avenue. (Uptown the taxi was taking on its passengers, the mother, the father, the hawk-nosed boy, the red-haired girl, at the hotel.)

Who, boychick? Jacob wondered. Who could hurt me? Big-boned, black-bearded Papa, a man invulnerable. That was how Manny saw him, so why should he ask such a question? Because the rabbi had scared him. That's how the little hump-backed man worked, with fear.

He said I'll wander. I don't want to wander, Papa. What's wander, Papa?

Wandering is walking, Jacob explained, walking without no place to get to. But you and I don't wander. We're walking to pick up the cart, then the produce, and then up to the square.

We're not going to shul, Papa?

When did you figure it out, boychick? No, not today. Tomorrow, in the morning, we can go if you miss it. Me, I don't miss it. I'm glad I have a reason not to go. All those men humped together like cattle in a barn. Maybe in the cold weather it feels good. But I remember it mostly for the heat. What for? what for, boy? In the old country it went well for those who believed it, but here it's a new world, a free country. And I'm free to walk in the other direction from the rest of them. (Down Fifth Avenue the famous taxi freely drove.)

Why was Mama crying, Papa?

Crying? From the joy of it. From slicing onions for the eggs. Because she once had a dead dog and she remembered today was its birthday. She remembered her dead dog.

Can I have a dog, Papa?

In the house? No, no, darling, but sometime like your little friend Arnie you'll have pigeons.

Really, Papa?

Really.

Here was the store yard where Jacob kept his cart. If he had had a horse he would have hitched the animal to the front. As it was, he stood in front of it and pulled while he directed Manny to push from the rear. In a moment they had it rolling up the alley and out onto the street. Jacob sweated despite the cold, and was thinking to himself—and how do I know? Here I'm guessing, because I know him so well I can figure it—Thinking to himself, I'm working, and with every foot forward toward the square I'm stepping on the remains of a Commandment—and this was even before they stopped at the wholesale place to pick up the day's fruit.

Reading changed my life, Jacob was saying to Manny as they hauled their full load. It was an accident, but it changed everything. Who would say that a hostler's son would ever learn to read Hebrew, let alone German and now English? And how he told him an old story, one I'd heard from him a million times but still a charming story. One spring, he said, we hauled a load of hay into the city and the wagon broke down and we had to wait for the repairs and for two days I had nothing to do but talk to the students drinking tea in the cafe where my father made me sit while he watched the carpenter work on our cart. It was a game. They showed me letters, taught me a few words, and I listened while they discussed such matters as the origins of creation and the movement of the stars. That was the first time I heard about the lost continent. I love to talk about it because it reminds me of that wonderful stay in the cafe where for once in my life I could pretend that I was a student and not a wagonman's boy. But you, Manny, you will become a fine student, and perhaps make a living at it too. After all, this place is better than Atlantis, because it's a found continent, not lost. Here's a curb now, come around to the side there, watch your step, don't spill no apples, don't catch your foot. So. Now it didn't take you no two days to learn to read, did it, boychick? No, it took one. You're a little sort of genius. And this new world will open up for you. One day I'll have a store. And we'll work together, Bloch and Son. Or sons, maybe. Who knows but what sometime a brother and even a sister might come into the world? Would you like a brother? Uh-huh. But not a sister? Oh, pupkin, the things you've got to learn! Watch it now! There, up, hup, there! Pretend we're back on board that ship—remember how the sailors!—there! And Manny looks up toward his father over the orbs of oranges, apples, lemons, over the half-moon clasps of bananas, touching a place here, a piece there as if for luck, thinking of sea birds, of the roll and swell of the waves, confusing them with the fields of waving wheat he's heard so much about.

The two of them walking, father and son. Approaching the square.

And in the distance, the wind whirls away with the sound of

bells bells bells bells bells

(I can hear them clanging still), and the father, sweating, stops in mid-step, looking down at the cobblestones. Cars chug around them. Father panting. Hard work, eh, pup? he says to the boy.

The boy nods, pressing up against the cart out of fear of the passing machines.

And closer now the clanging—wavering in air, fading in, out, out, in, out

BELLS BELLS bells bells bells BELLS BELLS

as father and son halt in their passage. In the middle of Fourteenth Street. And from the east comes a clopping, clopping, clopping, a truck hauled by a horse of

GRUENBERG'S DAIRY

and from the west, now they can hear it, the

BELLS BELLS BELLS

of the fire truck.

Fire somewhere in the city! Man and boy glance about, and the man looks down, as if peering beneath the cobblestones. This land once belonged to the Indians, he says.

The boy is scared by the noise, by the rushing passage of vehicles. Hugging closer to the cart, his nose pierced by the cold odors rising up from the fruit, he fixes his eyes on his father. And thinks: Why isn't he moving?

And who knows why not? Who will ever know why not? Was it his heart? Had something torn loose in his chest? So he was resting there in the middle of the rushing chaos? Or was he lost in a dream of the Atlantis he always talked about, stopped there in the middle of traffic—dreamer and hard-working peddler all in one, poised in his crossing to the other

side where he would take up his stand, *would have* taken up his
stand, in competition with the hustling Irishmen?

Beneath these stones, he was saying.

Papa.

Beneath these stones . . .

BELLS BELLS BELLS BELLS BELLS

and the forceful forward clop-clop-clop of the rushing onward
wagon of

GRUENBURG'S DAIRY

and from the east and from the west the

BELLS BELLS BELLS BELLS BELLS

and ahead of the fire truck the taxi cab pushed almost on the
sound, the way a leaf gets pushed ahead of a wave of wind.

Was it Jacob's heart? We never knew. He never had had no
trouble, but it could have been trouble then, from the hauling,
the lifting. He could have been standing there to rest until he
felt he could get moving again. Or it could have just as easily
been his mouth. May he rest in peace, he had a mouth, he had
an imagination, and he was talking to the boy, talking to him
about Atlantis this, Atlantis that, and then it was too late to
move, because here came from the east end of the street the
dairy truck, and he didn't dare try to rush with the cart and the
fruit and the boy to the other side, and from the west end direction comes the taxi and the fire truck behind it, and the taxi
driver flies into a panic, and he hears the big bells and the
machine behind him, what does he do? He swerves to the left—
here, I have a lipstick, somewhere in my bag, here, give me a
napkin.

So you see what happens? The fire truck nudges the taxi and the taxi swings to the left just ahead of my Jacob and Manny and the cart, and the truck coming from the east, the horse from the truck goes into a fit, jumps, what do you call it? rears up, and the entire wagon tilts over on top of my Jacob. *Oi*, can you just see it? Such a thing, such a mess! The wagon spills over him like a wall of falling bricks! And, I'm telling you, what do we see now? we see a crash of truck and splintered wood and moans we hear, and shouts, and the horse, it's screaming like a man, and there's bottles all over, smashed, broken milk bottles, and a big lake of milk spreading out underneath everything, fruit and fruit, like little steppingstones in a lake of milk, and my little Manny picks himself up where he got knocked halfway across the street and he's cut and he's bleeding, not major just minor, but he's lucky to be alive because the fire truck kept on rushing right past, bells clanging, to the fire in the east—*BELLS BELLS BELLS bells bells bells*—it trails away in Manny's ears, and then he hears the screaming.

Papa! he yells in a rush across the lake of milk that's spread out from beneath the wreck of truck and cart, steppingstones of fruit trip him and he stumbles.

And picks himself up.

There is screaming.

And he sees the gathering crowd, the mob.

And he hears the screams rise higher and higher in pitch until

Pap!

a snap, a crack of a pistol. Birds scatter up all around and the horse sinks into a heap of itself.

Oi, and then what he sees next!

Oi, and then what he sees!

No boy should have to see.

No man should have to see.

No one in the world should have to see.

But he sees it. *Him*. His father lying stretched out in the pond of milk, fingers curled around half-moons of yellowish-brown sheaths from which the fruity pith has been squashed as flat as his chest. His eyes are open—looking directly upon Atlantis. What does his son do next? What would anyone do? He doesn't know what to do. And as the crowd follows the sound of the moaning—before the horse's, now his—he kneels on his father's awful chest, and then reaches out into the mess of milk and muck and—I'm telling you, and afraid I'm telling—the blood that spilled there, too, and up comes his hand with a piece of six-pointed glass. Here, give me another napkin, I'll show you what.

And this is how he lost his father?
Yes so look.

With the lipstick, it's messy. But I'm glad I use lipstick so I could show you. Today they don't use it—Sarah wouldn't be caught dead wearing lipstick, and your grandchildren, besides your one the youth leader, the girls? Well, whatever. Here. Look. The star. The six points. And if you can believe that glass shatters in a design—and who can say it can't because it did—then listen to what happened next. The way a life breaks. The way life goes. The pieces. The pattern. What happens next.

He's now kneeling, my Manny, and now he's crying, moaning, the shock has hit him, the shock is setting in. And around him he hears voices—*oi*, they will become so familiar!

Help him up, you idiot! a man's big booming order.
Pa, he won't . . .
Help him, damn it!

It was the cabby's fault, it was the cabby, the cabby, he hears a woman jabbering alongside the rangling of the men.

Help him. Oh, schmuck, here!

And a strong arm lifts under his and Manny is up on his feet, as loose-limbed as a puppet from a puppet show in his misery, his shock.

Your father? the man asks.

Manny looks up to see this balding man in a fine suit and overcoat, nose like a hawk, eyes like a fox, and the arm that holds Manny belongs to this man.

His father all right, a taller, younger man also balding says.

How are we doing here? comes a cop along to say.

And Manny, who has never stood so close to a policeman before, studies his uniform, such heavy blue cloth, shining gold buttons, and then becomes distracted by the approaching sound of

bells bells BELLS BELLS BELLS

as the ambulance roars in the from the west.

And the man takes him by the arm away from the crowd, the policeman accompanying them, and they ask where he lives and he gives them his address.

And they open the door of the stalled taxi and help him into the backseat while they go on talking, talking outside.

And he sits in the cab staring straight ahead at the back of the seat in front of him, and he loses himself in the smell and design of the upholstery, like a snail's whorl of a shell, spinning around and around into a tighter and tighter knot, and he's fingering the star-shaped shard until all the doors appear to open at once. A man climbs in, the smell of the street on his coat, the younger man in a suit, a big boy, with a high, nasal voice, and the woman, still jabbering—shut up already! says the hawk-nosed man, shut up—don't you dare! the woman says back to him.

And he sniffles in the woman's perfume and the odor of a cigar as the hawk-nosed man lights up.

And only then, his fingers responding to the sharp-pointed star, does he turn away from the pattern on the upholstery, lift himself up and out of the pattern (this was how he put it to me) and look to his right, on the seat to his right, and there he sees the little girl. When she got there he doesn't know. She could have been there the whole time or she could have climbed in with her parents, her brother. But nonetheless there she is. Pale, pink, freckled face. Hair like wispy reddish cotton candy from a carnival, all done up in a knot. Like a doll's hair. A little skirt she wears beneath her tiny fur wrap. White-stockinged feet that don't reach to the floor of the cab. And as he stares at her something happens in her eyes—and she wiggles her nose in disgust—and that's when he smells it too, and looks around for the source. An odor like the horse in its dying. Garbage. Manure. Filth of the gutter. And only when she opens her eyes wide—if a girl that small can feel horror, show horror—and points a finger at him, and cries out, only then, just as he lets another one go in his pants, does he understand what has been done to him, and what he has done.

The poor child.
    Poor.
    And this is how he lost his father?
    This is how.
    And this is how you lost your Jacob?
    This is how.
    I'm telling you . . .
    You're telling me? I'm telling you!
    But it has a good side, no?
    It has a good side? Sure, it has a good side. I'm sitting here drinking coffee with you. That's a good side. I'm still here. And Manny is still here.
    No, I meant, this is how they met, wasn't it?
    How did you figure it out?
    The hair. You described the hair. So it's *her*, isn't it?
    It's her. The *first* her. The mother of the *other* her. The opposite of the *third* her.
    It was her family in the taxi.
    It was her family. Her father, her mother, her mixed up brother.

The brother-in-law? He's mixed up?

You should meet him now that's he's a grown man.

I saw him at temple.

Up close you should see.

I'll take a look next time.

Take a good look. It's all part of the family show. After years away he shows up, and he's part of the family now.

Here.

I don't take sugar, so why are you passing me the sugar?

Darling, don't talk bitter.

Bitter? All of a sudden I'm talking bitter? Mrs. Pinsker, Rose, I am sweet. Very sweet.

It was only a joke, Mrs. Bloch. Minnie.

Some joke.

Don't get miffed.

All right, I won't get miffed.

And you'll tell me more?

I'll tell you. I'll tell you things. I'll tell you that when they brought my Manny home to me without his father . . .

Don't tell me if it makes you remember.

Remember? I don't remember, darling. And I don't forget. I'll tell you this. Manny said to me, the poor little boy, he says, Mama, you know, if they used paper bottles instead of the glass the weight of the wagon wouldn't have been so much on Papa.

He said this to you?

He said it. Of course, he said it. Would I make something up like that? He didn't know what he was saying. He was in shock still.

Shock? Shock? Who wouldn't be in shock? But *they* brought him to you? or the police brought him?

They did. The Sporens. This was their name. It still is their name. The brother, of course, he's alive. The mother, the father, they died some years ago. Terrible. They had their accident. He was in his house, a very beautiful home in Cincinnati, let me tell you, and he was going to go to the basement to look for a bottle of wine—it was a Sunday, they were at home together—and she says, Meyer, let me go for you. She was a cold woman in a way, the little I knew her I could tell that, but she also had a good side, a nice side. When she had a glass of wine, it came out.

She sounds nice.

She was nice this time. Already she'd had one glass. And look where it got her? She goes over and opens the door to their downstairs, to their cellar, the house, was on a steep hill, they have many steep hills in Cincinnatti . . .

I've never been there.

Someday you'll go.

At my age? I want to see Paris first.

You never saw Paris? We stopped there on our trip to Israel a few years ago.

Rome. When we went to Israel we stopped in Rome.

Rome we stopped too. But so you'll never see Cincinnati, it's a lot like Rome, they say, because of the hills—so she opens the door and reaches for the light, and in the reaching, loses her balance, and she falls down the stairs. Terrible.

Terrible.

She hits her head. Without a sound she lies there. And he comes to the head of the stairs, the old boat captain, that's how he started out, and he bought more and more barges, I told you already, and pretty soon he's got a fleet, he's got docks, he's got bigger and bigger ships, and you think a man like this could live a long time to enjoy it. But . . .

So what happened?

What happened? He comes to the top of the stairs, squints down into the dark. And he calls to her.

And she answered?

She couldn't talk. She was paralyzed. Her neck, you know? her spine . . . the cord . . .

So? Don't keep me in the dark.

Very funny. He pulls on the light and he looks down and he sees her, and he starts down the steps. And by the time he gets to the bottom he's already dead himself.

You're kidding?

Would I kid about such a terrible thing. It was his heart. He had an attack. From the scare. From the sight. And that was that. He falls over on top of her. And who knows how long she was

lying there with the weight of her dead husband on her body
before they found her.
Who came? Who found.
Who came? Who found? Guess who?
Her?
Her.
Oi.
Oi, is right. It was quite a sight, quite a sight. For a girl her
age. Something to see.
How old was she?
She was old enough, old enough to feel the hurt and know
the pain.
So it wasn't like when your Manny saw his father, your
Jacob, under the truck. She was older. He was younger.
Thank God for small favors. No, when he saw Jacob, he
went into shock. And he came home, I told you, and he says
this about the paper containers being better than the glass. And
he's holding in his pocket the piece of glass.
The famous piece of glass.
To this day, that's right, he carries it with him everywhere.
And his hand was bleeding?
His hand? His heart! His hand was nothing. So we band-
aged it. Or Mrs. Sporen did. They took over for a little until the
rabbi came, and the neighbors.
That was a help.
A help? What could help? Nothing could help? The dead at
least lie still. I was rolling on the bed tearing out my hair.
Make some tea, make some tea! Meyer Sporen is shouting
at his wife.
All right, don't holler at me! Meyer, she's hollering back at
him.
Mother, for Christ's sake! the boy is shouting.
And the girl is watching her mother help Manny undress.
Where's your clean clothes, darling? she's asking him, and
he's standing there like a dressmaker's dummy, his arms and
legs moving when she makes them move, otherwise not moving. In his pocket, the piece of glass, this, the one I drew you,
in his fingers the bandage, and now he's rubbing the fingers
again through the bandage.
Let me, Mrs. Sporen says, trying to take it from him, but
quick he whips it back and she stands dumb, looks around for

the toilet, leads him to that little closet with the bulb you turn on by pulling the string. When the light goes on she sees her dress. And for a minute she forgets about him. She sees the smear on her dress from what he has done in his pants when she was helping him out of the clothes, and she grunts in disgust, and there's the girl looking at her, looking at him, and she lets out a shriek, and he, Meyer Sporen, comes rushing up to the door and he says, What do you think you are doing? We're here to help, not hinder, and so stop complaining, and so what is it? We've got trouble with the lady here, so what? what?

And the little girl points, and her mother says nothing, and the father says, On you even dreck looks good. Now take over, make some tea.

I'll make tea, Papa, the little girl says.

You'll make, you'll make. You'll make what the boy made, a mess, so don't worry. Thank you, sweetheart, but here we need your mother to take over.

I'm changing his clothes, can't you see? she says to him, with a voice like a knife.

Why they're hollering, I don't know, I don't care, but I can hear them from the bed where I'm tearing my hair, and I'm thinking, why are they hollering? Soon enough they'll be dead too. They had years then, of course, but to me at the time years were nothing. Time had dried like laundry on the roof on a warm afternoon. Years like moisture all gone and only the wind was left, blowing my hair, my face, burning me in the chest, the arms, and I had no days, but a lot of time left, both at once, you know? I had time like a big tall glass and nothing to fill it with. And if it wasn't for Manny I would have died. But I heard them shouting, and I got up, and he was standing there while they were hollering, and he was covered with his own mess, and I took him, and they grabbed for him but I pushed them away, and I took him to the sink, and I washed my boy, and I cleaned him. It was good practice for the years to come.

You took good care of him, these years.

I took, I cared. I took good care.

And he's grateful. You can see, he respects his mother, he gives to her.

You can tell. Yes, he gives. And this gets him in trouble with you know who.

With her? *Which* her?

The first her. And maybe the second.

The second Maby?

Sarah, yes. The second redhead. Or third, if you count me, the mother.

Of course I count you. You don't count?

I count, I count on my fingers. I count the years since all this happened since my Jacob passed away. You know when I started counting? I started counting when after I finished cleaning him up I saw Manny standing at the window by the fire escape watching the birds. The famous birds. His little friend Arnie kept the pigeons and they would all day long fly up, fly down, and here he was my Manny standing there, watching, newly washed, not saying a word. Behind him of course there's a lot of words people are saying.

How do they live? Mrs. Sporen is saying.

Sha, her husband says. I grew up in this neighborhood. They live, that's how.

This is living? she says.

They're talking, while I'm back to my oi-yoi-yoiing.

Maby, he says.

Maybe what? I'm thinking.

Maby, he says again. Darling.

What, Papa?

That's when I discover that Maby is the little redhead's name.

Maby, someone's knocking, please answer the door.

Maybe I will, she says.

Not maybe. Answer it. Your mother's at the stove.

I'll get it, Mrs. Sporen says. She was standing in the toilet, the closet, actually, taking a drink from a bottle that she kept in her pocketbook.

I'll get it, the older boy says, and goes to the door. He had been sitting next to me, trying to comfort me. It didn't help much.

But here came the neighbors, Mrs. Tabatchnick, little Arnie's mother, the whole bunch, and that helped a little. Behind them in time came the police, the undertaker, the rabbi, other neighbors. I went on with my oi-yoi-yoiing. Eventually the Sporens left, returning to their home in Cincinnati from where they were visiting the city, Meyer Sporen's old neighborhood, traveling downtown in that famous taxi, the taxi that swerved and frightened the horse that pulled the wagon that tipped over on my Jacob and left him crushed flat in a lake of milk. *Oi-yoi-yoi-yoi-yoi* . . .

Before this I did not think much about believing. I believed, or I didn't believe, it didn't matter. But that day I learned that the Lord giveth and He taketh away, in strange portions, strange ways. Here, now, wait a minute. Take an intermission. I've got to go to the bathroom. The coffee, all of it I drank, I got to go so bad I can taste it.

Okay, so here I am again. So. Where was I? Oh yes. He started the next week sending me money, and he never stopped.

Sporen?

Of course, who else? It wasn't enough, so I went to work in the shirt factory, but the money helped, believe me, it helped. He had the boat business in Cincinnati, you see. On the river. The Ohio. And this runs into the Mississippi, and then into the Gulf. The boy, his older child, took a job on one of his boats and went out into the Gulf, and further south. The girl stayed at home. She went to a fancy school. She learned French. All this while I was working in the shirt factory and Manny is studying with the rabbi. That's right—the little, hump-backed rabbi took him over. On Saturday mornings he started taking me to shul.

Your father would never believe it, I told him the first time.

My father made a mistake, Manny said, may he rest in peace. He worked on the Sabbath, and that was a big mistake.

So what do you want to do? his friend Arnie, standing there with us asked him. You want to become a rabbi yourself? Come along, Ma, he tugs at my hand. Arnie? You coming?

I got to feed my pigeons and then I got to practice, Arnie says. He was a skinny boy, Arnie, but when he picked up that clarinet, I'm telling you, he made beautiful music. Manny, on the other hand, was stocky, he was always stocky, like his father, and when he got on his high horse you couldn't knock him off with a stick. He wanted me to go to shul with him. I went. His friend Arnie stayed home.

He'll be sorry, Ma, Manny said to me on our way down the street.

Like your father was sorry? I asked him.

This was a time when Manny and I grew apart, the only time. When he was under the wing of the old rabbi. He did nothing but study, study, study. It was like he went from childhood to old age without having a life in between. And he was a stranger to me. I got up in the morning, made breakfast, went to work, he went to study with the old man. And he became like the old man, even walking a little hunched over, his head hanging to one side as if from the weight of his studies.

What's the matter, you don't smile no more? I used to say to him. But could he take a joke? Like his ugly teacher, he looked at me in a different way then than he had before. His own mother, he looked at her like she was a foreigner. And treated her like she was nothing but his servant. And he told me nothing. Ten, eleven, he got older in body and in mind, twelve, thirteen, he had a bar mitzvah, and it was like an old man's bar mitzvah, Manny stooped over the Torah looking even older than his teacher except for the hair, because then he still had his original hair color of the wing of a crow, tar-roof black hair, and the old man had his white hair. Fourteen, fifteen, he kept on studying, and I kept on working, and the money came in from Cincinnati, regular like clockwork, sixteen, seventeen, those years flew away, let me tell you. And then comes the invitation to study in Cincinnati, and this brings down the house.

Because until then he had not told me his secret. For years he had kept it hidden to himself and his old teacher. And so because it was hidden from me I kept it hidden from you until now, because I wanted you to know what it felt like to be in the dark. You go along, day to day, working, cooking, cleaning, trying to give the boy everything both a mother and a father could give, and you live in the dark. You know? you're sitting there every day eating the toast, drinking tea, passing the sugar, and you know nothing of what's going on inside the boy you're sitting with. You wash his clothes, you mend his clothes, you make his bed, dust his dresser, comb, when he's little, his hair, make him wash his face, make sure he has a little sweet here and there, make sure he has his friends to play with, that he does his studies (though in this department I didn't have to worry, did I?), and what do you know? You know nothing. Dark. Darkness. Like in the middle of the night. In the middle of the day. In the bright early morning. Dark, dark, dark.

And then something happens, and it's like lightning in the storm. It lights up, darling. You see everything, but only for a second.

The offer came from Cincinnati. And he told me. Well, he told me first what happened the first time. He told me and for a little while I came out of the dark. He had to tell me something because of his hair.

It was still black then?

Patience, Mrs. Pinsker, patience. The first story he told was about a bird: he had been walking home from the store one late afternoon, a dark winter city afternoon, dark enough but now snow coming down on top of it, and he had been thinking, returning from this errand, that there must be a way that he could help me with the expenses without giving up his studies, thinking he could get a job after school for an hour or two, if he could find the right man who would understand his situation and hire him for only a short period each day, and he was thinking, deeper than the thoughts about work, as he often did throughout his life after the accident, thinking, if the milk bottles had been cartons, the weight would not have turned over the truck, and his father would have lived, and how to make paper containers for liquid, for milk; and he walked right into an alley. You know how you walk when you're thinking of things but not about the world in front of you? Right into this alley. And he looked up and he saw a wall in front of him and he turned and saw another. How could that be? And a flock of pigeons descended from the small patch of sky above the alley, a dark curtain already thick with snow, the evening the color of window shades no one for ages has cleaned, and Manny backed against the wall feeling a sudden deep fear, and unto him spoke a pigeon, the leader of the flock, saying, *Manny, you have strayed from the path but do not falter* — listen, Mrs. Pinsker, I'm telling you this is what he told me it said — *do not falter because your father sees your works and hath no questions!*

You're shaking your head. You're speechless. But he told me what the pigeon said to him. And he felt faint, everything went black, and the next thing he knows he's back out on the street, walking toward our building. He was, at this time, let me see . . . fourteen. And he didn't tell me, not then. Later. Usually I've been telling you what I didn't know until later. But here I wanted you to see that for years I lived in ignorance of my son's thoughts and needs. Only later did he begin to tell me everything. When he started writing letters from the school in Cincinnati, that's when it started, the telling of the truth. This first time with the vision he kept it secret, to me at least. The old rabbi he told. But not his mother. No. This was before the news came from Cincinnati. Years before. And then came the offer.

Oh, you're going too fast. You're making time fly. Like the pigeons you're making it, Minnie.

So can you tell me where did the years go, anyway? I wish only they had nested up on the roof like the pigeons. Then we could visit them. Then we could see.

It moves so fast.

It moves fast all right. It moves like those movies you see sometimes on the television, the ones about growing flowers, all speeded up, and clouds sometimes, clouds moving so fast it looks like the world is spinning away.

Time stopper they call it. I remember from Rick my grandson's school.

Not time stopper, Mrs. Pinsker. Time stoppage. The world spins, the clouds rush along, the flower grows, one two three four five.

Stopper, stoppage. It moves, don't it? It spins so fast. And now you got to wait a minute for me. It's my turn for the bathroom.

That you can't stop, *nu?*

So, more about the birds?

More about the bird: another bird. The second time this happened he had just had his battle with the rabbi about the offer to attend school in Cincinnati.

You want to go to the Union of All Hebrews? the old man
had raised his voice full of taunt and disparagement. This is a
school for goyim. Classes they have in English. You want to
study Talmud in English? Go read a comic book, boychick. He
reached over to pinch Manny's cheek, but the boy ducked. You
want to read a comic book? Go 'head, go 'head.

I'm sure they read in Hebrew, Manny said.

Goyim can learn Hebrew, too. Does that make them good
Jews?

I'm not a good Jew. I'm a good student.

The humped-up little man clapped his hands to his face and
slid back in his chair. Here in this greenish light of the basement
office my Manny always felt as though he were sitting in a
fishbowl. And here was the big fish squirming at the antics of
the little.

You're a good student. But you're stubborn like your father.

Please don't talk about my father. What's this got to do with
my father?

What's it got? It's got plenty.

It's got nothing to do with my father, Manny said.

It doesn't? the old man said. It most certainly does. It has
to do with saving your father. Your father died like a goy and
you're helping to make him a Jew. Who knows where he is now,
his soul, spinning around and around in the smoke, burning in
Gehenna, because he died like a goy on the Sabbath, and praying, he is praying, you will help to make him leave his pain. Do
you understand? And you go to Cincinnati, go to study with the
goyish Jews, the Jews who aren't Jews, and he'll spin around
another thousand years, because what's time to him when he
died the way he died? so you'll go, and he'll spin, and he'll burn,
and he'll . . .

You're crazy, Manny told him. You don't talk like a rabbi,
you talk like a priest.

A what?

You heard me. Manny stood up.

A what?

You heard me.

Get out, you forsaken little bastard, the old man said. Out!
He stood up and waved a hand at the boy. Out!

I'm not a bastard, Manny said, moving toward the door.

Your father died like a goy! the old man said. And you're
a stinking little bastard not worth my time. And this man hurled
his miserable little body at Manny and struck him on the shoulder. Out!

Don't do that to me! Manny said. And he without thinking
slapped the little old man on the side of the head and knocked
him against his desk. Books flew everywhere, pencils, pads,
pens, ink bottles went flying.

Out the door, up the steps to the street, running back toward
our building, Manny kept going. If at that hour I had been home
already, and not still working my fingers to the bone at the shirt
factory, I would have heard the downstairs door fly open and
slam shut behind him, and I would have heard him pump his
feet, pump, pump, pump his way up the stairs, all the way up
to the fourth floor, fifth, past our door, and up again, higher,
to the sixth. And he's climbing, not only climbing stairs, he's
climbing years, he's going back in time and he's going ahead in
years, pump, pump, pump, pump go his legs, his heart, and
he's thinking, Papa! and he's thinking, You worked! you worked
so hard! and he's thinking, How could he say that? that rotten
old bastard, that slump! And he's thinking, He's helped me,
helped me so much, but how could he say that? How? How?
And he's reached the top floor, and he's wrenching open the
door to the roof, and he's thinking, What for? what for? Oh,
Papa, Papa, and he's feeling as though his heart has been
drained of blood, now an empty shell, now an empty bottle, a
cracked, shattered glass bottle of a heart, and he reaches into his
pocket, and he feels the shard, and he stops short of the edge,
looks down, breathing, breathing, and looks up, looks around
at a sound, sees Arnie's pigeon coop, hears the cooing and gur-
gling of the nesting birds, and he steps back from the edge,
catches his breath, the brat, I would have said if I could have
seen him then, the little brat, daring the air beyond the edge to
lift him somewhere without pain, daring it, saying, I dare you,
lift me, I'll leap into your arms, you air! and finally, stepping
back again, back again, and lifting his head to the horizon, seeing the spires of the greater city beyond the flat roofs of our
neighborhood, looking east toward the river where our boat first
docked, southeast toward that island, that pier in the bay, and
west toward Cincinnati from where the call had come, and north
again to the greater city, the towers, the spires.

Hands in his pockets, fingers of one hand curled around the shard, breathing hard, still breathing hard, and the stink of the street rising up to his nostrils, the stink of the pigeons in his nose. A wind coming up from the river. Heat of the roof in the late afternoon sun. Sun sloping toward the west. The street below, throbbing beneath his eye, the street beating like a heart—thunka-tunk, thunka-tunk, calling up to him, saying, want me? want me?

It happened then. Again. It happened first as a speck in the sky, first a speck, then a bird swooping up and then swerving around, and stooping down toward the neighborhood, past the higher roofs, toward our roof, the pigeon from on high, swerving in toward him, fixing its eye on him as it floated past, and opening its beak to say, *You want to be both rich and blessed?* as it sailed past on its broad, white wings untouched by city soot.

I d-do, stuttered Manny to himself aloud.

Follow me then, the bird said, turning around and swinging by the western side of the roof again, then swooping up over his head and swinging past the sun, making a shadow as it swerved past the sun, and then down again, toward the south side, and around again, where it feathered its wings and landed atop the coop.

You want? it asked him.

He knew the voice. He fell to his knees.

I want.

Then, I say, follow me, it told him, cocking its head first to one side, then the other.

Where? Manny asked.

Where? the voice said. *Where? Watch!*

And now the other birds inside the coop fluttered their wings all at once, all together, like a chorus line waving arms, legs, and then like an orchestra behind a solo singer the birds commenced to coo and gurgle and bleat and bleep and blutter-bluster, birdlike, birdlike, but loud, louder than he had ever heard, and the pure white bird who spoke with his father's voice, gave a flutter, gave a shudder, and pushed itself off into the air from the roof of the coop, soaring higher, higher toward the west. And soon it was no more than a moving object as large as his hand, and then as small as his thumbnail, and then as tiny as a dot on a clean white piece of paper, and then it was gone.

My Manny lingered a while on the roof before he realized
that he was still on his knees, kneeling. So then he arose and
walked slowly toward the door, and he descended slowly the
height of the entire building, down the flight after flight of steps
to the street, and he met his friend Arnie on his way out of the
building, and Arnie took one look at him and bumped up against
the side of the hall.

Oh, my god! he said and nearly dropped his clarinet case.

That night, I was stirring the soup, and in the door comes
Manny, his hair turned almost completely white.

That's how he got his white?

That's how. White as snow from that day on. Except for the
little dark streak down one side. They missed that part.

They?

You know. Whatever. The way it turned. It turned all over
except for that little streak.

It looks very becoming. I always thought that.

It makes him look distinguished now. But at sixteen it didn't
seem that way.

You took him to a doctor?

Why should I have done that? He wasn't sick. He was
scared. His hair changed. This doesn't happen every day, but
it doesn't mean he's a sick person. In fact, after this happened
he seemed to me a lot happier. Mama, he said, I have made up
my mind. I'm going to the Union of All Hebrews. I'm going to
get myself a good education and I don't care what name anybody puts on it.

A smart boy.

He was always a smart boy. He was always smart. But I worried, you know, I always worried about just how smart he was.

Ladies?

Oh, you surprised me. You sneaked up so quiet I didn't even
suspect.

More coffee, ladies?

More coffee, of course. Mrs. Pinsker?

For me, sure, thank you, yes.

The waitress stepped back from the table.

I don't need it. Already I've got a coffee lake inside me. But
I don't want to hurt her feelings.

That's why you drink more coffee?

That's why I'm drinking this cup. She's very nice. She caters to us.

She has nothing better to do with her time. It's not so busy now just before dinner.

It's that late?

It's that late.

After this cup I should go home and make dinner. But tonight I could be a little late. With Manny and her away on vacation.

We should eat together here.

Why don't we do that? The car is going to wait for me no matter what. It can wait a little longer. You think it's good here? Here I never thought of eating.

It's the mall. It couldn't be good, it couldn't be bad.

You're right. The mall is the mall. But we could try it.

Sure we could try it.

So when she comes with the coffee we'll ask her for a menu.

Sure, sure, we'll splurge, we'll tell her. We're having dinner. She'll like it. It will give her something to do.

You don't think she has a family of her own to think about? She's going to be happy because we're staying around to eat? Don't kid yourself. I bet she's a grandmother, just like the rest of us.

You want to ask her to sit down and tell us her story?

Don't be so sarcastic. I'll bet she has a story just like I do.

About her son the minister?

Or her son the doctor.

Or the janitor.

Don't be so cruel. There's enough cruelty in this world. We all got children.

Excuse me. I was making a joke. It's true. All grandmothers got children.

I'm glad she didn't hear you. Some joke.

You're miffed because I make a joke, Minnie? You would prefer that we don't eat together?

Sit, sit. I prefer that we eat. I don't want to eat alone. I'm enough alone. I was enough alone ever since Manny went to Cincinnati. I was alone. Mrs. Tabatchnick was alone. Mine only went to Cincinnati. Hers went to Europe already. To the war.

To the war?
To the war.

But there was a war on in Cincinnati, too, let me tell you.
Manny took the train west, and it was a dark ride, at night,
through the cities with the lights browned out, through the dark
fields, the woods, over the eastern mountains. He felt so strange.
Never had he been west of Sixth Avenue, and here he was on
the other side of the mountains. For him it could have been at
that time almost California, nearly Japan. But of course as it
turned out he didn't have to travel very far at all to begin his education into foreign ways. No, sir. No, sirree. It began on the
train—he saw young boys his own age in uniform. Soldiers
home from war or on their way to war. And for the first time
in his life he paid attention to what was going on in the world
outside. Before that, it had been his studies and Mama, Mama
and his studies. So if in Europe they had been killing the Jews
that was in Europe, and he lived on Second Street, New York
City, America. He had been born in the old country, of course,
and the old rabbi had taught him in the style of the old country. And from studies to Mama, and Mama to studies, that you
could say was living like he had never left the old country. But
there was a part of my boy that was— still is—so American I can
hardly tell you. Even if he lived the old country life he was living it on Second Street, in New York— and when he opened his
eyes and saw what was going on around him, when he saw the
soldiers, and talked to them about the war, and picked up—at
long last, he put it in a letter to me soon after he got to
Cincinnati—a newspaper it was like a curtain falling away
between his eyes and the world. He saw, he saw. For the first
time he saw. He saw his own little world, and what a little pud-
dle, as he put it, it was alongside the big sea. And by crossing
the sea he could learn to see. Living in this country made it possible for him to throw off the old ways, the old cloak, he called
it, and to make a way for himself that was more suitable, more
American, and also for him more comfortable, and, I think he
always thought about others when he talked about this part of
it, more useful. More useful to himself, more useful to others.
　　Of course this doesn't happen over night. On a train ride.
In the dark. But he sat up the whole night talking with the
soldiers, and thinking. And he remembered how far he had

come, the boat trip across the ocean he remembered, working with his father he remembered, the accident he remembered, his studies he remembered, even his Mama he remembered. But now came the time in his life when he met new things, new ideas, new people, and he noticed the difference between what he remembered on the one hand and what he knew firsthand on the other in the present.

Hitler? they talked about Hitler in the train in the dark.

And the war, what war meant. These young soldiers talked—and some of them drank. They passed around a bottle. And my Manny drank with them. Before he never drank a drop, but on the train, in the dark, with the boys almost as young as he was, he drank. And they talked about the contribution, the effort they were making. And he kept quiet about what he was doing, but he thought to himself, he was going to make a contribution, not just with his body but with his mind. He was going to study even harder, and he was going to change the lives of other people not by war but by peace. Not by deeds of battle but by deeds of peace.

You know years later, many many years later, I mean last month, just last month, when he was in the hospital, I was in the hall outside his room, he was sleeping, and *she* was off somewhere, and Sarah was in school, and I was talking to Sally Stellberg's Doctor Mickey, you know, he's so wonderful, he was always there, always ready to help, and what a relief it was to me to see him always there, let me tell you, so I was talking, and I said, Doctor Mickey, tell me, here is a man who has so much, he's a scholar, a teacher and rabbi, he's a businessman on the side, he's got a beautiful wife (well, she is beautiful, with her face, with her hair, you've got to admit that), and a lovely daughter, and yet he always seemed lately so troubled, do you know what I mean? Isn't it possible for a man to be happy? Isn't it possible for a man to say to himself, Look, I have a lot of wonderful things—and of course I didn't even mention his mother, his dear Mama who fed him and clothed him and cared for him all these years—why isn't it possible for a man to be satisfied when he has so much?

If you could tell me, Mrs. Bloch, what makes a man satisfied, he says to me, then I could help many more people than I do with my prescriptions.

He's such a wise man, Mrs. Pinsker. Our friend Mrs. Stellberg must be proud. Such a wise mind. Answers he doesn't give. He makes questions. What satisfies a man? I was asking him. I was asking why my Manny never seems satisfied when he has all of the things a man could want. He wants, he wants. No matter what he's got he wants more, more. And not in a selfish way. He's never been selfish. He's always given generously of what he has had, and he's always gone out for more. In a way, the trip to Cincinnati, that was a way of getting more for me as well as for him. He wanted a better education. He wanted to open up the world for himself. And look where this ended for me. A lovely house where we all live together. A car and a driver of my own—this from the business, of course, and not from the temple. From the temple he has never taken, he has only given. You know that. Everybody knows that. You're nodding, you understand. Good.

So there he is, riding in the train through the dark country, and it comes to him how much he has lived under a cloak, behind a curtain. Not like his little friend Arnie, who could barely come up to his shoulder—he's already going off to volunteer for the war—and you can be sure Mrs. Tabatchnick still thinks about that, you can be very sure. No, but Manny's making plans to volunteer for other things—to volunteer for the world. To make his way in the world. It's near dawn. He's got whiskey on his breath, and in his mind a million ideas are churning all around, mixed together, the past, the present, things he wants to do in the future, though the future is the darkest part, darker now than the forests outside the window of the train—and he's wondering at how far he has come in less than half a day, and he's wondering just how much farther life will carry him, because something has changed inside of him, something he cannot yet understand or explain, but the color of his hair seems to signal it to him, like a flag, like a new blossom on a bud sprouting out in time stoppage photography. There's a war on in Europe, and there's a war on inside himself. And the Allies have Churchill, the Allies have F.D.R., and in his head he's got his father's voice, the bird that spoke in his father's tongue, and this helps him get through the ride, through the night. Now if this sounds crazy, let it be. Who knows what other boys keep in their minds to themselves? This is what he told me, long long after. And if he heard voices then at least the voices told him

to do good things, not bad. Go west, young man. Go to the
school that will do you good. And do good to others. Build a
life. A way of life. A plan. A business that spreads out the good
to other people.

So he arrives in the new city, and there's a war on inside
and out, but to look at the outside you would never know it. Not
in the morning. It's bright, sunny, a beautiful day, above the
Union Station the birds soar, the clouds scatter past, and Manny
is standing there waiting for his host, his sponsor, his patron
you can say, to arrive. He didn't know that they walked past him
several times before finally stopping, staring, and Meyer Sporen pointing a finger at him, and saying You? It's you?

I remember *you*, Maby says. But your hair! What happened
to your hair?

And Manny retreats into himself, curling up inside like a little child, though he's still standing there, looking up at the girl
on the platform, his hand on his suitcase, his coat open, shirt
roughly wrinkled, one corner sticking out from beneath his
belted waist. She's so pink, freckled, fresh, fair, young—he can
hardly believe that voice comes out from that small pink birdlike mouth. It's music that slides up and then down, up and then
down, an imitation of something she heard from the lips of people she greatly admires, the voice of an actress, the voice of some
woman whom she might like to adopt as her mother. (Oh, if I
could have been standing there with him, I would have
whispered in his ear, *Watch out! watch out!*)

And now he's remembering.

And he's trying to disappear inside himself because he
knows what she's remembering and what she's about to say.

You, she is thinking. *You did it in your . . .*

Oh, and now he wishes he had leaped from the deck of the
ship, wishes he had died with his father crushed under the
weight of a thousand breaking bottles of milk, drowned in the
milk, in the blood pressed out of him! If he had only been the
horse, the horse against whose head the policeman pressed the
pistol! *Pap!* and he'd have gone, never to have had to live long
enough to step into this moment! And he can tell, it's happened
before, he's drawing blood from his fingers with the shard.

Yes, it's me, he muttered, and tried to smile. Tried to cover
it over, overcome it, comb it smooth, oh, I wish I had been there
to help! to brush his thick white hair, to make him feel neater,

more handsome. He's so embarrassed, you know, because through all this she's how do you say? exciting him! That's right, he's looking at the pin, her hip, the way it pokes, the ruffles across her chest, the blouse, the face, the hair.

Oh, she says, it's you all right, and she laughs a kind of laugh that spreads across the air between him like those same ruffles, unfolding but never completely opening.

Here is where I really wish I could have been standing there, invisible—and why couldn't he imagine my voice? I didn't talk to him enough? I didn't help to raise him like both his mother and his father? and whose voice does he call up at a time like this, the temperamental dried-up old prune of a hump-backed rabbi who never told him outside of Talmud anything worthwhile? Manny, I would have said, Manny, Manny, boychick, stand up to her! Oh, if I could have been a pure white pigeon, the bird swooping down! I would have said to him, Manny, stand tall to her now or forever she will always keep the upper hand!

You never liked her because she was mean to him? or she was mean to him because you never liked her?

Who can say? A little of both. Look, I liked her at first. Why shouldn't I? Her father was so generous to us all the years. The accident made us like family. It brought us together and kept us together. So you think it was an accident that the girl and the boy should get together? Let me tell you, this was fate. This was what they were supposed to do. I'm only complaining about the way that they did it.

It hurts you so much to think about it that it brings tears to your eyes?

Tears! Not tears. Itches. My eyes itch like crazy. I went to Doctor Mickey, he checks me out, he gives me an ointment. I rub it in. After we eat I'll go home and rub it in. But let me tell you about Manny's itches. Oh, did he get an itch!

He fell in love?

It was love, let me tell you. They clicked together like two magnets. The letters he wrote to me about her! They were poetry.

So it wasn't bad after all? You made me think you thought from the start it was bad.

It wasn't bad, it wasn't good. It was what happened. Now if I had been there I could have helped him handle what happened, but who could have turned him away from what was supposed to happen.

Stop rubbing your eyes. Sure, my children are the same. They got to school, they get married, they have children. Except for one difference.

And what's that?

Stop rubbing the eyes.

I'm stopping. I'm stopping.

The difference is the ones that are near don't call and the far ones don't write.

Well, let me say without too much fanfare that Manny wrote to me every week while he was away. For years he wrote to me. About his school, his studies, his business classes—Meyer Sporen put up the money so that he could also take classes at the University of Cincinnati just down the street from the Union. And Manny never asked but over the years I asked, I asked myself, what does this man want? Years ago he made up for whatever bad feelings he may have had about the accident, but he keeps paying and he keeps paying. So why does he keep paying?

Was it that he wanted a nice boy for his daughter to marry? Stop with the eyes, darling.

I'm stopping. I'm stopping. If that was what he wanted, then he got it.

Ladies?

Yes, we'd like to see a menu.

Here you go.

Thank you. Now Mrs. Pinsker, you look at this. I'm going to show you something else. Some things I brought with me.

So what did you bring?

Letters I brought. Lucky for you, I carry them with me.

Lucky for me so I'll look at them. But first. Here. So how's the fish?

The fish is nice.

I'll have the fish. Minnie, so you?

I'll have the fish too.

Two fish.

Two fish. One. Two. You can always count on the fish.

Dear Mama,

It's only a few weeks and I'm settled in already, feeling a lot like home. My room, up on the sixth floor of the dormitory, has a fine view of the river, looking southeast to where the Ohio comes down out of the West Virginia hills and squirms its way past the city, the city of hills as they call it here, comparing it to Rome where I've never been so I can't say. But if the city is supposed to look like Rome, it doesn't sound like it. A lot of people speak German, that's the accent here, along with Southern, something you'll have to hear to believe. The latter I mean, not the former, which you hear all the time in the city. *The* City. This is not The City by a long shot, Mama. This is a city in imitation of The City. The one thing it's got going for it, in terms of my own needs, is that it's just small enough so that when I talk to Meyer Sporen about what's going on in my business classes I get to hear about the main currents and big deals of Cincinnati commerce, the banks, boat, factory, insurance deals, all that stuff. How could I hear that in New York in our neighborhood?

Anyway, I don't mean to dwell on the business part. My work is going well, Talmud, etc., and I'm taking history classes, something I hadn't done before, world history, I mean. They emphasize a lot of stuff that the old rabbi would consider pure goyish hogwash—almost literally hogwash, Mama, *traife*. I didn't know how far I'd have to travel from the city to get some sophisticated teachers—there must be some but I never met them, did I? Not the way Arnie will go to Julliard. I mean, where was the equivalent of Julliard for me? I'm just lucky that Meyer Sporen kept in touch with us all these years. Otherwise, where would I be? Maybe—I can't write that word anymore without smiling, I'll explain in a minute—I'll still go into business some day, I'm certainly preparing myself for that, but at the same time I'm enjoying my studies, pushing myself with good results, you'll be pleased to learn, but I'm not hurting myself. I'm eating well, I'm getting plenty of sleep, and think of the exercise alone I get climbing six flights of stairs several times a day to get to my room. It's just like home! Speaking of home, the Sporens feed me about once a week, and even if Mrs. Sporen is a little strange she has a cook who makes great Jewish and German meals. Oh, and why do I laugh when I write the word—

"maybe," because, of course, of *Maby*, the daughter. I'm teaching her Hebrew. She went to good schools here, and she learned Latin and French and German, but no Hebrew. So while Mr. S. doesn't want me to feel an obligation, still I do. I volunteered.

I miss you, Mama. And I hope that you don't think that just because I was raving about the Sporen's cook's meals that I don't miss your cooking because I do. And I miss your company. I miss Arnie, too. You said that he's supposed to play in an army band? Let me know when his mother hears more. And please send me his address.

Well, I've got to run now. I've got a class in modern criticism, that's how to read difficult Biblical texts, and a public speaking class, and an accounting examination over at the University of Cincinnati. And oh yes, and Economic History from the ancient Assyrians, our old neighbors up to and past our own 1929 when American businessmen jumped out of windows, poor fools! Everyone in the dormitory here tells me they don't know how I do it, working in both worlds, as they put it, but *I* can tell you. I work as hard as I can. That's my secret. I like to think that I've inherited my strong points from Papa. Do you think so? He was that kind of man, wasn't he? And when he worked on the Sabbath he did it for our sakes, I know. And I'm doing the same, aren't I? Joke question: What kind of a Jewish boy would work on the Sabbath? Answer: A rabbi. End of joke. And end of letter. I miss you. I'll see you on vacation. Meanwhile it's off to the races . . .

> **Your loving son,**
> **Manny**

Dear Mama,

I got your postcard. I'm glad that you saw the show on Second Avenue. What a treat, my mother at the theater! I'm proud of your going, and with me away from the city and not eating you out of house and home perhaps you can go more often. I was sorry to hear that I missed Arnie when he was home on leave, but keep me posted as to where he is in Europe and so forth. Here everybody's talking about the war, because it's now on two fronts, and with all of the horrible news that we get about what's happening you feel sometimes that there's not much an individual can do, whether he's a rabbi, a barge owner, or even a soldier or a president. The world out there isn't the fairy-tale Atlantis my father thought it was, is it, Mama? with no disrespect to Papa, may he rest in peace.

I'm off to class.

Your loving son,
Manny

Dear Mama,

I don't know if I can write this, feeling suddenly as bad as I do. It just hit me without warning. I'm so homesick that it's in my stomach, in my chest, in my gut, in my head, in my joints, in my muscles. I was pretending to feel so blasé about it all, being away from the city for the first time, and the Sporens watching out for me, making sure that I have everything I need. Sometimes I think, and I don't mean to question his generous impulses, but his son still hasn't come home, and from what I figure he's been away several years. The father and son never got along. I can even remember *that* from the day of Papa's accident all that long time ago. Maby doesn't get along with him. But she's not close to her mother, either. So she's living sort of out on a limb in her own house, talking to me about going away somewhere to college, but who knows? She can't do it without their permission and she's sure they'd never give it. She's very smart though and should go to school. I know, I know, you probably think she should marry a nice Jewish boy and make a home . . . who do you have in mind? That's a joke, ha, ha! Seriously, I think it's important for a smart girl to go to college and I am trying to convince her to talk to her parents about it. "Talk to them?" she says. "They never hear what I say." "Manny," she says, "I think I'm a changeling, some other kind of creature born of another race and magically transplanted into their household." "You mean you think you were adopted?" I asked her. Because she had said that more than once to me since I've known her. "No," she said, "I'm a changeling." "And your brother? He too is a changeling?" "He's just a mean fairy thing," she said. "What do you mean?" I asked. "You heard me," she said. I was shocked to hear a girl talk like that. I never heard things like that even on the street. Sure, Arnie and I used to run around, though not so much because I was busy working and studying and he was busy with his music lessons, with practicing. And so perhaps our experience was a little more limited than most, but not that limited, and I never heard a girl talk that way about her brother. Or anyone. She troubles me. But also I have to admit she attracts me. Don't be jealous, Mama, but it's true. I don't want you to think I could ever love anyone the way I love you, and I'm not even saying that I'm in love with her. But we always promised we would tell each other the truth and so I'm telling you. Do you think I should still talk to her? I'm still tutoring her, but I don't know . . .

But enough of the letter, Minnie. Here's the fish.

It smells good.

It looks good. It always looks nice here even if it's the mall.

The mall. The mall. Today everything is at the mall. I remember before the mall. Everything was in the neighborhood, you didn't have to drive nowhere else. Because how could you drive if you didn't have a car?

Today we drive. We fly. To the moon.

Tomorrow the moon. Fish on the moon. The mall on the moon. *Oi*, I should be so lucky to eat on the mall on the moon. What we would eat there I don't know. Fish? Moon fish? What do you think? Are there fish on the moon? In the mall on the moon? And this same dark woman will be serving us? Moon women? Moon men? Grandmothers, grandmothers on the moon? There'll always be grandmothers. On the sun. Moon. Stars. We'll always be here, talking, making nice for the children, for the grandchildren. Here. Look. The fish is getting cold, Rose. Eat the fish. Enjoy.

Is it moon fish?

It's fish fish. Not a fishy fish but a meaty fish. A fleshy fish. Sole.

Sole. Moon sole. Soul. Soul moon. Eat. I'll eat.

And talk?

And talk. You want to finish that letter. Read more letters. But I didn't bring more. More I have at home. Sometime I'll show. Letters. Diaries also I have. And papers. Plenty of papers. These he gives to me for safekeeping. He trusts me. Don't you like a boy who trusts his mother? What more could you want? The moon?

Why not the moon?

So I'll give you the moon. And you know what that is?

What?

The truth. The moon is the truth. Everybody wants it, but it's always hanging up there in the sky just out of reach.

And this you can give to me?

On this subject I'm trying.

So tell me more.

I'm telling. First a bite of fish. And then more moon.

It was the woman who decided it. You know, it's always the woman.

He was teaching her Hebrew, and she asked him if they could read poetry in Hebrew. So at night he came over to teach her, and one night, this was in his last year, after his classes, after his dinner in the dormitory, where, I assure you, he ate well but not as well as he ate at home, he had stopped, you see, eating so much at the Sporens because of the atmosphere, Meyer Sporen becoming louder at the dinner table, the son still absent, Mrs. Sporen constantly sneaking off into the other room to take a drink, and Maby the daughter living in another world from which now and then she would visit, in the form of saying nasty things to both her parents, and teasing Manny.

So one night she tells him, after a year of reading together in the downstairs parlor, Come up with me, I want to show you something. And like a fool he climbs the stairs. Like a fool— like a boy so much in love he couldn't pee or eat a potato without thinking of her. It had been that way with him ever since that time he saw her at the station and he looked up and saw her beautiful white-ruffled chest—this is how the world is decided, by either seeing such things or not seeing and that changes everything—and in Manny's case he saw, and so when she invited him up after all this time—because she had other things on her mind all those other years, crazy things, they all show up later, sometime I'll show you, you'll see, you'll see—anyway she invites him up, and he can't climb the stairs fast enough— oh, if he could hear me tell you this he'd turn red, he'd say, Mama, Mama, please, do you think you could read my mind? How do you know how I felt then? And I'd have to remind him that he was a good son, that he wrote all this to me, that he told me everything, even though now he would like to forget it, now that's he's on his second honeymoon in Bitch Heaven, Beach Haven some normal people call it—the bitch herself leading him up the stairs . . .

Come and see this, she says to him, and takes his hand.

His fingers felt like hot sticks! Her cool touch, almost clammy, it didn't matter, it set his hands on fire! She leads him, by the hand, the heat rising to his wrist and climbing to his arm, the fire, burning, along the hall and up to the window at the end, the alcove overlooking the river. There's the moon hanging over all, turning the river to a silvery sliver that looks like water that spilled and then froze between the southern hills. Whenever he studies water, gazes at it, into it, he thinks of his father, tries to remember the ocean passage, recalls his father's stories about Atlantis this, Atlantis that, the city in the sea, and before he knows what he's doing he's telling her all about it, and she's laughing out loud, telling him how crazy it all sounds, and he draws back from her, a little hurt, a little insulted.

And I suppose all your talk about changelings isn't a bunch of bull? he says to her.

She gave him a funny look, a deep look that in a way scared him a little, for reasons we all found out later on, but also a look where he could see a bit of play-acting on her part too, a look that wanted to say, So, who can know what we really are after all? and perhaps I really am a changeling, whatever that is. Remember now that he's been studying Talmud, reading philosophy, history, and doing his accounting, his business practices, his little classes in managing things, all of it very practical each in its own way from the Torah to the economics, and maybe some rabbis they've got their eyes on the mysterious, on what God means when he says this or that in one place in the Books of Moses or another, but Manny was never interested in that part of it—in a way he had decided to study it because he wanted something hard but something he could hold on to—he could have the rules from the Ten Commandments, he could have maybe a little fuzziness in some of the arguments from the old rabbis, but there was always the *hard and fast* rule that you could always figure out one way or another and *pretend* at least that you knew what was going on in the Bible or in your life or somebody else's life or all of this at once.

Like that piece of glass he carried around, something he could feel under his fingers and think, This came from the bottles from the truck that killed my father, and I will always remember that day, and it will never change for me, hard and fast. Maybe it was a little magic trick he used on himself, a little bit of pretending, but he used the glass star as a way of giving himself good luck, of protecting himself against the kind of trouble he could see coming in her eyes. And he had used it before, when he had stumbled into the alley and looked up and saw the pigeon that spoke to him in his father's voice! The pigeon! the vision! Am I seeing this? am I hearing things? he asked himself always, and touched his fingers to the sharp-edged souvenir as a way of bringing himself back to the reality of his pain, the loss of his father so young in his life and so early in his *father's* life, and the pain would always put him back on the right path, the trail he wanted to take toward making a success for himself in the world both as a good man and as a man who can buy for himself and his family and his mother the things of this world that everyone, unless they're lying, want to buy and pile up and keep.

And through all this thinking and remembering he's still looking into her eyes and he sees in there some very strange things, first a park or a playground, a schoolyard, like that, with little demon children playing on the swings and push-go-round, and then a shift of light, like a big storm over the rooftops just at sunset when the colors swirl around and turn orange and purple and darker and finally dark, and he sees a garden, and a tree, an apple tree, *kinnahurra*, a tree from Eden he explained it to me, this is what he saw, which makes her, and makes him, well . . .

Come, she says to him, and takes him by the hand, down the hall, into her room, where her parents are I don't know. He doesn't know. If she knows, she's not telling. Always before they had done their studying together in the downstairs old-fashioned parlor, where the ship captain who built the old house could tell his daughters to sit if they had male visitors, but now they are upstairs—and it's so quiet it's as if somebody has turned off the sound on a television or turned off a hearing aid—and they're going to study, she explains to him, because he looks and there in her hand is a Bible, and in a minute she's leading him into her room, and she points to the bed for him to sit and she sits on the floor and she tilts her head a little, you know the cute way my Sarah's got, obviously she got disinherited from her mother who to me has never shown such cuteness but must have had it in her when she was Sarah's age or just a little older, because this is the time that we are seeing her in right now.

Read, she says.

He knows just what she means. They've been studying together, studying Graetz' *History of the Jews*, studying the *Encyclopedia Judaica*, at whose suggestion his or hers it doesn't matter by now, does it? Big books, heavy books, but tonight, they're reading the *Song of Songs*.

He clears his throat, feels just the tiniest prickle of embarrassment, since how well does he know this girl though by now it's been a few years? Not so well. He's seen her at meal times when he's been invited, but she's always kept her distance from him, even after the time he watched her coming down the stairs. She's his twin, she says to him sometimes, twin lost in the woods. And now and then she'd talk to him after services on the holidays at the Union of All Hebrews, since Meyer Sporen liked to keep track of Manny. He had an investment in the boy, of course. His own son, at that time, he considered lost. He was off on the ocean somewhere. Did he write? No. Did he telephone? No. Did he send a telegram? Nothing. And the reasons, well, Manny learned all this soon enough, but not during his first few years there, and not even up until this moment, but soon, and then it was soon enough, and it was enough, too, I'm telling you.

And my Manny opens to the proper page, and he's feeling at the very instant that he begins to read the twinge in his you-know-what-and-where that turns his face red. But she pretends not to notice the way he shifts his leg on the bed, the way he leans closer into the pages even as he raises the book closer to his face. He was a boy who had known very little about life except hard work and what love his mother could bring to him, which is a love every boy needs but different of course from the love that comes to a man from a woman, and this he needed, too, without even knowing, and the reddening of his face, the feeling in his legs, his . . . It came from not understanding how much he needed, but she understood, and she was tempting him even with her eyes, with her . . .

Well, I'll just show you. So he's opening his mouth to read, he's wet his lips for the *Song of Songs* . . .

I am a Rose of Sharon / a lily of the valleys . . .

Can you imagine him reading this to her at this moment, alone in the room, alone in the house?

Catch us the little foxes, / the little foxes, / that spoil the vineyards / for our vineyards are in blossom.

He looks up, she's standing, unbuttoning, can you believe this?

I come to my garden, he's reading, digging his nose deeper and deeper into the page as though if he tries hard enough he can disappear face first right into the poem and never have to deal with the life that's going on in front of him.

I come to the garden, my sister, my bride, / I gather my myrrh with my spice, / I eat my honeycomb with my honey, / I drink my wine with my milk.

She's a bony girl, but pretty, the same prettiness you can see coming out in Sarah these days, the slightly knobby shoulders and elbows still available if a grandmother wants to rub them for luck, but also a thickening in the tush and the chest, a reddening of the skin, the knees looking good, the calves, and here she is, standing in front of him, sliding from her shoulders her ruffled blouse.

I went down to the nut orchard, he reads, to look at the blossoms of the valley / to see whether the vines had budded, whether the pomegranates were in bloom . . .

And that was that. In a few seconds she had the book out of his hand, pushed him down, undid his trousers, slid them right over his shoes. Sister, bride, myrrh, spices, eat the honeycomb with the honey. Before he could turn around my little boy was no longer a little boy, and the Bible study, the famous reading of the big poem from Solomon, it was over.

Some over, I'm telling you.

So here now she's coming, the black girl with the check. The whole time we've been sitting she's been standing, working, waiting.

We're the last people here—but look here's more coming in, the night crowd.

Sure, we're the day crowd. And when Manny and his beloved come back from their vacation I won't be able to stay out so late.

What about your granddaughter? You ain't been cooking for her?

Today she's supposed to eat with a friend. And sleep over. Tonight the grandmother stays by herself. But she's used to that.

I can never get used to living alone.

Who can? Could I? When Manny left for Cincinnati, I'm telling you, it was like Jacob died all over again. Except that he wrote.

He wrote very nice letters. I'm glad you showed.

I'll show more. I've got it all, all the writings. Come over some time and we'll read together.

I would feel like I'm prying. After all it's not like they're famous people out of history. They're just people alive today, the rabbi of my temple, his wife.

All the more you should want to know about them.

Very funny. Very true. But look, darling, here's your car pulling up outside, I can see it through the window in the light from the parking lot lamps.

You see it? Where?

There, by the entrance.

You can see? I can't see.

Put in more ointment you can see.

Sure, my ointment. I'll put it in. I'll get better.

It could get worse?

Dr. Mickey said we'll see. Meanwhile we're trying the ointment. So it could get worse? So what else is new? I don't know a life where things could get worse? So come on, here's my driver and we'll drive you home and next time we get together we'll have another meeting and maybe you'll tell me things and I'll tell you things and we'll meet in the mall on the moon.

Ladies?

But here she is, so now let's pay the piper. Piper. Piper schmiper. Look, such a handsome fellow the driver is. A nice Spanish boy. Manny hires him from his corporation in the city. A legitimate business expense. To go back and forth from here to there. So he doesn't have to drive himself, or take the bus. The rabbi on the bus doesn't sound so good, does it? Or the rabbi looking for a parking space? Look, it didn't used to be that way, but now that he can afford it, I don't say why? I say why not? And it's getting dark, and here's the check, and it's time to go and I hope I didn't shock you with my old stories about the famous poems by the King Solomon, the love story, the truth about my family, this life I live?

Darling, Minnie, I see now it's not such an old story, I'm telling you, to me it's news, it's news.

A Mother's Prayer

Since I cannot stand up in the synagogue or temple to pray I make this silent request of you, God, whoever You are, wherever You are—a burning bush, a naked back, a cry in the night, a great big white, flapping, winged bird. Whoever. Whatever. Dear God. Please keep my children from harm, my one child actually, the rabbi, and his children. I did nothing in my life except to make this child and I would ask You now to keep him from harm. He had a rough youth as You know. The life started off just fine. But then he went out with his father on that Sabbath morning—and did You punish my Jacob for working on the Sabbath? I hope not. If You answered yes, I would turn my back on You, God. I would ask You please to leave the house of my life. But say that You didn't do it—say that You were busy in the synagogue with all of the people, the devout ones who went to shul that Saturday morning, and say that You didn't see the problem, the taxi leaving the hotel, the fire that got so big and smoky somebody called the fire department, the milk truck starting off on its rounds. I know that God is God and that You have eyes on everything. But say that these people in the shul, the very religious men, the ones who would not talk to my Jacob because he disobeyed Your Laws, say that they diverted Your attention for just a minute, and so even though You knew about the taxi, the milk truck, the fire wagon, and my Jacob and my Manny walking with the cart, say that You knew all this—still for a second, just the tiniest part of time, like the part of the body an eyelash is compared to all the rest, for this eyelash of a split of time You looked away, or You blinked, or (could it be?) You were looking at it about to happen and You let it— no, I'll think that You were listening to the prayers, watching the men lean forward, rock forward and back, forward and back in their devotions, and You missed the instant, just as You would later miss the killing of the Jews in Europe—were You called away then to another planet? did You have another world of Jews who wanted You to hear their prayers?—and that was when it happened. Look, I can understand, You liked the singsong, high-low quavering, wavering of the tunes, who doesn't like to hear those old-time melodies out of the Orient, the East? It's beautiful music, maybe not so much American, but then later we will hear lessons about the connections between the Orient and America, the Jews and Indians, and if we beat drums or tom-toms or wore feathers in our hair, the Jewish Indians, would our music be any less acceptable to You, O Lord? You looked away, the crash crashed, and the glass shattered, and the truck came down like a fist on my Jacob's chest, and I want You to know that after all these years I could possibly begin to forgive You, if, a big IF, You take better care of my Manny and his children from now on.

Book Two
Twilight

S ally! Mrs. Stellberg! I thought you'd never get here! Welcome, welcome to this apartment so high up above the park. And did you think that you were never going to stop once you started climbing in the elevator? And could you catch your breath? Me, I've had no breathing problems, not that I ever had such problems, but the eyes, the eyes . . .

It's very high here, darling, Mrs. Bloch. Me, I prefer Jersey where it's low, at street level.

Look, I know what you mean, and far be it from me to miss a meeting with you at the mall. But it's not so easy for me to get around much anymore—I don't want your sympathy, I'm just telling you the truth—and if you can get around without too much trouble you're a very lucky girl.

I'm lucky, Minnie, but I'm not a girl no more. No, coming in on the bus today to see you I decided that I'm not a girl anymore at all. A young man, my grandson's age, he got up and gave me his seat and didn't say another word.

Romance, Sally, you've got romance.

I've got veins and arthritis is what I've got, Minnie. But talking about sons . . .

Talking about sons, and moons, and daughters, and planets. Yes, so, I invited you here to tell you more.

Other girls . . .

I thought you weren't a girl no more.

Very funny. Some of the other girls they tell me that you've been inviting them here to tell them, too.

Other girls, other grandmothers, it's true they've come to see me ever since it's so hard for me to see them. Rose Pinsker, Mrs. Applebaum, Mrs. Sugar. All of them girls, all of them grandmothers, they come to hear my story, and sometimes they tell me theirs. And you, you didn't like what I told you so far? You didn't want to know further?

Of course, I want to know. That's why I've come all the way in here.

And they too all wanted to know about what happened to my son and their rabbi, and they don't have a right to know? All the grandmothers, listening to stories, telling their own. They—we—don't have a right?

They have a right to know. So don't get so excited, Minnie. You think that I'm jealous of them seeing you? It's a long way in here by bus . . .

Next time—and don't think I'm getting hoity-toity with you—next time I'll send for you the car and driver.

Next time you say. So why didn't you save me the bus trip this time. It cost me four dollars the fare . . .

Sally, you're complaining about the fare?

Minnie, Minnie, I'm making a joke. Look, it does me good to get out and ride the bus. This time I met a boy, next time maybe a man, a nice young sixty-year-old. Maybe I'll see one on the way back. We'll talk a little . . .

You're such a risky grandmother, such talk from such a respectable woman.

Now I'm a woman. A minute ago I was a girl. So I can't act like a girl?

Act like the grandmother that you are. Go in dignity. Don't talk to strangers. For you I'll have the car to take you home.

Thanks but no thanks. I'll take the bus. I'm not used to such a style.

It's not a style, it's a luxury. But don't knock it. From my Jacob's cart to this car with the driver, it's a long way, and when you've traveled as far as I have you don't turn down a ride.

Me, I haven't traveled so far. Just over the bridge.

And a long way besides, for you, too, you'll admit it if I push you, and for all of us, the girls turned into grandmothers, a far trip.

All right, all right, Minnie, you're convincing me. I deserve the car to drive me home, I'll take the ride.

I'm glad, darling. If it was afternoon maybe I could listen to you talk about the bus. But it's dark now, and the air's turning cold, the night is coming, it's almost here.

You're here alone?

I'm here alone. My Manny, and Maby, they're on a trip to Israel, the middle of the East. And I'm the one in charge of Sarah who's at school now, you know, up in the Green Mountains, at the Vermont college called something-ton or other, very small, very fancy, and very—you know—free, she tells me, or at least that's the way she wants it to be. As to how free, we'll see, we'll see. You just missed her, actually. She drove down for the weekend in the little car, very small, very fancy, and not so free, that her father bought for her when she promised if she would go to this place that she would work hard and not forget about us. So the only time she's here on a trip since school began it's the middle of the week and her parents are away on a trip. She couldn't have planned it better if she had planned it. She needed some things, she said, and goes into her room and starts packing jeans and sweaters and shoes and a load of bedding, and I'm saying, You need these things for school? You have these things for school, darling. And I'm trying to figure out what she's doing, I can't see so good now with the problem, like I told you on the telephone, so I have to lean over real close so I can see the packing, and she chases me away, she says, Grandma, please leave me some privacy.

Privacy, I should leave you? I told her, Darling, privacy you'll get from me when I'm in my grave, God forbid, and for now I want to know what you're doing. Your parents are away on their trip— they're in Europe and Israel now, on a trip *her* doctor said would be good for her. So I'm in charge.

Mama, you think you want to do this? Manny asked me for about the tenth time before they left.

She's in school, darling, and I'm down here. So if she has a problem up there she talks to people up there, and if I have a problem down here—because that's what you're asking, really, isn't it? I pick up the telephone and I call the doorman, and he calls for me whatever I need.

So you'll be all right?

I'll be all right.

I think that I must do this, Mama. The doctor thought that a change of pace would be good for her. And . . .

Don't explain no more, I told him. It will be good for her, it will be good for you. Take pictures. You'll show me when you come back.

And you promise, he says, you'll keep up with your eye medicine so that you can see them?

I promise, I promise. I don't tell him that I think it don't matter no more the medicine. Because the specialists Doctor Mickey sent me to they're already talking deteriorating nerves, and they want to try a beam, a this, a that, and we'll see, I say, when my son comes back from his trip, we'll see about putting a beam in my eye, see, and we'll all be happy together. They like my spirit, they tell me, they laugh, they joke, they treat me royally, like I'm their own mother. I *am* your mother, I tell these doctors. I am *all* your mothers so you'd better be careful. And they laugh and laugh again, sweet boys, like your boy the lovely Doctor Mickey, Mrs. Stellberg, I'm sure.

So Sarah picked through her things and packed up her things, and I said, You're taking all this up to school?

And she gives me a funny look, and a silence, and then she says, Sure, Grandma.

You think I believe her? It's warming up there, she needs more sweaters? In Vermont it's spring almost and she needs sweaters? So where are you going? I ask her.

Back to school, Grandma, she says.

She's always been an independent girl, Mrs. Stellberg. Very tough on her parents, a little tomboy sometimes, especially now she cut her hair so short when she came back from the first year at school, but I like to think she got it from all of us, from Jacob, me, the explorers who came from the Old World to the New, and from her father who went from here in the city to Cincinnati, and got his education, and came back and made a very good head of the congregation and then set up with the brother-in-law the new business, the holding company, and then the package factory, the boxes they make, the crates, the bottle tops, and then they bought the machines that make the bottles, and then they turned their barges around and sent them back to the ports and added to their fleet bigger boats for the ocean trips, I'm telling you, it's growing and growing, whenever I turn around he's buying something else, because they're quite a team as it turns out, Mrs. Stellberg, the brother-in-law who doesn't like the public so much but knows everything about business, and my Manny, who has such a good public presence, and people trust him, the ethics man, the man in the plain black suit, he is up in the front, and even the fancy old men with their gray suits they never even sat with a Jewish person, let alone did business with them, they trust him too maybe because of his hair, and the quiet way he has, I don't know, to me he's my little Manny, and she, I was telling you about the granddaughter, she's my little Sarah, except I hear her on the telephone she's talking to a friend and can you imagine she says, Hi, this is Sadie. Sadie! So who's Sadie, I say to her when she gets off the phone, and she jumps at me again, she shouts at me, Grandma, she shouts, why don't you let me live my life. You're just like the rest of them!

Just like the rest? I said to her. Of course I'm just like the rest, I'm your grandmother and I love you, and your father loves you—oh, she made a face when I said that—and your mother loves you—and youch, another face—and I said, So that's the way I'm just like the rest of them. Me and the rest of them, we're your family, we're your own, and if we love you that's not such a big crime, is it?

She looked at me with that funny squint, one I noticed early in her life would be her way of looking at things, and the way she's standing, holding her head to one side, squinting, it's not only her but somebody else in the family, not her mother, although she has her mother's coloring (and my coloring) and not her father, although she's a little heavy in the hips and shoulders, a little stocky like him, but it's the brother-in-law I see, the one I hardly know, the one who came back from the sea after the death of the Sporens together, that awful mess I told you about? Yes, I remember telling you, at another session of our grandmothers' club, and she's looking, looking, like a judge, or maybe like a wild animal who has just come out of the woods and sees a human being standing there and is wondering, Is this person dangerous or does she want to play, and then she steps up to me and takes me around the waist and lays her head on my shoulder and says, It's not such a big crime, Grandma, no.

And the next thing, this tough cookie is shaking, quaking like a leaf!

What is it, darling, I ask her, putting my hands on her head and pressing her even closer to my bosom. Grandma hurt your feelings?

She just shakes and quakes, she can't force herself to speak.
Never as a little girl did she cry like this. Her mother never cried,
and I think she learned from her mother somehow that crying
was wrong. So she always bit her lip or pounded her hands
together but she never cried.

Gr-randma! she says, quaking, shaking, trembling.

There, there, darling, I say, tell me what's wrong. Some boy?

But she says nothing more, just quakes, trembles, like a leaf.

Darling, you can tell grandma, you can tell your bubba. You
can tell.

She's stuttering now, n-no, I c-can't, I c-can't, Grandma, and
the next thing you know she's pulling away from me, and she's
out the door.

You didn't see her on the elevator? or in the lobby? She left
just a little while before you arrived. With the keys to her car
still lying there on her unmade bed. And half the things she
packed still sitting there on the floor. So she'll be back sooner
or later, if she really wants these things for school. Or whatever.
Frankly, I don't think that she knows what she wants. For a girl
who's had everything, toys, clothes, boys, friends, school,
books, records, a car now, trips everywhere to Europe, she
doesn't know what she wants. She wanted a car, he gave her
a car. Three cars the family has! and Jacob and I had nothing
except the cart that he pulled like a horse all by himself! With
little Manny, that last time, pushing from behind, of course.
With little Manny, pushing—and he's still pushing, pushing his
way to the business he wants to make into something bigger
than just in one country, because of the boats, he tells me when
I inquire, because of the boats.

So now here, look, she left papers, folders, notebooks scattered all over the place. Just before you got here I started to pick
up. And this I picked up, this folder with the papers. So what
is it? A school assignment? Let me see. *Oi*, I can't hardly make
out the letters at all. Last year I could see letters. Now to me
they're all blurry. I'm going to have to have the cataract operation he says. He, your Doctor Mickey. So until then you'll have
to tell me because I'm not blind, I don't read by running fingers
across the page like some blind. But what does it say? Read a
little darling, be my eyes a while, and the cook will bring the
food.

I'll be your eyes for a while, Mrs. Stellberg said. And then I'll be my own mouth and we'll eat?

You're hungry? So we'll eat.

But first I'll read.

You'll read.

I'll read. But first I got to adjust my glasses here. Here. Now. *Mr. Eskin,* it says at the top, and then *Language and Lit.,* and *Personal Essay,*

Jewish Halloween, it says,

by Sarah Bloch.

So what's a personal essay?

You're asking me, Minnie? I don't have the daughter who goes to the funny school up in the country. You tell me.

So don't ask, Sally. Just read, why don't you.

I'll read. Again. *Jewish Halloween. Personal Essay. By Sarah Bloch.*

Sarah Bloch.

Sarah Bloch. Here, can you at least see her name.

It's dim.

It's dim? It's in big letters, practically in crayon.

She writes her personal assignment in crayon.

I didn't say in, I said practically in.

Practically in. Practically out. Read now darling before the food comes.

Putting on costumes has never been fun for me. Ever since I was a small child I always found that I had problems just getting dressed in my everyday clothes for school. As the daughter of our town's rabbi, I was the object of a lot of close observation, or so I felt. Each morning I wanted things to be perfect, to dress perfectly, to know my lessons well, to talk without a stammer. Now I see that rather than call attention to myself as someone without a fault what I really wanted to do was to become invisible.

What? Invisible? This is about wanting to be invisible? *Oi,* the poor girl! the poor girl!

I don't think she's so poor.

Don't be funny. So, go 'head. Read me the rest.

I learned this lesson well the evening of the annual temple Purim party my freshman year in high school. Rick Sommer, the temple activities director, liked a good party.

Excuse me, Mrs. Stellberg, but just a little explanation. This is Rick, Rose Pinsker's grandson, by the way, and a very nice boy, she tells me. So go on. Read.

He called Purim—which is a minor festival in which Jews celebrate their rescue from a murderous Middle Eastern tyrant by means of the loyalty of his wife, Esther, to them—Jewish Halloween. Because everybody gets dressed up in costumes based on the story from the Book of Esther.

It's a name I never liked. And I never liked the holiday for the reasons which I've already said. But Rick kept after me, as he often did for sometimes very little obvious reason. I think that he suspected something about the fears public events like these produced in me, and he had some strange thing of his own which made him want to tease me about it. Teasing, I suppose, if you want to take Freud as your expert, is sexual in nature. It's a friendly accepted way of saying, I like you a lot and would like to make you feel the same. Except that it makes you feel uncomfortable. Because it's dishonest. Because it covers over the sexual feeling with humor. Well, not that sex isn't humorous—oh, is it ever! It's a real joke, except . . .

This doesn't bother you, Mrs. Stellberg, Sally, does it? The talk about sex, I mean?

Sex never bothered me. Talk bothers me less.

Good, I didn't think so, but I wanted to check. After all, these are modern times. And this is what they write in college these days especially, you know, at that kind of place, an experimental college. A personal essay.

. . . somebody forgot the punchline. It just keeps going on and on. "Are you coming as Esther?" Rick said to me at a meeting of the Temple Youth, our group that was sponsoring the event. "No," I told him, "I'm coming as her husband." I didn't know what I had said at first, but after a while with some help from a kid at school I figured it out. The night of the party was going to be bad enough because of the fact that I had decided I wasn't going—coming—through the hassle of trying to look like a queen. I know I am an attractive girl and look a lot like my

mother, and I have her coloring and her build. But I don't feel inside what I appear to be because somewhere along the line I never learned how to act pretty. I could easily blame my mother for never transmitting this bit of knowledge along to me, but she had—has—her own troubles. My father wouldn't know. He understands zero about girls, and I wonder how much he knows about anything outside of the Bible and his business. But that's another story. Or is it? I don't know yet where I fit in. But I was explaining, before I allowed myself to get sidetracked, about Jewish Halloween. Or maybe this is what the holiday is all about—confusing identities and the inability to heal anybody who has that problem including yourself.

So here I was, trying to figure out what to wear to the costume party, when all of a sudden it occurred to me that I was telling Rick the truth. I didn't want to go as the queen, I wanted to go as her husband, the king, or maybe her brother if she had one. But where was I going to get boy's clothes? I knew boys from class, of course, but never very well. All they could do is look at me and see how pretty I was but they never let the me behind my skin come out. They thought they were my friends but they were friends with the skin and bones of me only. I couldn't go to them anyway because it wouldn't be a surprise if I did. Word would get out quickly that the rabbi's daughter was coming as a boy. I couldn't use my father's clothes either because he is broad enough but not tall enough, and anyway all he ever wears are those deadly black suits and white shirts. I wanted something a little flashy—something that would call attention to my new costume in a sharp way.

So I had to go to Rick. And that was what got me into trouble. He was a college student who worked weekends at the temple and it worked out well for him most of the time because even though he was older and more responsible he was still young enough to know what kids are like and what they really want. Except in my case. I guess he never ran into anyone like me before. And I was after all the daughter of the rabbi, his boss. Well, foolishly, then, I went to him to ask for help.

"Come on down to New Brunswick," he told me. "I have all my clothes there in my room. Take the bus down and I'll drive you back." So, foolish maiden that I was, I took the bus one Thursday after school, thinking that he meant to drive me right back. I went to his fraternity house, the Zebes, an old white house with pillars painted black and white so that it looked like a striped zebra. And I met him in the living

room and he invited me upstairs to his room. It was just before the dinner hour by the time I got there, and the house was deserted because most of the boys were down in the dining room. Upstairs it was quiet, dimly lighted, and smelled of after-shave and gym clothes, a funny mix.

Should I keep reading?

What do you mean, should you keep reading? Of course you should keep reading. I want you should hide things from me? I knew maybe she was having trouble with a boy. I could hear something. I'm the grandmother. The mother can't hear it. She's too nervous, but how nervous we don't yet know. But I am always here listening, like a rock is near the sea, and what washes over me washes over. I'm still here . . . So read . . .

As an only child I never lived with the mess of other people my age. Because I was so pretty I never had a lot of female friends. Girls not as good-looking didn't like to have me around. Boys I knew a little better but still at a distance. Being the rabbi's daughter didn't help. I read a lot. I took guitar lessons. It helped to soothe me when I was alone, which I was a lot of the time, though my guitar caused me a lot of trouble on Yom Kippur one time! Being my mother's daughter didn't help either since she was usually alone in her own little world, and then she started talking about trying to write to keep herself happy in the same way that I tried to use the guitar. And maybe I learned that from her? From Maby? (That's her nickname, because as a child she always used to reply with a "maybe" whenever her parents asked her if she would do something.) Maybe? Maybe.

"What do you think of this?" Rick said after a few minutes of rummaging around in his closet. He was holding up a large turban that someone had worn once during a fraternity carnival.

"Hey, perfect," I said and tried it on. It was heavy, and I had to practice to keep my head from wobbling when I wore it. And while I gawked at myself he found a large pair of harem pants that could have been either for a man or a woman, and some wooden shoes.

"All just right," I said. "I'll try this on."

"You better change in here," he said. "The brothers will be coming up to use the bathrooms."

So he left the room and I pushed the door shut and went over to the mirror and took off my sweater and blouse and skirt.

This is for a school assignment? It's funny talk for a school assignment. But then that place is a funny school. I don't know, Mrs. Pinsker. It's got markings on it? Her professor gave her a grade? You tell me. Here, let me see. *Oi*, I can't hardly see the writing. So what does it say?

Everything would have been all right with Rick except that he came back in too soon. Or maybe he did it on purpose, it's difficult to say. He came back in and saw me there in my panties and bra and he came up to me and put his arms around me and I could feel him next to me . . .

This is enough?

No, it's not, it's not over. Keep reading. She's upset and I want to find out everything why. If I can, which I can't because you can't know everything. But go 'head.

. . . and I felt cold all over and moved away from him and told him to please leave the room. Asked him, anyway. "Sorry," he said. And he left.

Ah, so you see. He is a very nice boy after all. Nice to my Sarah. His grandmother would be proud. Excuse me. Read.

And I changed into the costume and saw that it would be fine, and changed back into my sweater and blouse. Rick was embarrassed when I told him that I was ready to go. He had made a pass at the rabbi's daughter and he was sweating. But I told him not to worry and I chattered away on the ride home, as if I were the one who should have been nervous because I had made the misstep and not him. That incident made me wonder. About a lot of things. But this essay is supposed to center around the Purim party, Jewish Halloween, and so I'd better get to the night of the party.

A springlike night, warm air, clear skies. I'm feeling wonderful as I step into my baggy trouser costume and fit the turban on my head. And then I hear Mother on the stairs and I remember that she is supposed to chaperone the party, and my heart sinks. There's a noise in the hall as she bumps against a door. And she's got to drive me there as well as take over the party? She's knocking at my door, and then steps in before I invite her. "Hey, Mom," I say. "Don't I rate a little privacy?"

"What's the matter?" she says. "Are you a boy or something? I come in when I come in. So excuse me," and she turns around and staggers back out . . .

"Dad?" I'm calling through the house. He doesn't answer but I find him in his study.

"Dad? There's going to be trouble."

"What are you talking about?"

"Mom," I tell him. "She's supposed to be chaperoning this Purim party? and she's . . . "

"She's what?"

"You know."

"I don't know."

"You do."

"Don't tell me, darling, what I know and what I don't. Now inform your mother that you're ready and I'll drive you to the party."

"You'll drive?" I asked.

"I'll drive."

"And you'll pick us up?"

"If you can't find another ride home, yes."

"Okay."

"Your costume looks good," he said.

"Thank you," I said.

"Maybe you'll win a prize?"

"I don't think so," I said. "They couldn't give me one because I'm your daughter."

"Of course," he said. "Poor girl. Always penalized."

He smiled, and I had to smile too. His eyes sometimes nearly hypnotized me that way, they are so powerful. And his hair. Even me, his daughter, can't help but notice his beautiful white hair.

"We'll make it up to you," he said.

"That's okay," I said.

"No, no," he said. "I was just sitting here going over some travel brochures. All these years as a rabbi, I said to myself, and I've never been to Israel. What if we were all to go?"

"That would be all right, I guess."

"You guess? You don't know?"

"I know it would be all right. I'd like that."

"Because who knows how long I'll be a rabbi, yes? So I had better take a look around."

"What does that mean, Dad?"

"What does what mean?"

"About how long you'll be a rabbi?"

"Oh, darling, every year I think I want to quit. I'm just talking."

"But what would you do if you quit?"

"Your uncle Mordecai wants me to come into the business full-time," he said. "And it's a very tempting offer."

"Well, I think that you should do what feels right," I told him.

"Is that so?" he said.

I nodded, feeling the turban wobble on my head.

"That's what you advise the rabbi to do?"

I shrugged, holding the turban steady.

"You look like a vizier," he said. "Giving me advice from inside your crystal ball."

"What's a vizier?" I asked.

"An advisor to an Eastern monarch. Like Haman. So how come you didn't dress like Haman?"

"I didn't want to be a bad guy," I said.

"You want to come as a good guy?"

I nodded.

"You give me good advice."

"Can I give you a little more?"

"Sure, Mike," he said, using an old expression I've heard grandma say before.

"Let Mom stay home and you come and chaperone."

He moved his beautiful white-haired head a little, as though some insect or tiny electrical shock had given him a jolt.

"I can't."

"Why not?"

"She's got to do it."

"She's got to? But what if she can't?"

"I'm not her father," he said.

"Neither am I," I said.

"Don't be a wise guy," he said, and looked down at the papers on his desk.

"Please listen," I said.

"Get ready, I'll drive you."

"That's all?" I said.

I went to get my coat and he fetched my mother. In the car on the way to the temple he smoked a cigar and mother said nothing but I could smell her breath. Oh, the perfume of my parents it was lovely in that time. Zillions of kids had gathered in

*the hall by the time we got there. My father dropped us off. I had to
help my mother to the door and I nearly lost my turban several times
since I was using both hands to help her. It was like we were dancing.*

*Inside, the real dancing had begun and I left mother at the coat room
and went over to listen to the band. It was Barry Katz and his rinky-
dink quartet, but I didn't care because all I wanted was a lot of loud music
to cover over the noise in my head. I don't know what I was waiting
for but I didn't dance with anyone, I just stood there rocking until Rick
came over and said hello.*

"How's it going?" he asked.

*"Fine," I told him, "just fine." But it wasn't fine because out of the
corner of my eye, I could see my mother standing at an angle over alongside the punch bowl, and I thought, You are really stupid, Sadie, that's
my nickname for myself that I invented, why didn't you just suggest
that your mother stay home and that Rick chaperone the whole thing?
Isn't that what he gets paid for. Except that he's not an adult, my father
would have said, and we need an adult there. And mother is an adult?
I would have said. And he would have gotten really angry. So here we
are, me in my turban, and a lot of princesses around, and a lot of other
Mordecais beside me, and a few million Hamans with dark thin mus-
taches and evil paint around their eyes, and our rinky-dink band was
playing an old song, "Blue Suede Shoes," and some people are rocking
back and forth. And then it's "Blue Moon" and Rick comes up to me
and asks me to dance, and I can feel him against me and I can feel the
metal-like coldness taking over in me again, but now there's no place
to run to since we're here at the dance for a while and I feel sick because
I want to say something to him but I don't know the words.*

*"Rick," I say to him, just to say something, "Don't you think it's
funny that Purim really is like a Jewish Halloween?"*

*And he sort of pulls his face back from mine, and his eyes do a funny
thing—later I understood (or learned) that that was his way of thinking seriously about something—and he says, "Hey, you know, that's
cool, I never thought of that!" And he pulls me closer to him, because
I guess by this time he had gotten over his fears of scaring me off, and
gotten over his worries about trying something with the boss's daughter, or maybe even that he thought it would get him somewhere, trying something with the boss's daughter. I don't know. I might have
found out a lot more about him, and about me, except that just then
the music came to an end. A break, guys and gals, Barry Katz said into
the microphone, in a phony style that he must have picked up listening to band music on the radio or television. Hamans are drifting by,*

and many many princesses. I'm beginning to have half a good time, despite everything. "Want some punch?" says Rick. I've even forgotten about my mother. When all of a sudden — just like in a ghost story or a fairy tale, that's right — when all of a sudden, there's a screech from across the room by the table with the punch bowl, I see a long white arm flash up over the heads of the costumed crew of kids, and then there's a loud crash!

Rick and I run over like everybody else. And we find my mother stretched out on the long table, having fallen and knocked the bowl over onto the floor. We're walking through a pool of punch, a pink pool, and at first I'm thinking, Oh no, it's blood, but it's only punch, and Rick reaches over and helps mother to her feet, and she sags against him just like a little kid who's really tired and I'm trying to straighten her dress, and my turban falls over into the pool of punch, and I'm crying suddenly, and she perks up when she hears me, just like some puppet on a string, jerks straight up, pushes herself off from Rick, and points a long bony-fingered hand at me.

"You look like a fairy!" she says.

"Mother!" I could only whisper.

"You look like a fairy from a fairy tale," she says again.

"Please," I said. "Rick?"

But he didn't know what to do — it was one thing to try to get close to your boss's daughter, but to get tough with the boss's wife? It was awful, all the kids gathering around, and her standing there pointing that finger at me.

"Take it off," she says to me next. "Take it off and we'll see what you have on underneath that junk!"

"Mother," I pleaded with her.

"Mother!" she threw back at me, mocking.

"Mrs. Bloch, please," Rick put in, finally realizing that he was going to have to step in. And he took her by one arm and me by the other and we walked her out of the hall, while behind us the quartet was playing again, playing "Rock around the Clock," and we went up to the pay telephone in the hall and called my father, because Rick couldn't leave the dance, and my father came and drove mother home, leaving me at the dance with a dripping turban, a heart made of lead, and Rick expecting me out of gratitude to kiss him on the mouth. Later on in the evening, I did.

Minnie, there's a note from her teacher here at the end. I suppose it's from her teacher. *Sarah,* it says, *this was supposed to*

*be a personal essay, not a creative essay about your personal life. And
there is no conclusion. Please see me.*

Please see him?

That's what it says. See me. Please.

She's a polite girl, Sally. So I'm sure she saw him. And since
I heard nothing about it I'm sure it all went well. And in case
it didn't I'll ask her. And Manny too I'll ask when he comes back
from his Israel.

You don't know what happened? You usually know
everything.

I usually know everything? Only God knows everything. Do
I look like God to you? I'm only a grandmother, like you, just
another grandmother worrying. In the worrying state. Not no
longer Jersey but New York and still worrying. I'm worrying
now even that it could be my Sarah is packing because she's got
boy trouble like she used to have with Rose Pinsker's Rick. And
where does she think she's going? Not running away with some
boy like this I hope not, because here is the poor grandma and
I can hardly use my eyes no more, and I'm holding down the
fort, the babysitter for the big daughter while the parents are
away, and I don't want to lose the daughter to some wolf. Let's
hope not. But what a comment from the teacher. He didn't say
about what a good writer she was, only complaining about what
she didn't do.

Oh, but doesn't the time stoppage fly by, I can remember
when Maby gave birth to the pride of her grandmother's eye.
While we're eating I can show you pictures I have of the little
thing, and now she's out running around, suffering from the
boys, in college, and did we used to say time flies, Mrs. Stellberg? Time is like smoke, like wind, like water, it's there, it's not
there, you're in it, you're not. Here I am one minute holding little
Sarah in my arms, cuddling her, singing to her songs to help
her sleep, like this, like *Ah, ah-a, ba-bee, mama is a lad-y, and her
name is may-be, and you're a lit-tle bay-bee,* like this, like this, and
the next thing you know my little baby is a lady, *Sadie* she calls
herself on the phone with her friends, and I'm sitting here with
you, with nothing in my arms but smoke, wind, water. I wish
only it were water then at least I would have something left over.
I could wash with it, drink it, feel it on my skin.

After she was born we lived, all of us, in Jersey, just across
the bridge, a lovely place close to the country, close to the city,
like I was saying, just perfect for nearly everything we needed.

You like it, it was your hometown, Mrs. Stellberg, I know. You raised a family there, two families you could have raised and still not done better, isn't that right? And we settled in, trying our best to make the best of all the good things that were coming to us. And come they did, they came and came. The congregation was good people, and Manny's father-in-law, he died, that horrible way, like I told you at the mall, and the company goes to Manny and the long lost son who comes back from a South American somewhere, that all came to us. And so while maybe to some people it looked like my Manny was trying to lead a double life, I could see in those days in my mind just as clearly as I can today that he's instead got twice as many blessings as the normal man, as the average. And if these things come to you, don't knock them. Hold out your arms. It's a duty, a blessing is a duty, and you have to accept it as it comes because if you turn your head away it's going to knock you in the block.

This, darling, Sally, is my philosophy, and maybe I should put it in a sermon myself. Did I mention the sermon, the one that started all the trouble, the talk about the camps? I didn't say what it was about? With the other *her*, what else could it be? She came from the camps, she was a little girl there, her parents got arrested, and she got arrested, and they died so she could live. And that's it. A horror story, her story, and forever after you have to respect a person who has had to suffer such torture. That, too, is part of my philosophy, if you want to know. But I've told you anyway. Even if you didn't want to know now. There. Here. Look, the girl is getting ready to serve. But then I was telling you about the sermon, and I think that's one that you missed. It was a bad time for Manny, in those days. Because along with getting a good blessing there are other things you have to put up with. For example, Maby was having a lot of trouble with her problem, the kind like in the little personal essay Sarah's teacher complained about. Sarah. Or excuse me, *Sadie*. I should remember that that's how she likes people to call her now or else I'll get my head snapped off. And why shouldn't I call her that if it makes her happy? It doesn't hurt anybody, does it? But there are things that hurt, and let me tell about one of them. And don't get ants in your pants, darling, about the sermon because I'm going to get to that. But first, a little appetizer.

The business of Maby and the food.

You don't know none of this because nobody else ever heard about it. Except for Manny and us. We heard. Believe me, we heard. Like an alarm this went off in our ears. A burglar alarm. We were living in the old house, the new house that the congregation gives, you know, the brick one over on Locust from where he walked the day of his fall, and my Manny is in his study, as a matter of fact working on the famous sermon on the Holocaust, and the daughter, Sarah, otherwise known as Sadie later in her life but now only still Sarah, she's in her room listening to records, Baby Dylan or some such person, I am in the kitchen fixing our supper, and since when was I ever anywhere else at this time of day, late afternoon, New Jersey afternoon, in what season? autumn, winter, spring, does it matter? I'm thinking, thinking chicken, chicken, what was I cooking? fricasee? and from the big market I had some fresh soup greens, so it had to be spring, yes? and I was in the kitchen, upstairs is the granddaughter and the music, and my white-haired boy is in his study, preparing his famous sermon, but where is the mother of the daughter, the wife of the rabbi? Good question.

No, no, wait a minute. It was soup greens and springtime, and it was Baby Dylan on the Victrola, but my Manny wasn't home yet, he was on a condolence call, someone's father, mother, that I don't remember, had just passed away and he had stopped to see the family and so he comes in the door and says,

Hello, anybody home?

So cheerful he could be in those days. And what happened all of a sudden that his cheerfulness went out like the tide at the beach and never, never came back? I'm asking you, because I don't know the answer. Well, I know and I don't know. I'm giving you answers but I'm giving you questions. Here is a man, coming through the door with a smile on his face, a little tired, but basically a man who knows what he wants to do in life and is doing it, making a living for his family, doing in the world what he does best, and he comes home and expects to relax a little—even a rabbi, a man everybody depends on, he has to relax a little too—and so he comes through the door and the music is playing, and that he tolerates, though he has never been a great fan of music, and in fact he never reads the books, not even books by rabbis everybody in the congregation is reading, and the funny thing with him I learned over the years, and this goes to show you that even someone's mother can sometimes be surprised by what her child is up to, and believe you me don't think I haven't been surprised since, but what relaxes him I was going to tell you is something that would seem to everybody else like work, it is this business in the city, with the brother-in-law, this is his hobby, and he makes it grow and puts in the hours, just like he was building a toy house with blocks or matchsticks or making a garden, the way other people make a hobby in the yard.

What can I say to him sometimes to make him see that he should be doing something soothing instead of the business all the time, on the telephone all the time, in New York every spare minute of his time ever since the father-in-law passed away and the brother came back from South America? Can I say to him, Manny, darling, you want to get prematurely gray from worry? I cannot. Can I say to him, darling, Manny, you want to make people think you care only about making a dollar? That I can't do, because he also puts in so much time at the temple that to everyone in the world it's clear that he loves the work, loves the people in the congregation, wants to help them, especially the families that are broken up because of a death, because of a divorce, because he remembers what it was like when he was growing up without a father.

So here comes the hard-working man doing a double time life but not a double life, not then, he didn't see it that way at that time, at that time it was still how can he be rich and blessed at the same time. Well, let me tell you, he was trying, and he was succeeding. So here he comes in through the front door at the end of the day, the end of part of one day since he will work in his study after supper for hours, and so the day doesn't really end for him yet, and he comes through the door and if he's not smiling, and he's not whistling, and he's not behaving like the happiest man in the world, he's not slumping in over the threshhold either, he's not beaten down like a dog the way you sometimes see men look after working all day in the business, whatever they do, men who come in and the first thing you know they're a little tipsy already, and that's the evening, the sun has set.

But not my Manny, on him the sun is still shining. You can tell by his face that he's got something on his mind—that night it was the sermon—but not something that he can't accomplish by applying himself. Which is how he works, steady, steady, at one thing at a time, and I think, Sally, this is something he learned from my Jacob, the steadiness, the plodding along like a horse before a cart, but of course I'm not calling him an animal, don't be silly, but it reminds me of my Jacob and the way they set out that morning, for the cart, loading the cart with the fruit, and then towing and pushing the cart up toward Union Square, and the taxi heading for them, and the milk truck, and the swerving taxi with the fire engine at its back, and the rearing horse, and the falling truck, the crash of the glass, the broken bottles, the crush, the weight, the crumpled body of my Jacob, the lake of milk, the blood, the half-orphaned boy.

So Jacob comes home—*oi*, did I say Jacob? I meant to say Manny. So my Manny comes home in a state which is for him almost close to whistling and walks into a wall. I don't mean this actually, darling, I mean it's *like* he walks into a wall. Because I am in the kitchen and Sarah is upstairs listening to her music, and Manny walks in and the telephone starts to ring. Like in a play or a movie.

Ring ring ring.

I'll get it, Manny calls.

Oh, your daddy's home, I call to Sarah from the kitchen. She of course is upstairs listening to her music but through the noise she can hear the telephone—she has a magical ability to hear the telephone through any kind of sound. And she's already on the receiver when he picks it up.

What, Mama? she's saying.

Hello, Maby? Manny is saying.

Maby's voice comes through very well.

What?

Where?

Both father and daughter sound surprised.

Please come now! Maby's crying, screaming.

Hello? Rabbi Bloch? It's a man on the other end now, gruff voiced, but not trying to be rough. Can you please come down here?

The police never tell you everything. It's not that they want to make you guess, I think, but you have to ask to hear it all. So Manny asked. So they told him.

At the supermarket? Sarah said to him as he went out the door. They caught her at the supermarket? How disgusting!

Don't speak about your mother in that voice, Manny said. I was listening, I could tell that he didn't really mean it—I mean, I could tell that he felt some of that same disgust as soon as he had heard the news.

It had been coming to this over the years—I didn't know about the Purim party until just now when we heard Sarah's— pardon me, *Sadie's*—story. But I knew she had a problem. How could I not know she had a problem? Ever since her mother's death, and her father's. And it was as if with her mother gone the world called on her to pick up the glass that her mother had set down, or dropped, actually, and Maby picked it up and took her mother's place without spilling a sip. Except that she spilled quite a bit from that point on, she knocked things over, fell down, splattered food over her clothing, and I should know this because by that time I was running the house, not just cooking but cleaning and managing—everything. Did the rabbi's wife have time for such things? She would have had little time even if she did nothing but go to meetings at the temple, and on top of this Maby had plenty to do with her problem. It takes time to drink all day. Time slows down for you. *Oi*, if I had only known what it could do for you with time I maybe would have done some drinking myself—whiskey clips the wing of the bird of time, the bird flies slower, slower all the day, until it finally may not even get off the ground . . .

Well, she'd done it this time, climbed into her car and driven over to the market, left the car running while she went inside, packed her basket with groceries, and rolled it right past the checker and out into the parking lot.

In the parking lot she got abusive, as they say, when a basket boy came running up to her.

What do you mean? she said, hands on hips, stopping for a moment as she loaded the groceries into the back seat.

Please, lady, the boy said.

Get away from me or I'll call the police.

He didn't know what to do. He was standing there, this pimply faced high school student, probably one of the boys who used to stare at Sarah from a distance because she's so pretty, he stands there almost in tears. And he looks around, waves toward the store, and a manager or a manager's assistant who had been watching from the window picks up the telephone and calls the police. From his point of view he wasn't going to wonder about what was going through her mind, he was just going to do his job the way the rules said he must. You stop a shoplifter? Call the cops. So he called. And Maby meanwhile was loading the groceries into the car because she believed that she had paid for them. Or at least she could not remember not paying, so here she is, loading her groceries into the car when this boy tries to stop her. What does she do? She does what a lot of women do. He grabs her arm, what does he know? She picks up a can of asparagus and dents his head with it.

He molested me! is the first thing she says when the police car pulls up alongside her in the parking lot. What a temper she's got! Her hair, her flaming eyes!

He molested me, officer, I'm so glad that you got here when you did.

The boy was more glad. He was standing next to the car trying to hold back his tears, the blood dripping from between his fingers, such a slice Maby's cut with the edge of the can.

Now what did the policemen know? They had a call about a shoplifter and they drive up and see this beautifully dressed woman, a beauty herself, and this boy in his apron, cowering, crying, bleeding, standing against a car, and for a moment they believe her, and turn him around and push him against the car and run their hands up and down his body, as if they are looking for things he has lifted, not she. He was wearing an apron, they should have known, but such is the power of Maby's appearance that they got confused, and it wasn't until the assistant manager came walking out to meet them that they got things straightened out, apologized to the boy, and began to ask Maby some questions.

Of course I paid for them, she said, her voice rising high in indignation.

This is a little cop she's got talking to her, and another one a little bigger only talking to the manager. They don't know what to do. They would like to say, bring the groceries back and we'll check them out for you and forget about it. Except that they've got the boy bleeding from the cut in his head—and now there's blood on his hand, on his apron, and a few customers watching this scene in the parking lot.

Still they could have gone back inside. The cops had even begun helping her repack the groceries in the sacks in the cart when Maby grabbed the little one's hand.

You can't do this to me, she said. Do you know who I am?

Please, lady, the cop said, holding a bag of onions, looking quite silly, probably feeling even worse.

Do you know? Maby said again, taking the onions from him. He felt even sillier now.

Please lady, give that back or put it in the cart.

I will not stand for this, she said. Do you know who I am?

The little policeman stopped trying to pack the groceries and in that voice policemen can put on, or maybe it comes natural, says,

All right, lady, *who are you?*

He might have said another time, I don't care who you are, and just taken her in. But maybe she piqued his curiosity, so he said,

All right, who?

She was clutching the bag of onions, and her face turned pale, and her eyes, those greenish grey eyes, turned watery, and she said,

I don't know. I don't really know.

All right lady, the cop said, we'll help you get these things out of your car.

Fine, she said, as if that was what she was after, someone to unload these groceries from her car and carry them back into the supermarket, as if that was what you did, brought groceries from home to the supermarket and then looked around for some gallant policeman to come and help you take them in.

She's hurt my boy, the assistant manager said.

I see that, the big cop said. So what do you want to do about it?

He molested me, Maby said, her hands suddenly tearing at her hair. She had worn it coiled up in braids that morning, it gives her such a little girl look, makes her appear younger than Sarah sometimes when the light is right, and now she was pulling at the braids. Pulling, pulling.

Just take it easy, lady. Now son, the cop says to the boy, did you touch this woman.

Touch? I didn't touch her, I didn't do anything except try to get the groceries back.

He grabbed me, Maby says.

I tried to get the groceries, the boy says.

Look, the cop says, I think we'd all better get out of this parking lot and go down to the station and straighten this out. Mrs.? He turns to Maby.

Not me, buster, she says to the cop, and slides into the front seat of her car which all this time has been standing open.

Please? says the cop. And who ever heard of a cop saying please?

Even at this point the cop believes he still has things under control. But he hasn't figured on my daughter-in-law, Maby, because she turns the key in the ignition and without even pulling closed the door throws the car into reverse, knocking aside the little cop and scaring the feathers out of the other cop and the grocery boy and the people who had stopped to watch. But the little cop—quick thinker—jumps for the car, reaches inside and yanks out the keys, and she gets knocked back by his elbow against the seat and when the car stops she is crying. Maby cried all the way to the station house, and by that time they definitely knew she was a little drunk. You see, when they asked for the registration, as they have to do, I suppose, out of the glove compartment rolled a bottle she'd been carrying around, whiskey, whiskey, yes.

After they looked at the registration, it was the police that got upset. Some of them like to arrest big shots, but these two fellows, they were not happy about having captured themselves the wife of the local rabbi. But I'll tell you, with everything she was doing, the poor troubled girl she was at that time, it's a wonder they hadn't met her sooner.

So here we are at the station house, and it's not such a pretty picture. Fortunately there's a matron on duty at this time—it's late afternoon, remember?—and she's sitting with Maby on a bench along the far wall covered with pictures of presidents. Listen. Maby presses against her, shaking, sobbing like a little girl. The woman comforts her like she's her mother. So the world gives us all sometimes, the motherless, the barren alike, the chance to behave like mothers. The lights haven't yet gone on. It's almost twilight outside, and there's still enough of an afterglow from the sun that just slipped down behind the western woods to give the inside a dark, cavelike appearance when first you step in the door.

When he came in Manny blinked against that dark. He
didn't see Maby sitting there but walked right up to the desk and
spoke to the sergeant. The sergeant waved him toward the place
where Maby and the matron sat, mother and child, like one of
those Christmas scenes, the kind the gentiles put up in front of
city halls. Mother and child. Not a bad idea—and they got it from
the Jews. After all, darling, wasn't Mary the Virgin a Jewish
mother? Comfort, darling, that's what it's all about. Everybody
wants someone to comfort them, and who is the best comforter
of all? We all know that. The father, he's good, I'm not knocking the father but when push comes to shove it's the mother's
arm the person in pain wants holding around them. From the
first it has been that way and it will be that way to the last. And
if I'm sounding like the Bible that's because such things are in
the Bible, and if they're not they should be.

So. Here is Manny's chance to help his wife, to show her
how much he cares. Because you know by now that she's a
drinker, and that she was the daughter of a drinker, and what
do they know except that the person who should be comforting them cares more about the bottle than them. Her mother
treated her that way—and who knows but her mother's mother
treated her mother that way, and so on back many generations.
But here I am sounding like the Bible again when I'm only trying to tell a story. So. This, as I see it, was her problem—is, too,
maybe, if the doctors don't help any more than they already
have—and what does Manny do to help her? I'm afraid to tell
you, darling, because it only makes it worse.

Good evening, Rabbi, says the desk sergeant.

Good evening, Sergeant, says my Manny, the rabbi.

You've come for your wife? the sergeant says. She's sitting
right over there. And he points toward the bench.

Oh, says Manny. And he walks over to them. And Maby
looks up, and Manny looks down, puts his hands on his hips,
and says,

What have you done?

Not, You poor darling, not, Can I help you? Comfort you?
Not even just kneeling there and putting his arms around her.
But,

What have you done?

Maby looks up and smiles. A minute before she was crying, now she's all of a sudden throwing him a smile, as if he had in fact shown her how much he wanted to comfort her. As if it wasn't the opposite of everything that she ever wanted and needed out of life—and it's easy for me to say this now, of course, when I didn't understand any of it while it was going on—but of course the smile is a weapon, a defense against the pain. The rabbi, my Manny, doesn't see it that way, though. He sees it as a way of making him into a fool—he came home, picked up the telephone, heard the desk sergeant say she was in trouble, he jumps in the car and rushes over to rescue her, and what does she do but throw him the biggest smile he's ever seen cross her face? And the smile says to him, Boy oh boy, have I made a fool out of you!

So what happened then, while it might seem strange and without any reason, happened in part because of this smile. What I didn't know at the time was just how ready Manny was for the Florette business. Stop the time. Freeze the minutes. And you could take a walk back and forth like on the rocks across a stream down in the park, from the time Maby heard the news about her parents' dying and her drinking and this arrest and Manny's desire for someone in his arms he could talk to and feel close to. That's it. That feeling. It's what nobody talks about, darling, but it's everything.

So for months now he's been walking around like he's got a hole in his heart, at the temple, in New York, with Sarah, even with me, his mother who never asks him for nothing and always gives more than he thinks to ask, more than he wants. But could I give him this what he wanted then? That lies beyond the limits of the powers even of the mother.

But she had retreated, and he felt her absence. In the years when he was just building his talents, when he was the young rabbi and she was the young wife of the young rabbi, it was easy for him to ignore some of the things that bothered him now, at this time we're talking about, and it was easy for her to believe that what she was feeling inside—wait, I'll show you later, the emptiness of a hole in the heart you should never know and your children should never know—that the awful cold wind that blew right through her chest sometimes not just when she was asleep and had nightmares but also, worse, when she was awake and smiling in the middle of a tea at some temple, at the club meetings, at the supermarket, like this moment now, and from her side it was so painful all she could do was try to kill the pain the way she learned from her own mother. It took a while for Manny to notice. Young love, darling, it's all alike, like one of those big races where everybody starts off from the starting post all bunched up together. It looks like everyone is going to finish—and then, after a half a mile, after a mile and three quarters, some of the runners begin to drop out, or limp at least, and you can see that not everyone is as well equipped as everyone else in this race. That's when to the person looking on things get interesting. To think that our amusement comes from such pain from other people!

Bitch! he spit at her through tightly closed teeth, and he swung his hand and clipped her on the side of the face.

She made a little noise, like a balloon might when the air pishes out through a puncture, and she grabbed her face. Why is it? Her he hit, and a year later he smashed a guitar?

The matron meanwhile stood up and like a professional backed my Manny away from her. She'd seen a lot of couples go through this—mainly the negroes are hitting each other all the time is what a lot of Jewish people think, until they find themselves like my Manny, with a stinging palm and a crying wife, and a police matron and a desk sergeant standing next to him, a few seconds away from a personal riot.

Take it easy, she says to Manny, and he calms down quickly, mainly because he understands how close he stands to getting the sergeant in a situation where he'll have to do something official. In most police stations, darling, more people use their fists than pull guns and believe me the police are quick to respond. And if you wonder how this grandmother knows such things you haven't been listening to what I've been telling you. But sometimes it gets away from him. It scares him when he loses control. And then, because he's frightened, he loses more.

I'm fine, I'm fine, Manny says, running his hands nervously along the front of his dark suit. And see what happens? This is the effect he has on people. In a second, they're back to where they were before, as if the man had not slapped his wife in front of them, as though the wife isn't still on the bench, holding her face to her hands, sobbing so loud that you could hear it outside in the disappearing light. This distinguished man, not so old but not so young either, this man in the dark suit with the striking thatch of brilliant white hair, my Manny, he's got the power.

I'm sorry, he told her on the way home. But you should be sorrier than I am. This to me shows that you've crossed over the line and that you are going to have to see that doctor in New York.

Until then what had she done? She had tried talking to your lovely Doctor Mickey about her problem, pardon my saying, because I believe he is a very fine doctor, but all that he prescribed for her was a good diet, lots of sleep, and some pills that did nothing for her. Everything had been all right until Sarah was born, and then she had bad dreams, but even the dreams were something she could handle until her mother and father started dying in them again, and then everything came crashing at once and the days turned into times as bad as the dreams at night. But my Manny didn't know this then. For all of his experts working at his company with the brother-in-law in the city he didn't know much, as it turns out, about what was going on at home. Without me, I think, he would have found out sooner.

But I think that in a funny way, Sally, it was the presence of the Mama in the house, my life, that gave him the impression that things were going all right. I mean, after all, who cooked and who cleaned and who was there to dress Sarah in the morning when her mother couldn't get out of bed, and who was there for a long time to pick her up after school, and to plan her school outings with her, and to help her with her homework, and to help with the decisions about what to wear to the club meetings, and what to do on a Saturday when she had three, four equally desirable things she wanted to do? Who was there? You know who was there—the grandmother, that's who. But there is a certain limit to my powers, do you know what I mean? I could be there in the day, I could be there in the night, but I couldn't wake in the dark and go down into my daughter-in-law's dreams and turn her fears around into something that would make her laugh instead of shout out in the middle of the night.

You're laughing. Why? Because I admit that there's something in life more powerful than the powers of the grandmother? Sure, there is, and you know about it, from raising your own children. There are the waters of life, rising, rising like the river

or the ocean during a storm, and there's the grandmother standing between the rising waters and her family, like a wall, a dike,
a dam. But you can only do so much, you're only human, even
though sometimes the demands they make on you are more
than that, and there's only so much holding back you can do,
and only so much suffering you can take into yourself and turn
into comforting. *Nu?* Isn't that right? Isn't that the grandmothers'
way?

That Purim party, that's when Manny first saw how she was
fooling herself about the way she could conduct herself in public. Can you imagine how he felt when he saw her, and his
daughter, with the punch dripping from her turban. The look
in Sarah's eyes? Jewish Halloween? I'm telling you, it all comes
in costume, darling, nobody knows who he is, or she is, what
they want, what they are, until almost always it's too late.

Did Manny know he was going to slap her? Did he ever
think that he had it within him to slap his wife in public? To slap
her even in private? Slap? He never even touched her hard with
a finger let alone slapped! He never used with her a harsh word.
Now this is not to say he didn't feel frustrated with her, because
the older she got the more like a child she became. And it
seemed to him, it worried him, that the oldest she ever was for
him was when they first met as adults and that year after year
she was getting younger, until now, in the car, or back there in
the police station when he had slapped her he had been filled
with the frustration of a father with a misbehaving child, the
frustration of a husband who wants his wife to act like a grown-
up and she behaves instead younger than their own young
daughter. When her mother and father died he expected that
she would have a reaction—he wasn't the rabbi of a hundred-
person-plus congregation for years and years not to expect that
her grief was going to take terrible shape in one way or another.
But Maby's way of responding was not to grow older at last, to
turn into the adult that people always wanted to become when
after their parents die they understand they finally have the
chance to be. No. Her way was to collapse the years into herself and turn once again into the little girl he met the first time
they met ever, the first time, in the car, after the accident, when
he was in shock, holding onto his piece of glass, digging with
it the blood from his fingers, soiling his trousers.

·   ·   ·

My nose is still good, you know. And I can smell the dinner, it's almost ready. And even though my eyes are bothering me so much I can still look you in the face and see you smiling, because you're remembering that accident of Manny's, not his father's death, and it's as if—no, no, I wasn't criticizing you, because that's the way it happened, all together, as if it is supposed to have that effect on me, you, whoever listens, so that we think not about death and the blood but the little boy who had an accident. And we smile a little, and that's the living taking the place of dying.

You're not sorry, she said. Maby said. You're glad that you had the chance to punish me, in public.

Punish? Punish? Manny, driving them home, turns from the wheel and says this twice. And for what? he says then.

Not for something, for nothing, she says.

Punish you for nothing?

Because I'm not the rabbi's wife, because I'm not anybody's wife. I'm not a wife. I'm too . . . too . . .

Too what?

Too . . . I don't know. I don't know the words for it.

So find the words.

So find the words, she says, repeating after him. Easy for . . .

Please don't make fun of me, Maby, he interrupts.

I wasn't making fun. I was making serious. I was saying seriously that I don't know the words. That you know the words. You know the words in English and Hebrew, perhaps even in Aramaic, isn't that what you studied?

I took a class.

I never took a class. I never took a class in English, I took only French but I never took a class in Aramaic.

You studied English.

I never took a class in it.

You had English in school. Everyone has English in school. Even I had English in school on the Lower East Side where hardly anyone speaks English, or hardly anyone did when I grew up there.

So you have the words, she said.

There are words, Manny said. You may have to look for them, but they're there.

If they are, she said, I don't know how to find them.

Take a class, he said.

Now you're making fun of me.

I'm not, he said. You talk about writing and reading and finding the words. Take a class in these matters.

In these matters, she said.

And now after complaining that I was mocking you, you are methodically mocking me.

Methodically, she said. If I could find a word like that I would be all right.

You can find it. I found it. Look, Maby, I had no words in English. I had my mother's voice, I had my father's voice, I had the voices of the boys on the block, the rotten old rabbi's voice, and it wasn't until I got to Cincinnati, thanks to your father . . .

Thanks, Father, she broke in.

Will you let me finish? I would like you to hear this.

Finish, she said. I would like to hear your words.

And stop the mocking?

I will stop the mocking.

Good. I'll go on.

Go on.

So I took the classes because I recognized that if I was going to speak before large groups I was going to need some discipline.

I need discipline, Maby said.

And I read and I wrote little papers for my classes and all of this helped enormously.

They now drive up to the house and Manny steers into the driveway, but they don't go in. It's an inky dark Jersey evening, blue-black clouds stretching over from the east to west blotting out whatever afterglow might have remained in the sky when they first came out of the station house, and here they are, man and wife, sitting in the parked car in front of their own house, talking, which they have done little of since they first read together, many years before, the poetry from the Bible, the *Song of Songs*, Solomon's song and in the house, the house well lighted and comforting against the dark, the grandmother, me, passes back and forth from kitchen to dining room, setting the table, and upstairs is their only child listening now to the new group, called the Stones, like in the Bible where who shall cast the first one? because she was listening now to the things that made her stand up and dance and snap her fingers, which is good, don't you think darling? that our children today can feel

so good that they can do that? I wish today when I saw her she
only looked so well. Oh, I can almost taste the meal the girl is
cooking. I wish Sarah would come back and eat with us. Are you
getting hungry? Here I invited you for a meal and all I'm giving
you so far is the appetizer. But wait, wait.

Inside the house life goes on, the grandmother setting the
table, the granddaughter upstairs listening to music. I said this
already, I know. And the grandmother is worrying, wondering,
where are they already? Where are they? The granddaughter of
course, their daughter, is thinking about nothing. She's happy
as she can be—though there's a question of how happy this is
compared to the pleasures of other girls her own age—snapping
her fingers, swinging her hips to the music, imagining a dance
without costumes, without shame, the bump and push and
bustle and the fancy steps of children at play, grown-ups to be,
who have no cares, no worries like the grandmother down the
stairs. So inside the house life goes on without much of a
thought or an idea of what is going on outside in the driveway
that could change, will change, does change everything for
everyone.

Outside the house in the car in the driveway my Manny and
Maby are still talking.

And this writing will help me, you think?

It would give you a way to focus your thoughts.

And I need that, don't I?

You seem to.

You think that's all I need. Just a class or two?

Are you taking a mocking tone with me now, Maby?

Manny, would I do that? It's perfectly normal. Your wife gets
arrested in a supermarket parking . . .

Pardon me, but you weren't arrested. They didn't press
charges.

So what was I? You have the words. Was I detained?

That was more like what happened. Yes, detained.

Does that make a difference?

A single word can sometimes make a great difference, yes.

Then why don't you use a word with me? Why don't you
use a single word?

You're raising your voice. Please don't raise your voice. I'm
sitting right here next to you.

Right here next to me? Right here? You're not here. You're in your study writing a sermon. You're talking to committees. You're in the city at a board meeting. Let me tell you about a bored meeting. You want to know about a bored meeting? Meeting with you is a bored meeting. Right now you bore me. Life with you is a terribly boring meeting, do you know that?

Is that why you drink?

It's none of your business.

Maby, please. He touched her arm, but she squirmed away.

No, he said, I want to know. Do you drink because life with me is so boring or is life with me boring because you drink?

If it isn't Mr. Paradox! Well, well. Why don't we apply some of our feeble psychological training to the question of our wife's unhappiness? Who knows where it could lead?

Enough with the irony, please.

You should have thought, enough with the slapping, please, when you slapped me in front of those people.

I'm sorry. But think of the times that you have made things difficult for me.

But you're the spiritual leader of the community. Certainly you can overcome a little personal adversity. I mean, where would you be if you didn't have a little suffering of your own when you have to deal every day with the suffering of others? You could end up sounding like a real prig when you give out all your advice if people didn't think that you had problems of your own.

So you drink for my benefit? I didn't know that, I wasn't aware. Thank you very much. I should be more appreciative.

This is when she slapped *him*—a real openhanded smack right across the mouth. He could taste blood dripping from his lip as he spoke.

This makes you feel better?

Did you feel better after you hit me?

I felt terrible then, I feel terrible now.

If it's any consolation, I feel nothing now.

Is that why you drink? To feel nothing.

I asked you not to mention that.

It hurts me to talk about it. But we have to talk.

Talk to the wall.

What?

Your mother says it's like talking to the wall. So talk awhile.
Talk to the wall. I'm the wall.

Maby, wait a minute.

Yes, Rabbi?

Oh, don't do that, please.

All right, Rabbi. What shall I do?

Oh, you're impossible.

I'm going in.

You need a drink? I'll get you one, and we'll talk.

None of your business.

Why, Maby? Is it because of your mother?

The mother, Mrs. S., always the poor mother takes it on her head, and where would they be without her? Where would they be without us? Without, for instance, his mother, me, who would be telling his story?

None of your beeswax, she said. I'm going. She opened the door on her side and got out of the car. It was cooler now than when she had staggered across the parking lot behind the weight of her loaded cart, and quiet too. Some nights she could in warm weather walk out onto the porch, in the middle of evening, and listen, a glass in her hand, until the traffic from the highway miles away died down to a low thin line of noise and only the crickets chirped and the ground around the house gave up, or so it seemed to her, a little steady whisper that she pretended was the growth in the dark of the next morning's grass and flowers. A nice girl she could have been if it hadn't been for that woman she called her mother? Whose mother isn't some of the reason for whoever they become? It's the mother, it's the father, a mix of both, and in her case the father had little to do with it. It was chemistry, mother chemistry, the mother drank, and her mother drank, and all her grandmothers and great-grandmothers and great-great-great-great-great-grandmothers drank all the way back to a cousin of Eve. Paradise, to this kind of woman, you can see only through a little whiskey haze. Eve, now she was Jewish too. Like the Mary the Virgin, a married woman, if you think of it, and so not a virgin probably after all but then Mary wasn't either except for the time she was supposed to have had the baby from God or the angel or the bird that was God, whatever that cock-and-bull story is the goyim tell about it. Imagine, a married woman and they call her a virgin? Like a young girl, like my Sarah, they make her out to be when she's as much a woman as Maby or me, even, or you, except for you and me, darling, we went out of business when our husbands passed away. Of course I don't want to put words in your mouth—please, don't make a face, I'll tell the rest of my story. Isn't life something? Here I'm in the middle of a tragedy and I'm thinking about the tale they tell about God turning into a bird and swooping down and making a woman pregnant. Can you imagine a woman today coming home and telling her husband a story like that?

But listen to the story Maby told my Manny while they are standing there in the dark driveway while I moved back and forth inside the house and upstairs the music plays, the pretty voices sing about homesick blues. She told it so he would know, and, let me know if you understand because I'm not so sure even after I heard it if I did. If I do now. So listen carefully, Mrs. Stellberg.

You think that I started drinking after my mother died, don't you? she said, leaning against the side of the car, pulling at a long thick strand of her hair. You think so, I know you do.

I do, my Manny said. He's looking at her, looking at the lights and shadows in the house, his mouth moving back and forth before the light, and upstairs the shadow of his daughter moving back and forth across her lighted room, and the house engraving itself into the sky as the last light fades, the house sinking into the shadows like one of those ships you hear about that runs into rocks and the thing sinks out of sight—the house, which had not been such a bad place to live, nice big rooms downstairs, snug bedrooms upstairs, a good kitchen, a pleasant place, the nicest of the houses we lived in after Manny was ordained and went out into the world of rabbis and houses and work—this house appeared to him to be fading quickly from his vision, and he grew fearful, as if he already understood by the tone of her voice that she was going to tell him something terrible that would change everything. How could he know that everything had already been changed? He could sense something, but what did he know of the truth? A nice house, he was thinking, and I'm sorry that I've made her feel bad, he was thinking, and I shouldn't have lost my temper, he was thinking, I should have tried to help her. I should have tried to help you, he wanted to say. But she was already caught up in her story.

My brother and I were very close when we were younger. Despite the large difference in age we found ourselves together all the time because my mother discovered quite early in Mordecai's life that he didn't enjoy the usual rough play that boys are supposed to like, but preferred staying indoors with her, doing the things that she did around the house, do you know what I'm saying? He was a bit shy, I suppose, is the way people would put it. It's not the way it really was at first. I think at first that he was just a little fearful of my father who was a big boisterous man stomping around the docks, a man always slapping people on the arm, the back, with his big fat cigar clenched between his teeth, shouting, cursing, shoving people around, Hey, you, do this, do that, shut up, come on over, put that down, pick that up, launch that barge, shove that load, tie that line, I remember his voice, I've got it impressed on me from the times that I spent down at his pier and on board the barges. You've seen him at home, and once on the barges, the trip we once took down the river, do you remember? I'm sure you do. Well, picture me as a young girl, a little older than when you and I first met at the scene of the accident that took your father's life—now I know you don't like to think of it, you're fidgeting, you're suddenly upset—but then jump ahead from there about five years and picture me then, still thin but tall for my age, my hair as red as a freshly painted barge in my father's fleet, and Mord, my brother, about twice as tall and with hair just as red, at that time he hadn't started to lose it, the two of us playing together at home, playing house, and you can't blame me, can you? because he was there for me to play with, and you can't blame him, really, can you? because he just couldn't bear to go out with my father because of the roughness of the way he treated him, it was just something in his nature, like his hair, or being left-handed, some people are just that way, and because of it my father picked on him terribly almost from the beginning, from the first time my brother refused to jump from the pier onto the boat or from the boat onto the pier, I can't remember just which way, I guess it was trying to get him to jump from the pier to the boat, and Mord wouldn't do it, he wouldn't jump, he looked down into the gap between the pier and the deck and saw the water swirling up and around and he wouldn't do it— and so my father picked him up and threw him across onto the boat and Mord hit his head and cut his hand and began to wail, and our father leaped after him and yanked him up by his shirt collar and said in a hard whisper in his ear, Don't you cry on my boat or else you're going over the side.

Are you wondering what my Manny's thinking through all this speech? He's thinking about the past, about his father, rubbing, rubbing his souvenir glass until his fingers are getting raw again, something that he hasn't done in a long, long while, remembering the accident, the sounds, the smells, the curling wispy smokelike trail of blood in milk—and then what she's saying catches his ear and he's recalling his Cincinnati days again— Why don't people really listen? maybe you're asking, why isn't he listening? this is an important thing she's telling him, this is his wife, she's telling him news about herself that he ought to pay careful attention to, he ought to listen hard, he ought to make notes, why does he drift off into dreamy recollections of his own story? Why doesn't he bear down hard with his mind on the story she's telling him the way he's pressing his fingers into that glass, that glass, *oi*, the bloody star that he carries around.

Are you listening to me? she says, catching his face in the reflection of the light from the house and noticing that he's staring into the darkness like he's watching a movie or a slide show from his past. I'll bet if I were one of your beloved problems from the congregation you wouldn't be thinking about something else.

Please, he says, continue.

I'll bet, she says, if I were one of these famous companies you want to take over you especially wouldn't get distracted, would you?

Please, he says. I'm sorry if I give you that impression. I'm listening quite intently.

Or are you thinking about someone else? Do you have someone else whose . . .

Please, Maby, he says, don't make trouble. Tell me what you want to say.

I don't want to say it, Manny. I never would have said it, Manny, if all of this stupid business hadn't happened, if you hadn't walked to the station house when I needed your sympathy and slapped me across the face, no, I never would have told you this, but I'm going to tell you this because I want you to know what you're up against, and it's nothing I would have told you ever if I didn't think you were so dumb, so blockheaded . . .

Why are you doing this?

Because you are so dumb, so thick skulled . . .

Maby, so what is this all about? Why are you speaking to me like this?

Can't I speak to the rabbi in a truthful way? Doesn't the famous . . .

Maby, please.

But you've never understood and in a way I never wanted you to understand because who wants to live with this out in the open, who . . .

Who wants to live what, with what? Will you kindly tell me?

Not when you have that in your voice I won't tell you, she says. Not when it's in your voice that same violence, the smack in my face, the . . .

And you didn't hit me?

You hit me first. And my father threw my brother across the space between the pier and the boat.

So he was a crude man, I knew him, I know all that, but he had a good side to him, he helped me over the years, helped Mama . . .

Did you hear what I said?

I heard, I heard.

He threw me across that space.

He took you down there?

He deliberately took me along the next time he went down to the pier with Mordecai, and he asked me to make that jump and I refused, and he picked me up and threw me and I landed on the deck. Except I didn't cry. I wish I had cried. But I was angry at him and I decided that I would get my revenge against him by pretending that he hadn't touched me, and so I clenched myself up like a fist and I didn't cry, I was aching, hurting, but I didn't make a sound. Oh, I wish, I wish that I had let myself go then, I wish I had known then what it was inside me that kept me all balled up like a fist, so that I could have screamed, wept, wailed, shouted, shrieked like the baby that I was—because if I had let out even a whimper, Mord wouldn't have hated me, and he wouldn't have plotted his revenge.

Revenge? Manny says. Standing there in the driveway of his house, the handsome white frame house the congregation gives him, standing there with his lovely wife, her beautiful face, her red hair, her pale like cream complexion, and inside the house his Mama, me, passing back and forth across the light, and upstairs the daughter, little Sarah grown now so big, snapping her fingers, humming, dancing lightly by herself, a happy girl, singing about how I want to hold your hand—and how many scenes like this do we see? such happy things? and how much pain lies behind the curtain? how many fingers digging into the glass, bleeding fingers, and how many minds concentrating now on the scene from the past where the pain shoots out, slashes out whenever the mind turns to it, like a bullet? like a knife? like a hurtling rock? My Manny, standing there in the driveway, a normal man for his age with a few extra large talents that separate him maybe from the others who can do only one thing well, so he can do several things well, a man frowning, his face lined with questions, his hair catching the light, looking slightly silver now instead of the pure white of snow it seems usually, my Manny asking for revenge? What revenge?

Revenge. Revenge the kind you've never heard of short of the stories that victims of the Nazis can tell.

Florette Glass?

Florette, that one, the stories she's told at discussions. Over there Jews, other people . . .

But mainly Jews.

Jews and Poles, and gypsies I read about too, Manny. But do you want me to go on?

You sound so sober, he wanted to say, I do want you to go on. He didn't say that, but he kept quiet, and she continued her story.

Over there they attack special groups, but over here who gets it but the people we call normal? They practice atrocities, revenge. Over there in Europe they single out religions, beliefs. Here it's psychology.

What an odd thing to say? What do you mean? My Manny leaned against the car, and if there had been enough light from the house to display his face you would have seen a puzzled look pass across it.

Here people whip people, beat people, attack people, rape people for the cause of their own revenge. Here atrocities begin in the mind and live on the bodies of other people.

Maby, I don't know what you're talking about. Your father mistreated you? It sounds more like he wanted to show off to your brother, he wanted to encourage your brother. And what did your brother do in revenge that was so awful?

You smug fart-mouth.

What?

You say that. You stand there and say that?

Maby, please calm down, one minute you're talking sanely, and the next you're cursing me. Please, please. What words, what language!

The language of revenge, she said. The language of American psychology. I've been reading psychology, trying to figure out my case.

Your case? What case?

Oh, Manny, come along, come along, what case do you think? My suitcase? A case of soda pop? Come along, dear Manny, come along.

Please explain to me.

I've been explaining. Don't interrupt. Or interrupt. As you like it. As you like. The case. My case. My father, brother. And mother. Musn't forget dear mother. Her case. Not a hard case. A soft case. Her head snapped open like a suitcase that fell down the stairs. Open to the world.

Maby, I want you to come inside with me.

I like it out here, Manny. Why don't *you* like it out here? Does everything of merit have to take place in a room? in a book? in a ledger? In . . .

We don't have to do this to each other, Maby. Please . . .

Take your hands off me!

The night air, it's cold . . .

No colder than what I feel inside.

So don't come inside, so we'll stand here, so you'll tell me about you and Mordecai, the sibling rivalry, the battles. Maby? He speaks too softly in the dark.

Don't Maby me. Give me an answer. The answer I never gave.

Here . . .

I—said—don't—touch!

Again the violence as she pushes him away toward the other side of the drive, and he stumbles, regains his balance, and comes toward her, dark in the drive, in his dark suit, his hair in the light. But lucky for him, for his conscience, he raised his hand but he didn't strike her down. Once that night had been enough. That slap in the face in the station. He never needed to lose his temper with her again. With Sarah, he still had his temper to lose — that time to come in the back porch, with the guitar, her song, with her remark, it was still ahead in the future, but here, now, in the driveway, in the darkness that folded around them like a winter blanket, the slap in the face was in the past, and there was nothing he could do to bring it back. Sooner bring back his mother-in-law, bring her back and help our friend, the mentor, the generous Sporen, not to bully her into drink, sooner catch her hand at the wrist and keep her from raising a glass to her lips that day she died, the day she went tipsy tripping down the stairs and snapped her neck, sooner hold her lips tight by pinching with your fingers her lips, sooner that, this, any other thing, before you could take back the slap the husband, Manny, my Manny, gave to Maby, yes, my Maby, the daughter-in-law, almost the daughter, that afternoon before a small crowd of uninterested police.

You talk of time, you talk of time stoppage? We talk of passing minutes, hours, days curving around and back again in memory so that it seems only like yesterday, maybe even like tomorrow — do you know what I mean? — that I decided in my heart that I would not marry the bad-smelling rabbinical student from the city, *kinnahurra*, so long ago that it might be tomorrow, and what if I had caught my own wrist and stopped myself from traveling after Jacob? What if I had never pushed myself just the little that I needed so that I could have the comforts I have now? what if? what if? What's done is done, me and my Jacob, Sporen and his wife, my Manny, and the slap in the face to the daughter-in-law, the passage of stoppage, the moving of time, and here we sit, sniffing the air and smelling our dinner, and it's now, not then, now and now and now, and it's also when I'm telling you then, now in the driveway, and he's getting very nervous, my Manny, very nervous, but even if he's caught himself by the wrist his own hand, he's watching — in the dark, but with the eye in his mind — his own wife's features fall apart like sand washed over by the waves that splash up at the beach. It was that quick that it happened, and he was standing right there. One minute her voice was calm and she was talking to him (even if maybe she was a little upset she wasn't hysterical) and the next he could hear the strain in her throat, like a car going into another gear he explained it to me later, and she was driving across a border.

I want to know about Mordecai's revenge, he said, lowering his hand as though it were made of metal, lowering it as if it did not belong to his own body, carefully lowering his hand to his side and asking again, What did he do that was so terrible?

He was thinking of Mordecai, bald, thin Mordecai, who as far as he knew never ate, who lived and drank and breathed, and ate only the business, the business, who had so little time for himself apart from the company—they have a new office on Park Avenue by the way, a nice suite of rooms, one secretary for them and another just for the telephone, I'm telling you, I don't know how he does it but he does—but I'm telling you when he was standing there in the driveway listening to his wife tell him this story it was as if he had no luck, no good looks, no talent for the congregation, no ability to talk about the religion, not a pinch of sense for the business, not even to know how to stand and talk to people, not nothing—he is a man listening to his wife tell him a story and he's hearing it as if he's hearing from a stranger.

You want to know what happened? she said. I'll tell you what happened.

And this is the play in his brain that Manny watched, as a spectator filled with, I don't mind telling you, very shocking feelings, with regret, with the feeling you call remorse.

But here's dinner. And can we talk of such things while we eat? So why not? Why not? It's a story more sad than disgusting although it gets disgusting, I'm telling you, something you might not want to hear with your soup. But by the time you get to our age don't you think that we can eat and weep at the same time? We have to sometimes do both at once, and if we say awful sometimes we're saying only that it's alive and we've seen it all before, and here in fact is the soup. Don't it smell good? Me, I don't cook anymore, but the girl, she's got my recipes, I tell her and she writes it down, and this is the old-fashioned soup that I used to make for my Manny all the time—the same soup I had on the stove the night all this was taking place in the driveway, in fact . . .

So of course I'll tell the story, her story, she's talking, she's explaining, and like I said, he's making a play, a movie even, in his head.

On a barge on the river. Her father's barge. One of the big boats in the fleet. He's standing there in the driveway and he's seeing this in the eyes of his mind, smelling the soup maybe, but not smelling it, feeling the air growing colder on his bare cheek but not feeling it, aware of the pressure of his soles in his shoes on the dark tarry surface of the driveway but not standing there, seeing as she talks, the barge, the river, smelling the river not the soup, the river he remembered from his stay in that city, fresh water slightly tainted with the odor of the gasoline from the boats, but at that time a fresh river, not the filthy waters today we have, the pollution, the stink, the smoke, dead fish, no fish, here was a pleasant broad stream where the children could come and play if only the father hadn't first flung the boy across the space, above the water, between the dock and the deck.

Because ever since for the boy it was not such a beautiful place, ever since for the boy it was not a place which he would remember with fondness, it was not a place the boy would think back on fondly while sailing the seas—and isn't it amazing how from the place of water where he had the trouble with his father he went out over the water again, sailing from one country to the next, from continent even to continent, and here he was, another one of us, passing over water, sleeping at night to the rocking of the waves, listening to the music of the engines, feeling the vibrations in the bones of the ship in his own bones, and when he later returned to land for a long time after he longed for the roll and slope of the deck beneath his feet? The boy, the girl, brother and sister, brought here by the father who wanted for them only the best—and wasn't it tough enough for our futures when our parents who wanted for us only the best began to work their way with us? And you can imagine when these children go into the world who have parents who give them only the worst— because if you think about Sarah, *Sadie* now as she calls herself, who didn't want the best for her? and how she is becoming so sad, and her father wants, and her mother if she could figure out what she wants, if she could come up for air out of the ocean of her depression—boy and girl on a boat, and it's a lovely day, and it's like a picnic up on top, the food for them set out, the fishing lines, because then you could fish in these clean waters, and now you could catch only bodies and garbage and dreck, the wreckage and the trash, but then there was fishing, oh, there was the fishing and the water you could even drink, and the sun, and the light wind, and the father went off on some errands, telling them that he would be back in a while, and they were alone, which nowadays you wouldn't do, but in those days, days of trust with people, days of doors unlocked, and at night the peaceful sleep of dreamers who fear no strangers, evenings filled with walking and talking, and children playing without bother, horses standing about waiting for travelers, the wind tickling the tops of the growing wheat, deer trotting down to the edge of the forest, nibbling at the stalks of grass, the bark, no dogs to fear, no hunters—but this is another time even further back still I started talking about, the time I knew, the places I knew, the fields I played in while I was that age, and the sun and wind and wheat and earth, the furrows, the watering streams, birds in air, frogs in chorus, and down to the edge of the wood trot the tiny deer, fragile, easily frightened, and no hunter raises his gun, and I sigh, loving the feel of the wind in my hair, the way it caresses my dress, lifts my apron as if with the exploring fingers of a mother studying me for neatness, and if this was a time back further still, then it's a time to think about when you picture the children in the cabin in the barge on the American River, the Ohio, the name from the Indians, because for them it was like for me, and for you, for all of us, my Jacob, my Manny, and as it was for Sarah, as we know, before the party where her mother made her weep, a time for all of us, before the time stoppage, before the stop motion, before the end of the circling back to the beginning when the conclusion seems too much like the start, and we all sigh, and say, Oh, not again, and then, Oh, yes, I wish, again, and again, and again.

The little girl felt something of this. What did she know? She played in childish simplicity, unaware of the ball of spite that grew hard, and, at the same time, larger, in her brother's chest. He knew no innocence. Not since his father had tossed him across the void between the land and the deck. He'd had a hint of these feelings once before, when his sister was first born and he felt cast aside, when he got elbowed away from the center of his mother's attention, a normal emotion under the circumstances, though in this case with some kernel of truth since Mrs. Sporen, with all her problems, particularly the drink, she could barely take care of one child in some way resembling normal, let alone two. So she cared for one and ignored one, and that one, the older brother, grew resentful. But then resentment alone doesn't make you harm someone, it only makes you hate. He, Mordecai, the older brother, might have merely ignored his little sister if his father hadn't tested him above the waters and found him wanting. But when his father tossed him into the air he landed with something that he hadn't possessed when he took off, a desire burning in his chest like a field fire for revenge against the man who humbled him—and against the sister whom that man held up as an example.

Isn't that something, the way a few seconds changes a person's life? One minute the older brother, the next the hateful enemy. The father might have forgotten altogether, the sister might have forgotten altogether—to them it was only a moment's annoyance, a joke, a misbegotten minute of comedy. But to the brother it was something never to forget, and like a banker he compounded his hurt until he struck at Maby.

In the barge, the boat, at the bottom of the boat, in the cabin, at the water line. They were playing, moving dolls and toy soldiers in and out among the pillows on one of the bunks while their father was out on the pier. Without warning, Mordecai leaped on his sister and held her down on the bunk while he pressed a pillow over her face. She struggled, kicked and scratched, and he pressed down harder, harder. She couldn't breathe, she couldn't scream, all she could do was pummel him on the arms with her little fists, and this annoyed him, and he let the pillow go in order to grab her hands, and then he started hitting her in the face, on the chest, and then he grabbed her by the hair and yanked hard, yanked ferociously, so that she screamed, and he made her scream again, which shows that what happened next was something that just happened, because just who would want someone to scream and make everybody on deck come running (although at this time no one was on deck, not the father, not any of the crew)? He yanked, and she

screamed, and if anyone had been up on the deck they would
have come running because the scream was loud, her scream
slit the air like a razor, and the next thing to happen he was pulling up her skirt and pulling down her pants and poking his needle into her little eyelet, poking and poking, because you see he
got stiff like he had to make a pee and then he did what he did
because it brought all of his hatred and resentment to a point,
and he poked and poked, and she kicked and kicked, and finally
she pushed him with both hands hard on his chest, and she
rolled away from under him, falling from the bunk onto the floor
and turning over on her stomach, weeping, shrieking, punching at the floor. She threw a royal fit, is what happened, kicking, kicking, pummeling the floor, the wall, and when her father
came back she was still lying there, her mouth covered with spit,
her hands red and raw from the punching.

What are you doing? her father shouted when he came
down from the deck.

Not, Are you all right? Not, Who did this? Not, No, no, poor
baby, poor thing. But: What are you doing?

What are you doing?

And here is what all the men in this family have done, with
the exception of my Jacob, and he passed away so early that,
who knows, but God forbid, he too might have done the same
if he had lived.

What are you doing?

Sympathy? A healing touch? None, none of this. Not like
your boy, your son Doctor Mickey. Not this man. Not them.
And here is where the men go wrong, don't you think? Because
they can't get over the need to pin the blame on someone, the
blame for the mess of life, the blame for the spills and the accidents and the things people drop and leave behind. They want
a reason, they want a mama to clean up after them, they want
to hear anything about why something happened except that it
just happened and now there's a need to do something about
it, even when as in this time on the barge on the river that flowed
clearly and carried barges south and west, on the spring day on
which this happened, in the state with the Indian name, on the
river with the Indian name, it was a man who was at fault.

Am I contradicting myself? So what? So I am? so if you were
a man listening, as Manny was listening, my Manny, in the
driveway on that night when he was supposed to have written

his sermon about the death camps, and was interrupted by the mess that Maby had made, and was listening to the story of how the mess began, if you were my Manny, that man, you might have done what he did then, said what he said, and saying is doing when the words make things happen, don't you think? Of course, of course. And what he did was make a truth out of the old saying, men are all alike, because he stood there and listened to what she said, and then he responded as her father did—he might have been a mouthpiece for the ghost of her father—standing there in the dark, his mama passing back and forth in front of the lighted window, upstairs the daughter beating her hands together to the tunes of the beatle bugs who want to hold her hand, saying, him standing there saying,

But what? but what did you do?

Let's admit it wasn't easy for him. He could listen to such stories coming from people from his congregation, he could read about such things in the newspapers, but hearing his own wife tell of such a thing, listening to her confess to this, he could not, I'm afraid to say of my Manny, even my wonderful Manny, he could not take it. This, he admitted later, much later, was on his mind, images, pictures of the scene, the girl with her skirt over her tummy, the panties down, the slit like the eyelet of a needle winking up at her brother, and the boy forcing himself into her—may you forgive me for telling you such things so clearly but when you need to know you need to know—in and out, in and out, as if he, my Manny, were jabbing himself with a needle, except it wasn't a point of steel but the tips of the starry shard that he was fingering then, as always when nervous, anxious, in pain, and the pain came in waves, in his hands, and it complemented the pain in his mind, in the images that stuck again and again, needles, sharp needles, in his brain, in his eyes.

This headache stayed with him forever after that. A man cannot just get rid of such visions, in and out, in and out, the needles pricking him behind the eyes.

You know very well what I did, she answered.

Dis-gust-ing, he said, my Manny. Dis-gust-ing.

And Maby, the wife who was the girl in the story, she turned on her heel and started away across the lawn.

Where are you going? Manny called after her.

She didn't say a word, she didn't even look over her shoulder, let alone turn around.

I meant Mord, he called after her. Because he realized now why she was running—she was running now. Mord, that's who I meant, he said, because by this time he had even convinced himself that he had meant Mordecai, the brother, the brother-in-law, the revengeful boy who had harmed his little sister and then ran away—and stayed away because he knew that he was not welcome— Mord, his business partner, Mord, the man older than he, gaunt, always looking famished, as though he needed a mother to feed him, Mord, whose life was mysterious to Manny up until then, until it was the hateful saga it suddenly became for him, as the headache deepened in his skull and the darkness thickened in the driveway, yes, by now he did mostly mean Mordecai, was mostly convinced.

But what if she had made up this story? What if she had made up a tale of vengeance to cover for some dreadful act or acts of her own? What if she had led the boy on herself to the terrible time on the bunk in the barge? What if, worse, she had made it up to slander him, to thicken the slander and thus hide some of her own wildest fears? Because Mord the man was not the boy, Mord the man was his knowledgeable partner, the man who made all the business possible, who showed him how to join one board, then another— showed him the paths to take, who played Aaron to his Moses, general to his minions, using him in strategies of which he never knew the completed arc until it came to pass, which meant when the holdings showed up on the books.

When Mord came back from over the sea, Manny had been nothing but an overtalented religious leader—and I say this, remember, as his most fervent admirer, his mother—with a yen for another kind of life and no awareness of just what that other life might be. Oh, he'd ridden the barges his father-in-law owned, and he'd seen on paper the steamships he had purchased, and some of the loading docks, some of the warehouses, but he had never turned his mind to the thought of making them his, not until Meyer Sporen died and left most of it to his daughter and son-in-law, with a small portion set aside for the prodigal Mord as an afterthought, the kind of codicil, my Manny called it, set down by a man who didn't want to take a chance on being denied entrance to a heaven if it existed. Mord the man had nothing to do with Mord the boy, as far as Manny was concerned, not the man who returned from overseas, from the tropics where he had been living for many years, not now and not then, because Manny hadn't before needed to make the association between the lanky young fellow a number of years his senior whom he had met at the scene of Jacob's accident and death and the man who returned, because it hadn't before mattered, but now, no, now there was a painful association for him between the boy on the barge and the man in their New York suite, the man behind Manny's growing successes as the head of several small companies they had acquired just that year, the man who projected another round of takeovers for the coming year, the boy on the barge and this man were now the same person, and how it mattered, it mattered too much. How could he work with the man who had defiled the sister who had become his wife? He couldn't—couldn't work with him, couldn't talk with him, couldn't stand to breathe the air in the same room with him, and so my Manny turned his rage around, turned it in two ways, one more visible than the other, the first being the way in which he turned it against himself, and the second being the way he turned it against his wife. And on that evening, in the dark laid on like paint from a house painter's brush, he turned it first against his wife.

You come back, he shouted as he had never done before, him, my Manny, solid, stolid, quiet, steady, rational—that's the right word?—always with the hand in the pocket clenched around the star, but never showing that side of himself to the world, and he's running across the lawn shouting at his wife who by now has disappeared in the shadows beyond the next house.

Where are you? he calls.

There is no answer in the dark.

Maby, where have you gone?

No answer.

So husband and wife play hide-and-seek, on a spring night in the New Jersey dark.

Where?

No answer.

Come the hell out! he calls, using language like never before.

And this draws a laugh from her, where she's hiding, in the bushes, in the dark.

Come out!

Come find me, Manny, she says, come find me, Rabbi.

Bitch! he yells, again with the language.

And as though this is her true name she steps up to him from behind and gives him a big push. And down he goes, and she's running past him, onto the sidewalk, onto the road, and down the street toward the corner, to the road that leads to town.

You come back! he shouts after her, picking himself up and limping—he's hurt his foot—in the direction she's running.

Such games! You'd have thought she was a little girl again, leading him along in such games. But despite her laugh, and her agile running, this is not a child, not even a young girl, but a woman filled to bursting with great sorrow. How do I know this? I know, I know, I have lived with her, heard her sobbing in the night, and I know from some of her writings, of which I could show examples of the pain that never ended in her, that flowed always, sometimes with the force of a stream in springtime, sometimes only seeping, like water in wet moss on a mountainside—and where do I imagine these things if not from her own voice, from her world, the words she writes, I've known, I've known—because sympathy, that is the word, *sympathy* is what makes the world go around, isn't that what they say?—so I know this, and you'll know this, and the sad, deep truth, the news that hurts the most, particularly to a mother, to *the* mother, is that he, my Manny, the man who needed most to find out, never knew about sympathy, or he didn't know he knew. His head was aching, this was a sign, but he didn't know. His foot was aching now that he had fallen forward in the dark, shoved down by his seemingly playful wife, but he didn't know. He didn't know and he didn't know and he didn't know, and he ran off after her along the street, well, not ran, but limped, his imitation of a run because now he felt the urgency that he hadn't known before, now he felt the same despair and humiliation that would descend on him, if she were to rush for the second time in the day into the arms of the police, and so he hurried as fast as he could.

Running running running.

As I'm telling you this he's resting on vacation in a hotel somewhere in the Holy Land. But as I'm telling you, in my mind, in your mind, if you're listening the way you should—if I'm telling the way I should, he's running running running.

And in a way he will always be running.

And falling like the fall he took just before the time I began to tell you the family story.

Get over here! he called out to her as he saw her leaning against the hood of a neighbor's car. Her chest was heaving like a bird's in flight, and her eyes, even in the dark he could tell, her eyes were wild.

You wait for me! he called after her. And this time she did look back, looked over her shoulder, as she cut across the lawn and ran behind the house.

A dog leaped out of the yard and barked at her. Way down the street inside the lighted house the mother, this mother, stood silently in front of the table now set for a meal of which no one seemed about to partake and heard the faint yip-howling of that same beast.

Help! Maby yelled, and ran right into her husband's arms.

He tried to help her, to help her home, but she struggled, and twisted free.

No! she screamed, no!

Lights flashed on in the front of the house where they struggled, and poor Manny, my Manny, blinked against the sudden brightness as Maby, a captive in his grip, kicked him in the shins and again raced away.

How long can this go on, you ask? How long. How long? Rivers are long, nights are long, space is wide, the air is deep, my memory and the minds of my children are long and deep and wide if they say to themselves what the truth is. And to tell you the truth it went on for another few minutes, running back and forth across the street, and some people by now had come out on their doorsteps, attracted by the noise, and my Manny was begging her, saying,

Please, Maby, it's enough now, enough is enough.

But enough wasn't enough. She ran, tripped, fell face first onto the roadway. Manny leaned over and yanked her up by the hand, as though she were a child or a rag doll, a child's rag doll, a rag doll's child, and she swung her other hand around as she rose to her feet and clawed his face and the sting of it matched the smart of his fingers, and the blood ran down his cheek.

By the time he got her upstairs and undressed and into bed, your Doctor Mickey had arrived. Manny feared a lot more kicking and screaming once she understood what was happening, but he was wrong. When your lovely boy gave her a shot she just lay there, not smiling, not frowning, staring up at the ceiling as though some picture show was going to begin there, a movie on the ceiling. Who knows what she thought she was looking at that night? I, the mama, stood in the doorway, ready as always to help. My dinner was dried up, ruined. I had no patience left for anyone or anything. But what did that matter? We were all upset. Even Sarah had recognized that something out of the ordinary was going on, had turned off her Victrola and come down the hall with her most serious expression on her face, the one she usually saved for discussions of friends and music.

Is she all right? she asked. What happened to her, Grandma? Was she, you know?

I don't know, I told her, and took her by the hand. She allowed me to press her fingers to my bosoms, like she was little again and I wanted to see her nails.

But, sure, I said, she'll be all right. Doctor Mickey can fix anything, except if you fall and go smash. So he'll give her something to help her sleep and in the morning your mother will feel fine.

It was the father I was worrying about, because Maby went right out but my Manny and your Mickey had a conference in the study, and the expression on Manny's face after that was also his most serious face, the one he reserved for accidents and funerals, and with those claw marks he had the appearance of a man to whom an accident has just happened. I noticed his fingers when he took out his handkerchief to dab at his nose — raw and red and sliced from the shard. Here was a man already marked out by the color of his hair, so distinguished that you couldn't help but notice him in a crowd, and now up close I could see these smaller but just as distinctive marks on him, the stripes and slits made by nails and glass, stripings for a day or a life filled with a turmoil and hullabuloo like nobody, or maybe everybody's seen. You see, on top of everything else — remember, but you don't, because even I didn't — was the fact that he had to write his sermon on the concentration camps so that he could deliver it at the service the next evening.

·   ·   ·

So here's the house now quieting down, a night like this, seeming normal, the music off, the creaks and shifts of the wood and stone, resting of the bones of the residence, sleep on the horizon, undress and lay your weary body in the welcome crib of dark, babies, grandmothers, it's all the same what we need at this time, some because we have so much to look forward to, some because we have so much to see over our shoulders, we look behind. I wash, I sigh, I smear my face with cream, throwing good money after bad for years, the cream on this wrinkled property, but this is America, and we have hope forever, and the same person, me, once a girl, who sailed the seas in search of a new life with her husband in a new country, she uses even at an age when she should—*kinnahura*, I shouldn't say this but I'm saying it nevertheless when I should be thinking about what the undertaker will do for my face at the funeral home. I'm using the cream and oil that promises all of the crevices and streaks and lines and bumps and spots and gouges and veins and ridges and hollows will fade away and I will appear as if young again— and I'm squinting into the mirror and the face before me looks like someone I know, if only because the dark is closing in and I can see it only in the barest outline, the faintest form. Sit, flush, wash, a night like any night. And into the welcoming bed-clothes, and into the welcoming bed.

For Sarah the same, except for her no cream. All the world lies before her, and she knows no sin, no pain. Not even has she crossed a river, not even has she had to work, not this child, fruit of a garden her parents and grandparents planted, blessed with the riches of the new world without ever having had to dream or wrestle or sail over waters, fly over empty space, here she is, sitting, gushing, flushing, washing, brushing the beautiful straight teeth, the lovely hair. No wrinkles on her face, and no sense of ever having done wrong either, this American child, who, even if she dreams of horrible beasts and fears great falling walls of brick and mortar, as she did, long afterwards I learned this, will wake up refreshed, as if she's returned to the womb overnight, beginning again as she did on the day of her birth, all peach flesh and willpower, bouncing up and down in her sneakers to the music of I want to hold your hand, another day to live as if the others did not exist, present, past, and future in the jittering finger snapping of the instant after instant she calls her life. She was a little tired, she slept. I was weary, I collapsed. Her mother, my daughter-in-law with the funny name, she was drowned in medication, veins churning with drugs, ropes to bind her in the hospital of sleep.

Only Manny, my Manny, remains awake. He's sitting in his study, walled in by books, magazines, notes, photographs of old teachers, Maby, Sarah, me, and he's staring down at a blank sheet of paper on which he must soon begin to write the sermon he must deliver the next late afternoon. But what to write? what to say about this awful time in the life of our people, in the life of Europe, in the life of the planet. Better to have been born on the moon than to have been a Jew in Hitler Germany he could say. Or, better to have lived in Hitler Germany than to have been married to the woman who nearly drove him this evening into a crazy state of violent distress? He's thinking that—his thoughts drift, wander, stray. Maby. She has turned into a monster, and now she needs the kind of care only an institution can offer. That's what Doctor Mickey suggests. Why let her suffer and slide into a worse state of detachment and distraction and, to be frank, a kind of lunacy, when she can go into a place for a few weeks of intensive treatment and come out with a program that will keep her on an even keel? I know just the place, your wonder-making Doctor Mickey said. Owl Valley. It's not far, it's modern, a warm place, good care, not cheap by any means, but the best in the state. I'll do it, Manny said. For her sake, I'll do it. Do it for your own sake, too, for God's sake, Doctor Mickey said. Near, good, warm, the best. I'll suggest it, Manny said. Don't suggest, Manny, Doctor Mickey said. Not suggest—take her there. We'll take her there together. Her face drifted in and out of his view, like a raft in the temple swimming pool butted here and there by the wind. He saw her, he saw her not—he saw her, he saw her not. This woman, the only woman he had ever known, the only woman in his life except his mother, me (Sarah didn't count as a woman, then, being just a little more than little girl, at least as far as Manny was concerned). He had without ever thinking much about it attached himself to her, for what he supposed—when he thought about it—was life. There was too much else to think about, work, work, the two kinds of work, to consider ever finding another way to live. Accept, is what he told himself, you must accept. Accept. Good advice to give to others, and advice he ought to take himself. But how can you advise yourself? He'd listen to your Doctor Mickey, and he would help her heal herself, help her to rest, take stock. And then she would get back to the odd but ebullient and appealing personality that she was when they had first thought of marriage. When they had first . . . kissed, was how he put it in his mind . . . which shows you how much he hid from himself in the realm of private matters as opposed to the way he did business, where he considered everything that had to be considered, no matter what the cost.

The paper. Still blank, and he was drifting.

Death camps.

Jews going up in smoke.

Bones.

Blank white ash.

Blank white paper.

What could he say that hadn't already been said? Here was a speech he wanted to use to greet the survivors who had come to the congregation, and to celebrate and commemorate. But what did he know? he knew nothing. Blank. White paper.

Silence.

The house creaked and yawned, like a ship in which he took passage across a great dark sea, in time, in space.

Blank.

The paper.

He had read everything, and understood nothing, knew only by rote, could spew out lines from the Talmud, from histories, and it was all, he felt in his blood, make-work. The ignorant congregants, they were impressed with the smallest bit of knowledge, but what could he say that was interesting to himself? Nothing.

What could he say that was new to himself?

Blank.

The paper.

He sighed, and the house squeaked, settled in response. Outside the study window he heard a noise, a fluttering of wings? He lighted a pipe, unusual for him. He had the sense that he was waiting, and not just for the dawn. Tomorrow he would have other work to perform, other duties, and there would be no time for the writing. And so he must accomplish it now. And a chill passed over him, and he hugged his coat tighter around his shoulders and arms. The pipe smoke curled up toward the study ceiling, and the wings beat at the window, and he knew that he was yet again to be visited.

Manny?

Yes, father? he heard himself say, in spite of his fear.

Manny, I have a suggestion. A solution for this nothingness on your page there.

What is it, father? he said, hearing his own voice tinny and shrill, a boy's voice in a man's throat.

Silence.

Father?

Silence.

Perhaps I ought to move in to Owl Valley along with Maby, he said to himself.

And then the voice returned.

Manny, that was the answer. Silence is the answer. Nothing is the answer.

Nothing?

Nothing.

I could get Doctor Mickey to prescribe something for me, he told himself. I could get something that would help me sleep, something that would at least help me relax. Hearing voices, for a man who has two jobs, nearly a double life, in fact, it wouldn't be such an admission of weakness if now and then he took a pill to help him relax, would it?

It wouldn't, said a voice.

Manny jumped to his feet.

What the hell? he cursed. His eyes rolled up in his head and he swung his arm as if striking out at something visible to him but no one else, and then he keeled over onto the rug.

It was light when he awoke, to the sound of me asking him if he was all right. I had found him there on the rug in his study, his knees curled up to his chin, his hands clasped around his knees, like the baby he had been in my womb.

I was working late, he explained. I had to get my sermon done, and I was upset, I suppose . . .

He supposed, can you imagine?

. . . from Maby's upset, and I had just figured out how to do the sermon when I fell asleep.

On the floor, darling?

It looked comfortable.

Darling, I can look at your face and in an instant know you're not telling the truth.

Can you, Mama? And he made the little laugh he laughs sometimes with me, when I catch him like this, and with nobody else. So he learned some things that night, and most important he made his sermon, and let me tell you it was a big hit. You were there to hear it, no? So you heard it, but you didn't hear it. I don't want to make a joke about something so serious. Remember? Twenty minutes of silence in honor of the dead of the camps. Before an audience that included, as it turned out (and oh, did it turn), some of the living who had survived. Twice as many words and twice as much time couldn't have done it better.

That's what *she* told him when she met him on his way out of his office door at the end of the service. He was exhausted, my Manny. Standing there for twenty minutes. In silence. But thinking. Thinking of the dead. The torture. Murder. Mangled bodies. Murdered babies. And all of the things he had done as a young man while these things were going on. Most Jews here didn't know, he decided. And they could never truly know, unless they went through it themselves, which, God forbid, should never happen. And so a paradox. And so the silence. Silence. Now to see Maby, to see if the drugs prescribed by Doctor Mickey had calmed her. To Owl Valley. On Monday. With the Doctor. And he wanted to remember, too, to have the good doctor prescribe something for his own sleep as well. It had been a long night for him, long awake in his study and then the voice of his father, he had heard it, clearly as if from the beak of the visiting white bird of his youth. And if he hadn't been a grown man by this time, with all that he knew, he might have been frightened.

I couldn't believe it was so right, Florette said to him as he came out of his office.

Oh, he said, thank you, I wanted to do the right thing.

You did, Rabbi, you did, she said, pressing her hand against his.

I'm glad, he said. Although it makes me sorrowful to have to think let alone talk about such a subject.

Such a subject, yes, she said, staring into his eyes.

Do you think he needed more than that to think what he did at that point? With Maby being what she was? For all that time? He did not, he did not need more. And if you understand, then you understand.

I didn't realize, he said, you are Mrs.? His voice trembled a little with fatigue.

She reminded him of her name.

You moved here when? he asked.

She reminded him.

Not that long ago, he said, looking down now at her hand in his.

She nodded, a presence of flesh and perfume, past and present.

Would you like to come in for a moment? he asked, stepping back into the office as she nodded her head.

Here in America, he said, Manny seated alongside her on the sofa, a rule he had never broken before even with the children who came to speak to him, always sit behind the desk and the other on the sofa was the rule, and here he had broken it, sitting next to her, still holding her hand. Here in America we just don't know . . .

But you don't *want* to know, she said. You . . .

That's what I was coming to, he said. That's why the silence. Because to know is to suffer, and why should anyone suffer unnecessarily what those, you, knew? Could it stop it from happening again if more people knew? No, I don't think so, because to *truly* know is only to suffer it. The paradox lives.

Though I am painting about it, she said.

Are you? I'd love to see your paintings, he said. Still holding her hand, and wondering to himself if she wore a number up on her wrist or above. But it was not that that fascinated him, no, it was not anything he could put into words, it was a certain electrical charge that he could feel, he explained later to me, a certain electrical field, he tried to say what it was. This had never happened to him before, except for the time that he met Maby, and he could only tell himself that he was mistaken even though he was sure that he was *not* mistaken.

You'll have to come to my studio and see them, she said. They're in my studio, in my house.

Your house, he said, I should know where you live.

And she explained to him, and he remembered from a list that he had seen, because he usually remembered everything that he saw on a page, and he told her that he would come and see the paintings, and perhaps they could allow others to see them, too, perhaps a show?

No show, she said. Just you, Rabbi.

Just me, he said, and that was an agreement.

And perhaps you'll let me paint you? she said.

Me? Why me?

Because of your face, she said, and your hair.

I'm not a model, he said, trying to make a joke.

But I've been watching you, she said, and that makes you a subject.

Not an object? he said. Thinking, I feel this tremendous pressure and I'm talking to her in joking language from philosophy?

The pressure didn't let up the rest of the weekend. In fact, as the next week began, it got worse, and worse. On the drive west to Owl Valley, a lovely old Victorian building with a number of modern cottages—like the extra additions on a motel, was what they looked like, what they still do look like—he was thinking about this encounter with the woman in the temple, the survivor of the camps who painted pictures and wanted to paint him, all the while driving with your own Doctor Mickey, and Maby, the poor daughter-in-law, my poor girl, so drugged that she behaved like a sleepy child. He should have been thinking about what had driven her to this point in her life, and I don't mean a car, I mean the childhood event that she carried around with her—because as you know it upset him plenty just to have heard it, and he still didn't know what he was going to do later in the week when he had a meeting in the city scheduled with the brother-in-law, the famous brother Mordecai, otherwise known as Mord.

But so now they are driving west across Jersey, watching the shopping malls and bald spots where gas stations and houses used to stand, and the grease and the dead trees turned into greener hillsides, the road becoming hilly, the earth curving, and soon the horizon becomes beautiful, with only here and there a billboard, here and there a house, an abandoned filling station, and it is like another state, and you can imagine streams and rivers and farms and all of those things that used to be here throughout the East when the Indians ruled, where now only the rich gentiles to the west commute to the city on their neat little train lines. And there are birds here, and deer, and perhaps now and then someone sees the droppings of a bear. And are there wolves? I don't know. And what do they call them? mountain lions? There are perhaps *almost* mountain lions, call them hill lions, because there are not real mountains but only the beautiful tree-filled hills, I can close my eyes now and see them as clearly as if I am driving with him in that car. The dozing Maby, the clear-eyed doctor sitting next to her, ready at any moment to give her comfort. She was going in for observation, for tests and relaxation, to get her away from the booze, to get her away from the stress that pushed her close to the booze.

It must be a relief to finally come to terms with this, Manny, Doctor Mickey says.

A relief, yes, says my Manny, steering carefully at a speed just within the limits of the law. (He didn't tell you all this, your boy, the doctor? Well, he keeps good secrets. But my boy, Manny, he tells me everything and that's how I'm telling *you* things, even secrets about your own son.)

His head—tumbling through it are pictures of Mord and Maby, the survivor woman Florette Glass, Mord, the company offices, the barge, wondering about Florette Glass, thinking, What are you thinking, Manny? get off it! get off it! wondering about how long Maby would stay, this would free his time, slightly, if Mama, if Sarah, oh, what he was thinking? nothing that you wouldn't imagine a man in his situation wouldn't be thinking, but to think about it, when you were he, it hurt, it hurt, and to tell it to you now, it stings a little too, let me tell you, it stings, it bites, like the cuts in the fingers made by him with his little shard of star. They sting, they sting.

. . . the facilities, Doctor Mickey was explaining to him.

It sounds fine, my Manny says, coming back to the discussion.

And of course the insurance covers it, from . . .

I don't worry about such things anymore, Manny said. What did he know in fact about money worries since old Meyer Sporen had died? Not much, except his worries about making the company, his and Mord's company, grow faster and faster.

Oh, what a thing is a man's mind, listen in on his thoughts the way he told me he was thinking, and you add in the wondering about the company, and you get a pretty picture, I'm telling you.

Maby, Florette, Sarah, me, the company, the takeover of the bottling plant they wanted to begin next week, and Mord, what to say to him, the boy with the needle in the eyelet, the mess at the barge, the old man tossing him across the abyss, over the water, over time, Maby her drinking, the story hitting him, my Manny, like a ton of bricks, the money from the deal, the cash to come, the board, new board control, the suit he'd wear to the meeting, the same plain black suit he'd worn to all of those meetings because it seemed to work like a charm, they see me and they think confidence, they have confidence in me the studious rabbi, what doesn't he know about these things? what couldn't he tell us both about the business and the ethics of it all? and Mord telling me this and explaining, and me not listening, and me explaining, Mord, you are the genius and I only look like the genius, and I know precious little but what I learned in my econ classes a long time ago and what I feel I can do by way of doing right. And what my voices tell me, of course, I musn't leave that out of any consideration since as of this weekend I do declare it appears to be true that after a long absence the voice seems to have returned.

. . . observation . . .

Observation? Doctor Mickey was saying. Observation? And my Manny is thinking, They ought to put me under observation along with Maby, because all of this boiling beneath the surface, the distinguished man with the white hair and the dark suit, put him under observation and study him, a man who hears voices and believes in luck beyond all limits set upon the world by his religion, and now add to this a man who can't wait to lock up his wife so that he can visit another woman.

Wouldn't that kind of thinking make you want to draw back in fear if it was in your own life? Like the kind of thing you see when you're out in the yard in springtime and you turn over a rock? If it weren't my Manny I would think so too. But as his mother I know him better than anyone else, and as his mother I can tell you that he never wanted to hurt anyone—that he wanted love, he wanted to be held, he wanted the kinds of things grown people need but can't get from their mothers. So?

if I tell you now things that might sound wrong, who's finally to say what's right, what's good, and what a grown man shouldn't do no matter what?

Because, as they say in bedtime stories I used to tell to my darling Sarah (when she was still Sarah, and not the Sadie person she has become) no sooner had he taken care of settling his wife in at the rest home at Owl Valley—a place, I have to admit to you, I haven't seen, because, to tell you the truth, there are few things in the world I mind thinking about but staying, or worse, *ending up* in a place like that I don't want to discuss, I don't want to know, I don't want to *look*—and he and Doctor Mickey drive back to the town, and then Manny says goodbye, and races right over to the house of the painter.

He had arranged it. So don't think it was an accident that she was home. She was expecting him. They had tea. Tea, of course, what did you expect, liquor? My Manny hardly ever touches liquor. Now and then, at a party, he'll sip a glass, but never a lot.

And they're talking.

And he says, and she says, you know that kind of thing.

But through the talk he's staring at her, she's staring at him, the looks behind the talk, they're saying a lot they couldn't use words for, not when they hardly know each other, not so soon.

How long have you been painting?

A long time, Rabbi Bloch. Ever since I was a small child. Drawing, I was drawing then.

Please call me Manny, will you, please?

I'd be happy to. Manny.

Thank you. So this was before the camps? or after?

Before. And I drew when I was inside. With whatever materials I could find. Sometimes a guard would take pity on me and give me things, sometimes guards would find my things and tear them up and throw them away.

Would you say it kept you going?

It did keep me going.

And after, you kept on painting?

It was the only good thing I knew. My parents were dead, I had no friends. Drawing, painting, was all I had. Rabbi . . .

Manny, please. Manny.

Manny. She's lighting a cigarette now. Putting down the pencil she was using to make a sketch of him and lighting a cigarette. This was her only·vice as far as my Manny could tell — she smoked and smoked and smoked. She was wearing a peach sweater dress and stockings in her own house as though she had been expecting him to arrive on her way out to some function at the temple or in the city, and when she crossed her legs the stockings made a swishing sound to which my Manny listened intently, listened to her inhale and blow out the smoke, swish, and the insuck and outrush of air. In the space between the sounds he could hear the noise of his own future, a faint faint whirring like the echo of a voice shouted far off in some hills. Does this make sense? It's what he told me he heard, what he imagined, do you think? But then this is the boy who heard what the white pigeon told him, and did it, and he's not crazy, he's a big success, he's got the temple, and he's got the business in the city, and if he hears things and he keeps it to himself does the rest of the world have to decide whether or not he's a little odd or if he's a success but crazy, who knows? He was listening to his own future, he told me later, and whatever that meant to him it had to do with the woman, the woman smoking, the escaped-from-the-camps woman smoking who in a few minutes would show him her sketch and he would say, That's me, I suppose, but a me I never can catch when I look in the mirror.

I want to paint you soon, she told him then, because there's no way I can get your hair and your eyes in a drawing. I need color.

Color.

And now, we finished our dinner we'll have some coffee, but first I got to . . .

Ah, never mind the spill, Sally, the girl will clean it. I'm so clumsy, from the eye problem I get clumsy because I reach and it's not there, and I touch and it's over to the side.

But while they're talking about the painting, and they're both trying to figure out, as people in this kind of situation do, how they can say to each other what they really want to say, I'm going to continue on my way to the bathroom, and then I'll be right back.

·   ·   ·

So. I made it. You thought maybe I got lost? I'm the woman who gave birth to a financial genius, to a man who figures out he should give silence instead of words on the subject of the camps of the Nazis. You think I couldn't find my way to the toilet and back?

Color, I was saying. His hair. She wanted the right color.

That is what attracted me to you, she said. Because now they're sitting next to each other, I forgot to say, I guess, ha-ha, it happened while I was in the toilet, they're next to each other, and he's kissing her, and she's kissing him, her mouth tasting of many cigarettes, and he's so uncomfortable in his suit coat, he stands up, and strips his coat off, and that's when she says, That is what attracted me to you, your hair, she said, the color of your hair, it's extraordinary . . .

Like me, he said, and sat down next to her and threw himself on top of her, and she didn't do anything but throw herself back.

You're shocked, I can tell, because of what I'm saying, about my own son, your rabbi, but why should it be a secret? If it's something I want to tell, it shouldn't be a secret, should it? Because I'm telling you, because I'm trying to figure how it all came to be the way it came to be, one woman in the rest home, a girl on the street, look, hours now and she hasn't come back. How did it happen? Was it me? Or my Jacob? Or my own mother and father, something they did or said? Or was it Adam and Eve, the things *they* did? Or was it God Himself, or Herself, my Sarah-Sadie jokes about it these days now that she's a big shot student in college, was it God? did He or She just decide that it was all going to be this way? the rabbi of the congregation and the woman who survived the camps taking their clothes off in her living room? Look, he's pulling off his undershirt, and she's turning her back so he can help her unhook her brassiere, and then she takes him suddenly by the hands and she says,

Don't you want to get comfortable?

And my Manny nods his head, yes, of course, and she leads him, both of them half undressed, and he's staring at her large breasts, cones in shape they are, her nipples dark coins, and there's a small line of numbers beneath the brown curling hair on her arm above her wrist, breasts, numbers, breasts, numbers, this is what he stares at on their way up to the second floor.

She is a hairy woman all over, he discovers when they get upstairs. No, no listen, look at the look on your face, if you could see it, but listen look, they get upstairs, what's the big deal a man getting undressed, we've all seen it, but to him, my Manny, he's only seen one woman, and I don't mean me, because he never saw me without no clothes except when we lived in the apartment on Second Street and it was very small and no place for privacy, but Manny was small then, and for him as a man he had only the redhead, and she is like a little girl, look, her I've seen plenty of times, flat-chested, not a lot of hair and what hair she has is reddish-blonde and so it looks like when she is naked you can see beneath her skin into the pinkish tissue of her underself. This was a sight he was used to, and what you're used to seems natural and everything else strange, a freak almost.

So when they're in the upstairs room, her bedroom, with her paintings hanging all around—dark colors, shapes he never saw before in paintings but things he could easily imagine in dreams—she's slipping out of her underclothes, and, oh, let me tell you, for him it's very strange, because in the dark light of the room in mid-afternoon, the curtains closed, the paintings hanging all about, he imagines things, he sees her all hairy and he imagines for a second that she has a snout—wait, and then he recovers and sees her climbing into bed, and it's like a forest from her navel nearly down to her thighs, and—wait, look—then he imagines, listen, in the heat of it he's like a little boy again, in the dark at night in our old place, and he's seeing these frightening sights, that she's got a snout like a wolf, so hairy she is, and then he climbs in alongside her and he's over the fear, and they're embracing, and for Manny, my Manny, it's like *he's* the one been taking drugs all weekend instead of the wife now in the rest home, because he has the sensation as soon as he's holding her and she's holding him, he swears this, that lying there horizontal he is falling, falling, down into the opening of the forest grove where the underbrush lay thick and overgrown, hiding the passage but showing the way all the same, and for the rest of the afternoon he got lost there, a little boy, a grown man, and for the rest of the afternoon he did not rest until it was over.

He didn't rest even then, as a matter of fact, not in his mind. For years he had been climbing into bed with Maby, and nothing like this had ever happened, the trip through a fairy tale, the voyage through trees. Wait, it was like that, he described it. He had seen things, sure, and he had heard things, because this is the boy who heard the voice of the white pigeon and grew up to be the man who heard *more* voices, and he had heard a voice just a few nights before, remember, when he was wrestling with the talk about the camps, but of all the things he had heard, it was not like this, because this was something that drew him in *all over*, not just sound or sight but smell too, and touch, but also this time with a sensation like electrical in his heart, and in his nose up where it meets the face, behind his tongue, at the roots of his teeth, at the sockets of elbow and knee and in my Manny's toes and ankle joints, something that he had never imagined before let alone believed happened to other people. So it was, this feeling, yes, in his marrow bones, and he did not know what to do about it or what to call it but only to live through it or with it or whatever else he was going to have to do.

Do you mind, she said, after a while, if I smoke a cigarette?

And he began to laugh wildly, the way he imagined Maby would be laughing if she were not sitting in a clean room in the rest home looking out at the trees enshrouded by fog, the clouds that drifted close to the ground in western Jersey where the forests flourished, where the state was not the state where the rest of us still lived, Maby sitting in her room with a river of drugs running through her veins keeping her calm and cool and collected, the way she would be laughing if she knew that after all these years, after the studies and the struggle in the early days to take care of the congregations, and the early days in the business after her father died, the business that was growing now so large that he was worrying almost all the time about living a double life, and which to choose, which to give up, that after telling his mother all because his mother was the only woman in his life for so long, and after thinking that he would live forever, because that was the custom, with his red-haired bride from the Middle West, and after discovering that he could not go on much longer because of what she had told him about her and her brother, *that* burden added on to the *other* burden of the congregation and the business, the choice between living a life that might be blessed and a life in which he was rich and growing richer, that after all this he had finally, finally, found a way to let go. Very funny.

A Daughter's Prayer

Where were You in the dark? Where? Where did You disappear? You walked with me as a child. I remember hearing Your voice in the closet behind my toy chest. God, I said to You, where did You put my Mickey coloring book? Where did You put my Mouse? And You answered, You said, Girl, it lies in the bottom of the chest. And I went there and looked and, lo and behold, there it was. In the old days—I hear this in the class, I hear it in sermons—You spoke to us in a burning bush, You spoke to us in a cloud and pillar of fire. Why not use Your plain voice now? If You're not a man, even better to speak. What if You are a She? or an It, something between the two usual sexes? What if You have both the one thing and the other? What if You are a dual sex? What if You are a woman, though, what if? do You have periods? do You feel the cramps come on as the egg sets out on its journey? do You mourn for the death of the egg? do You care for the egg? or do You hate the egg? Do You think about the egg as a life? Or is our world the egg from Your ovary? Are we the life on the evolving egg? Are we the children of Your universe? Or if so, how did we get fertilized? If You are a woman, did You have intercourse with a male god? And how did that happen? Did He force you, as I know how force can be, or did You go into a trance, as I know how a trance can take over, or did You decide that it was time and that You had to find out what it was like, which I did? And did You like it? Or did You find that it was something not for You? And if it was something not for You, God, did You find that You kept to Yourself for a long time? And then did You find that You looked for someone like Yourself so that You could find pleasure? And is our good weather on this planet Your pleasure, perhaps? And is our hate and fear and killing and war and anxiety, is it Your cramping? Your periods?

Oh, I know I don't know—oh, I know I care but I don't know how to find out. I don't know how to find it. But, Dear, dearest God or Goddess, if You are a female, then I want to tell You that I need You now. I need to know. I need You most. I need You fastest. I need You now in the dark, and in the light. I want to touch Your body, Goddess, I want to hold Your hand.

Book Three
Evening

N ow you've finished your meal, the latest of your grandmother's suppers.

And you've walked a little around this place where my son has put me in the style that I never knew I'd see. And while you walked maybe you looked out the window at the lights of the city – thinking, Could I? Did I ever imagine that I could climb so high and look down upon these places? Look down upon these people? But Rose, look, by accident and by design we climb higher and we get older and we look down and back along the way we came.

And we'll have some coffee, because it is that time in the meal. Here, the girl is bringing it. See? Her? Black? The granddaughter maybe of our old friend the waitress in the mall? Could be? But I don't ask, I never ask questions like that unless I can feel that someone has the answer in her mouth and wants to spit it out. They're all related anyway, from Adam and Eve in the Garden of Eden, it goes back, black, white, red, brown, maybe someday a miracle we'll hear about blue, green, and who knows what else could go on? Because even I know – I know – that there's a mixing sometimes at the beginning of things, like when you make soup there's a mixing and a thickening and all the bones and juices, spices and seasonings simmer together, so who am I to say that no matter what I think or what I want things have happened and things will happen?

And how are *you* now, darling? You've been in the kitchen all this time? And you've finished cleaning up almost already? And thank you, darling, we'll have some coffee, of course. Rose?

Mrs. Pinsker? It's the decaffeinated. It won't keep you awake
only just a little while. Me, some nights I drink it and lie in the
dark, lay in the dark, whatever, and it's like being awake in a
small closed box or hole in the ground, and in this cave, the hole,
on the walls I see pictures, things from my life gone by, because,
you know, it's restful for me when I'm having so much trouble
with my eyes, that I have a little perfect dark, dark like old velvet, like satin, dark smooth to my eyes the way the material is
smooth. And what does it remind me of? It reminds me, this
dark, of the feeling of Manny's tallis, his prayer shawl, the same
material, and the yarmulke I made for him when he went to
Cincinnati so long ago. I feel, and I feel the time, I feel old time,
and if I could have my fingers in my head or my eyes in my
fingers, that is what it would feel like, and I could see it like it
was yesterday, no, like today, now. No. Not right now. You
can't be in two places at once. But at night, at times almost like
these, when I close my eyes to see and try to contemplate the
many sad mysteries of Jersey and New York, the stories I need
to tell you, the stories you didn't know you needed until you
heard them, then I call on the powers of my eyes and fingers,
the strength of my old memory and deep heart feelings, whatever I have, whatever I give, to show you in your eyes inside
the way things moved in this world where I once lived.

So.

This is how it began, on the one side, this new stage of his
life, on the one side, the side we don't see, like the way the moon
has the side we see and the side we don't, and this is the side
we don't. The moon, that's right, where even shopping malls
may exist on the side we don't see. Moon malls. Moon men in
moon malls. My Manny, in this time of his life, he could live
there and be happy, the first rabbi on the moon.

Because this was how he felt, with the arrangement with
Florette Glass on the one hand and the tending needed by Maby,
who from then on was in and out of Owl Valley, on the other.
One side of the moon, and the other. But you only see one side,
and the other you have to guess about. He lived on both sides,
but he only saw one, was how he felt. And which was the light
side, which the dark? Sometimes it would change for him, some
things would change, and he would be happy one way, sometimes the other. He couldn't figure it, he couldn't predict. But
it's true that after her first stay at the hospital, Maby appeared

to get a lot better. And the house got a lot better. And to me, his mama, before I knew, it seemed to me that he was happier, too. But of course I didn't know about the arrangement with Florette. What did I know? I knew only that she was painting his portrait, and I trusted my son to sit still for a picture because that was what he said he went over to her place for. But did he sit? Not still. They loved each other, they rolled around.

And what about Maby? Was she sitting still? Not her, I'm telling you. With the permission of a new doctor she started to see in Montclair on recommendation again from Sally Stellberg's Doctor Mickey, she enrolled in writing classes at Rutgers Newark. Which meant she had to drive a lot, to the doctor, to the classes. So she wasn't sitting still neither.

So who was? Why should anybody? Sarah also wasn't. She was back and forth to Rutgers all the time now, because the youth leader, Rick, your grandson, he was finishing up the law school there and she liked to talk with him. That's right, you didn't know? So now you hear it. Much older he was than she was, but that didn't matter to her because when she wanted her way, let me tell you, she got her way. And who do you think she takes after? Her father? Her mother? Her grandmother? All of us, that's who!

But Manny, too, he was going back and forth in a number of ways, from Florette to Maby, Maby to Florette, and also from the temple to the office in the city, from the city to the temple. And this meant something that if you didn't think of it before you had to think of it now. The brother-in-law. Mordecai. Mord. How was he going to work with him now that he knew something of the circumstances that surrounded his early exit from the Sporen house in those days when the old boat owner was still alive. He ran away from home. And it was a good thing he was running, wasn't it? Because you can imagine his father would have killed him if he had caught him.

Of course he didn't know. Do you think that a little girl tells something like that to her parents? She takes the blame on herself, and she eats herself up alive inside. She's a victim, and she comes to be as much a victim of her own self, her feeling-guilty self, as she was of the one who made her a victim in the first place. But of the man, the boy that he was, and the man that he is now who made her feel this way in the first place – well, of course, old man Sporen, the father, helped her to feel this way, too, and in that way, he should share some of the responsibility—but it's the brother, the boy he was, the man he is, who is the main person—oh, it's so confusing sometimes, boy, man, girl, woman, father, mother, daughter, son, one behaving like the other should behave, the other pretending to be what he is not, or she—but the boy, I was saying before my confusion started weighing on me like a load of groceries in both arms, and I can feel it in my feet, too, let me tell you. I was telling you about the boy, who, like my Manny, became a man the hard way. If he ever did become a man. The boy, I mean. Mordecai. Mord. Not my Manny, because with my Manny there was no doubt that he was what he was. Why else was the Glass woman painting his portrait? But Mordecai. Mord. That could be another story.

Time for coffee now. Sip coffee, and while in the kitchen that young girl, somebody's grandchild, cleans up the dishes, or maybe she's done them already and she's thinking about going home, home to see her young children, she has some children, and a husband, hard working, a hostler maybe like my Jacob, I'll tell you what happened when Manny for the first time after he heard the news about the past from his Maby went to see the brother, the brother-in-law, who was responsible for the past.

As usual, he went in on the train. Well, I shouldn't say as usual because only in the last few years it was usual. Before that, he drove. But then when he worked more in the business than he did, say, at the seminary in the city, he took the train in. Because he had to go to midtown instead of uptown and to midtown it's easier to take the tubes and walk to where you want or take a taxi than it is to drive. And come to think of it you could mark the beginning of the big change in my Manny's life from the time he stopped driving the cars and started taking the train. So . . . that morning he got up and got dressed—Maby was, of course, still out in the country—just like on any other day when he had made the trip into the city, and I met him at the table where he was already reading the paper, the *Wall Street*, and I ask,

You want some eggs, darling?

He shakes his head. No thanks.

A big day in the city, you could eat some eggs, I said.

I don't think it's going to be a big day, he said. Just to make talk, he was talking. But I could see something unusual, the newspaper in his hand, it was shaking, he was trembling.

You're all right? I asked him. You don't have no fever?

Fever?

This word he reacted to. Because he had a fever then, he had the Florette Glass fever, and it made him sensitive, sensitive, of course, because here he is the rabbi, the leader, the father, the husband, the son even, and he's having an affair with the woman in his congregation while his wife is out in the hospital in the woods, so who wouldn't be sensitive to that? The fever of his life made his hands shake, for the first time, and it was worrying him because he didn't want to lose control, he believed that he couldn't afford to lose control, he was sure that everything he had accomplished in his life up until this point was the result of never having lost control. He believed this, but if it was true or not is another question.

So it was a good thing he took the train. On the way to the station he appeared to have so little power over the automobile that it wobbled and wavered, like a boat on water. His palms were sweating like it was summer and he'd just come out of the water. His underarms, all water too, what we call, you know, here and in the old country, *schvitz*. And in his pants, too, he almost wet, this later he explained to me, as he thought about what would happen if he talked to Mordecai the way he thought he ought to—call him *rapist, pervert, destroyer of innocence,* trying to think of his wife as a girl, a child really, and of his own daughter, and how he would respond if it had been Sarah to whom Mord had done this terrible thing. But his heart sank when he understood what would follow such a confrontation—the entire train ride in he mourned over the loss of the company, the collapse of the partnership, the end of everything he had worked for. Green hills, white houses, churches, vast parking lots, towers, then factories, train yards, power lines, walls, walls, walls—and in the station the crowd of thousands, not usually a force that my Manny did anything but yield to when he had to as he walked, threatened, it felt like, to close in on him and crush him between their hips and shoulders, so that when they stepped away the police would find him, a white-haired man pressed flat to the floor in his fresh dark suit. Shaken, my son walked on to find his stairway to the street, weary already of the thought which had come to him only a little while before, that he had become utterly without care for anything but the company and that to his brother-in-law he was not going to say a word.

A mother understands what's right. And for him this was what he needed in his life, that he shouldn't feel ashamed, although at first he did. If I had been with him, I would have said, *Never*, don't be ashamed. In that crowd, in that station, he wanted to disappear and change his life for yet another although he had by that time already changed his life one time more than most, or was nearly ready to, in any case, nearly ready. This was the spring before his fall from the dais — and so many things were building, building up inside. Like the storms in the systems on the weather maps you watch on TV? Oh, and if I could see them again clear I'd be a happier woman. Because my eyes. And yours, *kinnahurra*? They're still good? Then bless them, because that is a gift that came to me I didn't know was so precious until it started to fade. To see. To see, it would be wonderful to look out the window and see the lights of the buildings across the dark space of the park — how do I know what I'm missing? When we first moved here, darling, I could still make it out.

More coffee? My Manny is drinking some in his office after his trip on the train. Amazing that you can take the same ride you've made so many times before and this one time it all seems different. To my Manny, it was as if he had not passed under a river but crossed over a border. Several lights on his telephone were blinking and he was staring at them but not responding. He was thinking about Florette, about removing her and then his clothes and climbing into bed with her, and about the paper box company he and Mordecai were going to swallow, like a long thick South American snake swallows a baby kid or goat. Except my Manny knew that they could digest it in shorter time. The last things on his mind were his wife, his daughter, and, I have to admit it, because I'm in this too, his mother. Why not? We faded away to nothing more than a faint reminder of another life, the way your stomach sometimes growls to tell you that it's working. That's how faint we were in his day at this point, natural to him of course, but not present. How far he had come to reach this moment, when he could forget everyone he had been working for all these years! But I don't blame him, you understand. He had arrived at an important time in his life, when he had to say to himself, What is it all for, what am I doing this all for? to keep a girl in clothes and school books? to keep a mother warm against the winter weather? to keep a wife in and out of a hospital and shot full of medicines? No, it's more than that, more than that, and if the bird that visited him from time to time didn't swoop down out of the sky and give him the advice he needed, that was because right now he didn't have to go outside himself for news, for weather reports, for wisdom, for inspiration, for advice on how to proceed. All he needed was his brother-in-law Mordecai to show him where he was supposed to stand and like a good actor he played his part. Options rolled in, companies stumbled before him, the money added up, and my Manny, in less than half a lifetime went from peddler's boy to king—or what we call in this country the same thing as king. He was a president, executive officer, board member, he might as well be a moon man except that he goes to the office in the city and he and Mordecai look at reports, they talk it over, they telephone money men, bankers, they talk it over, and they draw up plans, and then they make more telephone calls, and the next thing you know they own something else, and Manny, my Manny, the nice little boy who used to help his father push the cart on the Sabbath, who made up for all that by serving so many years as a rabbi, and a fine one you'll admit, yes? He's sitting on yet another board in his dark suit and white hair, and he's got the respect of the others, and more important, he's got control of yet one more company. In less than five years, four of them, the bottling, the paper, the box, the ships, and the one they started out with, barges. But now they've got more than barges, they've got ocean ships. And shipping routes south, and warehouses where they need them. And my Manny is getting upset because he has to divide himself between the temple and the companies, and the other thing of course that's upsetting him now is the two women, between Maby and Florette, and you're smiling but don't ever think that except for what you're about to hear me tell him on the telephone just now, in a minute, when I tell you what I told him, I never asked him to do nothing for me.

Yes, my call was one of the those winking lights on his desk board, because I was upset at breakfast when he didn't eat, when I saw how much he was sweating, when I could feel his nervousness crackling in the air like Jersey summer lightning, and when his secretary told him that among the others on the line I was waiting to speak to him fortunately for him he took my call first. Because just when he said,

Hello, into the office walked Mordecai. Where he was returning from I couldn't say, but he was always just back from some place or other, South America, Texas, California, Detroit, even Israel is a place that he goes to and comes from. He himself, let me tell you, darling, is quite a story, a match for my Manny, no doubt about that, and to think that they all met — except of course for Florette who at the time was not born yet, and lucky for her not yet born because she had a future in the camps still to suffer through, and little Sarah who, of course, was also away in the future — they all met at the accident where my Jacob passed away, in the Union Square, and ever since in one way or another we've all been together. He has quite a past, and if I told you all of it you'd be sitting here until tomorrow morning and your own children would be wondering why you weren't at home to answer the telephone. Not that my driver wouldn't wait, he's a very nice boy, a South American, his name is Daniel, which is a French name, I understand, but somehow with the French and the South American he still speaks English, and he takes good care of me, like a grandson I never had.

And isn't Manny a good son, too? Because when from the switchboard comes the word that I'm on the line and it's an emergency — this voice comes to him through the speaker on his desk because, remember, he hasn't touched the telephone — he says, Put her on the line.

Hello, Mama? he says.

Darling, I say. I'm breathing hard. I'm worried, frankly, that's what it is. You're all right? I ask him.

Yes, he says, is that why you called?

He's staring up from his desk at Mordecai, remember, who has just walked in, without knocking, without buzzing, of course, that's his way, and he's talking to me across the river.

I was worried that you didn't eat your breakfast.

Mama, he says with a laugh, you're always worried.

Your hands were shaking when you held the newspaper. That's something I shouldn't worry about?

Mama.

Tell me I shouldn't worry.

You shouldn't. He looks up at his partner, wonders what, just what he's going to say first, there's the news about Maby in the hospital, there's the news about . . . but then he catches himself. Because Mord doesn't learn about Florette. Why in hell should he hear about Florette? But Manny is thinking a mile a minute, and the borders between his thoughts, or do I mean the boundaries? they're falling away in his mind, and like on the train he's working his fingers raw on the shard, rubbing, rubbing so when he finishes talking to me he's got to excuse himself and go into the bathroom and run water over the wounds and put on Band-Aids in two places.

Your mother? Mordecai said, sitting on the desk top. His big bald head caught the light from the ceiling lamp and appeared to be as beautifully polished as the surfaces of the furniture. To Manny at this time the brother-in-law's skull seemed about to burst out of its skin. Mord had picked up some weight in the few years since he had come back to this country and taken up the business with Manny. As Manny remembered him he had been tall, bony, thin. But this man could easily have lifted up the father who had tossed him from dock to barge and heaved the big man who tortured him across that same empty space over the water. At fifty plus, he had strength the boy he had been never dreamed of. In a funny way he owed this all to Sporen.

I'm starting to tell you this, and I said it would take all night. You want to hear? Listen. What happened between him and Manny didn't last all that long. Manny finished our telephone conversation—he was feeling better, I was feeling better because he was feeling better—and, hello, hello, isn't it amazing, how a mother's call can have that effect?—and he didn't take the rest of his calls but sat down with Mord and he talked, they talked, he explained about Maby, where she was, how long the doctors thought she would rest there, he wanted Mord to know, he explained, after all, she was his sister, and then they had a lot of arrangements for the business to discuss, they hadn't talked face to face in weeks, but it was true, they had a meeting here, a meeting there, and they needed to talk strategy, that's what they called it, Mord the mastermind, Manny the soothing presence—and during this time, while Mord is looking so concerned about his sister, and so serious about the preparations for the week, Manny is saying to himself, Say something, say

something, but how do you say something to a man some years
your elder about something he did (if he did it) as a boy? When
Manny couldn't, as it turned out, connect the little boy he had
been to the man he had become, and couldn't connect the man
he had become first, the student, the rabbi, to the man he had
become now, the corporation man in the dark suit whose presence soothed gentile (which doesn't mean gentle) boards into
submission, so what was he going to do, crucify his partner for
something his hysterical wife remembered like a bad dream?
And did it happen at all, he asked himself as he sat there, what
if it was only the fantasy of a woman lost in drink? It could be
the truth but it could be many other things, some of which
Manny had heard over the years from members of the congregation. If there was one thing he learned in that job, it was that
there was no such thing as an adult, so why couldn't he include
his hysterical wife in that number? And why shouldn't he sympathize with his brother-in-law, particularly when, if they quarreled they would get into a mess that could bring down all their
holdings on their heads? They had met by chance—the deathly
accident that took my Jacob, and again by chance yet another
time after the untimely deaths of the pair of Sporens—and
worked well together only by chance, an act of chemistry,
Manny had originally decided, not unlike the kind that brought
him and Maby together and now clasped him and Florette in its
fist like two pieces of clay to be joined and molded—and what
chance had wrought did someone want by design to bring
down?

   You hear stories these days about the coloreds and how they
felt when they were slaves—and I listen carefully because, and
I want to talk a little quietly here because she's still in the kitchen
cleaning up and I don't want to hurt her feelings, and it was
terrible, sometimes even the masters would sell a father and
mother here, a child elsewhere, and like I say, I listen, because,
you know, how it's been that way in the Bible with the Jews,
and I can tell you, my Manny knows his history inside out, he
was a student, and then a rabbi, and so I want to tell you that
even though it could sound bad what he's done with the brother-
in-law *it is not at all like that*, like that with the slaves, the
coloreds, the Jews, it is not like he is selling his wife down the
river because he doesn't bring up the subject with the brother,

with the brother-in-law. I believe this. I have thought about it.
Believe me. A son of mine I wouldn't have behave that way, and
he didn't. I'm telling you.

So.
You know, I'm wondering where she is. She should be
getting back by now from wherever she is. Sarah, I mean. Sadie,
as she calls herself. Sarah, Sadie, whatever she calls herself, she's
still my little granddaughter. Except now, not so little. Maybe
she went to her mother's? It could be, it could be. But so late?
On the highway after dark? I worry about her. I always worry,
I know, so who doesn't? You worry, and you worry. But the
worst thing you can't do anything about. The worst things—I
told you the Sporen story—you do yourself.
To yourself, I mean.
Excuse me. Why I should be crying all of a sudden, I don't
know. To yourself, I was saying. To your own.
For example, what Meyer Sporen did to that boy, I could
sympathize why he was so rough to the sister. A mother can
understand, though, I'll tell you, I don't think *his* mother did.
She didn't, because she couldn't. From her you could figure
some terrible thing had happened in her own life when she was
little, and to her parents, either the mother or father or both
when *they* were children, and on and on, back further and further, until you get to Adam and Eve in the Garden of Eden, and
you have to think, maybe the story in the Bible should tell the
truth about what happened, because maybe what happened
was, instead of eating the apple and getting God angry, maybe
they *hit* Cain who hit Abel—or, worse, darling, imagine, maybe
even it was God who hit Adam, and Adam hit Eve, or at least
made him feel worthless, and this feeling he passed along, and
along, and down all the generations—I'm telling you, one
mother, even this one, can't hardly make up for all of the abuse
the human race has given to itself, *and* gotten, all the years.
But I was saying. What Sporen did to that boy Mordecai you
already know. But what it *did* to him, that only came out later
in his life. When Mord ran away to sea. How do I know this?
I see it, just the way I heard it from my Manny, and if you don't
think he, the man who used to be the boy, the brother, the
brother-in-law, didn't tell it to my Manny, then you got another

think coming, because to my Manny he talked, they talked and they talked, like the Catholics with their confessions, his story, the brother's, the brother-in-law's, it fits in not because it makes you laugh but because it could make you weep. So here he is, standing there talking to my Manny, and on his shoulders, in his brain, he's carrying a lot around with him. You have this tableau, you call it? My white-haired Manny, and the older man, the hawk nose, the balding head, the slightly hunched shoulders, and he's carrying with him despite the man he looks to be the boy inside who went to sail the ocean where islands dotted the horizon.

So the brother-in-law, he saw the seas, from his father's barge that sailed the river down to the Gulf, and then out to the sea, warm waters there, and warmer still, unlike the spitting ice from the whitecaps where we watched the waves, yes, for him, warmer, warmer, warmer still, and through the canal, the one named after the hat, and on to the China part, his first big trip, and he was not so young that he couldn't appreciate the enormity of what he had done—put Cincinnati, his sister, his mother, father, behind him—and not so old that he didn't feel, along with the guilt a little bit of playful pleasure, and not so old that he didn't feel some homesick too along with the pleasure, and not so old that he couldn't appreciate the beautiful first sight, the flying fish, the sunsets, the sound of the engines churn-churn-churn-churn-churning him to sleep on nights when he didn't watch the stars fade to nothing and the sun come up over waters higher than he had ever dreamed, the waves, sometimes splashing across the sky—or so it appeared to him—and sometimes the sky spilling down into the trough of the waves, after a storm a sky so multi-colored it might have been the original roll of material that God supplied for Joseph's many-colored coat. Oh, he loved the ocean, and he hated it, too—and oh, we are an ocean-going people, a water-crossing people, ever since our ancestors rushed between the Red Sea waves the Lord pulled back to let them pass, and we crossed over Jordan, after awhile, and even their Jesus, who used to be, as they tell it, one of us, didn't he supposedly walk on the lake at Galilee? a nice Jewish boy, standing on the waves? the son, the brother-in-law, like me and my Manny, and my Jacob, and his father before him, too, he's crossing the water, and walking on the deck if not on the waves, walking, walking all the way to China.

And he was thinking about what he had done to his sister, and what his father had done to him, before and after, and he discovered that he didn't like thinking so much about this, and thinking about anything else much he didn't do, and so he took up the hobby of the older sailors, he took up drinking, and he liked it because he didn't have to think about what his father had done to him and what he had done to his sister, and he remembered now and then that what he was doing was his mother's hobby, and that he probably took after her rather than his father, and if he had done something awful to his sister, it was probably because he was jealous that she was like their mother, that she was made like their mother, and one night while standing on the deck, with nothing between him and the dark ocean except a thin railing, the air as dark as the water except at the top of the ocean of sky the stars poked through, winkling, twinkling, as the ship's deck rolled and heaved, and he felt such a longing for the water and sky and stars, felt such an urge to fling himself into the ocean, forgetting that he would not fall but rise into the stars, forgetting that he could not breathe the air but would instead inhale and cease to be, and remembering everything that had happened even as he thought about forgetting, that he left behind his hopes for merging into the starry watery dark and sank into himself, and up out of himself, like the way the mountains rose out of this same sea bottom in places around the world (according to my Sarah's geography books where I used to look at the pictures with her), a mountain range of despair rose up, and he wanted to take himself by the hand, take himself, do you know what I mean? in hand, and tear himself apart.

If thine eye offend thee, pluck it out, they used to say. And he wanted to get rid of the offending part, maybe he was drunk out here already, and if so, he was lucky, I'm telling you, he didn't feel so loose and lonely that he climbed over the rail and slipped over the side into the deepest part of the ocean sky, the dark deep where the stars go out from the blackness of it all, but no, he didn't, even if he was drunk at that moment, he didn't, but he did descend, descend he did, into the bowels of the ship, into the sleeping part where his little bunk lay, a niche in the inner part of the rear, the stern of the ship, and there he drank from a bottle he had bought in some port, rum it was, and he wept quietly to himself, and the bottle slipped from his hand in the night, and he wept on with an urgency matched only by the ship's engines churn-churn-churn-churn-churn-churning, already you're sorry for him, aren't you? the bad boy, the boy who hurt his sister and you're sorry for him? Well, he was a boy then, he was a mother's son, and a father's son, and you already know how they hurt him to begin with, and how he passed the hurt along, and here he is in his bunk, his bed, and he should be sleeping, a boy asleep in the niche in the ship, sleeping to the heaving of the sea and the churning music of the engines, a peaceful picture it could have been, but it wasn't, because he was weeping and then he was moaning, and he was choking, and he was cursing himself as best he knew how to curse. Now if I could have been there I would have known what to do, I would have taken him in my arms and rocked him like a baby— *ah-uh-ah-uh, bay-bee, Ma-ma is a lay-dee*—and I would have comforted him, taken away his drink, given back to him the peace he threw aside when he learned how roughly his father treated him, when he discovered in himself his urge to hurt his sister— because if you turned it inside out it wasn't the desire to hurt but the need to show her his affection that drove him to it, except that the affection got turned inside out and he hurt her beyond any limit he could have imagined. If he had torn loose one of her limbs he couldn't have hurt her more—or hurt himself. If he had killed her and then himself that might have been the only way he could have hurt both of them more. And oh the pain that it caused him as well as her, and I would have taken him in my arms, taken the place of that mother the drunkard, whose own parents hurt her, gouged out of her a well that she had to fill with drink, and so I musn't sound so harsh, and I apologize, but I would have taken him, and helped him, and soothed him to sleep, me and the sea, the sea and the engines and me.

But I wasn't there, and his own mother wasn't there, not that she, the drinker, could have done any good, and he had no father as far as he was concerned, not the father who had grabbed and thrown him, which, when he didn't think about what he did to his sister, was a large part of what made him weep, the father throwing him, the casting out of the son by the father is how he felt it though he didn't at this point in his life have the words, no, there was nobody from the family, there was only an old sailor, from the family of the crew, and this man, gray-bearded smelling of rum, and tobacco, and the sweat of his labor, this man, awakened by Mord's weeping, crept alongside him in the night, and he comforted him, took him in his arms and comforted him.

What am I saying? I'm saying, I'm saying. I'm saying that this poor boy had to travel many miles over land and sea before he found a little bit of . . . don't you know what I'm saying? Worry more about how I know what I'm about to tell you instead of why I want to tell it. But I won't tell you that. You'll have to guess how I know it. But what happened? The old sailor, the young boy, what do you think? What do you imagine? You think it could be worse than what the father did to the boy and what the boy did to the sister? I don't know, I don't think so. To make a pattern you need cloth. To make a pattern you need scissors. To cut, to sew. To sew you need a needle, you need thread. To thread the needle, you need a good eye and a steady hand. To hold, to thread. Do you see? I'm not sure I see. But the thread, the needle, the eye of the needle, the point of the thread, the point of the pin. To make a pattern, cut the cloth, sew. Do you see? Different from what happened with the sister, but the same, in a way the same. The boy, he was trembling, weeping in the arms of the older sailor—probably not so old as I'm saying, probably only old to the eye of the boy, the eye he saw with, not the eye to thread, that eye, no, to that eye was he old? I don't know—but the older sailor, the man, the boy, whatever he was, because maybe even he didn't know what he was, how could he be sure when he was doing what he was doing, the mixing, mixing of young and old, boy and man, and boy and girl, too, that too—he, the sailor, he was trying to help, not to get pleasure and comfort for himself only, I don't think, although isn't that always part of it?

What am I saying? I'm trying to say it, but it's not easy, you know. After all, a grandmother—a grandmother speaks—a grandmother speaks a certain language—a grandmother speaks a grandmother's tongue all her life, all her life as a mother and as a grandmother—a grandmother speaks and the words, the words sometimes they don't say—because they can't say—all that she sees, all that she hears, all that she knows—because the words don't, the words don't do it, do they?—see, hear, eat, drink, live?—do they say it? do they make you see? eat? drink? rest? fear? love? hold?—or hide?

The sailor, he held the boy a while, and as he held him, he played with him, do you know what I mean? I don't mean games like cards, I mean he played, and the next thing you know they're off in a shadowy bunk, a hammock, it's not clear, all of it isn't clear, but it's like I'm seeing things, I can picture it from the words I heard about it, the sailor, the boy, and the sailor helps the boy undress, and they caress, and that's a rhyme that tells you what they did, are doing, have done, the dress, undress, caress, caress, a rhyme for that time, because it's like out of a fairy tale not for children. The sailor, petting the boy, the boy weeping, mewing like a lost little kitten, long, skinny, hairy boy, bearded sailor, the little boy looking for a father who won't throw him across the abyss, the older sailor looking for a boy to care for, each of them lost, each has lost something, lost themselves, who knows why? but each a mother's boy, and wouldn't their mothers, if their mothers knew, know why?

And then the bending, and all the time the touching, and the touching and the stretching, in the dark, in the half light, casting shadows, rolling with the waves, and then again the needle, the threading of the needle, the making of the thread, the cutting of the cloth, the pattern, the pattern, a long hup and a hush and a straining whine and a cry and a sigh.

And then a resting, a lying down alone, a washing of the waves against the hull, a thudding of the engines in the quiet of the resting, of the lying down,

and then,

and then again,

the engines,

the waves . . .

So you see, this is how the battered boy found some affection, and so what if it's that kind, the kind we don't usually talk about, the kind, what would my Manny say (he's said it to me), the kind in the tent in the desert in the dark, the Bible says, but does the Bible bring affection to the battered boy? Even a dog needs affection, and this boy, long limbed and with a hawky nose, and already starting to lose on top the hair, this poor boy needed someone, we all need someone, and don't get me wrong, I'm not defending. I'm not defending what happened with the sister, I'm not defending what he does with his life after that, with the sailor, with other sailors, with men, with boys he like himself used to be, I'm not defending, I'm merely describing, but who is it for this grandmother, let alone a mother, or an uncle, or a sister, or a brother-in-law, who are they—who am I to say?— what's right, what's wrong, darling, short of murder, short of torturing somebody with a knife, a gun, who am I to say?

The Bible. The Bible, I told you I know what the Bible—I told you my Manny and I discussed it, the Bible, what the Bible says about the things in the dark in the tent in the desert, but there are deserts and there are deserts, and tents and tents, and dark and dark, and these are modern times, you know, and I'm not saying that you bend the rules until they break, but I'm saying that the rules they change and twist and bend and that's life— the rules live, too, and the rules change, like people change, and if I don't understand it I can at least understand that I don't understand it, the grandmother speaks—she says the words— the language comes to her.

Blood.

If blood could talk, if nerves could, in the two minutes they spent together in the room just after my telephone call, all of what I just told you they might have said right then and there. If blood could talk, if nerves. Let's imagine that they said this, with their nerves, with their veins. And then they sat down, and they made a deal. It didn't take longer than that. It had to do with a partnership they had already concluded just after Meyer Sporen's death, an agreement they had made between the two of them to run the company the boat man had left. They extended it now—it included not only operating the company, and building it up, certainly that they had done, it now included, from my Manny's side at least, a new small unspoken agreement. It included the fact that he put the company ahead of his love, his family, anything he cared about or believed in that might stand in the way of making things work.

It can only help Maby, he told me, a long time afterward, when the heat of her revelation to him had cooled, and she, too, had calmed down considerably, with the help of pills, doctors, and the nice trees and grass and air out in the country at Owl Valley. She brought some of it with her when she returned home, the calm, the pills, the desire for doctors. The first, she kept with her, deciding, with the help of the doctors, that she

ought to do something with her life. And what she decided was,
as I said before, taking courses. Manny would have preferred
that she work in the temple organizations, but that was something she never did with much enthusiasm and he wasn't about
to force her, seeing her delicate state, to do it now. Instead, he
listened patiently while she explained that she was going
to enroll in a creative writing seminar at Newark Rutgers. He
nodded, agreed. And he bought her a new car. Touching, no?
Well, look, he was behind her a hundred percent. He made a
point from that time on never to lose his temper with her, never
to criticize. And if you don't think my Manny could make a decision like that, you don't know what he did—by decisions like
that—to make his company, the brother's company, the brother-
in-law's company, grow. I mean, little companies they picked
up like kid's toys from the playroom floor—and stock options,
whatever that is, I hear him talk, these he gets from all of them,
and from the companies they buy they milk money and buy
others. My Manny. In his white hair streaked dark and dark
suit—he walks into a board room and no one, let me tell you,
is bored, my dear. They sit up, they watch him, they listen for
what he says, because he has learning, he's read in the Torah,
in history, and this is a twist for them, all of them like lawyers
and business people only, or maybe a few studied history at college, but this was all for the ancient history. I'm trying to explain
to you how he does it, trying, too, to understand it myself. But
he does it—maybe it's magic. Maybe he's got some formula he
uses, hypnosis, halitosis, outrageous how he does it, Manny,
my little boy turned wizard of the Walled Street. Look, he
learned a lot from the brother-in- law, I don't want to take away
from Mordecai, Mord, but he has something in himself, the part
that talks to birds.

And for a change he uses some of his magic when he listens
to his wife. He doesn't shout, he doesn't say put your time into
the temple, he listens, he nods, he agrees, he buys a car. After
all, by this time he wasn't tied so closely to the temple himself,
he only thought he was—after all, another year and he would
take a fall, and rest, and then resign so that we would move here
and he would put all of his time into the company—the companies. So it doesn't upset him that she won't be helping with the
auxiliary and the rest of it because it was all by this time auxiliary to him. In a way, I hate to say this, it always was, all of

it. He did it, he did it well, but it was all a steppingstone, rungs on a ladder. Don't get me wrong—he did it because he was a good boy and a good man, but when he saw that he could do it, it was in a way for him over and done. And he was ready for a change—in a way he was ready for a change whenever he was doing anything. From the first time he went out with his father, may he rest in peace, the first time they walked together to the square, he was ready for a change. And didn't he get one? He got a big change. We all got a big change. And sometimes I wish we didn't have any changes big or small. Sometimes I wish I hadn't been so particular that I didn't like the smell of a student from the city. If I had held my nose and lived my life, things would have been different, wouldn't they? Jacob, my Jacob, he might have been—but no, because whenever I think this, I remember about Florette, and I remember the numbers on her pale white skin, and I remember that if I hadn't been so particular I would have stayed, and I would have been put in one of those camps, and my Jacob, even if he hadn't become my Jacob, he too would have been caught, and we both would have gone up in big puffs of smoke, and there would have been no Manny, and no nothing, not this apartment, and the cars and the trips and the food and the gifts and the everything, no Maby, not for us, and no little Sarah, little Sarah-Sadie, and so where do you think she is at this hour, it's time she should be getting home, don't you think? But as I was saying, there would have been none of this if I hadn't been so particular. So who wants no change? So who wants to stand still? You stand still you might as well be dead—you stand still you *are* dead. And that's that.

So where do I think she is? At a friend's apartment, or someplace waiting to go back, waiting to pick up a friend she promised to drive, where else? She packed warm clothes to take back with her, is all. She came, she packed, so what? She's like her mother, you know, she won't talk about where she's going, where she's been. But her mother, I'm telling you, she paid. *Oi*, did she pay. She was in the hospital, the home, whatever you call it, and then she came out looking like she had paid. And she took her classes and then . . .

It gave her something to do.

She wrote about things she did.

She made up a little but a lot she put down just the way it was. I know. I was there for most of the time. There was a teacher, a Professor Bair, a writer of books, novels he wrote, and he came in from the city one night a week and taught the class, and Maby, she drove over from here in her new car, and she wrote stories. Look, here, wait a minute. You see . . . I know where she keeps them. I know where they are. And I'd love to hear . . . so you could read it to me? Like we've done before. We could listen together? I know she made one about a trip they took to Israel after she came home from Owl Valley. I forgot, I should have told you, the one thing she wanted was the classes, and Manny said, certainly you should do that, and then he asked her if she wanted to take the trip, a vacation to Israel, and she said, sure, she would do that, it would take her to places she had never seen before. And so they went, and the doctor, the one she was seeing at Owl Valley, he said, Maby, you should do more traveling, it agrees with you. And she wrote this, and other things, I heard her talking on the telephone to someone from the class, or maybe it was the teacher, the writer, about the trip.

So.

We'll look.

Here. In the room. The study she uses when she's home. Here it is. The filing. Here. The folder. Here. The writing.

What do you mean you don't want to snoop? This is not snooping, snooping is something else. This is learning. Here. Now. You got it? And so let's see what it says.

But there's more than one? I want to hear more. She got out of the hospital and went to this class for months and months. I at least ought to hear what she did—think of all the suppers I cooked for nobody, Sarah away at some school activity, Maby at the Newark Rutgers, Manny—well, I'll tell you where he was, though I think you can guess. Later, I'll tell you. Why not? If I know all this the world should know. At least you should know it—frankly I wouldn't tell the world before I told my friends. And I wouldn't tell my friends before I told myself, so I could under-stand it. And I wouldn't tell myself before admitting the whole thing was weighing me down like a ton of water. So I admit it, it's weighing on me. So I'm talking. You think I didn't tell you before now because I wanted to keep it a secret what I feel? I didn't know—so who can know what they feel before they tell somebody else? Only my Manny thinks it's possible to live that way—and only lately, since he stopped talking to his mother did he start to feel that way. And he'll talk again to me, I know he will. All his life he talked, and he'll talk again.

So. You're holding on to these pages? You want to look at the top page at least? You're ready to snoop along with the grandmother? What's it called? *Notes of a Rabbi's Wife After Shock, Drugs, Chaos, Night?* What kind of a title is that? And it starts in the middle of nowhere?

. . . I have come to love the work of my hands, spinning and weaving. Three days a week I am awake long before light and lie in bed contemplating the class to come. Breakfasts never thrilled me, but even the moist eggs and dry toast lure me on, and I chew, and I chew, and I swallow, building my strength.

"Good morning, Maby."

I open my eyes to see her white-lined eyes, her curling lip.

"I know you."

"Of course you do."

"And you know me."

"I do."

"A vow," I said.

"What's that?"

"A wedding vow. I do. You do. We do. We two."

"You're so poetic. Maby, would you like to try and write some poetry?"

"Try and? Why not? It's all done, isn't it? I went to school, you know."

"I think we know that. In . . . "

"Shhh! Not the names of real places. We don't say the names of real places."

"That still bothers you?"

"Always. Since communion."

"The weaving's going well, isn't it, Maby?"

"Um-hum."

"Did you copy that from a pattern? Something out of a National Geographic?*"*

"No."

"From some design?"

"No design."

"Looks pretty lifelike to me."

"Life has no design."
"Think so?"
"Know so."
"Well, so what?"
"My mother used to say, sew buttons."
"Did she sew?"
"She sewed seems."
"Seams?"
"Seems. She knew seems."
"Would you like to talk a little more about her?"
"She lived in sin."
"Your mother lived in sin?"
"In Cincinnati."
"A fine pun. Shall we talk about her?"
"She knew not seams."
"What?"
"When I was a girl we went to Coney Island and rode on the bumper cars. They . . . "
"Excuse me, did you say Coney Island? On one of those trips to New York with your father?"
"Coney Island in Sin-sin-atti. We had one of our own. We had many things of our own. We had sin-sin. We had original Sin-sin-atti."
"So tell me about the bumper cars."
"I don't remember what I was going to say."
"Maby, you ought to keep a notebook. Keep it at your bedside. When you have a thought, just write it down. And then we can talk about things that come to you. Would you like that?"
"I . . . would."
Eye. Wood.
Eye. Sigh.
Eye sigh for you. Eye die for you.
4 yew trees in a row. Four Jew trees in a row.

This is writing? This is craziness is what it is. And I can't tell you how much it hurts me to hear it, for the sake of the poor girl who all these years had such craziness inside her and it took a college writing class and the breakdown to come out, and for the sake of my Manny who lived with her, who made his life depend on her, and for the sake of my granddaughter in whose heart runs the same blood as this same poor girl, red, deep red, I'm sure, because they are both so strong headed, and strong

headed means strong hearted, but also it means wild and seeing things the rest of the world doesn't see—except for people
like me who see sometimes, and this I got to learn for the future,
without their eyes.

You know, Rose, sometimes you recognize these feelings
inside you, intimations of the future, invitations to the future,
whatever you call them, and about the little red-haired girl at
the scene of the accident I wish I could tell you that I knew better, because some things I can tune in on, like I tune on a radio,
but other times, the signals from the future fade, because maybe
the moon in the present or the near-past or early future, who
knows when, passes between my mind and the news I'm trying to get, like the way the radio crackles with the sunspots? You
tell me how. Because if I knew then—if I knew when I first saw
her—oh, if only I could have been a better grandmother even
though at the time I was only the mother of the boy still far too
young even to think about girls, let alone make a marriage with
one, and making a child that would make me a grandmother—if
only I could have known then, if I would have known the
minute she entered the apartment, dragged along there by her
parents when they brought my poor milk-truck-struck
half-orphaned Manny in the door, I would have grabbed my
little boy by the arm and dragged him inside and shut the door
forever in the face of this crazy bunch with their crazy little girl
who was not only about to make remarks about the smell in his
pants but who would grow up to give him a life that would
nearly drive him mad. And if my Manny could have avoided the
trouble from her, and if their daughter, my little Sarah, could
have been spared some of the trouble that has already come to
her in life because she is the daughter of you-know-who, I would
give up what time I have left ahead of me and go back to that
awful Saturday in that cold year, the Sabbath of milk and blood
and bells, and lay my own body down in the path of that taxi
to make it stop before arriving to kill my Jacob. I would make
a jump to stop that horse . . .

Now, I know that what you're thinking, what you could be
thinking anyway. I know that she had her own troubles that led
to this craziness, I know she had her troubles piling up in her.
And you had your troubles, too, I bet, Rose. And me mine, me
too, but at least you survived without getting too crazy
because—I don't know why. You're tough. And I'm tough? And

she wasn't tough? I don't think so. It doesn't look that way. And why not? That I can't tell you. This grandmother doesn't know every single thing, not the creation of the earth except what I hear in stories as a child and not the taxes that's always bothering my Manny, and not the reasons for war and the reasons for peace, except maybe I do know something about the last thing, at least a way to stop it because mothers and grandmothers they get tired. So? What? You want to hear my plan for world peace? Later. First you want to hear the rest of this story.

So, she's suffering a lot in the hospital, and do I have to tell you that it's not a picnic for my Manny either? After he fell she couldn't be his proper helper, and in fact I think that her own craziness was creeping up on her even then. They went on the vacation—to Bitch Heaven they call it, not Beach, not Haven, that's right—and who do you think was the bitch? Guess. They went to the shore and he didn't want to go back to the temple. He had made up his mind. Or his mind had made up his body, maybe I should say. He fell because he tripped, but not with his feet. Not with his feet first. First his mind tripped, and then his feet. And he went hurtling head forward like a diver or one of those men shot from the cannons at the circus. A bullet, like. A shell, you call it? But not a sea shell? I see. I can see him now, in the hospital bed, back at home, on the trip running along the seashore. Exercise, the famous Doctor Mickey said. Take it easy and exercise—so how can you do both? One High Holy Day Manny was walking to temple, thinking, What am I doing here, where am I going, walking, thinking. And then he climbs the dais, and then he sees a bird—a bird!—and falls. And now he's running along the beach, trotting maybe and she's tagging along after. And he stops, and he looks out at the water, the waves, white-capped waves, and he says to himself,

From that way, from over there, I came, and I've done things here, and what do they mean to me now?

He was about to answer his own question with *nothing* when a cloud passed across the face of the sun, and he felt as though nature had answered it for him with a big chill, and the covering of the face of the sun with a shadow, with cold wind on his bare skin. Up he looks and there's a dark-backed water bird skimming high above the waves, and he hails it, standing there in his black bathing trunks, skin prickled, goose bumps, his stomach hanging over the waist of the suit maybe a finger's thickness, his hair sucking in the light it's so bright itself in the sun, head like a whirlpool so, the way water sucks down into the drain—*swoo-uuck!*—and even though he had asked only what do you call? a remarkable question? the kind you want or don't need no answer for? everything of a sudden goes dark for him, and he hears nothing but the *scree-scree, scree-scree* of the bird swooping down on him, and the next thing you know he hears a voice again.

Manny, it says, and if sound can have a light, it's a bright light in the middle of the darkness that surrounds him, like a burning bush in a dark meadow, or a star against a black field of velvet, like that, all of the sunlight that was present a moment before condensed into the sound, and to my son, it's as if he is falling again, falling through the sand, falling through into whatever it is—some kind of rock, a shelf, a ledge I once heard the word?—and to someone watching him, such as Maby, the wife, who stops for a moment as she sees him, not sure that what she is seeing is real—he falls to his knees and spreads out his arms toward the waves, face turned upward into the sun—what's real to her anyway, after what she's been through? the woman who carried the hurt from the brother? the woman who married my Manny, who knows why? the woman who wrote the crazy mish-mash about the hospital? *She* should be the one down on her knees in the sand looking like she's going mad! *She* should be the one who's hearing the voice of a bird!

Manny, you must do what you must do. It's his father's voice, again, he's sure, the voice of my Jacob. *Go where you must go. Midway in this life, a point I never reached, you must take a new road.*

Now this is pretty crazy talk, I have to admit, and I'm the boy's mother. But this is what he heard, he reported this to me, and I've got to tell you that if I heard it I wouldn't believe it, because you know, it sounds like, what? poetry? something out of the television special on the Bible with Charlton Heston or somebody? but this is what he heard, he swears, down on his knees, in the sand, though, of course, he says he felt as though he was falling through the ground, through the floor of the world, that's the way he put it, through the floor of the world.

Take a new road, he repeats to himself, and he knows what this means. This means put all of himself into the business— throw himself into the business. But as much as he understands, he wants to know more. Even though in part of his mind he's thinking, I must be crazier than she is, I must be, because things like this don't happen, not to educated people, to rational people, to an educated man like myself, kneeling on the beach. He couldn't get up, he felt, until he knew more. He tried, but he couldn't rise. He kept on falling, sinking, and couldn't reverse it. He wanted to ask, But can I still feel blessed in that work? because wasn't that why he was hanging back from it? This much he told me, told me the truth of it, that he was hanging back not so much out of confusion as clarity, because that much he saw, he saw how much he was not confused but afraid, afraid that he would lose his special sense of himself in the world, his sense of himself as getting double goodness, the purity of his job as a rabbi, the money from the business, and what he wanted to know, he wanted to know if he could do this and still keep the high right sense of life that he maintained when at the temple . . .

And he might have gotten an answer from the bird, but just then up to him came Maby, running running she was, because she got scared, and she grabbed him by the shoulder and shouted,

Manny, are you okay?

Which pulled him up from the fall through the ground, yanked him right back her voice did, like he was tied to a rope that had just stretched taut to full length, and it yanked, and he felt the rope burn into his waist, like a tightening belt, and he turned with a scowl on his face, blinking into the sun that returned with her voice, and he stood up, and he snarled at her, showed his incisors, I'm sad to say, like an angry dog, and he said,

Don't you touch me like that, ever again!

How things change! They change, but they don't change that much, not that you can see. Look at this beach they're standing on, how it washes away and swells with the coming and going of the tide. Now it comes, builds, grows, then it goes, shrinks, sinks, washes far off toward where the breakers roll, the undertow carves it, the moon calls it, in and out, far and near, and here is my son, a scene I could have described to you earlier, much earlier, but who wanted to remember this, the way he spoke to her, after he had promised himself, but the tide, the tide, and there she goes, running again, running off along the sand?

Oh, if I could have been that beach I would have held him there on his knees. I would, if I had been those waves, washed over him to shut his mouth and stay his hand! I would have kept him from doing such harm to himself by speaking this way to her! But there she is, on the run again, and there he is, up and running after.

They had a lovely room in the hotel, a room facing the ocean. And they had had a lovely meal the night before. And in bed—don't blush, because with me it's no use, you'll be blushing all time—he had tried to be kind, he had tried to be gentle, and he thought he had succeeded. But what kind of a love is this where he has to try all the time, to think all the time, Now I must be kind, now I must be gentle? Because if it comes, it comes, right? And if there's no gentle, can you make it gentle? I mean, all the time? Can you think about it all the time? It's like a person with crutches, look I see these people, they have to think, Now where can I get down to the next floor? or where is the way down the curb that won't trip me? Where? where? There's always a way, and there's never a way that could have been. So he was gentle for one night, and then he has the trance on the beach, and it's all gone, blown away in the wind off the ocean.

Which is where she runs to—the ocean.

And my Manny, can he swim? You might as well ask if he can fly. He called after her, come back here, come back, but she's pushing out into the waves like she owned them, like they were nasty children she's knocking aside or stalks of corn she's wading through, except these children, this field, it keeps coming on toward you no matter what you do, and pretty soon she's up to her neck, and stroking, swimming toward deeper water.

Maby! my Manny's yelling from the shore, you come back here!

But does she even turn around? She keeps on swimming, stroking, until she's so far out you can see her head bobbing up and down with the incoming rollers. By this time, he's frantic, he's lost all of his ability to keep calm, and he's swearing at her, something he never does, and cursing himself for doing what he did, and meanwhile she's swimming along the horizon, nothing more than a little bump of hair and head, bobbing up, dropping down, bobbing up, dropping down.

Come back! he shrieks at her, and the cry sounds as though it echoes over the waves because of the scree-screeing of the birds. And like a crazy man, he's scanning the waters one minute, as if he might lose her, and then searching the sky for a bird who might help.

Please, Maby! he calls out to her, and all of his restraint, it falls away like the robe he tossed aside when he came down to the water's edge. Tears have filled his eyes—salt there, salt at his knees as he wades as far as he dares, poor unlearned swimmer, no talent for that, poor boy, and he's losing his voice, and a few other people in swim clothes have wandered over, attracted by the spectacle of a grown man with pure white hair shrieking like a sea bird at a woman beyond the breakers.

My wife, he says, helplessly, staring out into the waters, wishing that he had the courage to walk into the waves and never come back. Wishing that he had never been born to sail across this ocean. Wishing that I had never been so proud as to turn away the offer of that awful smelling student from the city, so that he, my Manny, poor unswimmer, never would have been born.

She returned to shore a few minutes later, her chest heaving from the effort of her swim. In her eyes there was something he had never seen before, a look, a certain way of telling him what she wanted to say even though she didn't have exactly the words for it. I can escape from you, maybe it was. I can go beyond where you can pursue me. Something like that.

And in his heart he felt a new emotion, too, forgetting as he did about why she had run out into the water to humiliate him, and he decided that this was a hurt that ranked above all pains, and that he had reason now to turn his back on her.

Some vacation, *nu?*

So he turned his back. He took his mind off her. Lucky for him, or unlucky? Florette wanted to paint his picture.

He was sitting for the portrait, see. If the one time he and Florette got together was an accident, sitting for the portrait was part of a plan. Hers. And, I have to admit, since he admitted it to me, his plan too.

As if he didn't have enough women in his life.

As if she didn't have enough men.

Oh, I can see by the look on your face you didn't hear that one before. But I've been telling you a lot of things you never heard before, mixed of course, like always, with things you knew but didn't want to think about or say. Sure, Mike, she had men. She was married? Sure, she had been married. But that was only one man. This woman, she had a history, and it was a crime to hear it when I finally did. A crime. She was in the camps. As a child, mind you. And they did things to her a grown woman should never know. What things? Let me tell you only what I heard, from her, of course, I heard from her, things she never even told my Manny, because she was too shocked and embarrassed to remember the things that gave her the bad dreams—the reason she came to him in the first place, or so she said—bad dreams? Listen, the things she told me, they make nightmares into a musical comedy. Rats, they used on her, rats! Rats in the you-know-where, they'd let the animal poke its nose up. And the fingers of dead men, these too they'd poke around with. Disgusting? Darling, there's no word for it—this world, the Old World, that's where it happened, to a little girl and to older women, and if it should happen here, God forbid, somewhere in the New World then we'd know that this world, this part of the world, was getting just as old as the other side.

So you see I have sympathy for her—her I don't hate. And I have sympathy for the other, too, for the daughter-in-law. She didn't have a bad childhood herself? She didn't have her own American version of the camps? She didn't have the Nazis, she had her family. And you can't get away from them, either, can you? Not if you believe her story. And of course I believe it. Not when she writes it down in stories she wrote for the class. Those I didn't believe. I know the truth so I know what she changes. Anyway—you call that writing? What's there but a host of *mishagahs,* mix-ups, confusions.

But look for a minute in your mind at the women in my Manny's life. One with the childhood of rats and the fingers of dead men, not to mention her parents going to the gas, and the other with her family around her but making the day into the time of nightmares. Two women—why does he attract them like this? Why not some plain ordinary girl, a nice mother, a nice wife, someone not too smart but not too dumb either who would help, and he would help, and she would feel grateful and she didn't want to do anything more than stay at home with me, the mother, and help with the house and the cooking? She wouldn't have to do too much because I like doing most of it. So it's three women out of the ordinary, if you count me. Four, if you count Sarah, and of course you have to count Sarah. But where is she? I can't see a clock. What's the—where has she gone, she should have been back hours ago!

I'm calm, I'm calm. I have to be, to think about these things, let alone talk about them. The portrait—he was getting the portrait. After he came back from the beach, after Maby went to the doctor again—this time she volunteered to get out of the house, I think, because, poor dear (I do sympathize with her, see), that was the only way she could get away. Until she thought about taking the classes. But that was a little later. But for now she goes back for a rest, she calls it, and he's sitting for the portrait, the famous portrait, that's right, the one you can see when you come into the foyer. With the wild brush strokes on the forehead, and the hair not white but the absence of color, just the raw canvas—she's got a style, *nu*? But is it the style you want our son to appear in? that's the question. The black suit, black as crow's hair, I like that—a magic suit, I call it, because when my Manny wears a light-colored jacket and trousers to his board meetings, he doesn't have such good luck with the things he wants to do. He told me. It's superstition, but he now wears only the black suit. Superstition. That should be the only thing he's superstitious about, huh? What with carrying around that piece of glass all his life, you'd think either it or his fingers would wear away. But he's still got it, and while he's sitting there for the portrait you can bet he's got his fingers around it, rubbing it, rubbing.

Why so nervous? Florette asks him. Are you afraid I'll catch your soul on the canvas?

She's worrying, actually, that he's thinking that she's just another widow looking for a companion and will do anything and everything to get one. Even if he's her rabbi. Maybe *because* he is her rabbi? Her rabbi. Her wild and sexy rabbi is how she thinks of him. Her heart leaped in her chest like a fish the first time she saw him, when she came from the city, moved there to escape the loneliness of life without her husband—and don't I know what that's like?—and she bought a little house in town, and joined the temple, and there he was. My Manny. With his hair, his suit. And his living fingers, fingering, fingering the star in his pocket—because didn't he? doesn't he? have his own souvenirs of death and dying?

But I'm telling you too much. You should listen.

Manny? she says.

I'm glad you finally brought yourself to call me by my name, he says in reply.

Don't move, she says. But listen to me.

I'm listening. But I have to move my lips to tell you that I'm not going to move, only listen.

That's good. *Don't* move. I want to . . .

What? You're talking to me like you're cutting my hair, not painting me.

You don't like my method?

I love your method.

Good. Then please, how do you say? button your lip.

I'm buttoned.

Stay buttoned.

I didn't make a sound.

You moved.

I didn't. I was only thinking about it. But we have such rapport . . .

Don't talk about our rapport, Manny. I'll get so heated up the paints will boil when I touch them with my fingers.

Now you're the culprit.

What?

You're making me move. Involuntarily.

Oh, you bad rabbi. You bad man.

Which one? Choice of one only. Bad man or bad rabbi.

Good, both.

Good.

Now stay.

I . . .

Hush!

I . . .

There!

So let . . .

Stay put!

No, he says, coming around, I want to see.

Have some respect, she says, holding him off at arm's length. Look at it this way, you wouldn't peek at a cake rising in the oven. So stand back. You'll see it when I tell you that it's ready.

No, he says, trying to push aside her arm, I'm the kind of person who would peek.

And you'd make it fall.

Is this an allegory? Or an artist's sitting? Let me see.

No.

All right, I won't take a look. I'll trust you.

Trust me. I trust you.

Now you're getting serious. And I was feeling playful, for the first time in forty years.

(Florette, my Manny's mistress, I thank you. Because he was not just talking the talk lovers talk. He was having genuine fun. For the first time, like he said, in a long, long time. But I'd better not interrupt.)

That's a long time to go without feeling that way, she says, stepping up to him and curling around his neck the arm she was holding him at bay with.

You know.

I do. And that's why we get along, don't you think?

It could be. Or maybe it's just chemistry. *Maybe.* I hate to say that word. I try always to say *perhaps.* Because when I say it, I think of *her.*

And you think of her a lot.

How can I help it?

Is it chemistry?

Physics.

What do you mean? She touched a finger to his chest. And he could feel it drilling into him, burning into him, like a finger of fire.

Nothing. I was just joking.

Well, she says, is this chemistry? She meant the way he was squirming a little under the touch of her finger.

He nodded.

You can move now, she told him.

And he put his arms around her, and when she realized that he was trying to move forward to catch a glimpse of the canvas she pulled him away, out of the room, up the stairs, to you know where. And there in that room, as they did in many rooms, in other rooms, in days to come, and some nights, and an occasional morning, they did things that they told me not of, not because they could not describe it, or because they thought that they would offend me, but things that they themselves, they claim, did not understand. Chemistry. Physics. People experiment, and it doesn't always work. But I believe in it, no matter what you call it if you don't call it love. They were like children playing, like two new grandchildren I had. Sometimes they'd get undressed—this much I know in case you're wondering if the grandmother had a total blackout in the news like they say sometimes from the government on the television—sometimes they'd get dressed up. Sometimes they'd stay at home, at her house, or sometimes they'd go out to the city. Sometimes they'd stay at a hotel in the city. Sometimes overnight. Business made him stay, he'd tell me at first. But later, much later, he confessed. After she, Maby, went back in again. After her trouble in the city.

I didn't mention that? Well, darling, I'll get around to that. You can stay and have one cup more, can't you? The driver, he'll wait all night if we want him.

So what was I saying? Oh. The staying out, their staying out, their playing like children. Of course he was on the leave he took after the fall in the temple. And she? She had a little money from her late husband, some investments here, investments there, and she owned her house, and so she had plenty of time. Who did she cook for and clean for and shop for and worry about? Nobody but herself. So she had time. She painted, and they played, and that was her life. Not bad, you say. Not bad, I say it, too. And she's not a bad artist either. If you can see the painting better than I can, you can say it's good, it's good. The lines, big, bold, modern, the shapes, modern, the plain colors more old-fashioned but attractive. You could even call her gifted, no? That was how she survived, you know. Drawings she made for herself. While all of the terrible things were going on around her at the camps, and sometimes, even terrible things were happening to her, she was making little sketches with stolen pens and ink, or at least thinking about sketches she would make. It took her mind off her hunger. A whole notebook she has from that time. She showed it to Manny. He cried, he told me when he saw it.

We each have our own trials, he said, hers was the presence of pain and suffering made palpable—oh, how he talks sometimes—when it comes to others he can talk, talk—and ours, mine, specifically, was the absence of palpable suffering and thus a suffering more inexplicable but no less painful in its own way. Did he say that? He wrote it down and maybe he gave it in a sermon, I don't remember. Or maybe he just wrote it down and I saw it somewhere in his papers when I was cleaning. I don't snoop, of course, but if something is out there, like Maby's writings, I might pick it up and take a look. Just in case I wouldn't throw out something that was valuable to somebody. Just looking—the mother, the grandmother was just looking.

While everybody else in the world, it seemed to me, was playing like a child. Maybe it happens only in this country, but all of them, and I don't leave out my Manny, they got to a certain point in life, adults, with a life, and they decided they were getting so old they better try to play one more time like children or else they might not have the chance again. I say it happens only maybe in this country, even though I never saw in Europe, I came here so young I never saw over there how it was, but they had a war and so it was hard to live like children after that, and here they didn't have no war, they had only their own troubles, but instead of making them older it made them want to be more like children again (which means, probably, that they felt how old they got but didn't want to face it, don't you think?).

I know he wrote that down, but I'm sure he didn't say it. It sounds too big for him to say. His best sermon was the one where he used silence—and that, after all, was the one that brought them, him and *her*, Florette, together. The silence.

But in his heart he wasn't silent. After his fall, after his time in Bitch Heaven, he wasn't so silent to himself. Because he talked to Florette while they played, he played with her, too, of course, I'm not kidding myself, I'm not kidding you, he played, the two grownups like children, my son the grandchild, I could joke with myself, but while he played he was making plans, he was talking with the brother-in-law, they were planning together, because once my Manny decided to go into the business full time there was no stopping him. And just like with the woman, with *her*, Florette, he could hold her in his arms and say to himself, This is where I was always supposed to be, because this was what he said to himself, and sometimes even he said it out loud to her—he began going into the city on a Monday morning instead of a Wednesday afternoon the way he did when he was still at the temple and only piddling around with the business, and he could say it as he rode in, say it as he took the taxi to the building, the tall glass and steel building (on Park Avenue, no less), he took a taxi at first and then he got the driver and the car, but that comes later, he could ride the elevator up the twenty, thirty stories to the office (the office they started in, because later they take a higher floor in a taller building), he can say to himself, This is where I was always supposed to be.

So he's riding up in the elevator and he's remembering the last conversation with her, Florette, trying to remember it as it happened, and what he recalls is how they fit together, like pieces of glass from the time he tells her about, the time of the broken bottles.

From the accident, he explains to her while they're lying in bed, him with his chin resting on his palm, her sitting up smoking a cigarette – the only bad habit she has as far as my Manny is concerned.

By this time she has told him about the animals, about the fingers of the dead (and once or twice not the fingers but the organs, do you understand?), she has told him about the men in the camps who traded food and pens and ink and paper for her favors, because that mattered little to her, the life after the encounters with the dead, and she had to draw to survive.

And he has told her about life with Maby, and how distant he feels, and how untouched and unloved he feels because of the distance.

And she tells him about coming to this country, about meeting her late husband, a successful man, relatively, and old, sick, and he died within the period of time that he himself predicted, and left her with enough to live on without worrying.

Enough except love, she says.

And who ever has enough? my Manny says. (A smart boy. Of course he had his mother's love, he still has it, but we know not to be insulted, we know what he means.)

Tell me about that time again, she says.

You're the counselor and I'm the person with the problem, eh?

We both have problems. It's just your turn to talk.

He glanced up at her, fingered the place on her arm just below the faint dark row of figures.

It's the accident, when my father died. For years I hadn't thought about it, and now it's come back in a dream. He's standing in the middle of the road, and the fire engine comes flying one way, the milk truck from the other direction, the taxi cuts off the truck, the horse rears up, the truck overturns and down comes crate after crate of milk bottles, crashing around us, crushing my father's chest. It's not an imaginative dream because it's so close to what happened. There's only one difference.

And that's what?

I'm not standing in the road, I'm driving the horse that pulls the milk wagon.

Very interesting.

Can you figure it?

Florette shook her head slightly, and she puffed, puffed on her cigarette. Afternoon light – the smell of some flowers in the vase on her dresser. A Sunday this was. He was trying to get the temple out of his mind at that point but he couldn't. Even when he had given up his duties he thought of them for a long while. Not strange, it isn't strange. He had a memory. Has. He remembered the accident, so he could remember what happened every weekend for years and years, like the way you're supposed to feel a limb that gets amputated long after its gone. No, he had to remind himself, he had only a visit to Maby at the Owl Valley home, and that was his only duty. Sarah, she was off with friends. About them I'll tell you in a minute. But so here he is, in the bed with the mistress. He's watching the smoke float up to the ceiling. Asking his question. Ah, what a life he has come to, he thinks. He has made several successes already and he's not yet fifty. But he wonders, Am I crazy? He's thinking about the dream, he's thinking about the birds he's seen in his life, about the voices.

Am I? he asks after telling her everything. Am I? What do you think? And suddenly he's crying – for the first time in his life since his father passed away, he's crying, and he can't help it, the tears they come and come and come, and, oh, I wish I, the mother, could have been there to take him in my arms, to give him comfort. Because she tried, but she couldn't help him as much as I could have done. But it's true, she cradled him in her arms, and she tried to quiet him, she patted him, she soothed him, she did everything but croon in his ear – the way I would have done – *ah-uh-ah-uh, ba-bee* . . . but he can't stop until finally she reaches her hand across him and crushes out the cigarette in the ashtray and uses both hands on him, massaging his neck and his chest, stripping away his sobbing like the old undershirt he was wearing, and soon she changes his weeping into groans of pleasure, the kind, you know, that come

with a particular moment, and that's the way she does it. Not
a mother's way — but a woman's way — and that is good enough
for my Manny.

Ever since my father died, he's saying to her later, and this
was such a long time ago that you'd think I would have gotten
over . . .

Just the opposite, she interrupts.

Perhaps, he says. But ever since then I've felt as though I've
lived on the run, constantly rushing toward some goal or other,
rushing toward it and then past it, school, Maby, a job, another
job, a child, the company, money, the expanding company. The
only time — times — I've felt as though I'd stopped, have been
when I felt the craziness come upon me, for just fleeting seconds,
when the visions came, messages from the birds, when I
fell . . .

I don't know, she says. Now she's smoking again, the
curling pillar drifting upward to the ceiling, the sun has shifted,
beams spread out in the cloud and she exhales like rays through
water.

And this time, he says. This is almost like standing still.
Time. Now.

(And you're maybe wondering why in all this he never mentions me, Jacob's wife, the mother? because I'm so close to him,
he told me once, it's like I'm with him always, and if I'm with
him, why talk about me.)

This time? she says, getting close to him again.

Like this, yes.

Like this?

Yes, like this.

This?

This.

And this?

This, too, yes. This.

And there's a silence.

Meanwhile Maby? Meanwhile Maby is in and out of the
hospital, and when she's out she's taking the writing classes at
Rutgers in Newark. You saw some of the papers. If you look up
on the bookshelf just to the left, there, you'll see some books by
the teacher who signed comments on the paper she wrote, Bair

what's his name, there, see? Are they still there? I see the shelf but I don't see each book too clearly. They're missing? She must have taken them with her to the hospital, is all I can say. Well, so, she's taking this class, this is just before the move, and driving back and forth to Newark by day and night. She was out at all hours. And my Manny, he was so caught up in his change of ways, with his idea that he was going to do the company full time—and not to mention, but I've already mentioned, his girl-friend Florette, who was not exactly a girl in age but who cheered him up, I have to give her that—so I'll give her—he was dis-tracted, and he knew she was out, but he didn't raise a fuss.

And Sarah, she didn't care, she was finishing her high school, and that means she was a little crazy, even a little boy crazy, and then she had her idea about going to Vermont—*oi*, what a year it was for ideas!—and she started dressing funny and playing with the paints and the clay, I'm telling you, the only one around here not doing something crazy was the mother, the grandmother. She went on with what she always did, the cooking, the cleaning, with maybe a little time out here and there for meetings with the other grandmothers, but the mother, the grandmother, she was the only one to keep things on an even keel while the rest of the house rocked and pitched, *kinnahurra*, like the boat most of us came over on, in a storm.

Here is Maby, a mother herself, caught up in the rock and roll, of all things, singing, humming to herself—now I don't mind if she is happy but could you call this happy?—in the car, on the way to her Newark class, and she's got the radio on, and she's heard the same music loved by the daughter, not the bugs, their music, some other boys, what do you call them? and she's turning the dial to find a station so she can sing while she drives, she's got one of those stories in her briefcase, she's going to show it tonight to the teacher, the writer with the animal name, what is it? Bair, I said, that's right, Bair, and have you ever heard of him, darling? He makes the best sellers? Myself, I never heard the name. So she's heading along the road, and she's singing,

> *Come on baby,*
> *Light my fire!*

With her hair cut short—she did it in Montclair the day before— the rabbi's wife looks ten years younger, almost like her own daughter, banging the heel of her hand on the steering wheel, in her mind she's getting ready to turn over the stories, and she feels good—of course when I learned about how she felt I didn't yet know the stories themselves . . .

> Come on baby,
> Light my fire!

This is music? They call this music? Give me the big noisy bands, first, give me Paul Whiteman, Tommy Dorsey, I love Guy Lombardo so much at New Year's, but this is their music they listen to now and you can't tell them anything, anyway, so you have to listen to it if you want to listen to their stories.

And she's got thoughts on her mind that are about as young—I don't say immature, because that would not show respect to the youth, and I think that if we want the youth to show respect to the older, these days, we got to give them the respect right back, or even first, maybe—as young as her daughter. She's thinking that she wants to be a writer, and she wants to impress the teacher and the class, she wants to show them how good she is. Because she's been through things, she's lived through certain things that might make good stories and she believes that she's done good work from them, out of them, because of them, whatever you say, and this is the only thing in her life she's ever felt good about thinking, the only time, believe it or not, that she's ever believed in herself. She's suffered her childhood in Cincinnati the way that you know, and she married my Manny young, and they went through the early years together, and she was not happy, but she didn't know just how unhappy she was until it all came to a head with Manny that evening in the driveway, not the slap in the face in the police station was what did it to her but the slap to her feelings in the driveway—and oh, I was inside, and I wish I had been outside, I could have helped, I could have done something, if I had been the air, if I had been the dark night coming on, I would have wrapped myself around them, closed their mouths with my fingers of darkness, told them both to stop for a minute, told them to think, to feel deeply about each other instead of just themselves, people today they're so selfish—and from that time on, it was in and out of Owl Valley, and here and there with different fads, clothes, shoes, in the stores, out of the stores, the hair long, the hair short, the stones, rocks, bugs, beetles.

> *Come on baby,*
> *Light my fire!*

And I'm telling you, she was flying, driving very fast, but with her eyes on the road, so she was safe, this time, and I think— because I was once a daughter, and still am a mother, even if now, as a grandmother, I'm a mother over too many years of time— I understand how she was hoping, how she was wanting, how she was feeling. Didn't she yearn for things the same way my Manny did? didn't she wish for the good instead of the bad? the happy instead of the miserable? the light instead of the dark? But what did she get? That I'm not so sure. She had bad luck, you could say, being born to those miserable parents, and bad luck to find herself alone with the brother who the parents had hurt miserably, too. And this made her into someone not exactly right, not exactly wrong. It was like—like she had a mechanical problem. It was like there was something minor wrong, but it made with the major. Like . . . you have, say, a flashlight, and one battery, is that what you call it? a battery, a connection is loose. There's a wire worn down, a nut, a screw, whatever. And it goes. You smell a little smoke, the lights flash on and off, and it's not working right. (I had a washing machine this happened to, and a stove.) So once she was all right, and the parents they made a dent in her, and the brother made a big slash, and that was it. We had only to wait for the day when it showed. How could my Manny know this? He couldn't know. I couldn't know. And could Maby herself know? Could she, I don't think so. If I had been that way, I wouldn't have wanted to know myself. I would have wanted help, but I would have prayed for help from God and never asked for nobody on this earth to help. And if God didn't answer, if he didn't send the Mr. Fixit, then I would have burned the way she did. And you would have. We all would have.

> *Come on baby,*
> *Light my fire!*

You bet. Come on baby, light my fire, she's thinking to herself as she drives. Sure, Mike. Come on, baby . . . The road ahead. Lampposts winking on as the sun falls back far to the west, twilight night. Before me down the long incline of the Jersey shelf, Newark lies. Dark city. Blacks live there, mostly. And Italians. They're dark, too. Like most Jews. Except me. Redhead. Flame hair. Fiery things. The road bends. The road tends. Freedom. My fiery legs in these slacks—the color of the earth. Grounded. A pun. Sarah's grounded. Means under house arrest. Means also in touch with the ground. Solid. Two feet on it. Not like me. One foot. Other in air. My other? Two feet above the ground. Always high. My mother, I meant. Not other—but mother. Mother. Light up ahead. And then turn. And turn again. And turn again. And park. Walk. These dangerous streets without good light. And in the center, the building. Classrooms. Guards. Against myself. Should I read? What if? Should I? Now class is here. And the others. Not the mothers. No one here a mother but me. Children. I am old enough. To read or not to read. And if I don't? He will think. And if I do? He will think. What? I have a feeling. Here they are. Here he is. Others. Mothers? Me only. Hello, I will say. Good evening, he will say. And so I do. And he does. And we do. And he suggests. I will read. And I do. And after. He says. And I hand it to him. And he suggests. And I say, Why not? So a few days later I drive in.

She drives in. Easy. But the parking problem, it's just awful. Bair lives in Greenwich Village where even during slow hours there's not always a lot of parking places. She drives around and around, she must cross Bleecker Street four or five times, looking, looking. Once she nearly gets into a fight over a space with a man in a dark sedan. But she gives it up, and drives around the block again. Finally, something opens up, about half a legal space next to a fire hydrant on the west side of Fourth Street. She parks, gets out, walks. The Walk, she's thinking, because now she's been seeing French movies where the heroine always seems to take a Long Walk through the City, usually Paris. She pretends her eyes are a camera and watches stoops, storefronts, people on the street, signs, cars, birds, trees in the little park at Sheridan Square. I could make a film. Be in a film. Be a film, watching myself with my eyes, she's thinking. And in the background she's making the background music . . .

Come on baby,
Light my fire!

And the organ music, the doodle-doodly-dooodly-dooodly-doot-doo!

You know that I
Would be untrue

Stops at a street corner. Gets her bearings. Continues on down toward Bleecker and reaches it, this time, on foot. And sees a parking space! Oh! she's miffed for a few seconds. Then she shrugs. A husky man in blue gym shorts stops, stares at her.

Hello, he says.

She blinks at him. Does she know him? Does he know her?

Where you headed, baby?

She turns the corner, hunts for a number. He's following.

Do you mind?!

Hey, baby, I know where . . .

The number! It's nailed above the entrance to a basement stairwell. Two garbage cans guard either side of the descending steps. Down, down, knock.

Hey, come on! the man calls down to her. He's behind her, still talking.

Oh, please be home, she's worrying to herself. It's broad daylight, sunlight, no threat, not dark Newark, but still. He's got a glass in his hand.

Hello.

Bair in the doorway, rumpled hair, beard plastered to his face.

Oh, I'm so glad. She turns and the man has disappeared.

Come in, Bair says.

Oh, this is. What? Dark, small, not what she expected. The famous writer's . . .

Sorry for the mess, he says.

You just got up?

He nods.

I'll bet you worked all night.

Nods again.

What's that?

There's a red shrine with a candle in the center nailed over the small bed in the rear of the one room cave.

Oh, he laughs. A friend of mine sells those. He gave me one.

A joke.

Yeah, a joke. Hey, would you like a drink?

She shakes her head.

Just one, he says. I can't talk to you unless you have a glass in your hand.

A joke?

No joke. It makes me nervous.

Just one then.

Just one.

You teach without a glass in your hand, she says looking around the cave. Did this used to be . . .

A basement. A storage room for the restaurant upstairs. Then they blocked off the stairway—it's behind that little closet—and made it into an apartment. Nice, huh? There's a shower in there, and a . . . here.

Is this . . . ?

All I have? Unless you want some warm beer. I bought some beer last night but forgot to put it away.

No, this is all right. But it's awfully . . .

Just one.

Just one but a tall one.

That's what you've got. And I can teach without it because teaching doesn't make me nervous. Only life. And work.

Teaching isn't work?

He drinks. Not when there's someone like you in the class.

Pardon?

Come, sit down.

They sit, she on a straight-backed chair at the table where he both eats and works, he on the edge of his single bed that takes up almost a third of the room. Outside the sun shines but little light penetrates through the grillwork down into this cave. He's talking about her piece of writing, a story from her childhood she wrote for the class, she read it, he read it, it's moving, he says, and daring, for her to tell what she did, very daring, but daring isn't enough, you know, because you've got to have technique to convey it, and the daring part has to be there in the technique as well, to tell a daring story in a plain way makes the story plain, to tell a plain story in a daring way makes the technique stand out, to tell a daring story in a daring way gives the reader a real sense of the life, of the experience.

Could I have another one of these, please? she says.

Sure, he says. See what I mean?

I think so, she says.

Is it cold down here or just her imagination? It's a day in spring, bright sunlight through the bars, but here in the cave she expects moss, it's so damp, dank, musty. Does he sleep with heavy blankets into summer? And then it must become a steam bath, no real ventilation. She smells musk, whiskey, food, dampness from the shower. So close. She takes the glass from him.

So when you do that scene on the barge, on the river, you don't want to muck it up with that stuff about the childhood. You want to make us feel her girlish self, her helplessness, and also her strengths because she's got strengths, no doubt about it, but the use of light, shadow, the water, the motion of the barge, all that can work to your advantage here, I'll get you a little more.

Now there's no doubt in her mind that he is sincere, he's telling her the truth, and certainly she is sincere in wanting to hear the truth, because why else would he invite her to his apartment? He could get anyone he wanted in the class and there are girls a lot younger, real girls, not mothers like herself with daughters almost in college, rabbis for husbands, drunks for dead mothers, dead fathers, someone with feelings who can feel and not just try to write about feelings that used to be.

So do you think it's any good?

Oh, hey, don't ask such an apocalyptic question. *Is it any good?* And will you be saved and go to heaven? We try, you try, and if we're lucky some good might come. Maybe you've got something, but you just have to keep on trying and see what it is.

Is that what you did?

Here, let me take care of that drink. Me, oh, sure, I wrote for a long time before anybody took any notice at all. I worked on newspapers, on magazines, I wrote about sports, I wrote about furs. I even wrote about robots once, what do you think about that? A magazine I was working for wanted a piece on robots and I had read all the science fiction stuff when I was a kid. So I did the piece.

Do I have to do things like that?

You? Naw.

Well, what . . . ?

You don't need the money. You've got a husband. You're a lucky woman. It's like having a Medici patron. I would have liked to have had a husband. Instead I had wives.

You had more than one?

Three.

Where are they now?

Around.

Children?

Around, and around. That's why I'm going up to Alaska.

You're going to Alaska?

Yeah, I just heard from my agent. I'm going to do a book on Alaska.

When are you going?

Right after the semester ends. In fact, one of my ex-wives will come up for a while and do some photography for me.

Your ex-wife?

One of them. She's a photographer. She needs the money so I'm going to let her do the pictures.

That's very kind of you.

It's very smart of me. I pay the money to her one way or another.

Is that why you teach the class? For the money?

No, for the love of the students. Sure, for the money. You think I meet somebody like you in those classes every time?

What's somebody like me?

You? Smart, beautiful, talented maybe. It's usually kids in camouflage and combat boots, the girls too these days, and they all want to write about parachute jumps without ever having been up in a plane.

What do you mean?

They want to write without experience.

I . . . don't have much experience.

You have your life. And you recognize it as such. They're all too young to recognize it as such. As such.

(I'm trying to help you picture this, Rose, like we're standing right in the corner of the room, in that shrine, maybe, where instead of the Virgin—remember, a Jewish mother—you and me we're standing there looking down on this scene. And, *oi*, if we could have the powers the Virgin is supposed to have, we could have helped her, we could have helped! Though, now that I think about it, maybe she didn't need so much assistance.)

My life? It's a shambles.

Shambles make for good lifelike stories. Neat lives lead to dull neat stories. Look, it's like a room without corners, it doesn't collect dust. The patterns in the dust, that's the interesting part, the shape, the designs. Neatness, hah! Here, let me . . .

No, that's okay. I don't think I'd . . .

Can't do it, lady. You sit here with me, you got to drink here with me.

It's lunch time. We could . . .

That'll just get in the way.

(Rose, if I was up there, in the shrine, now I'd be whispering to her, Daughter, I'd whisper, watch out, watch out!)

I better not, she says.

One more. And with the next drink comes . . .

What?

Don't look so serious. And nervous. This is supposed to relax you. With it, comes comments on your style.

You wrote some on the pages.

These will be firsthand, direct observations.

Tell me now.

After another.

I think I'd really better . . .

Please.

All right. But, please.

Please?

Please don't say I'm a room full of dust like the rest.

Shit, I'm a room full (I know, Rose, but I didn't say it, I just heard it) of empty bottles. That's why I'm going up to Alaska. To let in some fresh air. Like an arctic blast of wind. Full force. Room full of empty bottles. Let in some fresh air. What a bunch of metaphors! I'm supposed to be an artist and look what I serve up? Good thing I can revise my work, huh? I can revise my work but I can't revise my life. What?

Nothing.

You're disgusted. You're leaving.

I don't know what.

Here.

I don't want another.

One more. And then we'll go out to lunch. There's a nice
Italian place around the corner. Or there used to be, several hundred years ago.

I can hardly stand . . .

Then don't. Just sit.

I shouldn't.

We all shouldn't. None of us should. It should all be smooth,
airless, free of dust, without corners, pssssshhhh! Sliding down
the floor toward eternity, there we go!

Let's try the Italian place, please.

Right now? Okay, let me finish this. That's okay? You eat
Italian?

Of course. Oh, you think . . . ?

What do I know? You're married to a rabbi. Which is the
closest you can get to being married to a priest as far as I can see.

As far as eye can see.

Huh?

Nothing. But no, it's not like that. He gave up his congregation. He doesn't have one anymore. He's in a partnership here
in the city, with my brother. And he's thinking of doing that full
time.

Oh, so one of those worldly priests.

Worldly? I don't know if I'd call him worldly. But he's probably one of the strangest rabbis you've ever heard of. Though
he's not a strange man. I don't mean to call him that.

Tell me about him. Why did he give it up, his pulpit?

I'm not sure. I don't think he ever liked what he was doing.
I don't. He. His father died when he was young. And. It's like.
He went into it as a kind of memorial to his father. Except that
his father never believed. But he says that his father. Spoke to
him. Visited him. Told him. I'm not sure.

You don't sound sure. But who's sure? I'm not sure. I'm not
sure I understand. I'm not sure I want Italian food. Do
you? Don't tell me. But I'm sure of one thing. I'm sure. Alaska.
Frigging cold Alaska. That I'm sure of. With my frigging cold
ex-wife. Shooting pictures. Maybe she'll shoot me. That would
do it, wouldn't it? End it all. No more dust in the rooms. One
nice clean package shipped over to the morgue.

That's so gruesome. Don't talk like that. You shouldn't feel
like that. Look at what you have. You . . .

Puh-lease. Lady. None of that. Here. Give me that. I'll get another. Don't get up. There. Hey. See. Now. No speeches about what I have, what I don't have. I have. What I had. When I was a kid I had a bicycle. Brand new Schwinn my father bought me with his last goddamned paycheck after he got laid off at the plant. I left it out in the rain. Brand new bike. It got all rusted after a summer. Nearly broke his heart. Look what I got you, he told me, and look what you did to it. That's what I say to myself— here, hold out the—there—that's what I say to myself. You had this talent and you left it out in the rain over the summer. And it got rusted.

I . . . like your books. You shouldn't talk like . . .

You like my books? You like them? And do they like you? Have you asked?

What?

Italian food or what?

I . . . I'm not hungry. I th-think I'd better . . .

Not yet. Puh-lease. Not yet. Wait. I don't leave for Alaska for a few weeks. Stay until then.

Stay? I . . .

Stay a few weeks. We'll talk. My books will like you.

I've got . . .

Don't get up. It's not polite. Wait.

But you can't leave in a few weeks, can you? The class runs . . .

The class runs down. I'm going. I'm taking off before the end. Got to. Got to get up to the north before it all freezes over. Got to see it before the freeze. Here. Wait a minute. Sit back down. I'll get . . .

No, don't.

Don't say don't. For Christ's sake. Aw, shucks, can I say that to the rabbi's wife? Don't get insulted now.

You can say anything. But he's not a rabbi anymore, not with a congregation. But what's . . . ?

The ex-rabbi's wife. The ex-rabbi's ex-wife. The rabbi's x-rated ex-wife. Sorry. Sorry. Sorry.

I have to go. I'm sorry . . . if I disturbed you.

No, no, you didn't disturb, you didn't disturb. This pest hole, hell hole here, little light from my shrine, few books, needs company. Whyn't you stay a little longer? Did I give you an impression? I didn't mean to give you an impression. Honestly, so, now, we're going to talk about your stories. Which stories are they? Yours is the lyrical one with the doctor, right? I thought so . . .

Please, I'll . . . see you after class next week. We can talk then. I've got to go now.

Hospital. Talk about the hospital. And did you put a nurse in? I can't remember. Where's the manuscript? Nurse is what I need, before the freeze. Up there, no nurses, just ice and snow. And the aurora borealis. Seen that? Not me. But want to. Like a vision. Every writer. Needs a vision. Yours, you got the nurse. Right? Me, I have this. This glass. But need something outside. Maybe the ice. The snow. Alaska. What the . . .

I have to go.

His hand on her shoulder, but she shrugs it off. Ice in her belly. Up the stairs into the sunlight. Blinds her. She had thought. Hoped. What had she thought? What had she hoped? Poor dear, she was looking for a friend. And could this man be the one? Not in a million years! And so she felt as though she was out in the Alaska cold. She had invested her feelings in this, in this visit, in the writer, teacher, and now it had all fallen through. So in the middle of the beautiful day, hot late sun of morning (and it was heating up the trash in the gutters and the trash in the cans, lending an ancient rotting odor to the street, something like our old street, long ago, which, remember, was only a short walk away on the other side of the Village, think of that, only blocks away, but how far in time? how far? think of that) she could feel her disappointment boiling, cooking in her like it was fresh and now it was garbage and it lay there in the gutter, baking in the street.

She had counted on it, you see. She had counted on the writer telling her how good the writing was. She had counted on him saying to her, you should publish this in magazines. You should publish this in a book. She had counted on this to pull herself out of the hole she felt she lived in. She felt she lived at the bottom of a pit. This was the feeling she had, the feeling she complained about, lamented sometimes, sometimes screamed about to her doctor at Owl Valley. And she felt as she wrote her little stories that she was climbing her way out, that she was escaping from the pit. Never before had she seen so clearly what a trap she lived in, and never before had she felt so good about how she was going to get out. And she wrote these things, and she thought she was climbing, and he read them in the class, and, I suppose, encouraged her, invited her, and she arrived, and what happened? He couldn't talk about them or didn't want to talk about them, he didn't even try to touch her, that was worrying her, too, he didn't want to talk about the stories but not because he wanted her, he didn't want anything except to sit there and feel sorry for himself and drink, and she was nothing to him, absolutely nothing, she could tell, she could feel it, she was a prop in his life, and that understanding helped something to snap in her head. She concluded that she was a prop in my Manny's life, not a person, just something he needed to keep around, not a person but a thing. She felt that it was the same with Sarah as well, and if to me too she never said but she probably felt it, but she just couldn't say it when she was telling me all the other things (and it all fits together now that I've heard some of her little stories, the feeling that she was not a person but a thing, a prop, as she called it, something to be moved around in the lives of others) and to this she said,

NO!

That's right, she stood out there on the street and cried out, NO!

In the middle of the street in the bright sunlight, NO!

And people turned, even in the Village they turned, and she remembered that she had been drinking and tried to quiet herself down, and she looked behind her and saw that the door had opened down below the stoop and the writer, Bair, was sticking his head out the door, and he was waving to her with the glass,

Come back down, come back!

And she, the daughter-in-law, my daughter, her beautiful short hair, feeling the heat in her chest, the taut pull of her pink waist, the pinch of her sandals at her ankles, feeling the sand cave in around the trap where she stood, blinking at the sun, listening to Come back down, come back down! She started walking straight up the street.

This was her life. In a minute she put the little basement cave with its shrine, its temptations, its mistakes, its delusions, all this she put behind her. Now she had to find her car.

Wait a minute! the writer came loping up the street and touched her from behind on the arm.

What do you want? No, the way it came out was, What do *you* want? As if she had better things to do. As if standing in the middle of the street looking for a car she couldn't find, she couldn't remember parking, as though this was her idea of a good time.

I want to apologize. I want . . .

You're sorry. So you're sorry. I'm sorry. I can't find my car. That makes me sorry. It even makes me sad.

He made a loud vulgar noise with his mouth.

What? she asked.

Mode of registering regret and loss. Where did you park? Come on, I'll help.

You can't. You're too drunk.

I'm not at all drunk. Maybe just a little. Come on.

No, no, I have to get home.

I'm helping you get there. I'm helping you find your car.

It's not helping. It's making it worse.

Come on.

No, I can't. You go. She made a noise in her throat.

Well.

Well. Go.

I tried.

You tried.

I'll see you in class.

You'll see me.

He made one final lunge for her hand.

Come on.

Please let me be. Go to Alaska.

I'll do that.

Good.

See you.

Yeah.

My life on the street, she was thinking. These things in my life all seem to take place on the street, in driveways, in cars. Car. It took her what seemed like a long time to find the car and when she finally did she discovered that the windshield held a ticket. This she tore in a lot of pieces and sprinkled onto the roadway.

Kinnahurra, she says, like me. She's heard me a thousand times. To ward off the evil eye. A saying, that's all.

Kinnahurra, she says over and over as she's tearing up the ticket and then climbing into the car and starting it up. In a moment she's off and away, driving uptown to the bridge, and then across the bridge, the old way home. Looking upriver, she sees nothing familiar, rock ledges, the water, trees, trees. Downriver, there's the city, something she knows a little better than the natural part, towers, spires, glass, and steel. And she's thinking, He's up there now, behind one of those windows, looking out, but not north probably south, south because of Mord's holdings—she's overheard a number of conversations, just as I have overheard but never had any information, the way I have gotten it, directly, from Manny, from the brother—south because they're buying there, building there. North is the company she hears they want to buy in order to invest further in the south. North is also the school where Sarah wants to study. Study? Fool around is more like it. The girl wants to become an artist, a potter, that's the latest. I should understand, trying to write as I am. I should, but I don't. Should she? Why should she? Can the family stand more than one? Can Manny? He's paying. Him and his stupid star. And isn't he lucky? That I didn't. She pictures what could have happened if she had. Stayed. If I sat down again. He would have. With a hand. Kissed his lips. Whiskey he smelled of. Me, too. And how can I drive? Cars coming fast. And steer. And steer around. He would have lifted up my arms and helped me with. He would have helped. If he could have stood. If he could have stood it up. Nice man. Not a bad man. Why didn't I? A nice man. I like his. Not a bad man. Steer. Steer, girl, steer. Onto the highway. And forward. Not a bad man. He would have lifted. Light ahead, Jersey horizon. Light spreading up and lifted behind the horizon toward the . . . he's lying drunk now in his bed. How can he work? How does he, how do they say, *get it up.* And Manny, how does he? (Terrible this information here, I know, but what can I say?) He doesn't. Not with me. (And terrible that she doesn't know about the other, *her,* Florette. I know.) Does he with others? I doubt it. But the teacher, the writer, does he? In class he seems sober. Maybe after next class. Maby. Baby. Will you or won't you? Maybe, maybe light my fire. She thinks about it some more. She thinks about taking off the sweater, taking off the slacks. She's thinking about drinking more with him. Thinking, if I could, I'd ask, Can I go to Alaska? I'd say, I'll work and you'll work and you'll understand. Not like with Manny. He gives me money, and he's cold. Alaska. She's on Route 80 now, heading west, traveling at a terrific speed, and her eyes blink open, and she slows down and takes the next exit and pulls over and sits a minute on the side of the highway, cars whizzing past, chewing on a finger, tugging at the waistband of her slacks, and then after peeking at herself in the mirror she gets back on the road in the other direction, and in a few minutes she's traveling toward the city again, paying a toll, rolling over the river, this time the north to her left, the south to her right, the light in the south much brighter, as though near sunset the brightness increases as if at dawn, thinking, Am I really doing this? And answering, Yes, I am, he will hand me a glass and I will take one more, and then I will help him, and he will ask me, Another glass? and I will, and he will raise my arms, and I will lift up my arms unto him . . .

Now I'm really getting upset and worried about where the other one is. Not Florette. Not her. Sarah, I mean. She's been out for hours now and she said she was coming back. So where did she go? And where is she now? And who is she with? The questions a grandmother asks, they should be answered without fail because otherwise she only worries on into the night. I know where she's been lately. That I could tell you. But where is she now? Is she now where she's been?

She went down to Rutgers, some years ago, I told you, you read it, it was in her story—and this was not good. All the way to New Brunswick by herself—well, not exactly alone, which is why it was not good.

All the time, oh, all my children always in motion, in cars, going up and down in elevators, and in airplanes, too, of course, my Manny, flying back and forth between here and New Orleans, New Orleans! where they just bought a company, some boats, and a warehouse or two, and a pier, in motion, in motion.

This was after the move here, to Manhattan. So it was after he bought the company down there with the pier and the warehouse and the boats. Because soon after that—it was like opening a door into a bank, he said—a lot of money suddenly appeared. Don't ask me how you spend millions to buy a company and suddenly, right away, you have more to spend than you know what to do with, but that's what happened. And now listen, this isn't bragging, do you understand? This is explaining. This is recounting. Counting the blessings. If they are to be counted and recounted, if they are blessings is what I mean. Suddenly it was there. Just the way I say this word: suddenly. And it was there. Maybe it was creeping up on him, on us. Maybe it was in the bank, growing, increasing. I know. I turned around and—boom—it was there. A new car for me and the driver. The handsome Latin boy, Daniel. And the driver, for them too he drove, of course. But Sarah wanted her own car and she got. And she wanted the fancy college and she was going to get it—but that comes in a minute, in a few minutes and Maby the wife? what did she get that she wanted? If she could have told him, he would have gotten it for her. If she could have figured it out for herself she would have said it to him and he would have gotten it for her. Trips, he took her on when he had a spare week. Things he bought her. A new typewriter, my god, it looks like what you see on the astronaut's spaceship, such a machine he bought for her to write on. Everything he got. And nothing for her but the best, still this Owl Valley which was from the first the best for her, that, too, when she needed it, because by then she was in and out, from season to season like the changing of the leaves.

Oh, so the move? Yes, sure, I'll tell you. We moved. It was no big deal to me at the time. So we left one house and moved into another. It was only after I lived here a little with the heights, with the view, that I came to love it, and I remembered—all too much sometimes I remembered—how it was when we lived six flights up that we had to walk, and now we were thirty flights up and fly there in an elevator that rides like silk. You felt it? You felt that you didn't feel it, right? And the car downstairs waiting—waiting for you now, darling, to take you home across the bridge whenever you're ready. But just a little more coffee first, or a glass of water or schnapps or whatever, because the last thing tonight I have the energy to tell you doesn't take long.

.   .   .

Maby took the move in stride. Manny, of course, he made the move for all of us and wanted it, as it turned out, quite badly. The brother, the brother-in-law, he liked the move because it showed to him that Manny was finally making a decision about putting his life into the company. I took the move, I told you I took it. The only one who didn't seem to take it well at first was Sarah. Little Sarah. Except by that time she wasn't so little. She's already part of this because you read her little story about Purim. Jewish Halloween, she calls it. What a smart little cookie, don't you think? If I knew now where she was I'd feel like the smart one. When she was little we knew everything about her. But the bigger she got the more mysterious. She was the kind of child that everyone loved, chubby, roly-poly, playful, always smiling, never any trouble. Her mother took care of her and even with being one of the most sour people I've ever met in my life she the mother even laughed sometimes because of the child that Sarah was. She could make you smile. She could make you chuckle. She could make you giggle. And she'd smile and laugh and giggle and chuckle right back at you—such a mimic she was on top of everything else. Her father was busy, he didn't see a lot of her. But her mother and I, we saw her, we played with her, we dressed her, we watched her play with other children, although this she didn't like so much it became clear after a while. She was used to us, and she didn't like strangers or strange children. She was always with her mother or her grandmother, with her mother in the dressing room, putting on the clothes, putting on the makeup, and with me she was always watching me cook—oh, you should have seen her eyes open wide when I would say, Here, darling, you crack the eggs, you put in the milk, you mix the batter, when we would make a cake and put it in the oven and she would feel part of it, part of the magical rising of the batter.

But then they grow, and she grew, and little by little, like water eating away at the beach, she changed the way her mother felt, because she didn't accept her mother's problems, and her mother knew that, and an ocean rolled between them, and also between her and my Manny, because he felt that he was taking care of the problems, and he didn't need to hear anymore about them than he already knew—I know that was what he thought, but to her it seemed like coldness. If he could go back and explain, she might today understand, but it made a rift, a wedge between them too, and so you have something like the moment I described to you once before, the last time you and I talked, the time when on the holiday she quarreled and he lost his temper and picked up the guitar and smashed it on the ground.

Physically she changed too, from the little miss roly-poly to the thin girl, almost tall, still always though with her mother's coloring, the pale red hair, the freckles—oh, and does she hate these freckles! When they first came out she once asked me if she could use tarnish remover like from the silverware to get rid of her freckles.

Tarnish? I say to her. What's with the tarnish? You got no tarnish to remove, darling.

I do, she chirps up like a little bird. I do, I do. And she rubs her knuckles into her freckles, and she starts to cry.

You're a beautiful girl and you don't need to remove nothing, was the way I comforted her. And I wasn't lying. I was saying the truth. She's got her mother's height, just as tall as her father who is a man of medium height, wouldn't you say? But the men tend to be taller than the woman, and here she is getting almost to be a woman and nearly as tall as her father, which is all right, don't you think? And no more Miss Roly-Poly, though. In fact, I wish she would eat a lot more than she does. Thin is the god these girls worship today—not like in the old days when a man wanted to feel a pinch of fat between his fingers when he gave your waist a good squeeze. But nowadays, modern days, you never can tell one minute from the next what's going to be in fashion and what's not. So that for example my Manny's dark suits, the kind he's always worn ever since he got out of the seminary, these too may be in fashion for the men in the big companies when they see year after year how he wears only these and how it brings him success.

But oh yes, the move, the girl. I was telling, before I got caught up in the ride in the elevator, the heights up here, the view, did you see the view? I used to see it before more clear than now, it is so beautiful, at night especially, I don't need my eyes, I got my memories. The girl? Yes, where's the girl? She's out now in the night, the dark, she should get back, she should come home. She's not a child now, I know, she's in the college. The college. That was what I was going to talk to you about. Not the college she attends but the college where the boy went. Or still goes. Him I never heard nothing more about after this, at least not from her. But from you I hear plenty.

This was just after the move. The move back across the river and up, up onto these floors. High above. And you know, we should have known how children hate to move, they don't want to leave their friends? they don't want to leave their school? Well, we should have known because she was so happy to hear about the move. We saw that she was happy and we should have thought—the mother, the father, the grandmother—we should have put our heads together and figured it out, if she is so happy to move from Jersey to the city, it means only one thing, that she is miserable here, and if she is miserable here there must be reasons. But what if we had figured that out? and we discovered we were the reasons? What would we have done? Could we have changed ourselves, changed our lives so that we could make her life better? Who could have the power to do that? Who could find the strength? Who could say, I live this way but it is doing thus and that to my child and so I will live another way? You could change? Could I? When the way we live is fixed in the time we live it that goes back to our own parents and their parents and all the way back to Adam and Eve, the first family that ever lived together. They had a nice place to live, they had a garden I understand was very lovely. And they made trouble for themselves. They wouldn't listen to their Father, God. He spoke to them, told them what to eat, what not to eat, but they wouldn't listen. And look at the mess they made for their children. But what if—what if it was God who made the mess for them because He had a mess made for him by his own parents? If God had parents, I'm telling you, they *must* have made a mess. And if that's not how the world got to be the way it is, then I have no way of explaining.

So. We moved. Up high. Up here.

And Sarah's in her senior year at Dalton School—fancy, schmancy. A uniform even she's got to wear. Like in the Brownies. Miss School Girl.

You can imagine how she looked when she left school that afternoon and took a bus across town and then a subway downtown and got out at Canal Street and stood at the entrance to the tunnel and stuck out her thumb. That's right, stuck out her thumb. When she was little I used to say, stick out your finger, don't let me linger, stick out your thumb, chew me some gum.

And she would always say, jumping up and down, up and down so excited she was, stick out your thumb, gee, but you're dumb! Oh, and I'd grab her and tickle her and she'd laugh she'd have so much fun, laugh and laugh and laugh. So. There she was, sticking out her thumb. And gee, was she dumb? Twenty minutes went by before anyone would stop. They drove by, they slowed down, they looked. You'd think a father would have stopped, some man who had a family and noticed that this girl in her uniform she was so young she couldn't have driven through the tunnel if she had had a car.

Finally a car stops and it's a black man in uniform.

Get in, he says, opening the door.

She wants to run, but she's trying to get to Jersey, so in she gets and he tells her,

Close that door.

And they're driving through the tunnel into Jersey.

What do you think you're doing, he's scolding her. Standing there with your thumb out. Where do you think you're going?

She's scared. She's thinking, Oh, no, he's a Jersey cop and he's taking me over to the other side of the river to arrest me and book me (she knows all the lingo, let me tell you, booked, she knows, and all of those things, from the books she gets it, from the TV, from living in the city) and what am I going to tell Papa?

Where you going? the uniformed black man behind the wheel asks her in a mean, mean voice.

To see my brother, she says.

Where's your folks? he shouts again.

Back there, she says, jerking her thumb in the direction of the tunnel entrance. Now they're rolling under the river, and she's looking forward at the long tube ahead, the pale yellowish lights on his face, the strange color of his complexion. Suddenly she takes a good look at the patch on the shoulder of his uniform coat.

You're not a real cop, she says.

I am security, he says. Now you keep quiet. I want to ask you a few questions.

She's quiet for a minute, as if waking from a dream and looking around. Or falling into one and looking around. What has she got herself into? she's wondering.

Now where are you going?

To New Brunswick, she says.
And do you live there?
My brother's there, she says. He goes to Rutgers.
You're going to visit your brother?
That's right.
Light at the end of the tunnel, and they're coming up onto the road that curves around in New Jersey, with the view of the city, and the rest of the way—a lot of people think this is sad—the rest of the way is Jersey.
He goes to Rutgers?
That's right.
And you go to some fancy school in the city?
That's right.
Which school?
Dalton.
Dalton? I never heard of that one.
It's just a school.
I'll bet.
That's all it is.
And your brother goes to Rutgers?
That's right.
And you're going to visit him?
You know, if you're not a real cop, I don't see why you think you can ask me all these questions.
I am security.
Where do you work?
I ask the questions. Now. What were you doing out there? Were you hooking? Or just playing games?
Hooking?
That's right.
Hooking? You mean . . . ? You've got to be kidding.
Am I kidding? You are kidding if you think I don't know what you was up to.
I wasn't up to anything except trying to get a ride to New Brunswick.
(*Oi*, that man! If I had been there, I would have given him such a smack! Not to mention what I would have done to her! That girl! And so where is she right now? You think she's sticking out her thumb somewhere? She's got a car now, so what would she have to do that for? But then what was she doing that for in the first place when if she wanted to go to New Brunswick her father would have sent the car with her?)

So now you got one.

Are you going all the way?

I'm going to take you where you want to go. I'm . . .

Security, she finishes for him. This makes him laugh.

You're a smart little bitch, ain't you?

Really, she says. What kind of a thing is that to say? This isn't some TV movie, you know.

What's that? he says. TV movie? What's that? You trying to bullshit me, girl? Well, forget about it, you hear? 'cause along with security, you know what comes?

No, what?

Along with security comes heavy manners, that's what.

What's that?

You never heard of heavy manners? At your Dalton School, you never took up the question of revolution in the Caribbean?

No, we didn't, she says. Next year we're supposed to study the Caribbean in history. We're doing Europe now.

Europe, he says with a snort as they're turning onto the turnpike. Or maybe they're further down the road by now, I'm not sure of this.

You don't like Europe?

Europe, he says again with a funny sound in his nose. Old shit.

My father was born there, she says.

But the man from security doesn't pay attention to that. He's studying the oil tankers as they're driving past, the factories pumping out smoke, the bridges, the towers, as though it's them he steers by not the road signs.

Brunswick, he says.

That's right.

I take you all the way, he says.

Hey, she says, thanks. You don't have to.

I know I don't have to. But I will.

Hey, good, she says. Hey, good.

Used to have a uncle lived there, in Brunswick, he says. I know the place. University—lots of white kids, some black, a few spicks, Italians. You know what I mean?

I guess so.

Mixed, he says. It's a mixed place. He glances over at her, as if giving her a sly look, and she notices that in the daylight his skin looks beautiful, like varnished wood. Dark wood. But wood that breathes. She looks at her own pale, freckled hand, the knuckles, the tiny cuticles. This hand she wants to dip in clay and make pots, she's deciding right then and there. Don't ask why. Maybe because she's riding down the middle of the ugliest part of Jersey and she wants to make beautiful things to stand against the filth and the dirt and the smoke and the fire. Could it be? She asked herself but didn't get an answer. Riding through this wasted land, she calls it, from a poem she's reading at the Dalton School.

You like the mixed? he asks her.

Do I like it?

Do you like it?

I haven't thought about it. Noticing that her school skirt, the green and blue plaid, has risen up over her freckled knees, she tugs it back down. But I guess I like it.

The Muslims say no.

Do they?

They say no. And most white folks say no.

They do?

They do. You're a little girl. You don't know. You don't hear. But listen harder. You'll hear better.

I suppose.

You suppose right. And if they say no and the Muslims say no, I say, what the hell can the Muslims be right if they agree with the white?

I . . .

Not a question. That's my answer. I say the Muslims can't be right if they agree with the white. He looks around and sees the exit sign he wants—see, they are further down the road than I thought. They are driving right off onto the highway for New Brunswick now, and Sarah is feeling all right—given the circumstances—but she still doesn't know what she's doing there, I mean, she just left school and started off for New Brunswick, why? Does she know? She certainly doesn't. All she has is a feeling, go see Rick—Rick Sommer, your grandson, once the youth leader from the Purim dance. First, he was political science, now you should be proud, Rose, an assistant dean at Rutgers, the youngest dean in charge of students, and things like that. He's told you, I'm sure, you've heard—this is the so-called brother she is lying about. But if she feels for him like a sister, this is something she has yet to find out. Maybe it's what she's going to find out.

All through high school she's gone out with a lot of boys, and they either want to take advantage of her or go with her because she's the rabbi's daughter — *oi*, remember the pale-faced boy from the city who smelled so bad to me? that's what he wanted, something like that, not me, but what I stood for in some dream of a delusion — but what? the farmer's daughter? but who can know? he's ashes, now, along with so many of the rest of them who stayed behind — and if he was alive, by some miracle, what would he say? he wouldn't remember, I'm sure, because the young boys, they don't remember as well as the young girls, this, of all the things I'm telling you, I believe more than anything, because the girls don't need things like the boys, souvenirs, like Manny's piece of broken milk bottle in the star shape, because girls have memories better than boys, don't ask me why, it has to do maybe with the fact that they bear children, they bear them instead of just planting the seed for them, and the garden remembers better than the seed or the sower. I don't know. Who knows? This is just what I think, what I believe. And I'm telling in the middle of this story, I suppose, because what comes next I don't like to remember, sure, because it's painful, for her, for me.

They're driving through the downtown in New Brunswick, there where it's all cleared for the renewal except it hasn't yet started to be renewed and so it's just empty, block after block, like pictures of after the war in the old country, but here it's not supposed to be a war but helping people, building better places to live except it looks like a battle has happened here and they're just starting to figure out that they want to clean up the mess, and he's telling her, this black man in uniform, and come to think of it he could look like a soldier in a certain light, he's saying,

This ain't urban renewal, this is Negro removal.

And she's nodding, yes, yes, wondering, Why am I riding with him? if she's wondering anything. To be perfectly frank with you I don't think that in this time she was wondering anything, because considering how she told to me her story I don't think she knew much, she had a blank, a blackout, from the time she left school, not a blackout in memory but in — what do you call it? — in morals? in rules? in feeling herself part of what was going on? I don't know how to describe it because personally I never felt that way and though I never felt some of the things like my Manny or my Maby—yes, I call her that, *my* Maby, after all—I can sympathize, but with this girl, a modern child, I find it difficult to sympathize not because I don't want to but because I can't find the feelings. I look for them inside myself but I can't find them. I'm trying, so bear with me, darling, bear with me. I don't mean my feelings *for* her, you understand, I mean the feelings she feels when she's in a situation like this or like that, her feelings for the world—unless, God forbid, in a situation like this, her feelings are not there, and it's a blank in her heart, *oi*, I hope it's not so, but when I feel around in my heart to try and get a grip on hers I feel nothing, it's like trying to hug the air, and God forbid that she should live like this—no one should have to live like this, no one would want to live like this, day in, day out, through a life time.

So it was contemporary, no, I don't mean that, I mean, *temporary*, the way she was feeling or not feeling in the car on the drive through the town on the way—on the way to where? to see this boy your grandson she had been talking to for years, she just got the idea that she had to see him and talk about things, things she needed to talk about, things she needed advice about, because she had the idea that because he had seen her through some bad times with her mother and father, like the night of the Purim dance, he might be able to help her now.

With what?—that's the question. With the problem that she couldn't feel anything about anything except that she couldn't feel.

What's that address you want? her driver asked.

She had a street for her friend your grandson, Rick now the dean, she had a street number.

That's the other side of the river, the man said.

She nodded, watching buildings roll past, students on the streets in long hair and jeans, books under their arms, this was a school, a university, and it appealed to her somewhere in the back of her mind (so she was thinking of something if she wasn't feeling nothing). And then they crossed a bridge, and there was a large hill and they took a road up the hill and rolled past shabby houses, student housing a sign said, and the next thing she knew they were turning in to a vast parking lot near the round heights of a stadium.

Last stop, he said.

This isn't where I want, she said. Her voice was flat. She wasn't scared. She wasn't even annoyed.

Everybody out, he said.

There's nothing here, she said.

I'm tired of driving, he said, adjusting the lapel of his uniform coat. Security, the patch said. Two yellow arrows crossed on a green field.

I'll walk the rest of the way.

You know where you're going?

I'll walk, she said, her hand on the door handle.

Wait, he said.

What?

Here. He unloosened his pants then, and he tugged out his, what shall I call it? his dangling dark tube. She had never seen anything like it—poor dear, she had never seen circumcized, uncircumcized, felt maybe, but never seen. But did she scream? did she panic? A spider used to scare the girl, a mosquito, a fly. But if this new view of things gave her any worry whatsoever you wouldn't know it.

What? she said again, looking out the windowshield at where the stadium rose roundly up against the paling blue horizon. In her mind she imagined cheers, football cheers, rah, rah, Rutgers rah, and don't ask where she knew the cheer unless she'd heard it on the television because she'd never been here to this stadium before. In her mind she could hear music she remembered, snatches of songs from (of all things) the temple service, songs about the Sabbath bride, and her beetles, stones, doors, she heard them, I want to hold your hand, baby, light my fire, and she was feeling warm in her own temples, warm at her neck, warm in her shoulders, and her chest was tingling, tingling, as though I, me, her grandmother was rubbing her aching little chest with Vaporub the way I did when she was a sickly child.

Some guys.

What?

Some guys would want a blow job. (Feh! feh! such language, such talk! but this was what he said!)

What?

But I am not that type.

What?

You can use your hand only if that's what you do.

She shook her head.

See, I'm a nice guy.

Sure, she said, opening the door and climbing out.

I'm security, he called after her but didn't make a move to follow.

(Some security, I would have said and spit on his thickening stick before leaving the car, but my Sarah, Sadie, she didn't say no more.)

Next thing she knows, though, as she's crossing the parking lot the car starts up and starts following along behind.

Beep-beep! he taps the horn. Security!

She turns and sticks into the air her middle finger.

The engine growls louder.

She starts walking fast.

The engine growls nearer.

She breaks into a run.

There's a field, and a small woods behind the stadium, and in a minute or two she's in the trees, walking in what she thinks is the direction of the river, downhill, downhill. Once or twice she falls — her skirt and blouse by now look a mess, and by the time she reaches the road she's got mud on her hands and knees, the smiling part of her knee, dimpled, where the socks don't cover. It takes a while for her to walk across the bridge, because midway she stops and looks down at the flowing water, thinking, What if? but why? what if? but why? over and over, and she's thinking what if the security fiend follows her, what will she do so when he pulls up alongside her and calls through the open window of the car,

Hey, girl!

She will simply turn and keep on walking.

What would have happened if the real Rutgers security didn't come by I don't know, but a real cop in a real car with a mean look comes up behind the other driver, and he gets him to speed up, and then he slows down, and he leans from the window and says,

Was he bothering you? This man is also black, but in a different spirit, and she shakes her head no, and keeps on walking. He follows her across the bridge, with cars backing up, about three of them, behind him, and she sneaks a look at the sluggish brown river as she walks, and then as she starts walking in the direction of the campus, he speeds up and passes her, but then in a few minutes while she's still walking—it's some distance, let me tell you—he circles around and comes back again, watching, a real security man, and thanks to him my granddaughter gets to the college in one piece.

So she can fall to pieces. I don't know what's going on with her mind. Like mother like daughter? I'm not sure because everything I know about the mother, like I told you, makes me think that she at least knew what she was doing all the time and maybe couldn't help herself. While this girl could help herself but didn't always know what she was doing.

And then, so finally, she walks past a park and finds some buildings that look as though they belonged in a university, and there she is, there she was, she's reached her goal—if only she could say what it was.

But. Now.

I'm pausing, not stopping. In a little while it all comes to a stop.

But. Now.

I pause.

Because.

I pause because. A rhyme. I made another rhyme. Like a little child makes. Because. To tell you the truth, I'm feeling bad because to tell you the rest of what happened to her is so terrible. I might as well tell you what really happened at the football parking lot.

No. See. I didn't. I changed it a little. Because while I wanted you to know everything I made it a little prettier than it was. So. I'll grit my teeth. And no more fibs, no lies I'll tell you. For better. For worse. You won't be shocked? Good. Because if you didn't want to listen in the first place you would be out playing mahjong, or watching TV, or sitting alone drinking coffee, or talking with me or some other grandmother on the telephone, *nu?* Good. So you're here. And you hear. And you see. *Oi,* don't I wish I could see a little better like the old days. Here. Look. What happened after was not good with her, and what happened up there on the heights of the parking lot, *oi,* it was—this was it. I'll say it.

Here they are. In the car. (*Oi*, another rhyme. I'm driving myself crazy with these rhymes). And you remember when he opens his pants and takes out—his tube? And he asks for one thing? Well, I lied. He didn't ask for the one thing, he made her do the other. That's right. Isn't that terrible? The poor girl, you should have seen her. He held her head down, really rough, and he pushed her, pushed her, pushed her, and she didn't know what she was doing, and she bit him a little, and with the knuckles of his hand he cuffs her on the ear, and this makes it still worse. I'm telling you, she's crying, and he's making sounds like a crazy man, and it was awful. And then she pulls away, and he's sitting there with his head back, looking like he just took a drug, and then she jumps from the car, her blouse all mussed, the uniform skirt filthy, it's like someone has spilled soup on her clothes, and she runs toward the woods at the end of the stadium, and she hears him start up the car behind her.

But while she wants to run, she feels cramps and she has to stop, and she doubles over, and she retches, you know, she doubles over and wants to do it but nothing comes, nothing comes.

The engine growls louder.

She starts walking fast.

The engine growls nearer.

She breaks into a run. I'm telling you, the rest is just like I told you before. But this part, where I just told you it was different, it was hard for a grandmother to tell you that part, but I had to, because there are harder things coming next that I have to say. And I wanted to get you prepared, and I had to prepare myself. And if you don't believe me from now on, if you think there are other things I've changed already or other things I'm going to change, well, what can I say? So I had to go back and tell you what really happened. And now I have only a little bit more to tell you about Sarah, and I hope that you'll trust me. You'll have to trust me.

Good.

Because it's bad. It hurts to say it. To say it for me is to see it, and that hurts.

And after I finish you'll know why I get nervous even now, even when she's a college girl, when she goes out by herself.

Because you never know when something's going to happen. You never know. Because look here, even now, in this nice new apartment of ours we're having trouble with the electricity. What? Look, don't tell me you don't see it, the lights are flickering. Sure. Good. I'm glad you saw it too because, *kinnahurra*, I didn't think I was going crazy. Even here. In the heart of the city. Maybe especially here. You could look at it that way. Even here. Or especially here. Either way. It can get bad. It can get good. You never know. That's right. *Kinnahurra*.

So she's walking, remember?

And now there are many students that she sees, walking the walks, crossing the streets. And buildings with signs, the library, the gymnasium, many cars, and there are a few school girls like herself, and so while some boys look at her nobody finds it out of the ordinary, except if they look too close they see it seems like she's spilled soup on her blouse, in her lap. She wets her lips. She'd like nothing better than something to drink, something to chew on, a bath, shower, a towel to dry her hair with. Her hair—it's sticky with soup, someone has spilled soup in her hair, and this is on her mind, or should I say on the surface of her mind? because she's walking, pardon the expression, like, God forbid, a dead person, and the thought of what she needs rests just on the top of her mind, like a petal from a flower in a pond that's fallen onto the surface, or a leaf floating down from a tree above the pond, floating there, resting there, turning this way and that in a breeze.

Here! Someone catches her arm as she trips off the curb.

Thank you, she says, and keeps walking.

Can I help you? It's a boy, a student, long dark hair, glasses, stooped shoulders like he's been studying studying studying.

I'm looking for the dean's office, she says.

Which dean? he asks. There's the mean dean, the lean dean, and the queen dean.

What? she says. What?

I was making a joke, the boy says. But which dean are you looking for?

The—what? And she keeps on walking.

Hey! he calls after her. But she doesn't look back.

I wish. I wish life was more like a story. Because if that was true, this nice boy, he was a little wise guy, but he was trying to help, maybe he would have followed her, and would have helped her, like from the fairy tale of Prince Charming. But this was her life, not her story, and so he shrugged his shoulders and went about his business, going to study, probably, the way he looked, a good student, a nice boy with a little sense of humor. Maybe they would have gotten along, they would have dated, he would have come up to meet the family, and after he graduated, and maybe went to graduate school, and became, who knows? a doctor? a lawyer? a big businessman, maybe even gone into business with my Manny, there would have been something between them. But that's a story, a fairy tale, and what I'm telling you is her real life, and it's darker than a fairy tale.

So.

She passes a number of buildings, she passes paths leading to buildings set back from the road, and she crosses the main avenue and finds a little street where there aren't so many people to stare at her, and as she's passing by one of the houses where the boys live, one of the clubs with the foreign letters, a house with this—look, she showed me once, and I remember the odd look of them—here, give me again the lipstick like the last time and I'll show you on the napkin, except this is not paper, wait, here's a piece of newspaper, some sign like this.

Not like Manny's star that you remember.

Oi, signs, signs, signs. I see them a little better in my mind now that I don't see so good with my eyes, but it confuses me, and so you can imagine my Sarah's, *Sadie's* confusion when they call her from where they're sitting on the porch, these two boys, they're dressed in old clothes, and they're holding beer cans in their hands, and she's so thirsty that when they ask if she would like a beer, she says,

Yes, please, thank you.

Never in her life before has she had a beer, not more than a sip or two at least.

But in a minute she's swallowing everything in a can. And then another.

You go to school around here? a boy asks, one of his loafers dangling from the bare toes of his foot. He's got a smile on his face, half question, half wolf-at-the-door.

No, she says, reaching for another can of beer.

We better go inside, the other boy says. He's been staring at the thin strip of pink sky between the upper band of her knee sock and the lower edge of her skirt. We'd better, he says again. If we got spotted.

Spotted? the other boy says. Splattered. Smashed. They both laugh. And nod toward Sadie.

You want to come in? It's not safe to drink beer on the porch. Not with you.

What's wrong with me? she asks.

Nothing, the boy without socks replies. *No-thing*, honey!

So I'll come in, she says in a voice that later if she had heard it would have surprised her. So tough, so calm. The rhythms of that speech, half her mother's, I think, half, maybe, mine. But the will? Her desire to enter? Where did that come from? From some empty space? Who was in there speaking? She felt nothing, she later claimed. But who was speaking? *Oi*, my children, one who heard birds, the other falling sick, and this one, the next generation, opening up her mouth and the voice she lets out belonging to nobody she knows!

We are coming to the end here, I'll tell you, we are coming to the end of this part, and I'm sitting here shaking, shaking, you can see, because of what I have to say next. Look, my hands, my rings! Shivering, shaking! And if I told you I lied before it was because I wanted you to believe me now when I'm telling you the truth, because I want you to know that a grandmother would have to be crazy to make up such things about the dearest granddaughter—the only one, I admit it—she ever had.

To make up the part about going inside.

To make up the part about drinking more beer.

To make up the part about going upstairs to the room of the sockless boy.

To make up the part about sitting naked on the bed of the shoeless sockless boy.

To make up the part about lying down on the sheets on the bed of the shoeless sockless boy.

To make up the part about unlatching the belt on the trousers of the shoeless sockless boy.

To make up the part about the next thing that happened with her and the naked boy. The blood, the soup.

To make up the part about what happened with the next shoeless sockless naked boy. More blood, more soup.

To make up the part about the next boy. To make up the part about the next. Blood and soup.

But who could imagine this and not be crazy? Who could tell you the truth about this and not be weeping. Here. Listen. The sun went down. That's the next part. The evening shadows fell. That's the next. Now and then the door to the hall would open and another boy would leave, another come in. The room was quiet. It smelled of beer and cigarettes and aftershave, sandwiches, sulphur, fish. Sweat poured from the walls—music from somewhere played in her ear, a samba, and then a Frank Sinatra singing

> *You ain't been blue,*
> *No, no, no . . .*

The kind of music her mother should like, her father, but you know Maby, she was with the *light my fire* music, and her father only with the bare necessity for the services, what the cantor plays on the organ, he'll listen to

> *You ain't been blue,*
> *Til you've had that*
> *Mood indigo . . .*

but here she heard it, ghost music maybe, ghost of music that used to be played here, because nothing that was happening to her seemed to take place in the present, and so it could have been that she was living in the past, or even in the future, some time not her own, with the boys on top of her, the boys naked surrounding her, the boys joining hands in a circle and dancing together, sweating, as ferocious with each other as much as with her, weaving in a circle their jerky wicked dance.

After a time, as in even the worst of fires, the flames died down, and in the thick of the stinking smoke the boys began to get scared. The girl on the bed, swimming in sweat and oils, bathed in the spew of their masculine youth and the vapor of their breath, this girl, my Sarah, my Sadie, she began to weep quietly, and then she began to moan. And this scared them all the more. It was not the open-eyed gaze of the girl who now knows something—that was not the look that took over her face. No, no, she was staring at them through the veil of teary fear because into her mind came all that had happened that day, all that she had apparently made happen, or at least let happen, and she feared that she was going to join her mother in the hospital because she understood then that that was why she had dared the world to do something to her that afternoon and night, which it did, which it did . . .

So that she could become as sick as she thought her mother was sick.

But this was only a stage, only a stage.

They helped her get dressed, trembling all of them as though some wind from the snowy north pole had swept through the house. She was trembling, they were trembling. And just as she had now left something of her childhood behind, though certainly not out of choice (because she did not know what was going to happen when she started out that day), these boys had left something of their maturity behind as well, what little maturity they possessed. And what frightened them was now her calmness. If she had been hysterical they might have known what to do—might have bundled her out the door and into a car and taken her—well, where? they wouldn't have known, so why should I try to imagine? But calm as she was, and saying as she was now that she wanted to see her friend Dean Sommer—your grandson the dean!—they turned into a pack of whimpering babies. That those who break and pierce and smash and violate the whole things of this world can themselves be reduced to such ash and shard so quickly, it makes you wonder whether anything or not is real, or at least strong! Not even the hate is strong, not even the clenched fist, the forced entry, the power to smash! None of this is strong, not any of it! In the light of the first sun, when morning threatens, the smoke rises from the dying fire that has cooked the evening meal or scorched the hands of children, and it's still nothing more than what it is, dying sparks, the remains of the heat for good or not, the last of the warming, *genug*, enough, the end . . .

You didn't hear about the scandal, no. There was no scandal. This dean, your expert grandson, he pulled the curtain on everything, closed the door of the house where it happened, threw the boys out of school, put them on record with the police, and would have done a lot more—but my Manny, his old boss, asked him to keep things quiet. Once Sally's Doctor Mickey informed him that Sarah was not physically harmed he asked the dean to pull the curtain. He didn't want the scandal—he was just about to pounce like an alley cat on another company he wanted, and he didn't want the noise or publicity. It was enough for him what happened with her mother in the parking lot that time.

As for me, his mother, I could see what he was thinking about, and as the grandmother of his daughter I knew, too, that he wasn't doing what he should. The mother stood outside of it all—or slept. Me, the mother and grandmother, I was caught in the middle, and I was in my heart flapping around like fresh laundry in a big wind.

Then I got sick, and while I was in the hospital, where they studied my eyes, my Manny looked as though he was patching things up in his life, he bought her the new car, he took her up to the college she wanted to see, and he paid for her to take the trip she wanted, you see because at this time of his life the wife, my Maby, she was already in and out, in and out of Owl Valley, and when she was out he was good to her, a pleasant enough husband, and when she was in, he was with his Florette, and his business, and sometimes you couldn't tell which was the bigger mistress in his life, the woman or the job, and then he sent Sadie up to the college, and he had time for both his new lovers, the woman, the business, and sometimes he was very serious, and sometimes like a boy he never was because of after when his father died he became so sober and grown-up, and to tell you the truth, I think she, Sadie, forgave him for not making such a stink and a scandal. In fact, I'm almost sure.

But listen, do you hear a noise? I think I hear it, I think I do, a door opening, the sound of keys? Has she come back? My Sadie, after all this talk, has she come back? I can't wait to see her, to feel her hair, her face, her hands. But has she come or is it only my misery making sounds to me in the night?

If you see her, touch her for me, ask her for me, ask her for her own living grandmother because she talks to me sometimes but she don't listen . . . and I touch her but she don't touch back, ask her, Where are you going? say to her, like in the song from Baby Dylan, Where are you going? Where have you been?

.   .   .

A Former Virgin's Prayer

*Dear Lord. Lord of the world. The word. Globe. Sand sea and land,
wind, fire. Watch over me. Protect me as I set out on this voyage. Over
land, over sea. I know nothing. I fear all. And yet I could be something,
could I not? When I am trembling with fear, hold me fast, Lord, by the
shoulders and keep me straight and strong. When I am turning my back
on those I need most blow upon me and turn me around with Thy sweet
strong breath, sustain me, nourish me in my needy hour, cast not a
gloom upon me even in the dark but give me the will to move forward,
yea, even through the thorniest thickets, through the deepest,
roughest waters.*

    *Lord, succor to youth, guide to the unaware, I cast myself into the
oceans of the world and know that Thou will buoy me up. Wind in my
sails. Gravity of my world. Brain, belly, and loins I offer up to Thee
on the altar of time. May my gift be not found lacking. For if it were,
I would sink rapidly beneath the spume and buffeting, sink down, down,
so low as never again to find the air.*

Book Four
Night

Put on the light. You'll feel more comfortable. There.

Eyes can see better now? Good. As for mine, bad.

But what's to see now? Now that the light of my life has gone out? My light and your light also.

Here, let me touch your hand. The fingers. Such nice nails, such nice fingers. And your face? Let me feel your face. Since the lights went out, I like to feel the skin, the hair. Ashamed I'm not, am I? I never was ashamed. I was always proud, very proud. My Manny made me proud . . .

See how the eyes run? Dark but they still run tears. My Manny. Your Manny. Where is he now? Somewhere in the dark? Or flying on the back of that great broad-winged bird? The one that carried him off. But what, you're asking what? The bird that carried him off? Sure, I told you.

Here, you sit. Let me. Your hands. How smooth, darling, smooth. What are you doing for them? You're using a cream? You're using a lotion? Me, I bathe now and then, with the help of the little girls who work here, in a large tub of milk. How many cows must give to fill the tub in which I float I cannot tell you, but it must be a number, yes, because I am not a little girl no more. But imagine me floating in the lake of milk, the creamy stuff bubbling up at my old shoulders, laving my chest, the nubs called nipples, aureoles, where first he sucked, my little man, and now he is taken away.

Put on more light. I want you to see. See? Here? I found it. I feel it. In his pocket we found it. After. Feel?

All the years. They've worn it down a bit. But still the points remain sharp. It's a wonder it didn't shatter. And now we remain behind. In the dark. Put on more light. For me, there's no more left. I hear, though. I sniff the air, the way, you know, you see a dog sniffing? I can tell many things from the patterns of the breeze in the halls, in the room, which nurse wanders here and where, which doctor, by the scent of them, by the odors. One for example, I know, is fooling around with a woman not his wife—because I've asked him if the perfume on his shoulders one morning was his wife's and he said yes, and then came a day when he smelled of another. And the nurses I like, I like by their smell. And there is one I don't and she doesn't bathe. I bathe in milk, but she does not bathe at all.

Kinnahurra. I would like for the rest of my last few days to breathe in only good odors, the trees outside, the smell of the leaves, dirt. It's autumn now, and the year is traveling toward the end, not on the wings of some bird but on the rear end of a donkey, bumping along toward the end of the rocky dirt track that leads to nowhere. That reminds me of the old country. Here it's not so much country—in summer you can hear the mower powered by gas. But sometimes at night I believe my ears and listen to the snorts and fidgeting of a horse in the barn, thick-boned old dray. Back in the old country. But, I know, I shouldn't talk, because for me the old is good and for you it's bad. And for me it exists because it no longer exists, and for you it no longer exists because it existed.

Do I make sense? Do I cost dollars? I start talking and I can feel my tongue starting off like a bird that just heard a gunshot—*snap! pap!* and my tongue is on the wing, swooping, turning, saying words I never heard, Crash! it says, Kill! it says, Blood and milk and scum and stones and bullets, it says, *oi*, the medicine they give me, the medicine they give me, it makes my head swim and gives my tongue flight!

But thank God for the medicine! I take it for my eyes, for my nerve. Here on this part of my face I have a nerve that burns through to my bone. Sometimes I sit here and wait for it to erupt, like the way you hear people in Hawaii wait for volcanoes? If they wait—or do I hear wrong? Do they go about their business on those islands and get caught unaware? Or do they worship the fires within the mountains? Or do they believe in nothing but ocean and wind and sky and cloud and the heat from beneath the ground? Lava flows—pace of a dray horse it makes. New country, Hawaii. I would have liked one day for my Manny to have taken me there, except he was business busy at the end, busy, oh, I meant to say *at the end down there.* In the Americas, they call it. Where the brother-in-law lurked for many a year. Building connections. Making deals.

He was ready . . .

Eye . . . shit . . .

No, no, sorry, darling, sorry. Excuse this crazy tongue. Excuse. I'm not losing control. Blame the drugs. It's just that in so many months I haven't wanted to talk about this, not since. The. You know. And so. It makes for pain, it alerts the nerve in my cheek, the volcano feelings. New country feelings. You, who now know old country sorrow, it's difficult to understand. And if I had not come over in my youth, I would not be so easy to say this, that's for sure. Look, even the Gentiles, they have this problem. Because they too are all immigrants. Their people came over the water. And trekked over the mountains, dray horses, oxen leading their carts, wagons. Here first only were the Indians, the red Indians, and even they walked over from the old country, from Siberia, the first ones some cold summer morning ten thousand years ago, packs on their backs, children at their hips, or was it the reverse? across the land bridge that no longer joins the Russians to our Alaska, and one day they walked over a hilltop and saw the mountains of the country where we live now.

Mama, says one of the little Siberian Indians to his mother, I want a drink of water—in whatever language, if they talked, they said these things to each other, and the mother smiled down at the little one, a babe naked as the day she gave birth to it, and pointed to a pool of water in the rocks past which they walked. Mothers in those days were as good as they are now. They loved their children, they tried to keep them from falling too far and feeling the hurt. These first Americans, what wonderful parents they were! Surviving such a trek with their children, these Indian mothers, or the same for the Jewish mothers—there are stories, you know, told by certain religions that these first ones belonged to the lost tribe of Israel. That they sailed over here on large reed boats, whole families, many families, the entire tribe.

My Sadie was studying these things, is how I know. When she got to college it was around the same time that her father bought the big boat company down there. The brother-in-law went down on trips all the time, but my Manny, he didn't seem to find the time. And he kept threatening her, You'll go, you'll go, and all the time she was studying about it—in fact, she got to the point where she was talking about it so much he even used her to do research for a speech he had to make when he took over the big fruit company down there. And for a long time when he was heckled by those roughnecks, the demonstraters, and even the ones that called themselves Jews for Justice, he thought at first, poor fool, that she was standing by him, giving him facts, facts. Almost to the end. But not all the way to the end. And so when you get to the end, when you see what she did, you could cry.

But the facts, the facts—these she kept on talking about and I, the grandmother, the mother, I couldn't help but learn a little about these matters myself. The land bridge, or the reed boat, which is true? Not even the biggest scholars on either side want to make a final No to the other side. Maybe both sides are right? They both came. And why not? Look, here we got room for everybody. But I'll tell you one thing, my dear, my friend, my dear companion, the one thing I'll tell you is that Columbus Day is a joke. Today this holiday is a joke. So maybe it was an Indian, so maybe it was a Jew, so maybe it was a Jewish Indian discovered America, but it wasn't the Italian who first came to these shores. He came so late that when me and my Jacob and my Manny, when we sailed across over the ocean that flowed all around, if it existed, my Jacob's famous Atlantis, the prow of our boat was nearly bumping the stern of his boat, our front his back, I know these words from Jacob.

See, so the Europeans didn't make a discovery but only found something they wanted to take over. And cover over, not *un*cover. And this was the problem with my Manny, wasn't it? That he behaved in the end like he didn't know this—that he hadn't yet found out the truth that even my schoolgirl, my college student, could figure out, the truth about discovery, about the discovery of this part of the world, that it had been here already before he got here, before any of us got here, and that it wasn't ours to do with what we would.

All the tribes that got here before us knew this, but the Europeans who broke away from their tribes never learned it well enough. All together we knew this, but when we break away from the group it's something we forget. All our waking hours we know this, but sometimes in our sleep, in wild dreams of uncovering, we forget. All the sleep time we know this, but waking sometimes we act as though the day is not part of the night, and the night the day, do you see? I don't see no more myself, but I think of it, I see in my thoughts, I see my thoughts, and my thoughts see me.

The Europeans came to New England and to the southern shores, and over the mountains to the great river valleys of the south of America. When they saw the tribes they conquered them and took their lands, and you know what, darling? we've been paying back with interest ever since. From the first garden these explorers took from the Indians, we've been owing, and we've been paying back. Take my Manny now, my poor Manny, he was taking out but he wasn't putting back, not fast enough. But was that what happened? I don't know, I don't really know, I only know what I see when my eyes remain closed, what dreams may come to me in my state where I'm sitting awake and alert, the wind bringing the time of day and the season to my nostrils, to my skin, a blanket on my lap, my feet encased in slippers, the hands of the nurses upon me, and in my brain and blood this story I'm trying to tell you, my Manny's rise, my Manny's fall.

The first time came with the board meeting when he was really flying high. The brother-in-law, the brother, Mordecai, Mord—I'll call him Mord, it's easier, darling, on the breath— Mord, he and several of the analysts they had brought in to decide about the future of the company, they had fixed their attention on a large old and famous firm in Boston that was going through hard times. Talking about ships, they had been in ships ever since the beginning of this country, hauling ice down from New England to the warmer regions, and bringing back up to the colder part of the world fruit from the tropics.

It looks like the thing for us to do, Mord is saying, a perfect way to diversify and build at the same time. They've got ships, we've got piers. They haul produce, we've got the warehouses.

The ships are large, seagoing, we've got the barges and tugs. This is the chance we've been waiting for, for years now, Manny. It's a big leap, but I think we've got the agility to make it.

He touches the tip of a pencil to his hawklike beak, as if he deliberately wanted to call my Manny's attention to this birdy nose, a sign of his approval of everything that might be involved in the deal, everything both normal and natural and human, and all the aspects of it that could require some acting out of the ordinary, particularly because of the amount of money that was in question.

I'd like to say that my Manny could tell by something in this pose that to choose to follow Mord's suggestion would lead him to the disaster to come, but I can't say that. Manny, he didn't see. Because what was there to look at? The same face he had watched for years, the same creases in the cheeks, the same peering quality in the eyes, the hawk hunting for his breakfast.

And how much do we need? Manny asks.

(I liked this so much about my son, because he never changed in the way he talked—he could be asking about how much the temple needed to put up a new basketball court for the teenagers, he could be asking Sadie how much it would cost her for a new coat, he could be asking me how much it is for a movie and a dinner in the shopping mall—no, he didn't change his way, and lucky for him he learned not to change the way he dressed either, remember, at this meeting, where the brother and the consultants, the accountants, the experts, they're wearing the nicely tailored pinstriped suits, the beautifully polished brown leather cowhide, he's standing there in the same style plain black suit he wore with the congregation, the same dark tie, only his white hair flaring up like a fire of smoke giving a signal that here was a man you might have to deal with.)

How much?

And the brother says something, and the consultants each report some other things, and the accountant says something, and my Manny listens, listens, and then he asks, And we can justify this to the . . .

And the brother-in-law points to the map spread out on the large polished oak table, and he points his finger to a part of the map here, a part of the map there, and he swings his finger along the coastlines, in sea lanes, around isthmuses, through canals, all the time talking quietly.

And my Manny is nodding, nodding.

And the telephone is ringing—blinking, to be specific, blinking nearly off its cradle . . .

And in and out walk assistants, young women secretaries holding paper, folders, files, notes, tapes, photographs, and charts, more charts . . .

It's like an operation, really. My Manny was never a doctor like Sally's Mickey, but to see him surrounded by all of these associates and assistants, to see the look of concentration on his face, only once before did I see this expression when he was leaning over the Torah to read on the High Holy Days, like on the day he fell forward from the dais, like a surgeon over an open chest who leans in to see the bloody organ beating, beating, beating.

If I had been there you probably think I would have tugged at his coat sleeve and begged him, Manny, Manny, don't do this, it's too big, and if you make a mistake you're going to pay for it like you never paid before, it's not a little congregation, it's not like the bottle company and the opener company and the boats and the barges and the warehouses, it's a country, Manny, almost a whole country that you buy when you buy this company. Look, you think I would have said, taking him by the hand and leading back to the map where a moment before the brother was pointing, showing him, this, that, Look, I might have said, this could make you but it could also break you, and you're so high now—this office, this high floor, this building of glass and steel, and the apartment we own now, in glass, high above, and the cars, and the schools you pay for, and the hospital, I mustn't forget the hospital, because, let me tell you, to pay for the wife in the hospital costs him much more than the daughter in the most expensive college in the country—because apparently, and I don't make the rules, teaching someone to forget (and you, of all of us know probably that it can't be done, can it?) is more difficult and so much more expensive than teaching someone to remember—and the vacations, the traveling, and the food we eat, and everything we buy and do, except of course for his clothing, which he keeps as simple as it always was—from all this you could fall away and be lost, and lose it. But no. If I had been there, I would not have said that to him, my Manny, my still then yet rising boy. I would have watched a while in amazement, admiring him, the kid with the cart he

helped his father with, may my Jacob rest in peace, this little kid
he's grown so big and powerful and rich and wise. Wise, yes.
Sure, Mike, he was wise. How could you listen to all the reports
and the news and the accountants and the commentaries and
the advice and the analysts and the middlemen and agronomists
and weather experts, the ones who tell the plain facts about
money and the sea and the earth and the fire and the sky and
clouds and sun and moon, how to listen to all this and make a
picture or a pattern out of it and not be wise? Wise, yes. But how
wise? We get to see.

So if I had been there, would I have said, Caution, slow
down, you got enough, you could go too far and lose everything? Not this mother, not me, no. Because I had confidence
in him to do the right thing, because I had seen him at work over
the years, seen him work his charms on the people in the congregation and do right by them, seen him help the troubled and
the disturbed and the worried and the upset, this was his great
talent, not so much the part where he could tell you marvelous
things about the Torah and history but because of how he could
look into somebody's eyes and see down into their hearts where
the blood rushed, and the truth of their feelings that roared along
in the arteries and veins, and he could advise them so well, and
when he went into the business full time, this same power
worked for him, where he could make the new men he met feel
such confidence that he would handle their affairs, and his own,
with ease and dexterity and wisdom and caution to a certain
extent, but also with enough foresight and even—what's the
word I want to say?—abandonment? daring, yes, *daring!* that
when he came to an abyss he would draw back and consider,
and usually draw back far enough in time to make the run and
leap across it without any great exertion. Or so it seemed.

His hair.

I think in a way if he were just a former rabbi in a dark suit
without the hair many would not have believed in him, no matter how much he had already accomplished. But because of the
combination of the suit and the hair, the hair that looked almost
out of this world it was so gorgeous, so stunning, as though light
collected in it and reflected back in your eyes, I think that this
had, in some strange way, an effect on the people that he met,
on the boards, and in the meetings, and at the clubs, and on the

docks and warehouses, so that even the roughneck men with the gaff hooks in their hands kept peace in their hearts for him when he walked past.

It was a kind of miracle, don't you think? You who have known a kind of miracle in your survival? Or would it have been a darker miracle but a miracle nonetheless if you had not? I don't mean to press. Wait. You know the effect he had on you, the steady hand on your shoulder, the gentle pressure he applied to your life. Imagine how it was growing up with him, as his mother, watching, hoping he could keep his balance, expecting that at any moment he would tumble. Of course he had some talents, too, in addition to the looks and the luck. When he was a student, and then a young rabbi, he could memorize the things he needed to say, the poetry, the lessons, the parables, the learning, he could quote from here from there in the Talmud, he could find examples from books of history, from literature—though to me always it will remain the most impressive—and to you too, darling, I know it is also doubly true—that sermon of silence, the sermon on the camps, the talk of silence, the silence of talk—but he did talk when he needed to, and I'm not saying that he stood like a mute and nodded when the brother-in-law and the experts made suggestions. Not at all. He asked good questions, and he made suggestions, and all in all it was his company as much as anybody else's and he ran it like that.

Except of course he had doubts. Who doesn't have doubts?

And the night after that meeting where everything, or so it seems, got decided, he came to me after the late supper I cooked for him with my own two hands like the old days.

You like it here, Mama? he asked me.

Do I like it here? No, I don't like it. I want to go back to Jersey where I have to do this (I was cooking for him potato pancakes, a little bit of lettuce and tomato on the side) every night. I want to go back downtown, even, to the little apartment where we lived after your father died, alone, where I washed and cooked and cleaned without no help.

Maybe I can arrange it, he said, leaning over my shoulder and taking a delicious sniff of the *latkes*.

You want to go? Go 'head.

You wouldn't like it.

I wouldn't. It's true.

I wouldn't either.

No?

No.

And certain women I know wouldn't like it either.

Maby.

Maby, of course. She wouldn't like it. She couldn't take it. She couldn't afford to stay alive without the care we buy for her.

True.

(I went on with my cooking, turning the flat little cakes of shaved potato as if nothing in the world interested me more.)

And Sarah, she couldn't take it.

Sadie wants what she wants. And what she wants takes money.

Yes, Mama, he said. For a girl who talks against things (something she was doing ever since she started at the college up in New England) she needs a lot of them. Her stereo in the car, her stereo in the room at school, her—well, I don't want to knock her too much. I enjoy buying these things for her. But she couldn't take it.

Take what, Manny? What are you trying to tell me?

Nothing, Mama. I'm just talking. Just letting off steam.

You had a hard day?

Hard? Soft? It was my day, the way days go these days, not so bad, not spectacular.

You're having a big success?

(I slipped my spatula beneath the pancakes and turned them easily one more time. In a few moments I had scooped them up and stacked them on a serving dish. The odor was alluring, and also memorial-like, reminding me here in the new days in this beautiful apartment high above the city of the old days in the tiny apartment down in the lower East Side. It was as if, for a second or two, the past was as real as the smell of the past and I would turn and find my Jacob ready at his place at the table, smiling up at me through his dark beard, his mouth watering at the sight of my potato pancakes.)

I have a chance, he said.

Do you want to talk?

I want to eat your cooking. Mama, I eat at the most expensive tables in the city, in the country, but your food is still the best.

(I leaned over and kissed him as I served up some latkes for his pleasure.)

What a good boy.

Thank you, Mama. I guess I needed to hear that.

And I needed to hear about my cooking. I don't cook so much these days, do I?

Why should you? And the smoke it doesn't bother your eyes?

What smoke?

Oh, Mama. Here, let me serve myself.

Stop it, stop it. You think I'm some kind of invalid? Here. (And onto his plate I placed a few tomatoes, a piece of lettuce. A slice fell onto the floor but he quickly scooped it up.)

Mama, please tell me. You couldn't see where you were putting that, could you?

What are you talking about? I see perfectly fine.

Ma-ma?

So I missed your plate. You want everything in life?

I want you to see the doctor this week. I want you to see the specialist we talked about.

So I'll see him.

Promise?

I'll see him. And if I don't see him when I see him, what's he going to do? Give me new glasses? He can give me new glasses, but he can't give me new eyes. Anyway, new eyes I don't need because I see everything I need to see.

You'll see him?

I'll see him.

Good. Because I don't need to have this worry on my mind on top of everything else.

So tell me about everything else.

I fed him. He told me some things, a lot of what I knew, some of what I didn't, a lot of what I've told you already in the past, and some of what I've said since you came into my room today. A long story, a sad story. You know the part about what he was saying to you, about the burden he was feeling, the working day in day out, and many nights getting the proposal together for the big takeover. You spent one late evening with him, in the hotel room he kept for the two of you just a few blocks downtown, and he held you in his arms as always, closer to you than any woman besides his mother, me—perhaps because you are *not* a mother, because either from choice or chance and circumstance you are as much like his lover and sister than mother and wife—but this time not with the steadiness you felt in him ever since the first time you embraced. This time you felt him tremble, you drew back, and watched him blink and blink, as though he were trying to shake off a fever or a nightmare, and you said, My darling, what's wrong? You're shaking so.

(And I want you to notice I'm not jealous when I say all this, not this mother, I am not, certainly not, not if it makes him feel good about what he is doing, because I want—I wanted him to feel so good that he would love life, like his father, like me.)

I can't tell you, he said, drawing loose from your embrace.

Of course you can. It's me, Manny, you said, your Florette.

I know.

Then tell me. You'll feel better. Haven't I talked to you about things when they bother me? My nightmares, my dreams.

I too have dreams. But mine don't sound as good as yours.

Not even as bad as my nightmares?

What do you mean?

(He's up now, walking to the window, peering between the slats of the blinds as though he might be able to spot some messenger or watchman on the street twelve, fourteen stories below.)

I'm just talking. I'm just alive. I want to help you.

I don't need any help except to keep calm. And you can't poke around inside me and make me calm.

No, but I can squeeze you and pet you on the outside. (You get up and join him at the window.) There, there.

Ah, Florette. (He turns, embraces you.) I don't mean to make a mystery. It's easy to explain, just difficult to live through.

Your company?

My company. We're about to commit ourselves to the biggest outlay of money and stock that I've ever heard of, let alone participated in. So my mind's not here. It's in little pieces of paper in brokers' offices all around the country. It's counting, counting. I'm buying so much of another company that I'm not going to have enough cash left to take a taxi home when I'm through. So I'm borrowing, borrowing—look, you don't want to hear this. I've got it under control—except the man at the controls, he feels his hand shaking on the wheel as the vehicle approaches maximum safe speed.

So you're having bad dreams?

I'm having my usual dreams.

And what are they?

You know. My father, voices at my ear, someone trying to feed me with a teaspoon. I've told you about these visions. It's just static, the mind's static from a day of rough and tumble. When I had the temple, people would come to me with questions about their dreams, as though I were the psychiatrist they feared to visit, and that's what I told them. In those days I had a kind of theory, you know. The Torah was God's broadcast, and we were the static. Some modern thing to say like that. What did I know? I was fooling myself into thinking I knew what I wanted or even a little about what I could say about anything serious. The best thing that ever happened to me was an accident—when I fell off the dais. Or was that God's hand pushing me from behind? Who knows? Do you think I want to know? I knew nothing about my life then and I know little enough about it now. And how much am I going to learn between now and the end? This much? The space between thumb and forefinger? Look in the Bible and in novels and you find lives that have meanings either from without or within, do you know what I mean? God pushes in one meaning, and the vital living force of the character is the other. But in real life (and imagine now he's standing naked at the window, you, woman with the numbers on your arm, clutching his waist, leaning your head against his shoulder) you feel more forces from without that come from the world, not from God, you feel like a stick pushed along by the current of . . . of time, say, of the flow of the hours in the day and the force of the days gathering together one after the other behind you. I want things, I'm aware of these things—peace for my family—which I'm not sure I'll ever obtain, health for my family, my mother's eyes (and isn't he a good boy, worrying like that?) and I want to play a little more with this company. Play, that's what it is to me, you know. So why am I shaking when it's only a game? Because games are serious sometimes, too. Any businessman knows that. So I'll shake a little, and I'll worry a little about whether or not we're going to make this takeover work. Now Mord, take Mord, he's a fanatic. He's like boys I saw at the seminary years ago—they had God, and he eats, drinks, breathes, sleeps the company. I put in sixteen hours, he puts in twenty. I put in twenty, he stays up for

three days running and then catnaps and works a fourth. To him
it's not a game. He has bad memories of his childhood, anything
reminding him of his youth he runs from. Me, I'm the other way
around. Me, I wish I had it to do all over again. I wish . . . (he
pauses, thinks a moment about something long lost, stares out
the window again, watches clouds pass behind a tall tower,
waits for birds to swoop from cornices, sees none, breathes) I
wish . . .

What do you wish, Manny?

I wish . . . many things. I wish . . . I wish . . . I wish I
could figure out why it is I *can't* figure out my life, why I feel
sometimes as though I'm plunging headlong off the dais in a fall
that goes on for years, through the end of my days at the temple, and on to this life in the city, in the company, in my new
rooms, my new thoughts, and why I still dream about the old
days, about my father, about his accident, and I see birds, and
I hear, sometimes, voices, I hear voices in my head, in my ear,
and all of those dreams and visions, if that's what to call them,
all those things haul me back, back, back toward the first part
of my life—and sometimes I feel the tension of the torque, is that
how to say it? the twisting and untwisting, winding and
unwinding, screwing and unscrewing along the thread—until
it feels as though one day I just may split apart—what?

(You're kneeling before him now, touching the outspread
palm of one hand to his turned out kneecap, the other hand
clasped behind his knee joint, the other leg.)

And along with that comes another sense of splitness—I can
call it, yes, good, splitness—comes the feeling of getting pushed
along like a mouse at the claw's end of a great paw, God's paw?
I don't know anymore about the things I felt so confident about
in my younger days. So—I feel like the mouse at the mercy of
the God's cat paw. And other days, days such as this—look out
through the blinds, no, no, later, don't get up, that's good, that
feels good—other days I know in my bones that I'm in control
of it all, of my life, of my time, of my head and heart and lungs
and eyes, and that I'm making things happen for myself and for
those around me. I'm making . . . ah . . . ah . . . ah . . . ah!

Can you bear to hear this now that you can't touch him no more?
Can you bear to think about the connection you made between

your flesh and his? between your heart and his heart, the beating, the pulsing? And think how it was for the mother, for me, the one who first felt the kick and tickle of his life within her womb—did I know it would come to what it came to? Did I know when I felt my own heart winking at the sight of the bearded young hostler behind the team of oxen? Did I? Could I? Did I have a choice? It was my own mother and father who made me—and then I made myself—and made my life with Jacob, and we made my Manny—and he unto him begat Sarah, known now in her early adulthood as Sadie, and she, she, *oi*, what was she at this same time begetting that could help her erase the errors of the attack upon her childlike flesh?

It has to do with America, America the south, South America. I have to tell you, but I don't know just yet when to put it in. Telling you these stories, it's like cooking. When does the baking powder go in? when the sugar? when the salt? And at what temperature do we bake it? and how long does it bake? I never was much good at it—baking, not cooking. At cooking I was all right. But you know now I remember something about Manny that never came to mind all the time before when I was thinking about him, that for a time when he was a young rabbi, when a congregation was giving him trouble for one thing or another, as congregations sometimes do, he came home every night and he baked bread. That's right, my Manny the baker. And I had completely forgotten about that. And if I was telling you the whole story and I left that out, would it have been important? To leave it out or put it in? Who knows how much I'm telling you is too much—or too little? Sure, it could be that, but I don't think so. I think I'm telling you just enough, and not much more, just enough for you to know him as I did, but not enough to die with him. To feel the grief but not to die. You wouldn't want to be in the story that much, would you? To want something so real it takes you along with the people in it, making the good things, that's one thing, but if there's hurting, criminals, killing, and if at the end, like in this sad story, there's dying, do you really want to go ahead and become so much a part of the telling that you never come out alive? I don't think so. Just like with a meal you're invited to, you don't want to have to slice the potatoes and chop the onions before hand, you don't want to do the dishes and take the garbage out after. Only the enjoyment is what you want, the pleasure, and sometimes suffering is part of pleasure if you know that when it's over you don't have to clean up the mess.

But I was saying about the American part before I interrupted myself with my thoughts about the baking, after years and years of living his life in what seemed to be a straight line my Manny's days began to take on a different shape, a shape I see at least from where I tell you about it, a shape that you don't need light to make out but like me can figure out with the fingers you have in your mind alone in your room in the dark. You could say, if you still want to think about the matter of making bread, that his life was rising. All the years before it was baking but it hadn't yet started to rise—it needed salt, it needed yeast (none of the unleavened variety for my Manny because he wanted heft and depth and flavor, taste, texture) and so the years leading up to the time when he fell and rose up again to take a new interest in the company in the city, these were the years when the heat had not yet accumulated, the years when it was building but not yet hot enough to make the dough rise, and then came the time of real fire, of fierce heat, the baking years, and, oh, his life changed so differently, he changed so differently and sometimes you would think if you didn't see him—with his hair and his dark suits—that he might be a different person, but he was the same person only changed, changed by the heat of his life, darkening, no doubt, darkening, darkening, but the same person nonetheless.

But I was saying about the story before I interrupted myself—and thanks, my darling, here, let me feel your hands, your face—thank you for not interrupting when I'm doing such a good job of interrupting myself—I was saying about the American part, I wanted to say about it, of course, it was always present, it was there from the beginning, from the time I woke up to discover what I wanted, that I wanted freedom and escape and a life with a man I wanted and who wanted me, and that was the American part beginning right there in the old country, and it was there when we sailed here, and it was present, of course, when we arrived here—get up in the apartment and look out the window in the bedroom at the far end of the long hall and you can see the lights of the very place where we arrived, the same pier itself and the buildings nearby, little pinpoints of light now down below in the city dark, like stars in a sky turned upside down and become the ground we walk on—that was our destination, and this, right now, this was what we sailed toward, and here we have arrived, after lightness, this dark, after young days, this age, a New World? a country of the old.

But I was saying about that part—the part I'm calling the American part, even though it's all American—it was building, building, rising, rising. Because while my Manny was working on the takeover, Sarah, now called Sadie by her friends at college, she was working on her own little bit of business.

You remember when Manny and Maby drove her up to New England to visit the school? Nobody thought of asking the grandmother if she wanted to take the trip. Who knows? I might have liked it. But of course I was busy with other things, with the furniture for the new apartment—it was taking me months to get settled in here, let me tell you, here, I mean in the new apartment, not here, this room, the window that throws light on my face I can only feel but not see, not here, the gardens, the walks, I'll never feel settled here. But there, there I was setting up. Go to New England? Nah, I said, not for me, darling. But wasn't it sweet of him to ask? I can't go on.

Wait. Here. The tissue.

Thank you.

I'll go on.

So I stayed home and they went on their trip, and this trip, I'd like to think, was just as important in their lives—and what happened—as the trip in the taxi the daughter, Maby, and her parents took all those years ago, and the trip up to the Union Square my Jacob and my Manny undertook, and the smoke from the fire that called out the fire department wagon, and add in the daily trip by the milk wagon, and what do you have? You add in a trip like the college trip and you've got a life, and you've got deaths.

It was a cool, clear, cloudless day when they set out north from the city, Manny behind the wheel of the big car. Maby was in one of her friendly states and she had packed a picnic lunch for them which they ate at a roadside rest area about an hour south of the Vermont state line.

Do you want this? an art school? she asked Sarah as she passed her a half sandwich of liver paté—what we used to call on Second Street *chopped liver!*—and a napkin.

Why shouldn't she want it? Manny broke in before the daughter could answer for herself. She wants something, she gets it. When I was young I learned that lesson—you want something, you work for it, you get it. If you're lucky. If I could—here he waved through the air the half sandwich that he had picked up from the tray held out toward him by his wife—I would give her the sun and the moon. He smiled at her as lovingly as he did at anything in his life. Even me, his mother, he never often gave a smile like this.

But Sarah—soon to become Sadie—did not smile back.

I don't want the moon or the sun, she said. I'd like to go to this school, though. It has a good art program.

Art you want, art you get, my Manny said.

(Can you hear how after all these years he still speaks in the same rhythms as he used when we all lived together in the tiny hole in the wall on Second Street? This is—was—oi! was—one of the things I loved so much about my son, that though he accomplished things, and he changed, and, oi didn't his hair change color overnight, he never put on airs! So he left the temple, and people would say he left his religious days behind him because, you know I have to admit, he never went inside a temple again after that, never went to another service, but he didn't pretend he was anything that he wasn't. He was a former rabbi in a black suit and almost glowing white hair. Nothing more, but nothing less. A former rabbi with a knack for business. Or for calming the fears of people in the business, to be exact.)

Art I want, Sarah said, staring her father directly in the eye.

He stared back, thinking to himself, How far will she go when I do everything to make it up to her? thinking, If once we cross over the line neither of us will ever come back. What could I do? he had been asking himself for a long time now. Could I invent a feeling for her mother that was like love but wasn't love itself? Could I mend her spirit, hers, Sadie's, Sarah's, when I couldn't even thread a needle and start to work on her mother's? (Look, if it's the feeling of regret you're wondering about, the moaning tone he takes in his mind right there in the middle of a sunny roadside stop near noon on a lovely day, think about the darkness you carry with you into the middle of the happiest occasions. You of all people shouldn't blink an eye at me as though I'm only telling you a story! You who have lived in the dark at midday and drunk the black milk of morning at midnight, you! You who have embraced my Manny and held his shaking, quivering spirit in your hand!)

Some picnic they had, eh? If I had been there I might have done something to save them, I might have pointed out to them the lovely wildflowers blooming in little shapes of stars, spades, clubs, all purple and blue and yellow at the edge of the picnic ground, the pine trees standing nearby dripping with the sap of springtime, the bees newly present since the disappearance of the snow and cold. If I had been there I might have clapped my hand over my granddaughter's mouth before she spoke.

You can't buy me, you know, Father. You can give me everything I want, and I'll take it, but that's no guarantee that I'm ever going to love you again.

There—in the middle of the wildflowers, bees, the trees, the beautiful season—there, she said this. And it ate into his heart, my Manny's heart, like acid spilled onto cloth. It burned, it burned!

So what could he be thinking through all this? That he should have done something different? Sure, he should have done something different. He should have never lived! Because what else could he have done? Could he have saved his father on that cold Saturday morning when my Jacob pulled the cart out onto the street? Could he have said, Papa, let's go to shul instead because if we work today you're going to die? He's supposed to know that? God he's not. That I guarantee. Because he was my child, and while I was a Jewish mother I was not the Virgin Mary or whatever her name was. No, I was not! I met my Jacob long ago at the stream, and that was that, as far as my virgin condition was concerned. And so he was nothing but a man, but a man has his rights, does he not? A man has his dignity. And my Jacob had his. And he wanted the right to earn his living the way he wanted to earn it. And so he went to work on the Sabbath, and that was that.

He looked away from Sarah, not speaking back to her, staring up into the perfect pale white cloth of sky.

We'd better get going, were his words after a little while. The admissions person will be waiting.

Now if I had had the powers of a god or goddess, if I could have made weather, I would have called up storm clouds, great crashing thunder and lightning, like the noise of many gods gnashing their teeth in heaven – I would have called up winds, huge rushing torrential floods of winds, and I would have turned this car from its course. *Oi*, if I had been the goddess or the god, *Hoo!* I would have shouted, *hoo, hoo!* go back, you ridiculous mortals, go back to the city you came from, because up here your daughter's going to meet real trouble, and this will in turn bring the trouble home to you!

But nobody would have listened, I think, if I had had the power. Do children listen to their mothers? Do daughters listen? Do sons? I would have warned them if I could and they would have done it anyway. It's the law of life, on earth as it is in heaven, that what they want to do they will do, and doing it they will think they could not have done otherwise. *Oi*, I sit here with my eyes closed to what's around me, feeling the world to life with my fingertips, and I think, *Oi*, if I could have done it perhaps I might have simply struck them down right then and there at the roadside rest stop among the wildflowers and the neatly tended grass.

But no cloud blotted the sky as they drove north. And it was warming up, and it was a beautiful day, and *oi*, what bad things can come into the world at two o'clock in the afternoon, on a lovely spring afternoon in the country! Those people who put you in the camps, who tortured your childhood, did they get their ideas on cold cloudy days in winter? I don't think so – I think they could have thought up their monster thoughts at a picnic on a sunny day in spring. They loved music. They loved certain poetry, all this I heard from my Manny. And if they thought up murder in big figures on a sunlit day, why isn't it possible that the God we pray to decided in creation that evil would be there in a pure white cloud? that a good man like my Manny could try to do good for his family and himself and still make the worst things happen?

Oi, I would have rolled rocks down from the mountain to block their path! I would have made earthquakes to tear up the road out from under them! I would have hurled God's dinner dishes out of heaven, and His pots and pans, if I could have stopped them from reaching their destination!

The college. The quiet little art studies college in the hills of Vermont. My Manny thought something was funny with it from the first time he took a look – it was an old farm turned into a college, with the faded red barn and the chicken houses and farmhouse and other small buildings making up half of the campus. For this he was going to pay the highest tuition in the United States of America? He was a man on the verge of buying a shipping line and not so far away from beginning to ponder the value of buying half an isthmus—is that the word?—*down there* in the south of America. And so, because he liked to match what he knew in his mind with what he saw with his eye, he had a deep deep question about this school even before they walked in the door. But he bit his lip, my Manny did, and oh, I wish I could have been the muscles in his jaw and pressed his teeth through the skin of his mouth! Because then he might have had some idea of the pain that would come of this, and he might have said, Wait, no, this is wrong! I don't want you to do this! I won't pay a penny for this, not one!

But he felt so guilty about her, because of Sadie's trouble that time at Rutgers, the memory of it, it hurt him as well as her, and he tried to do the right thing, and the thing he tried to do was buy her these things that she wanted. And if she wanted to attend this place whose appearance suggested to him that *they* should be the ones paying the students to attend just in order to give the convincing air of a college, then he would send her. Of course, she had an interview, they had to read her records, they had to accept her—but even though she had one of the worst high school careers in the history of her school he was not in doubt of her getting in. All they would do was read the name of his business on the application—that would do it as sure as they would have had a different, if still positive, response if he had put the temple on the application as his place of business. Corporations or churches, it was all the same to people like this—they waited and wanted to be impressed, and so they were by money whether gained by deeds or misdeeds. It was all such a game to my Manny by this time—and he wanted nothing greater than to make all of the pieces fall into place.

How do you do? he said when the head of the admissions department, a slender, pale woman, pearls at her throat, offered him her cold and bony-fingered hand. He could see written all over her face the desire for his company's name and cash in the files and bank accounts of the college. This ship was sinking, he could smell it about the place. My Manny, he had some of that same instinct as his brother-in-law, you know. But if his daughter wanted it for a while, for as long as it lasted or as long as it made her happy, then that was fine with him. Nothing it seemed was too far out of reach for him anymore, and so nothing that any one of his family wanted was out of their reach. Except maybe some kind of peace? I don't know. Here he was riding high, talking quietly to the admissions woman while Sarah was taking her interview with a member of the art department.

Oh, if I could have started a fire and cleared the building and ended that interview—and broken the link in the chain that weighed my Manny down! If I could have hurled lightning at this crumbling old barn and crackled fire through its timbers! *Oi,* if I could have eaten giant onions so bad that I could have breathed and cleared the halls that way! If I could have smelled them out, stunk them out! *maybe, maybe* then the rest of it would not have fallen into place!

But she was in there, stayed in there, and came out beaming.

So? her father, my Manny, asked her.

She's wonderful, Sarah said, already becoming though we didn't know it yet the person she called Sadie.

She?

She was Lana Peale, an overweight painter from New York who had come up that year to teach on the college faculty. She had a face like a knife, eyes like a small animal from the woods, and no sense of humor, hardly. Only later did we learn that she stood on very bad ground with the dean and that she was volunteering her time in admissions interviews in the hope that she could make up for some damage she had done earlier in the year. The damage, as it turned out, my dear, was a freshman girl from her design class who sliced her own wrists with a linoleum cutter because Lana Peale told her that she would be an artist only if she lived to be four hundred years old. I love students, Peale told the Dean, and I love art, and you can see that from my work and if you don't think that I love students I'll show you. I'll help with the admissions committee, how's that? And they took her up on it. And so there she was, giving an interview to my granddaughter.

It was love at first blink. It didn't even take a blink, maybe only half a squinched look when Sadie came into the room. Both of them felt it like a piece of jagged glass in the palm of the hand—*suh-lash!* and the pain was there, and the beautiful feeling, was how Sadie described it to me—only for the first time last night when she finally came back from her wanderings—

but, oh, for how long I never knew where she was and didn't want to imagine!—here in the dark of this room, holding my hand, touching now and then a cool finger to my forehead, saying, Oh, Gram, oh, Grammy, Gram—she had never felt anything like it before except maybe for the time when she was dancing with Rose Pinsker's grandson, Rick Sommer, the youth advisor turned dean, at the Purim dance, that was, she told me, the last time (and the first time) she ever felt like that with a boy or a man.

It was like lightning striking me, Grammy, she said (which was why, maybe, when I was telling you how much I wanted to stop things from rolling toward the end I thought of becoming like lightning, like a big summer storm), and then she made a little noise on her throat, like she was thinking of something she desired. Since from the time she was a little girl I never heard her talk in that voice, with the dreamy part, with the little purr like a kitten's when it sleeps. What was this that happened to her? What do you call it? When my Manny fell in love with his Maby, it was so different, full of old-fashioned talk, from the *Song of Songs* they were reading, and if Maby behaved like a Delilah, like a Jezebel, then that was old-fashioned too. But this business between the women, you don't hear too much about it. There's nothing in the old books to explain it, at least nothing I ever heard. But it's there, here, in the world, a fact of life, like red hair and people who write with the left hand. But then I never heard everything—who lives long enough to hear everything? to know everything? the Jews thought they knew, you know. They thought they knew it all. They had the Torah, and they made commentaries, saying what they knew, and then commentaries upon the commentaries—see how much I learned over the years from my Manny?—but the years go by and soon you're arguing about the meaning of the commentaries on the commentaries and you forget about the first things you said, or they seem different, and what used to seem like such a simple truth has become so complicated that in the end all you know is that you don't know. And the Gentiles, the goyim, they're no better, because they overlap with what the Jews know and add their own complications on top of our complications and it's even more mixed up—the truth—than it was when it first started—back then, in the Garden, where the first man and first woman came to life, and they looked at each other—like the way

I looked at my Jacob the first time, it had to be—and so maybe that's the only thing we can know, that the lightning strikes whatever kind of tree is standing there, male, female, boy and girl, girl and girl, boy and boy, the lightning, the fire it makes burns the same.

For Sadie—if I could see and had a lipstick I could draw you an arrow—it went from the woman Peale to this college to trying to paint to—the disaster she made for her father, my Manny, *oi*, my Manny! my Manny! Here near the end I think of his beginnings and I turn to ice inside, ice! to think that it all should come to this, the boy, the years, the work, the love I had for him! Ice! Ice! Ice!

I'm sorry. I'll be calmer. I'll take it easy. Behind my eyes I see unfolding in time stoppage, like a flower, the year my Sadie went to college. It's a movie, sometimes, sometimes a song, a dance, a poem, and sometimes the bad odor when you lift the lid on a can of garbage that's stood too long in the sun.

I like the work you showed me, Sarah, the Peale woman said at the end of the interview and Sadie had put away her portfolio. I'd like you to come to my studio in the city and show me more.

(If a man says a thing like this to a young girl he knows, she knows, everybody knows what is meant behind the words. But what if a woman? if a girl, really, not that much older than the girl she speaks to, says such a thing? who's to know what she really means? Who's to suggest that she's just not being friendly? Oh, these modern times, I'm telling you, where sometimes, you hear of these things, even the mothers and fathers can't be trusted with the children! And if it keeps up like this even the ground we walk on—or used to walk, because this particular grandmother, me, she don't walk much anymore—even the ground you can't trust. You hear about it, earthquakes, talk of planets going to collide, moons falling, the sun going out some day. And I say, what does it matter to me? what does it matter if the child you bear and the children he fathered, they can't get together and live even for a few years in peace? I say, if that don't happen, then the rest could happen. I say, let the earth quake, let the stars crash, the sun spit and smoulder out like a fire in a trash bin. What do I care? I have no hope. I have no prospects.

I have no future that I see behind my closed-out eyes. Let it come, I say. Let it quake and shake and crash out and sputter—let it burn and burn and burn and burn, let the worlds collide, pieces of star shapes trailing through the airless spaces between the bones and tissues of void, a crash of a milk wagon of the heavens into the fire engines of hell. The only thing that comes of it is death.

See? The scene changes, time stoppage unfolds faster. Her mother's in the hospital scribbling star shapes in her notebook. Her father's on a business trip to New Orleans with the brother-in-law. Grandma is as always at home, in the apartment, getting the meals ready despite eyes so bad she has to run her finger along the edge of a knife to figure if it's the right one to cut with.

See?

She's walking across Houston Street, though classes haven't even begun yet, she's going to see the art teacher. Her portfolio, with some new drawings, it's banging against her leg. Her chest feels funny—like she wants to cough but can't quite. Her mind is a million miles away from the traffic and the trash on the street. She's thinking about how her father invited her to go to New Orleans, and she turned him down.

You don't want to?

He couldn't believe it.

I have things to do, Papa, she said, never, as usual, looking him in the eye.

Things? what things? You don't want to eat with me at those restaurants? It's superb, my daughter, it's wonderful. The seafood especially.

You eat the shellfish?

Of course I eat the shellfish.

You don't keep any of the laws anymore.

Sarah, none of that means much to me anymore. Except that I try to stay true to the morality behind the laws. The spirit, not the letter.

You *have* changed, she said.

Of course I've changed. The world demands change and we demand that the world changes in turn, my dear.

When I was little you used to spank me if I broke one of the laws.

I never spanked you.

You did.

You have a faulty memory. Perhaps you recall the pain of humiliation as physical pain.

I remember physical pain .

You are imagining it. The memory plays tricks on us, darling. But will you think this through again? Are you sure?

Is it some kind of . . . ?

Some kind of what?

Never mind.

Will you think it over?

Um. I remember. I remember that you once broke my guitar. I was playing on the High Holidays. And you smashed it.

I'm sorry. I was a fool. I apologize again. But didn't I buy you another guitar? And many other things?

That was after . . .

Yes, you're right. But are you . . . all right?

All right?

All right.

Yes, I'm all right. As all right as I'll ever be. This year.

My Manny shook his head.

Sometimes I don't know when I'm talking with you whether it's you or your mother I'm hearing. She is always saying things like that.

Things like what?

Like, I'm all right. This year.

But it's true. I'm all right this year. Next year I can't say yet. Can you?

I don't think like that. And I wish you didn't. Look, Sarah, why don't you just get on the airplane with me and we'll have a fine trip to New Orleans.

Watch the rabbi eat shellfish in New Orleans.

Will you stop that? I'm a former rabbi. But I'm also a human being, and I have my appetites and desires and that's that. Am I supposed to be better than everybody else? Am I like the Catholic who's supposed to be more Catholic than the pope?

I don't know what you're supposed to be.

So come to New Orleans and I'll show you some things you might enjoy.

What are you doing there anyway?

I have a little business to do. But we can have plenty of time for fun.

I'll believe it when it happens.

So come and see and believe.

Is *she* going?

Florette?

She. Her.

You don't want her to come, she doesn't come.

Some loyalty.

You want me to take her so you can say I was keeping you from going? Sarah, don't try to have it both ways. You want to come, Florette stays here. You don't come, she might come along with me.

While my mother turns into a mushroom at Owl Valley? No thanks.

So that was the whole point of this conversation.

I didn't know it had a point. I was just talking to my father. And he turned everything to shit again.

You led me into this, you know.

Listen to the rabbi. The devil made him do it. The devil in his daughter.

Please don't talk like that. Now let's calm down and try to talk about . . .

Owl Valley.

You cannot keep throwing that in my face.

Owl Valley.

Please stop it, Sarah.

Owl Valley.

I can't . . .

Owl Valley.

If you . . .

Owl . . .

Hit her he did. And sorry he was, too, like the time he hit her mother. But it was too late. By the time the stinging stopped in his palm she was already out the door and gone. She's walking across Houston Street, classes haven't even begun and she's off to see her new teacher.

I'm awfully glad you came, this Peale woman says, her legs folded beneath her on a bunch of large floppy pillows. This is how they sit in such places, like Arabs in tents. Above her head the high ceiling of a factory loft, the kind of place I worked in for years after the death of my Jacob. And today, artists live and play in these buildings. And the granddaughter of a former seamstress plays here too, watching the funny little cigarette in the pinched fingers of her hostess, watching the trail of white smoke pour from her pinched red lips.

I like your work a lot, she says to the Peale woman, meaning the canvases piled all around against the walls. They show giant breasts, nipples as large as the heads of children—in fact, some of the nipples take the shape of children's faces. Other paintings: they show parts of the woman's body which fifty years ago a girl didn't even know she *had*, let alone would show in a picture. The colors all stand out very bright, because of the veins, the skin, the tender flesh. If you didn't know it was art you would think it belonged on the wall of a butcher shop or a doctor's office, the work of a very angry person, the red, the red makes me think that. And so it's no accident that Sadie found it pleasing. So angry she was with her father, if she had a gun who knows what she would have done. But she didn't have any weapon to use against him except her life, and this, like a terrorist's bomb, is dangerous both to the one who carries it as well as the one who is the target.

I'd like to paint like you, Sadie said.

The Peale woman laughed.

I don't think you'd like it, my dear, I don't think you would.

Pushing herself off from her nest of pillows, the older woman fetched a little dark metal tin. From this she took out the special tobacco to make more of the cigarettes that make you dream. My Sadie, who never drank a drop in her life except the wine at holidays, and of course that unfortunate beer at Rutgers, and who never smoked nothing at all, she watched her heroine roll a little pencil of it and when it was time she learned to inhale and puff, inhale and puff.

Some time went by—the way clouds roll past your window when you're looking out at a big Jersey storm. It actually passed by her eyes. Next thing she knew she was rolling on the puffy pillows, her chest bare to the air, and the painter woman is playing tickle-tickle with her long fingernails on Sadie's back.

I never had so much fun, my granddaughter is saying to herself, I never had a pal like this before.

So by the time Sadie's school started they were great friends, eating lunch together all the time, and spending a number of evenings together, and even whole nights. It was a bit of a shock for my granddaughter when going back up to Vermont she had to live in a dreary little wooden-walled dormitory instead of the loft with the pillows and paintings.

I felt like I was being separated from a twin sister, she told me. Gram, I'd never had a friend before like this, not anyone. Mother never held me the way she does. Can I say these things to you?

Sure, Mike, I told her, sure you can say these things to your grandmother. Who else could love you so much to listen and not grit her teeth? You think your mother? You think your father? I know, I know, my Manny, he has his problems. And you should understand them—remember, his own father he saw crushed to death by the wagon, his own father's blood he saw spill out into the lake of milk. I told her long ago, I told her the story.

He saw his own father crushed to death by a milk wagon, she told her friend the painter. He saw his own father's blood spill out into the lake of milk.

I like the action, I like the color, the painter said.

How can you say that? Sadie was shocked—for maybe the last time.

He's not my father, she said. And from what you've told me about how he's treated you, you probably feel a lot more anger than sympathy if you'd admit to the truth.

Let's say that this conversation is taking place in the little apartment the painter uses when she comes up to the school during the week to teach. Let's say that they're sitting on the bed together, smoking that stuff. Let's say that the Peale woman calls this their advising session, and that they both laugh whenever she calls it that.

So the painter says, If I were you . . .

Yes?

I'd be completely unforgiving.

Sadie—she's torn now, like a piece of butcher paper, right down the middle. He can't help it, she says.

He's a free agent, Peale the painter says. He's free to act.

He's weighed down, Sadie says, feeling herself floating higher and higher.

A typical man, the painter says.

He's unusual, Sadie says, wondering at herself even as she defends him. This lightness she feels, is it good or bad? This strangeness in her life, the bittersweet taste of Peale's oily mouth in her mouth, the sharp earthy odor of the dreamy cigarettes, is it here to stay? Will life be like this from here on in? All that she knew from the past seemed out of reach and even if within her grasp unusable. All that she has heard about life from her father (since her mother spoke to her very little, very little) appears weak and foolish and even sick.

Have you told me everything about him now? Peale the painter asks.

I think so. Everything I know.

He was a rabbi but he no longer even goes to the synagogue? That's right.

Hypocrite, Peale says.

He changed his mind, he changed his life, Sadie says, amazed at herself that she's still defending my Manny.

Look, Peale said.

Look what?

Look, you can't go on talking about him from his point of view. It's your life that he's eating up. You're nothing but a slave to yet another male monster if you keep on seeing things from his perspective. Do you think I make my art by sticking to the male perspective? Do you think I could get my forms if I showed the female body the way men see it? Do you?

No.

You want to paint?

I do.

You want to be an artist.

Yes. I want to paint. And I want to make pots.

If you're going to be any good, and I don't know how good you can be, sweetheart, though I do know you've got something to start with—God knows you've got the pain in your life a woman begins with when she makes her art—but if you're going to go on with it, push on with it, you've got to make your own vision. You've got to give over the vision of the fathers. The vision of your father.

I . . . guess you're right.

You guess I'm right. You only guess? You don't feel it in your guts, you don't feel it in your womb?

I . . . know you're right.

Yes, you know it. You know I'm right. And she leaned over and kissed Sadie on the mouth. There. That's the seal of our pact. Sealed with a kiss.

S.W.A.K. Like a letter in grade school to a boyfriend.

Yes, love. Except it's to me, not a boyfriend.

Yes, Sadie said, and rolled over to where she could rest her head on her painter-teacher-friend's chest.

And now we have our pact.

And what's our pact?

We're going to get rid of the father who haunts your mind.

How are we going to do that?

Here. Painter Peale leans over and kisses Sadie tenderly on the neck. This.

Um. How?

Sadie closes around her friend her arms in a desperate embrace.

We're going to find a way to destroy him.

Destroy! Can you imagine! This is what it had come to!

Excuse, I got to wipe my eyes. Even the blind weep, darling, when in their minds they witness sadness. Hate. Destruction. Of their children hating, and being hated.

My Manny's building, and she wants to destroy.

In this building he's building. He's sitting in his office in his building, with the brother-in-law in a meeting. These are new offices, twice removed from the original where the company they first formed had its home. On a wall map, with pins stuck onto the colored shapes where they own buildings, piers, here a small shipyard, there a complex of warehouses, you could count fifteen little pinheads of blue, and another seven, eight of black. Glancing away from the wall, Manny stares out the window, and he can see down from this height all the way to the same pier where our ship first docked. And he can remember just how far in time and how high in the world he has climbed.

In legend, he says, in mythology, there is a plot to describe a passage such as this. A man wants, and the devil appears to him and offers him his desires in exchange for his soul. Devil! This is a metaphor, is it not?

If you say so, Son, I reply to him.

(Now we're talking together over supper on a night when he has come home late from another meeting in the series of meetings coming upon the big takeover. I've made a little salad, it's early spring, there's not such good tomatoes yet, but he's been asking for avocado, something I never even saw let alone served before we moved to this new apartment in the city, high up where we moved from Jersey, so I had the Gristede's man send some over, and some steak I cooked for him, too, and to tell you the truth it was also from the Gristede's, because the butcher shop was closed and—what?—no, this was a good thick bloody piece of sirloin, we hadn't eaten kosher for years, not since the move definitely.)

I say so? I know so.

(Oh, and a baked potato, of course, with a little butter—that's right, since he was eating this way it included dairy in the meat meal, and was it going to kill him?)

The devil is for the goyim, isn't it? Jews don't have the devil.

The *Gentiles*, Mama, don't have him either. He doesn't exist.

So what's with all their stories?

Just stories.

Just stories? I've heard some of their stories from Sarah when she was studying them at school. They're scary stories. And sometimes she said we, the Jews, we're supposed to be the devil. But so I told her, darling, we're not angels, but we're not the devil either. But Manny, darling, you don't believe in angels then either? What about your . . . ?

The birds? Mama, I don't know how to explain that. The voices came to me from the birds. What can I say? Perhaps it was my mind's way of telling me something I couldn't bear to recognize, or wouldn't understand as my own thought. I don't know.

If you don't know, I don't know either.

Such a good mother.

Such a good cook is what I want to hear.

Such a good cook.

Really? You like it? It's hard to hurt a steak. But is it rare enough for you, darling?

It's rare.

So eat a little more.

To tell you the truth, Mama, my stomach is in turmoil. I've got a lot of things on my mind.

(And then I said it. I take the blame. Were my words pulled out of me by some invisible devil? You don't believe in them, not even you? Then it was God who did it? And did God do all those things to you when you were a child? And if not God and if the devil didn't, then who? who? I said it. It was an innocent remark. What could I say? It was one of those things a mother says, and isn't that as innocent as it comes?)

I said, You got your wife on your mind?

(What did I know? I was thinking of her. I was thinking that in spite of everything else she was his wife, and she was alone and probably very lonely out there in that place. Owl Valley. With the green lawns, the shaped shrubs, the stately, stately trees — I been there to visit, I saw it. But he hadn't been there to visit in a while. And so I said it. Sarah had gone. She went there when she come down from school. But he hadn't. You marry a girl, you try to make a life, and then when she gets sick do you leave her there in the home? No matter how good it is — and he tells me, and I believe him, that it's the best place on the East Coast — no matter how good, do you leave a person there? Do you leave there a person you married?)

He didn't say a word, just looked at me, deeply, deeply. In his eyes I saw — I was watching when I said, *With your mother you get a meal and for dessert you get a lecture* — I saw in his eyes there was this empty space, a darkness and a nothingness, a large field of black like on it I could have picked up a lipstick or a crayon my granddaughter wrote with when she was a child and I could have inscribed my name, made pictures, drawn this star-shaped shard around which that very moment he was curling his fingers in his trousers pocket. It frightened me to see this — *into* this — because he was my son, who I tried to raise practically by myself, and I knew what he had lived through, and I knew the things he felt and saw, because he told me so much, the mother, his friend, and to sit across from him and look into that place it was very scary, let me tell you, because I had no idea how much he had changed, right before my very own eyes. In another man, an average man without the kinds of talents possessed by my Manny, in a man who would never climb so high, you could look and you could see, like vegetables and meat floating in a stew, bits and pieces of guilty thoughts and happy thoughts, hopes, prospects, fears. But I told you just now how it was with my Manny. Why I kept after him on the subject, I can only say, I must have been a little bit crazy at that time.

After all she's still your wife, I said.

And he nodded. What had I said that he could argue with? You said the same to him? I know you said the same. He told me just then.

Florette tells me the same. He said this. He said.

So what do you do about it? I asked him.

Him holding a bit of meat up on his fork.

I'll see her more often.

Often? It doesn't have to be often, I said. It just has to be sometimes. Sometimes is better than nothing, Manny.

It hasn't been nothing, he said. Still holding the meat on the fork. He had stopped eating, stopped chewing. He reached out for a glass of wine without looking and nearly knocked over the bottle. Wine, which I had brought out from his new collection in the study wall. Dry red wine—not the white sweet he used to like. It's all changed for him, see, even the wine.

Now maybe he would have gone to see her again sooner rather than later anyway. Maybe he would have. But when I remember it I worry that it was my remark that started him back there. The way he did. What he did. And this in turn. You don't know that part because he told me he couldn't bear to tell you. But I'll tell you even though it hurts me, like tearing the scab from a sore. Why shouldn't it? The son hurts, the mother hurts. That is a law of life. But as far as laws go, what happened in the next months, it showed me an answer to the questions he had on his mind about the devil or not the devil. If you could say anything on that question that made sense after what happened next, the answer was there to see. It always has been. It always will be. *Life* is the devil.

They were pulling up the long tree-lined driveway to Owl Valley when Sadie got cold feet.

What if she doesn't believe me? she asked.

She'll believe you, sweetheart, her painter friend and teacher said. You're her daughter, her only child. She'll want to believe just about anything you tell her.

But if she doesn't want to come?

She will, sweetheart, she will. How could she refuse the offer we're going to make to her? I wouldn't, would you?

I didn't, Sadie said. I'm living up there with you, right?

You shouldn't put it that way, Sadie. You shouldn't make it sound as though you're my subordinate. Here, park here.

I wasn't trying to. It just came out that way.

Think about the way you frame those statements, sweetheart. Your whole sense of framing is subordinate. We're equals, remember? Under the sign of the *gyn*?

Under the sign. Here we go. Sadie's voice trembled a little with anticipation, and a little fear.

Up the steps of the lovely wide veranda to the large oak door. Once inside, Sadie went directly to the receptionist at the desk.

She introduced herself and said, We've come for my mother.

Peale meanwhile was studying the portraits on the wall—gray-faced, gray-haired men, doctors they appeared to be, the founding psychiatric fathers of this place.

She'd probably like to take a walk, the nurse said as she led them down the long hallway toward the rear of the large converted Victorian house.

That's what we had in mind, Peale said, suppressing laughter.

My sister, Sadie said.

I'm her sister, Peale said.

The nurse looked from Sadie to Peale and back again.

Here we are, the nurse said, leaving them at the door to Maby's room. She took a last look at Peale, and walked away.

Bitch, Peale said.

Why? Sadie asked.

Just bitch, that's all.

Sadie pursed her lips, gave a shrug and knocked on the door.

No reply.

Sadie knocked again.

Again silence.

Just go on in, Peale said.

Sadie looked up and down the hall, and then opened the door.

Who? Maby said.

It's me, Mother. Sadie crossed to where her mother sat at the window. Her slacks were an ugly green—Sadie had never seen them before.

Who?

And my friend. Sadie gestured toward Peale who had come in and shut the door behind her. But Maby didn't turn.

We've come to take you for a walk, Mother.

Who?

Mother. We've come to take you for a walk.

Maby stirred, finally.

A walk? I've had a walk. They walk me twice daily. But I'm tired now. Later I shall arise.

You'll what?

I'm reading this poem, Maby said. But there was no book nearby, only a few novels on the shelf near the bed. Sadie stared at them while wondering how to move her mother off the spot—there was a title by the man named Bair, the one who taught her. The man she turned back once to see before he left for Alaska. Once. Maybe twice.

Come along, sweetheart, Peale said, taking Maby's hand and urging her to stand.

Who are you? Maby blinked at the painter, as if coming out of a dream.

She's my friend, Mother, Sadie said. A dear friend.

Come along, Peale said. We've got a ride to take.

We do?

We do.

Not back to the city. I don't want to go back to the city. Not just yet.

Up to the country is where we're going, Mother. Up to Vermont.

I would like that, Maby said. Where we took our picnic. I remember that. I enjoyed myself.

We'll enjoy ourselves a lot, Mother. We're going to spend a lot of time together. The three of us. And maybe more. We'll invite more women to live with us if we can find the right ones.

All of them are okay, Peale said. Some are just a little closer to a sense of themselves than others.

That's right, Sadie said. We want you to come with us now, Mother.

I'll need to pack.

We have some of your things in the car, Mother.

And your father? Was he glad to hear the news?

Oh, yes, Mother. He was very glad.

Very glad, Peale said.

We're going on a picnic, Maby said as they passed the nurses' station.

Today's the day . . . Peale was singing.

The sisters going on a picnic, Sadie said.

. . . the teddy bears have . . .

Maby laughed as they went out the door.

. . . their pic-nic.

But when Sadie opened the car door and motioned for her mother to climb in? Maby pressed her face against the side of the vehicle and began to cry. I have no things, she said.

We packed for you, Mother, I told you, Sadie said.

I have nothing to read, Maby said, her voice choked with tears, high-pitched, like a worried child's.

We're going to stay near the college, Mother. You can use the library.

Well, we'll have to be careful for a while, Peale said. But we can get books for her from the library, sure. But Mrs. Bloch, Maby? Maby. Climb in. We're going to have a picnic on the way, really.

Really?

Maby peeked over at the painter from behind her hand. It could be fun. I never had fun. I couldn't, do you see? Mother?

I couldn't have much fun at all.

Mother, please get in.

I'll get in, Maby said.

By six o'clock that night Manny was beginning to think about returning home from where he was—in Boston, at a meeting— and he called the house to tell me that he was going to take the shuttle. I had to tell him that the Owl Valley people, a nurse, had called to ask if Maby had shown up there at the apartment.

What? I could hear the airport noise in the background, I could hear static on the telephone, noises both loud and soft. And in the middle, my Manny's silence. What's going on?

They said that she left for a picnic with Sarah and a friend and she hadn't come back.

A boyfriend?

A girl, they said. A woman.

Jet noise, static. Silence between.

Manny, you're hearing me?

I hear you. It's the teacher, the one she's been talking about.

You think so?

Who else? Look, if they show up, you keep them there, Mama. I'll be there in . . . an hour and a half, two hours. I'm going to call Mord and have him come over.

Please, no.

I want someone there.

Not him . . .

Mama?

I'll call Daniel. I like him. He'll come up.

Okay, Mama. I'm going to catch the plane now.

And I could imagine my Manny, his dark suit, his white hair, the slender little briefcase in his hand, taking big strides toward the entrance to the airplane, a distinguished man in an undistinguished hurry.

He had been there for what turned out to be a final meeting with the board of the company next on the horizon—with the biggest shareholders from the board—and he was giving them assurances, assurances all afternoon long. There had been a faction of people owning stock, family members, younger people, who wanted him to acknowledge that he would turn around some of the company's policies in that part of the world, America the south, where it owned most of its property, and these he gave assurances to also, and so—surprised as he was that these Boston people wanted something more than just the money for their shares—he gave his assurances to the ones who wanted only the money that their money would be there—and before you knew it he was the majority in this biggest company of all that he had ever owned. My Manny the majority!

She has gone far enough!

This was Mord—who came over at Manny's call.

She has gone too far!

Mord claimed, he *claimed* that he woke up this morning and knew that something was going to go wrong.

He was writhing in a dream, turning his body to the tune of a Bedouin flute while beasts of burden—camels, horses, asses—tested the lengths of their tethers, hawing, spitting, snorting, and the moon rose over an ocean of dunes. There was music in this dream, the splattering of tambourines and the punching of drums, the jangling of wristlets and bracelets, a moaning chorus of camel drivers.

> *Zum bah nim*
> *Sum akh*
> *Zum bah nim*
> *Sum akh*

Some strange singing in dreams! And some strange goings on! For a man who lived like a monk—from all reports, including his own, this was the way he lived—there was also some funny business with a boy all greased up and dancing.

Some dark night, warm with cirrus clouds, flavored with citrus winds, he and the greased child had sipped mint tea together, and spoke in the language of the dream songs.

> *Mustah markhim zum bah nim.*
> *Alla goh beem, go beem.*

Words like this, like that.

And he had traced a map of the unknown country in which he lived while asleep on the sand, on the boy's dried, bony chest, turning his flat nipples into oases, his head into a hairy mountain—and elsewhere? Well, on this subject he didn't go into too much more detail.

But he said that when he awoke his scalp bristled with an electricity only danger can generate, his skin prickled with it. In his nose, the smell of camels, elephants even, the prominent odors of his neighbor the Central Park Zoo.

He was so furious when he arrived at the apartment I thought his bald head would turn so red-hot he could cook an egg on it.

I've called the police in Jersey and here, and I've called the F.B.I.

You called the who?

The F.B.I. This is interstate, Mama (hardly his mother I was, but he called me this anyway, and I let him, because who doesn't feel sorry for a man such as this, no matter what his successes?) They say that they have to wait a certain number of hours before they can start on a case.

A case? This is a case? A girl took her mother on a picnic. How can that be called a case?

This man, he was the only person in the family I didn't like, even if I had some sympathy for him. I wanted to wash my hands of him—he was driving my Manny so hard, showing him what he must do, one thing after another. And now he wants the F.B.I., *kinnahurra*, to come and chase my granddaughter?

It's that school, he said, pacing around the apartment. Manny should never have let her go to that school.

He's a good father, I defended him. She went where she wanted to go.

Well, look where it's got her.

Where has it got her? She took her mother on a picnic.

She's kidnapped her out of the hospital, he said.

Don't yell at me, mister, please.

What's all this? Manny asked as he came in the door.

He's yelling at me and we're not even related, I said to my son.

Mord?

Have you called the New England state troopers, Manny?

They've already found them, he said. I talked to them from the airport.

Where?

In Vermont. At her teacher's house. At her apartment.

They were having a picnic?

Yes, Mama, I suppose you could say that, my Manny answered to me.

They had driven directly to Vermont from Owl Valley, a trip that took several hours. The sun was going down when they arrived. Maby was asleep in the back of the car, but she woke up abruptly when they stopped at the apartment on the campus where Peale the painter stayed when she was up from the city.

It's too dark for a picnic now, isn't it? Maby said. When will we do it?

Tomorrow, Peale said.

Tomorrow, that's when, Sadie said.

And what do we do tonight? Do we go back to Owl Valley? It's a long ride, isn't it?

We'll stay here tonight, Mama. We'll eat dinner indoors. And you can come to class with me tomorrow. Would you like that?

I would love it, Maby said. And she climbed out of the car as enthusiastically as a child arriving at the house of a relative whom she loves dearly and desires to see.

Is this where you live? she asked the painter woman after they stepped inside. The walls were cluttered with more of Peale's giant woman paintings, breasts, ears, fluted noses, the Vs of thigh and crotch, tents of leg and hair, here and there an entire body or two clutching together as if falling through a terrible empty space.

Liberated territory of the super-gyn, the painter said. Right, Sadie?

Right.

It sounds like fun, Maby said. I never had fun when I was Sadie's age.

Or mine? The painter smiled, as she led her into the kitchen and began to look about for the makings of a meal.

I never was *your* age, Maby said.

The painter laughed. She lighted a funny cigarette and after sucking in smoke passed it to Sadie's mama.

What's this?

Try it, you'll like it, the painter said, pursing her thin cruel mouth into a crooked smile.

Maby took the little stick in her hand, studied it, took a puff and started coughing, choking. She kept trying. Strange, she said after a few minutes. She started helping with the salad while the painter cooked something in a skillet and Sadie set the table, as if mother and daughter had become daughters and the stranger, the painter, was the mother.

They give you a lot of medication there, don't they, Mama? Sadie asked as they were sitting down.

Maby nodded.

No more of that, though, the painter said. They drug us, it's the tranquilization of an entire gender, and we're not going to let that kind of shit go down anymore.

Hell no, Sadie said.

Strange, her mother muttered, staring at her plate. Are you thinking of driving me home now?

No, no, Mama, Sadie said. We're not taking you back. You're going to stay with us here awhile. You're going to get all that stuff out of your system. You're going to enjoy the country air. We're going to take walks, we're going to swim when the water warms up a little.

Does your father know about this?

Fuck the fathers, Peale said. Fuck and fuck and fuck them dead!

Strange, said Maby.

She doesn't mean kill them, Mama. She just means that we have to throw off the yoke of oppression all those generations of patriarchs have put on us.

And brothers? Maby said.

Them, too, Peale said, looking Maby hard in the eye. Why? Did your brother oppress you as well as your father?

Maby lowered her head until her brow touched the edge of her plate and began to whimper like a hurt little beast.

I'd better go back, she said after a minute. Sadie was touching her shoulder.

There, there, she was saying. There, there.

I should want this, shouldn't I? Maby was saying. I should, I should.

Mama. Sadie kept on stroking her shoulder. We're damaged women. We have to help ourselves repair ourselves. Do you see?

I see you.

What?

Maby picked up a knife from the table, sliced it across the tender underside of her right forefinger and drew in quick bloody strokes on the tablecloth:

Mother, are you . . . ?

I'll get a—Peale was rising.

But a knock at the door interrupted her.

You want adventure? You want to see what happened next? I'm telling you, I'll give you adventure, as if adventure is not my heart like it's beating now, thumpa-thumpa-thumpa-thump, thumpa- thumpa-thumpa-thump! family life! that's adventure! Go join a war, start a fire, build a city—the boredom sets in very soon. But raise children, watch them grow, and you'll know horror and love and fear and worry, you'll learn real pain and your wounds may never heal. In an accident you only die once, but in a family you go on living. Didn't I? Didn't most of us?

Peale went to the door, and the policemen, after muttering a few words, pushed their way in. Behind them came the two men in suits who immediately began reading to them from a little card. Maby burst into tears. Sadie started swearing. Peale, her eyes full of fire, made her big mistake. She picked up the knife.

The next thing she knew she was falling back against the kitchen counter, the victim of a very big swing of a fist by one of the police. Later, when she sued, this was a big thing, the punch. But everyone in the room saw the knife in her hand, and that made all the difference. They had so much on her at that point it nearly didn't matter about the attempt with the knife, if it was an attempt at all. They had Maby in the house and the dope on the table, if they wanted to use this against her. (Later, sad woman, Peale probably wished that she had plunged the blade into her own chest.)

Aw right, ladies. The men said this a lot of times before emptying the room. Sadie and her mother they took to the office where the campus police called Manny where he was waiting at the airport. The two men in suits escorted Peale into another room and talked to her for a while.

We took my mother on a picnic, that's all, Sadie told them over and over.

Some picnic, some picnic, the men said over and over. That's what I say too. It ended with the painter woman out of her job, back in New York and ready to kill, really. And Maby, very upset, back in Owl Valley. And Sadie, what was with her? She stayed in school, behaving as though she had made a silly error. As though wanting her teacher and girlfriend, Peale, and her mother, Maby, living together with her in a little house on the campus might have been all she was looking toward. As though she had not hoped that her action would in a brief terrific burst of emotion take her father's heart and sear it like meat on a fire and shrivel it into dried leathery tissue. Now that my Manny—though it was Mord who called the New York police, he was acting for my Manny, and so it all turns out to be the same, doesn't it?—now that Manny had blocked her game, not even knowing, of course, that it was a game, a dangerous kind of play but a game nevertheless, she turned quite serious, keeping her lips buttoned tight, but planning all the while when the time and place and scheme seemed right to take her revenge against her father not only for his inability to help her in her hour of need after the mess at Rutgers, and not only for forcing her mother out of the house and into the hospital—because she did place the blame squarely on him, and who wouldn't, if she had no sense of how life was as much to blame as the people who lived it?—but now, on top of these old scores, she added the new grudge of vengeance, the charge of taking her friend's life, the life of Peale the painter, spreading it across his knee and breaking it in two.

The funny thing was, although she still believed that she was fighting on, in part, to defend the wrong that he had done against her friend the teacher-painter, she became distracted from the woman herself. Now that the woman was in a way broken, Sadie often turned to other people for amusement. For instance, and this is not just a for instance but I'm just saying it that way, *for instance*, as if it just happened one among many because I don't want to sound like the trumpets and kettle drums at the beginning of the last movement of a symphony, *for instance*, she joined in a campaign that was growing in the city on the part of the group of crazy children called Jews for Justice.

Her father was writing a speech.

After all had seemed to have been said and done on the subject of Sadie's escapade with her mother, after Maby was back in Owl Valley more miserable and stranger than ever, after Peale was back in New York, out of a job and smoking so much of that stuff that her head was always filled up with the fog of illusions, and after Sadie pretended to settle back with her schoolwork and take up working with clay—and this is important, the part where the outside world begins to break in on the solitude of the immediate family—after my Manny's takeover of the Boston company became real, he was writing a speech.

He had, you see, his own illusions and delusions, and these were just as bad as those that appeared in the mind of Peale the painter born out of the smoke of that weed, or worse, because they came to him while he was supposedly sane and sober, alert and alive in the middle of the day.

His first delusion, of course, was that his daughter had settled back in school, while in fact she was merely biding her time. The first private delusion then. You got that one? And the second? It seems to be, to me to be, both private and public. Manny, my little boy from the old days, he's grown so wise and distinguished, and he's made such a success in taking over one of the oldest companies on the East Coast, that's suddenly convinced him that he can do something more than merely be big business. From rabbi to big business to what? He's on the verge, in his mind having already crossed over the line, of stepping into yet another walk of life—diplomacy.

You see what I mean about my baby? How he didn't need no dopey plant leaf chopped up into a tobacco to live his waking days in a dream? *Oi, oi, oi,* my Manny, my Manny, from where did all these dreams and fantasies speed out to you? the talking bird? the delusions in the mind? Listen: he had a lot of things going for him—he had, maybe, too much going for him, and so he got carried away. But the fact is he grew and grew, slipping out of one life like a snake's skin and taking on another, and there he was getting ready to change himself once again, when it all came down on his head.

This is how.

Rick Sommers, that darling grandson of our Mrs. Pinsker, the youth leader who became an assistant dean at Rutgers, he renewed his acquaintance with his old employer when they had to take care of the business of Sadie at the fraternity house.

What could he say at first? He was sorry, very sorry, that any of it took place. And since the former rabbi wanted to keep things quiet he was well pleased to do the same. After some appropriate punishment for the boys involved, of course. All of them were suspended and the fraternity was put on social probation—no parties—for a semester. A few of the boys in the group, none of those directly involved, grumbled a little, but compared to the possibility of a trial for their brothers, they had to admit the punishment wasn't so bad.

So here is this boy become a dean, one actor in the next to last act of this play. A minor actor, like the taxi, like the fire truck, but an important one nonetheless. Him I can see with my eyes closed, a light-haired fellow, handsome, he doesn't look very . . . you know, blue eyes, neat suits, a nice smile. Who knows what he was doing in his life except studying since he worked as a youth leader, and remember the Purim dance? Maybe he's engaged to a nice Jewish girl—to a law student or a doctor, maybe. And he's the kind of fellow who's very unhappy with the way he had to fix the problem with Sadie, unhappy for everybody all around. Unhappy with what happened to her, unhappy that the boys did this, unhappy with having to punish. College is paradise and he hates to play the snake. And in his cheerful thoughts a few years later he gets an idea, he's been reading the business section of the *Times*, following my Manny's progress with the growing company, with the latest takeover. And the idea he gets, is to have one of the campus organizations invite my Manny to give a talk, and in anticipation of this, Rick Sommers suggests that the school award my Manny an honorary degree. The president, whatever his name, loves the idea, you know, a former rabbi who in his philosophical wisdom becomes a successful East Coast business magnate. What else could better take away the bad taste of the unfortunate incident with Sadie?

And there is another actor involved here, too, a smaller part, I should tell you, but one that makes big waves. Say he's like the horse that drew the milk wagon. A nice-looking boy, a Jewish boy for sure, since what he did was organize . . . But wait, let's just say he's working behind the scenes, and it will come out in a minute when I tell you what he's doing. He could have been—he was a student there—might have been the same boy, remember him? that Sadie met on the street and who gave her directions, him or one of his roommates, why not? He had a plan. So here, listen.

Rick Sommers invited my Manny to give his speech, and Manny was so proud when he got the invitation. Like a little boy again almost he was. This is what I mean. Even at his highest he was never showing off, just feeling good, wanting his mother to know.

Can you imagine? he said to me over the telephone just after he got the call. And when he came home, hours and hours later, over the dinner I fixed for him—I sent home the cook and did it all by myself, like the old days—he was still talking like he was a child again, standing on the roof of the old building, looking out across the rooftops toward the uptown, saying to himself, one day I'm going to own a building like that, like that, the spires in his mind, the glass windows, the towers.

I have worked hard, he said.

Yes, darling.

I have worked harder than most men I know.

Yes, darling.

I studied the Torah like I had no time left to live.

Yes, my darling.

And I threw myself into a business I didn't know and learned as much as any human being.

You did it, darling.

I have led two full lives where most men they don't know what it's like to lead even a full *one.*

Yes, you have. But please eat a little, Manny. It's getting cold. There was a veal chop on a plate, with nice spinach I had cooked. And a salad of lettuce and tomatoes, this we learned to eat over the years. But here is his plate in front of him, his food getting cold, like he was a boy again, and talking about what he wanted, his dreams.

I helped a few generations of congregations get themselves together.

You did, darling.

And I took old man Sporen's business and I have, with of course the enormous assistance of my brother-in-law, parlayed it into a company that has now the largest holdings in a country greater in size than New Jersey.

I'm impressed, my darling. I didn't know that—bigger than Jersey? That's big, my darling, that's big.

Mother. Mama. I have accomplished many things . . .

Yes?

. . . but even this last one, the putting together of the package, taking over the holdings down there in the country . . .

In the country? In the Jersey?

In that country *down there*, Mama. You know the Panama Canal?

Sure, I've heard of it.

Near there, Mama.

I've heard of it.

After supper I'll show you on a map.

I'll look at it, I'll see.

I was thinking . . .

Yes, darling. Look, there, please eat.

I will, Mama. But listen. I was thinking that I would fly down—organize an inspection tour of our new holdings.

A good idea. But you should wear short-sleeved shirts because it's probably very hot.

He laughed. When I realized that I had made my little big Manny smile I laughed myself. Why not?

I'll remember that, Mama.

And you'll get yourself a lighter suit for a change, Manny.

I'll think about it, Mama. But what I wanted to tell you . . .

You're telling me.

I'm telling you, if you'll let me have a word . . .

Take four or five.

I'll do that. Mama, I've been invited to give a lecture at Rutgers. Now what do you think of that?

I'm impressed. So who invited you?

And he explained to me the whole thing. Of course it wasn't until later that he told me how he had in mind inviting mother and daughter, which as it turned out was a mistake bigger even than Jersey. But this again was the little boy in him—he wanted to give his speech in front of his family so that they could puff up their chests in pride. Me, I didn't need no puffing, let me tell you. And you think Maby did? No, sirree. And Sadie? She puffed—on the funny cigarettes from her friend the painter, ex-teacher, who saw her now and then in Manhattan when she was supposed to be up at the school it was costing my Manny a pretty penny for her to attend.

Believe it or not, he went through with it, and Sadie and the Jews for Justice, they all showed up.

As my Manny saw it, for him it was the high point of his long climb after his first fall, the opening of another part of his life, the first step on a trip toward becoming a part of diplomacy, an ambassador somewhere in the world, and all of this, he was sure, was to come from the way he handled his new holdings. The company he took over had the worst reputation in the world for the way that it treated people *down there*. People called them everything including slaveholders, and a lot of it must have been true because my Manny went out of his way from the start to explain all the good things he wanted to do to change this. In his mind, he was going to make the business, the fruit and whatever it was down there, work better than ever, and he was going to do it in a way that would make everybody, north and south, feel good. Included in this package of dreams, was, of course, the idea that he was going to show Sadie once and for all that he was not the monster she took him for. What he wanted to show Maby, that's harder to say. I suppose, big man that he was, he was just being a little more sentimental than I expected—his mother I could see he should have around at this time, but the wife who had such trouble and made so much trouble, did she have to be there too? It could have been that deep in his heart—and my Manny, after all, had a good one—he wanted to make a complete picture, the mother, the wife, the daughter, the grandmother who was also his mother, in his hour of greatest success. If everybody in the picture, present person excluded, wasn't a little crazy, it would have worked. Oh, darling, remember how he talked to you about it? Remember how you wanted to come but didn't even dare try to sneak in?

I want to see you, you said. I want to see you in action.

Impossible, he said. I'm bringing Maby, Sarah, and my mother.

Bring me.

Impossible.

I'll come by myself then. I'll stand in the crowd.

There won't be a crowd. You'll stand out.

I'll wear a mask. I'll paint my face.

Then you will stand out.

I'll sit down, I'll wear a veil.

Who is the lady in the black veil in the back row? The mystery lady, Darling, I don't think so. I don't.

I'll bring a pen. I'll sketch you, I'll make a record for you of your triumph.

My triumph. Not a triumph at all. But certainly something very satisfying to me. I wish only . . .

What? you asked him.

I wish . . .

You're weeping, you said. You touched a hand to his cheek.

My . . .

He was choking on his memory, pouring tears out from his wish.

What is it, Manny? you said to him, cradling him in your arms.

My father . . .

He wanted Jacob to be there to see him, he wanted to pull his spirit up out of the dark where it has rested all these years and put him in a seat in the whatever-it's-named auditorium and make the speech for him to hear, in front of all the students and teachers for him to see. And if my Jacob might be wondering what's the problem with the family – with the wife who doesn't look at the husband, and the daughter who shoots heat from her eyes, like lightning, at the father, and the father, however big a success he is, struggling to hold the family together for just this afternoon – well, he would look and see the success and that would be enough to return with into the dark, into the forever ended, into the black hole where my eyesight stops and the nothing of the rest of the time of things begins.

Forty-seven! Manny shouted, pounding his fist against the pillows of your bed. Forty-seven! Forty-goddamned-seven! (*Oi,* and how he cursed, for the first time he did this, and you can imagine, well, you saw it in his fiery eyes, in the reddening cheeks, the puffed up shoulders, the emotion he was feeling.) And I'm like a little boy! I have this speech to make, and all I really care about is that I could make it in front of my father! I have this company, and all I really care about is that I could show my father what I've done! I have this country, I explained it to you, an entire goddamned country almost, and it means nothing to me . . .

It means a lot to you, you interrupted him, stroking his head, stroking.

No, it means nothing. Nothing, because I cannot have the satisfaction . . .

Your mother will be there.

No! and here he pounded again, and doesn't it strike a little spark of misery into my heart to hear this? Yes, it does, but it is the truth, and that is all I know, sitting here in the dark, that is all that comforts me. So I tell you again, and I listen again as I tell you, and I'm sad as I was when I heard it the first time, but so what else is new? A mother is sad? So a mother is sad. And the sun goes down. And the stars come out, with a moon.

Once more in the night you drew him in, caring for him as I would have had he searched for sleep and comfort in my own arms, if he had become a real little boy again instead of only a man with white hair who felt young and helpless. But he was not truly helpless, as you know, because of what he did with you after you put out the light and took off his clothes, and yours, and cupped his aching sacs in your palms and sluiced his mouth with your tongue, brushed his eyelids shut with lips wet with saliva, and sketched his body for a finished drawing with your own, your own. No, no, what you do in the dark is not your business only when you do it with my son, because at times like these I am with him in his pleasure because of the times I am with him in his pain, we have been that close from the beginning, we will be that close to the end, and though he has ended he will not become an eclipse until my voice goes out like my lights.

Remembering his best and highest moments, I could cheer. Seeing the sheer drop before him I could tear my hair, pull my eyes, yank my fingernails out by the roots and turn my bleeding fingers into tree limbs, burning in brushfires, slaked by the driest winds.

Manny.

My Manny.

Where are you now? With your father? And do you hold his hand pressed to your chest as you did when you were a little boy? And do you glance with admiration at his thick dark beard, hoping for the chance to give it a playful tug? to show him how much you love him? to make him feel the pressure of your presence, your life?

You arrived, my son, in the college town in your long black automobile driven by the man from *down there*, one of the Spaniards you always had driving for you, and you enjoyed conversing with him in his language, a little of which you were learning every day, yet another tongue as you had learned English and Hebrew, and now learning the Spanish, a real smart scholar you were, sometimes enjoying more the thrill of learning than using what you learned, I think, and you had with you your wife, who sat silently, hands folded in her lap, in the thrall of the pills that kept her quiet most of her waking days, and you were to meet your daughter here in the hall where you were to speak—she had refused to come down with the two

of you in the car, preferring instead to find her own transporta-
tion, but that was all right, because you valued her independ-
ence now that she seemed to have thrown off the yoke of that
vile and vicious creature of a teacher who had caught her up in
her plans with even more of a tenacity than the hold the pills
had on your wife, her mother . . .

And it seemed right and fitting that this should be taking
place, you in the same dark suit and white hair that you had
when you first addressed your first congregation (though the
suit now was made of fine wool, but still the same dark shade,
black, black, yea the very essence of all the black suits you had
worn, and worn out, in your lifetime thus far), and Maby in her
light brown suit, a color that didn't become her hair—she paid
little attention to what she wore, although aided by nurses and
social workers she had made some effort to look smart and
tailored, because of the nature of the occasion . . .

And you, my Manny, as the long black car slid as if on silent
wheels onto the campus, could see the crowds of students filing
up and down the avenues, and saw the crowds thicken as the
car slowed down in its approach to the hall. You had now several
years of such appearances, before boards of elders from the
thickest stock of the gentile rulers, and that never fazed you.
You had years of wrangling with accountants and consultants
and specialists, in paper and machinery and oil and gas and
heavy construction and ships and now agricultural experts,
agronomists and econometrical engineers of the size equivalent
to builders of small cities and growing empires on sea islands
and isthmuses, these things you did and I never understood the
inner parts of them, how they worked, but then you ate my
cooking all these years in our childhood and you never wondered about the recipes, the seasonings, the heat and length of
simmering, the time for pickling, the role of fats and oils, and
just as you had mastered the study of the laws you mastered the
means and methods of these businesses, yea, better yet, you had
the impression that you could and would and had and did, and
you understood that after all was said and done you still had
yourself and your integrity, the ability to make the right decision at the lowest cost in terms of cash and human dignity also,
and pleasure, all of these you factored. I never knew how you
did it—to me it always seemed you had magical powers. That
you could walk into a room full of experts and make them see

that you had more expertness than they, more expertise, is that the word? and more insight and foresight and hindsight and sideways and upside down, all the powers in the world. Manny. My Manny. *Oi, oi, oi* . . .

Whew. I had to take a breath. But here you are, and your own breathing has become shallow, as if you are saving yourself for the big run, the speech. It has been weeks in coming, because you had so much to do, meetings, conferences, and more meetings, more conferences, and as the news of the takeover reached the ears of the reporters more interviews and more, and finally you decided that you would answer all of the questions that came up by giving the speech at the university, a speech in which you could state the policy of your company and your position as a man—my Manny. And you would use the occasion to give Maby the chance to try and come back into your life (and, oh, darling, my listener, I know how this hurts you to hear, but still it's the truth and I had to say it!). And you would use the occasion of the speech to show your daughter, the wayward and (you hoped not permanently) estranged little (I call her little but she's not little no more) Sarah-Sadie that you could do good as well as the other of which she thought you were capable of only. And you would use the occasion of the speech to speak to your brother-in-law, Mord, and give him some guidance for how you wanted the company to grow.

You walked into the hall to see that about two hundred people had already taken their seats and dozens more stood at the back of the room, waiting for your appearance. You smiled, and touched a hand to your blizzard-white hair. The first thought that came into your mind was this: this is a long way from Second Street (you thought of the street, the old apartment, the blood-stained butcher paper and horse dung and dead birds in the gutters). And in your pocket you fingered the star-shaped shard, old partner, souvenir of lost times. Would but that you could listen now to a bird speech, the guiding voice of your papa, but no, the noise drowned out all sense of recollection, and after turning to smile at Maby, you led her by the arm toward your host at the front of the hall.

Rabbi, said the boy turned man who once had worked for you, now with a slight thickening of flesh under his chin.

Mister, if you please, you said, Manny. But you smiled as you said it, making him feel at ease. That smile, that smile that won so many votes in recent days, won over shareholders by the hundreds, picked up shares by the millions! What a smile, the dawn breaking over the horizon on a summer day in the mouth of my only son!

And here is Sadie, in the company of her old pal, the boy turned dean. Brave girl to have ventured back here, the scene of the crime. But that was a few years past now, you assured yourself, and the memory of it had faded. Look how she stands tall, shows her own heady ways, tosses a brief hello to her father, and then scans the crowd, as if there might be someone here she knows.

And the dean introduces you to the head of the political science, or whatever, foreign relations, something, who has actually invited you, and you come forward to the podium and take a seat behind it. The professor, or whatever he is, steps up to the microphone to introduce you. You settle yourself in your chair, looking at your wife and daughter who have taken seats in the row reserved for them at the front of the hall.

You don't love yourself that much that you listen to the remarks the professor makes in his introduction. Instead you're trying to concentrate your energy on your delivery, something you've prided yourself on ever since you took over your first congregation. No, not *Rabbi* any longer, but *Mister,* but still you can't leave behind all that you learned, not the technique. And you're remembering the discussion you had with the brother-in-law just at the time that you decided to go ahead and accept the invitation to speak in which he leaped to his feet, an older man suddenly rejuvenated, and grabbed you—quite uncharacteristically—by the shoulders.

That's it, he said.

What's it? you asked.

Give the talk, state our new policy. The press will pick it up, what a boost for the reorganized stock. You've got to do it.

You didn't tell him about your sudden awareness of what you could do even beyond the business, how you could work with these foreign governments, and show your growing expertise as a man of diplomacy, and use the reformed company's role *down there* as an opening toward an eventual diplomatic appointment. These were what we used to call pipe dreams, or daydreams, but then, my Manny, you seemed to be one of those people with the power and the luck – your father watching over you – to turn your daydreams into real things. You didn't say a word about your new idea about going into diplomacy. And if you had, why he might have laughed, the brother-in-law, and that might have changed how you felt about it, it might somehow – but would it? – have prevented you from going through with this – but I doubt it – and that would – might – somehow? – have saved you? but for what? another way of going as quickly as you did? Oh, my Manny, this two-minute conversation with Mord, it started everything tumbling faster, faster, deciding then and there to use your talk as – what? (see the light in Mord's eyes) as – a – what? as a send-off for A TRIP DOWN TO THE HOLDINGS!

That was it, my Manny. You would take a business trip, a what-do-you-call-it? a fact-finding trip, like a congressman, like a senator, and you who head the new company will see firsthand for yourself what the old managers did wrong, and see how the operation functions now, and make recommendations for changes that will show the stockholders and the new board and the press and the public that this is a company for the future and show you, yourself, as a man – my Manny – for the future!

(It's dark here? *Darker*? Put on another light!)

Mr. Emmanuel Bloch, president and chairman, chief executive, all that is said.

And there is applause.

And you rise. And walk forward to the lectern, your speech in a folder in one hand, the other in your pocket for one more quick touch of fingers to the shard. RG'S DAI. And you take your place behind the stand, and you look down into the audience, into the first row, and you see your redheaded women, the mother, the wife in brown, the daughter in dark sweater and jeans, though the mistress – that word, ugly word, I'm sorry, I'm sorry – *she* is missing because of all the reasons you went through, the awkwardness, the shame, but you are here with him now, because I am putting you here, are you not? with him in the aftermath, in the afterfact, which is as good as any way we got of being anywhere other than where we are ourselves, as good as any way of living any life other than our own.

And you are with him as he blinks at the vision of the
women sitting below him, and he sees me, his mother, sitting
alongside them, and he blinks again, and I'm gone, and he
remembers that Yom Kippur afternoon when he looked down
and saw us and fell— flew?—from the dais, and he blinked again,
and his mind soared up to some crazy perch where it waited for
the voice of the dove, and then back again to inhabit the brain
cage in the body where he stood, thinking, I have done this
before, and I will not fall this time. No, I will not! I will not!

But he might have right then and there if he had not begun
his speech.

I am a businessman . . . representing a business that is sound
because of two established policies.

One, that its business dealings with others are mutually
beneficial to both parties, and two, that its employee-employer
relationship is animated by a sound social and economic con-
sciousness.

(It started beautifully, don't you think? Such an opening!
I am a businessman. Because it was true, and he knew that, and
he finally found it out, and for a man, my Manny, my sonny
boy, to know who he was, this was a blessing for the mother.
So many boys, they never know, they never know.)

The essence of good trade is that all parties shall derive
important or desirable advantages from each transaction. Mutual
advantages are the essence of inter-American relations today and
tomorrow. Our Western Hemisphere has become a community
of nearly half a billion people, Americans, all interdependent in
trade, prosperity, culture, and progress. The enduring good of
one American nation, in this case the United States or each of
the three smaller nations where we have much of our holdings,
is inevitably the good of others.

The socioeconomic philosophy . . .

(Why I remember this speech better than I remember all the
sermons he gave—except the sermon of silence—it beats me. But
it could be because this was something that I understood so
little of, and that because it was so foreign to me it stuck in my
mind. All of these words, those phrases! Oh, for years he studied! And to think it all began at that stream when I looked at my
Jacob, and he looked at me! And further back and further back,
I know, I know . . .)

The socioeconomic philosophy which motivates our thirty-five hundred mile trade-and-work front is this: good trade requires healthy, solvent peoples. You cannot do business with peoples or nations who have neither the money nor the credit with which to buy the goods you have to sell or to produce the goods you wish to buy. And a people we cannot do business with is a people who may be ripe to do business with the other side. With the communist nations of eastern Europe and their satellite island of Cuba.

The agricultural sphere of our operations is largely concerned with the sovereign American nations of the Caribbean area included in the phrase *Middle America,* and also Colombia and Ecuador in South America, with a small metal-mining interest in Peru.

Middle America. The phrase may remind you of a part of our own country. Consider this. Mexico and the republics of Central America . . .

(Consider this, if you had been there, he would have had you hypnotized, my Manny would. He was that good a speaker. Not just the words, but the voice, the deep commanding voice, with just the slightest bit of hesitation, the part left over from his days as the rabbi who had more questions than he had answers, just the slightest bit, so that if you have questions you feel as though he is already making them for you. And besides his voice, his hair—how could you not stare at that blinding white shock, the brilliant hair that drew in your soul, almost, through your eyes until sometimes it felt as though you had passed along the line of your vision like a tightrope walker between one pole and the next and you were sucked into the blank space of the whiteness of the color so that you lived within another place inside some dimension inside his head.)

Consider this. Mexico and the republics of Central America—Guatemala, Honduras, El Salvador, Nicaragua, Costa Rica, and Panama, with their dozens of millions of inhabitants who consider themselves—as we do, *Americans,* and who sell us four-fifths and sometimes more of their total exports, and buy from us more than three-quarters of all their imports, these countries, most of them, are actually closer to us here in New Jersey than is San Francisco or Portland, Oregon. Middle America is close to us, and destined to become closer. These nations, our partners in trade, and with their millions yearning to come out from under the yoke of petty dictatorships and the threat of Communist takeovers, need us. And we need them. We want the essential crops that flourish in the tropical climate of Middle America which we desire and cannot grow ourselves.

(Words! but in here, in his head, there is light. Words give off flame and heat, they point like fingers at a map, at a block of land, at time like the hands of a clock! This space where he has nursed his vision, it is vast and without ceiling, a hall without a roof, planet without cloud or atmosphere, nothing stretching between surface of rock and the farthest blinking star, oh six-pointed shard of flight! And here live gentle creatures, so different from the human beings we know as to make the feeling between words like *Portland* and *Salvador* and the noise given off by this white-hot light appear to be as unalike as space is from sound. Without eyes even I see father, mother, daughter, brother, and the father and mother of the father and mother and the brother, their bodies giving off light like shocking white, calm color, absent darkness, band of peace, a tribe wandering across a windless plain, grassy sward where picnics go well, while above them heaves a moon so large it nearly deserves another story.)

Bananas.

Pineapples.

Sugar.

Palm oil.

Coffee.

(Between these words, the fruit, the sweetness, the coffee, the oil, and the great swarm of doves rising behind the gigantic moon, what connection? what tie? this is what my Manny is asking himself, this is what to himself he is saying even as he is speaking these words—because he stands before this crowd, saying his business sermon, and inside his own brain he is falling, or flying, how to tell the difference in a space where gravity doesn't hold? faster and farther, up and up toward the moon, one of the birds, one of the beams of light that hovers like the rung of a ladder of light between the strange earth he imagines and the distant shard-shaped star.)

To name the major crops that our company grows and cultivates in the soil of Middle America.

(Did you know this? I didn't know this. But I didn't know as much about my Manny now, this became pretty clear to me after a while, all of what I knew about his modern life I had to hear from him in bits and snatches over meals, over coffee, in the last few months before this last flight of his life. His life! his life! If you had predicted it I wouldn't have believed – to go from talking about boys' things, work, his studies, Talmud, Torah, sermons on doing right and avoiding wrong, on family and friends, on fathers and mothers and sisters and brothers, on grandparents and grandchildren, these things everybody like him *except* him would have talked about until the end of their days, to go from this to talk of packages and bottle tops and glass and steel and boats and piers, and now of ships and fruit, bananas, palm oil, who who who would have known?)

The company's most important crop, of course, is bananas – of which it now owns and operates two hundred and fifty thousand acres in Middle America. The banana is one of mankind's oldest crops, and it is not native to the Americas.

(You heard that? The fruit he's talking about it, it too was an immigrant, like our family, and like the rest of us, except for maybe the Indians, and them, too, we all come here from someplace else. But from where? From the old country, or from the moon? When I tell you about this speech of my Manny's, or what happened on this afternoon, I got to ask you that.)

Chinese literature of three thousand years ago mentions bananas. They are called *the fruit of the wise*. But imagine if, instead of the apple that tradition has as the fruit with which Eve tempted Adam, it was in fact the banana – *the fruit of the wise* that grew on the Tree of Knowledge. In 327 B.C. Alexander the Great discovered bananas growing in the valley of the Indus in India. Later, history records the crop's further journey westward. In 1492, a famous year for us in America, the Portuguese found the fruit growing along the African West Coast where the people there gave it the name *banana*. At the time Columbus launched his voyage, the banana, some historians tell us, was growing abundantly in the Canary Islands. In 1516 Father Thomas de Berlanga . . .

(Because it's turning now, I got to tell you what's happening, in his head he's no longer walking in a fantasy. He's concentrating on the crowd – on the fixed, firm, attentive faces, mostly young, with here and there a professor wearing a dark beard – like the old neighborhood he's thinking when he allows himself a glimpse of the beards – and he's losing attention from his dream in his mind and beginning to focus on the audience because somehow or other—you know my Manny's magical senses—he's already got a feeling of what's about to take place even before there is any way of telling from the look of the crowd or the sound of the crowd or the smell of the crowd—because they're college students, mostly, and they smell of sweat and cigarettes and here and there a little perfume, and here and there a little dope cigarette—it's turning.)

. . . a Spanish Dominican, carried the roots of the banana plant with him when he sailed to Santo Domingo as a missionary. From there the culture of this ancient fruit fanned out to various points on the mainland of Central America and to one Caribbean island after another.

The fruit is old. But the banana trade as we know it is definitely new. The first bananas to arrive in New York were brought here from Cuba in 1804. By 1830 occasional clipper ships were bringing small cargoes from Cuba and the Bahamas. This trickle gradually increased, though as recently as the Philadelphia Centennial of 1876 red bananas wrapped in tinfoil were sold as an exotic curiosity.

It was not until the introduction of the modern refrigerated steamship at the turn of the century that the real banana industry was born.

(And he has one strange thought before it all begins to break apart, my Manny does, up there on the podium looking down upon those faces, listening for a moment to his own words— he's thinking, What do we know? what do we know? and the design suddenly came clear, it fell into place, all the pieces shifted into the pattern—and he saw that he was standing in for Adam, the first man, to whose lips Eve had raised the forbidden fruit, the delectable produce of the Garden, long, slender golden offshoot of the Tree, and together they had eaten, first him taking a bite, then her, then him, then her, until all the nourishing shaft was gone, and so they ate another, and another, and to the animals in the trees, the monkeys, and to the dogs in the bushes, the cats in the furrows, they passed along the food, and down even until the next generation, and the next, and the next, and now he stood, carrying forward the first tradition, assuming the leadership of this company whose power lay in its ability to clear spaces in the wet lowland jungles and plant with the thousands of hands they owned the so-called bits or rhizomes from which the first lusty young shoots would rise—and he stood as one with the first human shoot, the male Adam, and Maby with Eve, the first woman, but isn't it strange what my Manny's idea would do to me, his mother. It would make me, you see, into the mama of Adam, Creator, or, how do you say? Creatrix? the Mama God, not the Virgin but the Goddess, Maker Mother of all that lived, and lives, on earth!

But from this crazy thought his mind immediately fell away, as if it had climbed too high—and as he delivered the rest of his speech, as he outlined the company's holdings and its policies and its future projects, though he spoke with more conviction, now that he had convinced himself that there had been, working through it all, a reason why a former rabbi had taken over a company that grew and shipped and sold this exotic fruit, as he hypnotized himself and he hoped the audience with his explanations and projections, a boy with dark hair and tortoiseshell glasses took some steps that changed everything.)

This boy: now he might have been the one, like I said, who gave Sadie directions on that terrible afternoon as she was walking across the campus, or he might have been a stranger, another child, but he was, not, finally, an unknown—he became, even in his awful doings, in a way like a member of the family—as I see it now, because, like some man who fires a gun that kills a president or king, out of his action grows something so intimate as to be so personal that it belongs more to you than most of your own actions, because it changes your life and the lives of others close around you—this boy: say that his name was Alan Kaplan or Mitchel Markovitz or James Bloom or Norman Fruchtman, and say that he was raised, like many good boys my Manny had known—and like the good boy he was himself—in some congregation, synagogue or temple, Orthodox, Conservative, Reformed, whatever the direction it doesn't matter, and say that after a time he cleaved from the laws, and he discovered another way of living, say a way like my Manny's, a way of living in the world without religion, but say that this boy, he belonged to a time when his soul ached from the lack of the laws, and he wanted something to set him on the straight and narrow, and he found friends with the same soul-ache, and they became boys who wanted some different kind of political situation, a change of government, but at the same time they fell back into the line of the laws that raised them, and they talked and they read and they met and they wrote, on campus that's easy, and they formed a group called Jews for Justice, a catchy name, don't you think? some catch for my Manny I'll say, and they followed the progress of my son's rise in the business world, my Manny was only one among many they followed, but he was the one on whom they took their aim, because he had risen so high, and lived so near, and when they heard that he was coming to speak at the university they organized a plan, and the plan was to make a demonstration that would point up the truth of what they believed he was doing—carrying out the work of imperialism, as they put it, instead of following the laws of the Torah—some cartoon world they lived in, and where are they now? all in business themselves I wouldn't be surprised, or becoming dentists or shoe manufacturers, nice boys following their own fathers' businesses, or going to law school, or teaching college, Jews for Justice!

But whatever they were, whether right or wrong, touched by the finger of God Himself—or Herself—or Itself—whatever—or crazy in their devotion to the Torah of Maimonides or Marx (you didn't think I knew such things but from talking to my Manny over the years, from listening to him, I hear these names, I hear these ideas—a mother doesn't just teach, you know, sometimes, big miracle, she even learns!) here comes this Alan or Mitch or Norman or James, whatever his real name, and he's got his gang with him, the group or cadre or circle or cell or club, whatever they call themselves, here they come, shuffling in from the back of the hall, and they're wearing denim and scruffy beards and wearing yarmulkes—*yarmulkes!*—and they're carrying signs and they're chanting,

> RABBI GUATEMALA!
> OUT OF THE AMERICAS NOW!

and

> JEWS FOR JUSTICE SAY,
> OUT OF THE AMERICAS!

(So what is this? I should have stood up and shook a finger at them, so what is this that a Jewish person can't behave like any other person? a Jewish person can't make a business? can't

take over a company and try to make it better? because that was
what my Manny had in mind—he got the confidence and shares
and votes of the majority of holders exactly because this was
what he pledged to do, and they didn't want just anyone to take
it over, they had a bad time with it for years, they knew how
bad it was, they wanted someone to *make* it over by taking it
over, they wanted someone with a vision, with a knowledge of
the law, with a conscience, you see the business life isn't all bad,
they wanted my Manny because of what he promised to them
by the way that he presented himself both in his looks and in
his plans—but in this world things don't move in straight lines,
do they? even a grandmother who can't see no more knows
this—this world makes for motion by collision, and here was the
collision and the crash making a noise, and having an effect, as
loud and as great as the smash and destruction of taxi and fire
engine and milk truck and my poor Jacob's wagon—everybody
in a hurry, nobody in the wrong, and out of it everything is
changed.)

   Rab-eye Gwat-a-mal-a! they're chanting.

   Rab-eye Gwat-a-mal-a! they're shouting at the top of their
lungs.

   And my Manny stops his speech—the air swells with the
noise of those chants and the outcries from others in the
audience, some of them shouting down, some shouting up—
and he looks out upon the crowd like a man observing the rising waters of an ocean in a storm. He sees his wife clutching the
arms of the chair, and he moves slightly forward toward the
edge of the stage, around the lectern toward the edge, and some
professors rush toward him, as if they expect him to fall forward
right then and there—but he's careful, he's done this before,
remember? It's Maby who worries him, sitting there clutching
the seat as if she might take off and fly up to the ceiling and hit
her head against the roof and break through, against all laws of
gravity, and fly out of this world—and he motions for Sadie to
turn around, her back is turned, she's observing the demonstra-
tors who stand chanting at the back of the hall—and he calls to
her, but who can hear amidst all this din?—but she does turn,
she turns, and she doesn't know he's watching her, she doesn't
know that he catches sight of her for a second with her lips moving with that phrase, he sees her lips moving, and his heart turns
over in his chest, like a fish it turns, a fish diving up out into the

light and then diving down again into darker waters, he sees on
her pink lips, the mouth of his daughter, only child, the lips
moving to the chant,
    Rab-eye Gwat-a-mal-a!
    Rab-eye Gwat-a-mal-a!

Or maybe he didn't see her chant it? There was suddenly chaos
here, a lot of noise and motion and confusion. He could have
been imagining things, my Manny. As you know he's good at
that upon occasion, but not on an occasion like this. This was
business. He was always very alert when it was business. But
there she was, or so he thought. And don't think he didn't say
something to her right away after the rest of the speech, after
the reporters came with their flashing bulbs, and the campus
police arrived to carry off the boys with the yarmulkes and
shouts and signs.

    You're coming with us? he asked her as the police led them
out to the car. You'll come home with us?

    Us? she said, bearing down on him with a stare, something
she hadn't done in years, for years it was always look off to the
side, stare at the sun, moon, anything but look her father in the
eye.

    Your mother will stay at the apartment tonight. And I'd like
you to come back with us.

    I have to drive back up to school.

    Come in the car with us. I'll drive. And Daniel can drive your
car back to the city.

    I'll drive.

    I said . . .

    I'll drive the big car, she said.

    He felt unexpected heat in his chest, and he smiled, in the
middle of all the noise, the police holding back some reporters,
and some bulbs still flashing on and off.

    It's a deal.

    Be careful, her mother said as Sadie climbed in behind the
wheel of the long black car.

    Mother, that's the first nice thing you've said to me in such
a long time I can hardly believe it. She was steering the long car
away from the curb. Some students ran alongside it, waving,
chanting, you could see their lips moving, though the words
became a blur . . .

Rab-eye Gwat-a-mal-a!

Don't speak to your mother that way, my Manny said, sorry as soon as he said it.

I'll shut up, sure, Sadie said, pretending to concentrate on her driving. Anyway, she couldn't hear me. But I'll shut up.

I didn't ask you to do that, my Manny said. He sat in the front passenger seat—he had decided that he would sit there instead of with Maby so that he could speak to Sadie once they got rolling. Now as he glanced back into the rear of the car, behind the glass partition, he noticed Maby looking so alone and forlorn, that he was sorry that he had isolated her—New Jersey rolling past her window, lights of the city and then highway, refineries, rest stops, the darkness of the turnpike on her face. She said not a word, not the entire trip. Or if she did the space between front and rear stopped the sound from reaching to his ears.

Sarah? He was, in any case, more interested in conversing with the daughter than with the wife.

This car drives neat, she said. I like the overdrive.

Don't speed, please, he said, I don't need any more bad publicity than we already received today.

Oh, they're just crazies, Dad, she said.

Is that all they are?

Just crazies. Nobody pays attention to crazies.

And you think they're crazy?

Why are you asking me that? I just called them that.

But do you believe that they are correct? Or that they're crazy?

Uh-oh, she said.

Answer me, please.

How can I answer you? There's always a little bit of truth in what people like that say. And a lot of fantasy.

So mature of you, my Manny said. Is that what the college has done for you? Then I'm glad, after all, that you went there.

After all?

I don't want to argue with you, darling. I was just asking your opinion.

My Manny was remembering the sight of her lips moving, remembering her mouthing the chant. For him all the rest of it— the escapade with the art teacher, stealing Maby away, the police, the agents—all of that was a closed book. He wanted only

to know whether or not she was part of it, part of the demonstration, part of the outside world, part of all of that against
which he had to work in order to make his way, make his mark.
For him, my Manny—I suddenly understand it now that I'm telling you—it was him and the cart and his father, and the rest was
rushing car and rearing horse and yowling siren, the crash of
the truck and the smash of glass. Can you imagine? Can you
imagine what it was like to live this way? I've been trying to
show you, and I hope that I have shown you, I've been trying
to make you feel what he felt, and I hope that I've made you feel
what he felt—this endless sliding back, no matter where he
stood, no matter what, back and back and back and back to the
crossroads of the crash and glass. It was like a scar he wore with
the rough ridges of the wound turned inside rather than out.
Except for his beautiful hair that everybody noticed, he showed
no outward sign of his difference. But different, as you long ago
knew, he was, and would be, while he lived. This difference,
of course, the children never know. But if you could look into
the hearts of others, if you could see a field, or a forest of hearts,
my Manny's you would notice for its rough and strangely over-
bearing growth.

What do you want me to say? Sadie asked.

I want to know.

You care about my opinion? You really care?

Of course, I do, darling. Of course I do.

Bull. Shit.

Don't use—no, not bullshit. What I said wasn't bullshit.

He could feel the car picking up speed, as though she drove
a team of horses and not this long sleek vehicle of steel and rubber and glass, horses that she whipped and whipped until they
roared forward, slobbering froth, with thundering hooves. He
wanted to say, slow down, slow down. But he bit his lip,
fingered the shard, waited for her to say something, anything.
Could he tell that this was his last chance to hold on to her? He
must have understood, he must have known somehow that it
was now—on this turnpike, rolling past the lights of oil refineries, factories, moon cities of gridwork, tanks, wires, even within
the car the air flavored with the stench of chemicals unholy and
disgusting—or never.

I want to know, he asked her, what do you think of my latest
venture?

Your latest venture?

My new holdings. The big company. General Banana.

She laughed, and said that it was such a silly name. And the label, the long yellow fruit with the officer's cap and epaulets, that was sillier still. It was a comic book, she said, her father was turning her life into part of a comic book.

Should I change it then? he asked. Should I call it Middle American Bananas? Republic Bananas? United Bananas? What about maybe Bananas United? Bananas Away? Bananas Awave? or People's Bananas? Major Bananas? Bananas Ahoy?

Why do you ask me? You're not going to change it if I say you should. You'll change if you think you want to. Why fool around and ask me?

I'm asking you. Because I'm asking you. I want . . . to know your opinion.

Bull. Shit.

Please, Sarah. We said we weren't going to do that, say that.

(This is how close they came. He came. How close! *Oi!*)

You don't want my opinion. You're just buttering me up because you're afraid I'm going to do something terrible again.

I don't think I'm buttering you up, as you say. I want to hear what you think.

(This is how close!)

Silence, nothing but the hum of the tires, the purr of the engine.

Sarah?

Are we going to take her back to Owl Valley? Or is she coming back to the city? She turned and tilted her head toward the rear where her mother sat silently, eyes wide open, staring at the lights ahead.

Sarah, you didn't answer my question.

What question?

Should I change the name, the label? Should I make them get a new brand name?

Oh! Is that what you wanted to know? Sure, let them do it. Get a new one?

Keep the old one. It's funny, it's a gas.

So you like it?

Sure, I like it.

So I'll keep it. Because you want me to.

I'm flattered.

I respect your opinion, he said.

Is this the exit?

Can't you see? If you can't see you shouldn't drive.

I can see. I'm just asking.

Yes, this is it coming up. And Sarah?

What?

I want to ask you something else.

Ask.

Would you . . . ? Uh . . . I'm making a trip down to the new holdings. I'm setting up an inspection tour. I want to see for myself what's going on down there, what we've got. I mean, thousands of people work for us now, and I think that I should go and see for myself exactly what the story is, what the picture is. And . . . I would like you to come with me. I would like that very much.

Take that trip? All the way down there?

I would like that.

Silence—hum of tires, whirring of engine. And then from the rear of the car, a faint (at first) wailing, like an infant lost, separated from its mother at feeding, the whimpering of a child. And then the louder noise, something like a scream or the out-cry of an animal tortured by some larger child. Both daughter and father turned around to see, and passed the exit, missed the turn.

Pull over, my Manny ordered her.

Here?

Right here, he said. And Sadie slowed the car down, and they rolled to a stop on the shoulder, in the dark, swamp ground to their right, cars rushing past on the left.

Ride with her, he said. I'll drive the rest of the way.

She needs you, Sadie said.

She needs, she needs, he said. You go on. Get back there.

Something in his voice—his life erupted through it. She didn't understand that—all Sadie felt was the way it pierced her, like a splinter, a shard of glass.

All right, she said. And she said to herself, all right. And she got out of the car and felt the cold on her face and neck. It was snowing.

· · ·

Somebody once said that hate stories go well in winter. Ice and dislike, they're alike. So here's snow, and Manny planning his trip. And the snow came down for a while, as it only seems to do in New York and Jersey, like a beautiful gift that breaks after only a little while, before you can really use it. For a few days, a week maybe, everything lay covered in white, and then everybody mixes in the dirt and the soot and dogs add their part—I was still walking on the street now and then at this time, and so I can remember what that was like—and so did the garbage men, who scatter as they collect, and pretty soon the snow was bordered in black, like a funeral notice for the lovely stuff it was when it first fell, and it melted a little and turned into dark lumpy chunks, the bad memory of its old self, and many citizens noticed that when it came to nature this part of Jersey left something to be desired.

Except for people like my Manny, who never notice anything around them because their eyes stare ahead into the future and down at the work on their desks. What do the seasons matter to a man whose life stopped and started again once when he was eight years old? He was like the rest of us, sure, he ate, slept, and suffered when his child spoke back to him, but he was also different, living in a different kind of time. But if he spent all of these years living his life—he's my son, but I have to say this—indifferent, finally, to the business of being a rabbi, and indifferent, finally, to the pain and torture inside of his very own wife—if one day he looked up and saw clearly a few words of hatred rolling from his own daughter's lips, *Rab-eye Gwat-a-mal-a! Rab-eye Gwat-a-mal-a!*, he shouldn't have been all that surprised. But here is where he made his own trouble, I think, and if I could have been there, if I could have sneaked in like some ghost or thief in the night and lay next to his heart and alongside his brain and camped out in his nerves when the question came up of doing something about her, I would have urged him to leave well enough alone! Leave well enough alone! Or leave half-bad enough!

But here was his problem, his fault, if you can call it a fault, I don't know if I have even the right words for any of this, but call it now a fault, and here it is: that he couldn't be either completely indifferent to the feelings and desires of these other people in his life, mainly the daughter now, and before that, before her feelings went underground like a stream in a dry season, the wife, my daughter-in-law, *or* that he couldn't get enough of their love for him, because this was how they felt for a long time, before the feeling went sour, rotten, what's the word? I'm telling you so I should know but sometimes the sensations go beyond the way to say it, that he couldn't devote his life to those he supposedly loved himself! Here is where he lived a life divided, and if you live that way, eventually you discover that you have to give up something, because it takes two people to live two lives, or nine people nine, and my Manny was fast approaching the point where he was going to find this out.

She's coming with us, he said to Mord in the office the next morning.

Why not bring your mother, too? (Oh, I never liked this man, but when he talks like this, could anybody in the world have any love for him?)

I'm serious, Mord, I'm bringing Sarah.

You're aware of what we have to do down there?

We have to fly in a helicopter and look at some banana groves. We have to walk through some warehouses and hospitals, we have to look at workers' housing. This is what we're saying we're going to do in our press release. So I'm taking my daughter with me—it will be even better press than we'll get already. I *should* take my mother. That would be better still.

And my sister? Should we take my sister?

No joking.

No joking, Mord said. We'll take them all. We'll turn it into a family cavalcade. We'll get complete TV coverage. What if we dress in native garb—picture this, you in a sombrero holding a machete, Rabbi Gwat . . .

We're taking her, Manny said. And that was that.

(And oh how I wish the rotten hateful brother had been more forceful—for all of a bastard, excuse me, for all of the *bastard* he was, for all the damage he did, what if he had been twice as bad, perhaps then he might have blocked my Manny in his plan, and everything, everything, would have been different! But if he had been more that way from the beginning, then that too might have changed everything. Oh the puzzle, how everything fits and falls into place!)

You remember what else we have to do?

We have to meet a general.

We have to meet *the* general.

General Banana.

You're making a joke but it's not funny, Manny. The hawk-nose cut through the air as the brother-in-law turned stiffly to one side. Manny, we own the company but we control nothing until we can arrange for the ceiling of the export tariff on the fruit. The general controls the export tariff on the fruit.

General Banana, I'd like you to meet Rabbi Guatemala. And this is how the world runs, two cartoon characters shaking hands. Rabbi, mucho gusto. General, I'm pleased to meet you. Shalom, shalom.

Manny, will you . . .

Will I what? My life, it's a joke and a tragedy, a success so big I can't describe it and a failure so abysmal I'm afraid to look at it. I want to bring my daughter, Mord, so we're going to bring her. Look, it will add to the occasion. I read the file you gave me on our new general, and he has a daughter himself—she went to college in Massachusetts, so it will balance out, my daughter from her fancy school, and his from Wellesley. And what has to pass between us, it will pass.

(They're standing at the ceiling-high windows of their office, looking south toward the harbor, toward the states between them and the border to Mexico, and southward beyond to the countries that on the map give the picture—I saw them before I couldn't see no more—of the country where my little boy now owns so much jungle and swamp that's been cleared to grow the famous ancient sacred fruit of the wise, *Gwat-a-mal-a!* I can still feel the chant on my eyes, and the words, even though merely whispered by my granddaughter, they sound like the clanging of a thick metal door—the crash of a cart, the wagon smashed into smithereens, the glass—the little country next door, like a long thin neck of a bird whose breathing you could stop with the twist of a wrist.)

So how does my soul come to power so great? my son asked himself and asked, and talking tried to answer. Part of it I can understand, he answered himself, the part we all share, the drive ahead, the dreams and wishes for managing, for control. And part I don't know, the invisible wind that pushes at the back of some people, and pushes back against the progress of others?

Whatever the reasons, get ready, because here he is, Florette you knew him, from the gutters of Second Street to the forests of Middle America. It could be a book, his story, or a movie, even, imagine, in color, a famous star, a serious man in middle age of middle height with hair the color of glaciers, his eyes piercing dark points of power, the face lined now by events printed upon it, a father, lover, son, and husband, a man of family and a man of the world, a man of spirit and a man of business, my son the hero, maker of sermons, maker of speeches, counselor to the sorrowful, advisor to the worldly, he's taking off now, he's racing along the runway, picking up speed, prepare for takeoff, and he's up . . . and away!

So look down at the islands from the window seat of the jet his company acquired in the takeover and see the rock ledges they rest upon leading into the ocean sea like stepping-stones toward the blue-green underwater kingdom. Could it be Atlantis? Jacob's sunken Atlantis? I don't know, should I know? Picture this—dolphins guiding the airplane south, sending signals silently up into the cockpit of the ship, a band of invisible beams steering us all. Or the restive mewing—dangerous to all but elephant and dinosaur—of the red-tinted jaguar caged within pyramids on the Yucatan peninsula. Here is the Jewish Italo-Hispanic explorer, watching his crew members shuck their clothes and dive naked into the bay boiling with Indian women, Tainos, Caribs, all lost tribes. Or the famous tribe itself, appearing one day on the eastern horizon, a people aboard on reed boats, in exile, hungry, tired, sick. Was there a cousin tribe to greet them? Or were they the first? Did only the thick-coiled anaconda notice their arrival, and did he stir in his sleep in the undersea mud, an insignia of the danger and the charms of a region so untouched by human beings that hummingbirds hovered at the ears of the newcomers and deer the size of rabbits lapped water from cupped palms?

He had read—she had read—father and daughter had both read histories in preparation for this trip, had read legends and mythology and reports, his supplied by his company researchers, hers supplied ever since the night of his Rutgers speech by the kids from Jews for Justice, and as they roared through the space above the lands in question, facts and processions passed by the dozens in and out their brains. As for the bloodstreams, their nervous systems, it was a different story. For him it was a feeling of racing toward reconciliation and new fame. For her, the tale was revenge, though the vehicle of her plot had yet to become revealed to her. His, of course, showed clearly below them, even as the plane banked and went into the first turn of its large, lazy spiraling descent. Both of them could see, as if they were observers at a display in some lower-grade classroom, a country like a relief map, its green ocean borders, the darker green of its forests, and here and there a volcano poking through the tree cover, like a smokestack in the factory chain of the gods.

Oh, if I could have been there, if by then my sight had not vanished and prevented me from going anywhere I would have pointed a finger, I would have said in the best warning voice I produce, Look, I would have said. Do you see how far from home you've strayed, my Manny? Can't you notice that these volcanoes spit dangerous fire? You who once peddled bananas with your father, who now own fields of fruit as far as the eye can see, can you see as far as the jungle bleeds its green into the lighter green of the sea? Your vision has grown that much? Go back, go back, you're still my baby, still a boy, and everything you've done since then has grown out of an accident. If you go further you'll have a greater accident yet, and when it goes smash you'll take a country with you, not just a cart. Please, my darling, tread lightly, tell the pilot, it's your plane now, turn around, fly north, north, and take a chance on a crop in a colder country—buy a bakery, make paper again, cap bottles, sell boats. Spend time with your crazy wife, pick flowers for her, twine them around her throat and wrists, eat meals with your mother, take your daughter to the movies, on trips to Europe, to the Holy Land, buy a camel, a saddle, show her the old tricks. Kiss your mistress on her lips and kiss her brown puckered nipples, dive into the rapture of pleasure you never imagined when a child. Take your brother-in-law to the theater, buy him cigars, cravats, tuxedos, Arab boys dipped in oil, make a party, have a dance. Pour out the punch bowl at Purim time, buy and sell your old congregations. But turn around, my child, my Manny, my son, turn the airplane—the ship—around! Turn, turn, turn!

I would have said.

And to *her* I would have said,

Honor thy father and mother.
And she would have said,
Fuck, Grandma, what are you talking about?
And I would have said,
Please, what kind of language is that?
And she would have said,
I still don't know what you're talking about.
And I would have said,

You honor your father and mother now and by doing so honor yourself. Because when you are older, when you are a mother, you will want your own children to treat you with respect. By respecting them you're respecting the self you will become. That's all.

And she would have said,
Children? Children, Gram? You got to be kidding!
And I would have said,
And why should I be kidding?
And she would have said,
The last thing I ever want is children.
And I would have said,

And what's wrong with children? I had a child, you know, I had your father, he was my child, and if I never had him you never would have been here, sitting in this fancy airplane, landing in some little country your famous father just bought for a song.

And she would have said,
That's a good reason.
And I would have said,
What are you saying?
And she would have said,
That's the reason.
And I would have said,

Your grandmother can't see so well, she can't hear so well, so tell me what is it that you're saying.

And she would have said,
That's the reason. That's why. Because if nobody had children I wouldn't be here. I wouldn't be feeling this way. I wouldn't know this pain.

And I would have said, a little shocked but I would have said anyway,

Pain? What pain do you feel, poor darling?

And she would have said,

Imagine a razor blade slicing across your wrists every minute of your waking life. And at night, dreams of puncture wounds, rusty nails through your breasts. And . . .

And I would have said,

Enough. Enough is enough. Here, the plane is landing. Look at the scenery—beautiful trees, did you ever see such a jungle in your life? Such beautiful greens and oranges and yellows and reds and blues—there's a parrot, blue as the sky, a flowering tree like something out of a picture in a museum. Except here—as the wheels touch down, the bumpity-bump, remember when I rocked you, bounced you on my knee? The slowing to a halt, the hatch opening, and the heat rushing in, like someone opened a door to a room on fire. All right, since you're here, get on with it, I would have said. Get on with your trip, with your life. Help your father after all, be a good girl, listen to him, watch him. After all, blood is thicker than water, blood is blood is blood. Did I say he bought this country for a song? I was only kidding. He's got a piece of paper in his pocket that's worth a million dollars. Can you imagine that much money? And he's going to hand it over personally to the man who sets the export tariff—this much I learned—on the fruit he grows and ships up to the north, fruit of the wise, ancient bananas, full of wisdom, potassium, the works. You go with him. I want you to see this, I would have said. I want you to notice how your father moves through the world, and I want you to admire him, my little Manny grown big, into a man. Help him out, the general's got a college graduate for a daughter, break the ice, talk to the girl you'll meet in a little while after a trip into the plantation country. This is a help to your father. You're going anyway, so be a help, not a hindrance.

Into the jungle. A place of verdure—of windy places, of wind—a place of moist and fertile soil, yellow soil. A place with peaked places and grassy places, a place of trees, thick trees, a place of jungle, of stumps, underbrush, dense underbrush.

A place of crests and covers and crags and hollows, a disturbing place, fearful, frightful, dwelling place of the rabbit, the deer, the monkey, the ocelot, the bobcat, the serpent, a place from which nothing departs, nothing leaves, nothing emerges, nothing changes.

A green place, of green light and green wind, green heat, green water, green air, green fire. A place of thick green trees, with thick green leaves. A fearful disturbing place of green.

A verdant place of green swellings, green entrances, green hollows, green crests, green changes, green chances, green prospects, green ends.

And if you don't like the color green, too bad. That's all you get here, deep deep in the jungle where my Manny owned his land. The green things he read about in some poetry written by the general, the very man he was to meet at the main plantation for the bananas. This general had written these things about green many many years before, when he was still a young boy in a military school in South Carolina. In English he wrote them and then translated them into his native language—and as you can hear they are all about the famous jungle that my Manny was traveling through. He read them on the airplane because the brother-in-law, very worried about the meeting with the general, wanted my Manny to have some things with him he could talk about if he needed to. (*Oi*, he's such an arranger, that brother-in-law, such a manipulator, but then I suppose he helped my Manny with a lot of information about people he met during the various little takeovers they made over the years, and especially during this big one.)

Still, reading about something is one thing and living it is another. As far as the jungle went, my Manny was very surprised. On paper, he could clutch his holdings in one hand, and in his mind imagine the miles after miles of trees bearing the fruit of the wise, the workers' housing, the port facilities, the shape, even, of the country on the map. But once that airplane hatch opened and he stepped out into the special atmosphere of this country he spent a lot of time adjusting between the figures and knowledge in his head and the smell and feel of the land and, in particular, the jungle around him.

What did my Manny know, after all, about jungles? He was a city boy—and in these countries that Americans buy even the people they hire to run things for them, the local people, they're city boys, mostly, themselves. City is city, jungle is jungle. And if sometimes you hear that our city, as people say, that it's a jungle, let me tell you that they don't know what they're talking about. The jungle, my Manny discovered, is very hot and very wet and very noisy and very smelly and very stuffy and very strange—and if it's dangerous it's not the kind of worry that you have in the city at all. In the city do you worry about the bite of the snake called the pit viper? Do you look at the trees as you travel along in a Landrover, worried that a snake will slip from an overhanging branch and strike at your face? Do you, in the city, turn around at the scowl of a cat as big as yourself and wonder if it's stalking midget deer or fat ratlike creatures who grow to the size of ponies or yourself? In the city do you notice that by day the light turns greenish dark, as if you're staring at the sun from miles underwater? All of this you may do, in a way, but none of it you do really—it's a dream of a jungle, and the jungle a nightmare of a city, and for my Manny, and my granddaughter, and I suppose for the others in their group, the brother-in-law, some managers in shirt-sleeves who met them at the airport, and the several officers and boyish little soldiers who accompanied them as well, the jungle was, is, a thing apart from any other kind of life. A desert might have its own pains and pleasures—and life too beneath the city or on a mountaintop. But to call a city a jungle, I don't after hearing all what my Manny told me believe it for a minute. A jungle is a jungle is a jungle.

So here they are, rolling along in Landrovers on the way to the railhead that will carry them deeper into the territory, deepest, deep where the fruit of the wise grows best. If I had my sight, if I still had my lipstick, and a piece of paper, I could draw you a map. Here, the road from the airport in the capitol which they left at once, and into the suburbs and then east through the scraggly jungle, and then the only road through deeper growth, toward the western end of the railhead built by the company nearly a hundred years before when it slashed the country in two in order to roll fruit both east toward the port and west toward the capitol. If I could still draw I would make arrows for directions, north, south, west, east, but I can't do it no more.

She wanted to remember the route, Sadie did. She marked it all down in a book. Take good notes, the Jews for Justice boy (Alan, Mitch, James, whoever) had said to her the night before she flew down with her father, my Manny. Take notes, notes upon notes, note everything, and if you can, take pictures.

I don't know how, she said.

Get a Brownie, you don't have to be a genius.

I can ask him for pictures, for Christ's sake.

Oh right. If you can, do it that way.

Of course I can. He'll give me pictures. He'll give me anything I want.

Is that it? the boy had asked. Is that the problem?

What problem?

That he always gave you everything? And so you never had to prove . . .

Fuck you, asshole, she said, getting up to leave. (New Brunswick, an old dilapidated apartment, something that went from Hungarian mill workers to undergraduates, time immemorial. Roaches, stink of stale food. Our apartment on Second Street all over again—you'd think she wouldn't want to spend a minute there. But to a girl who has everything—except dirt—maybe it was somehow appealing.)

Take it easy, the boy said. This Rutgers boy. This Rutgers Jewish boy for Justice (Norman, Alan, Mitch, James), he believes what he believes, though ten years from now he'll be lucky to remember what he believed back then—and he's like the taxi or the horse towing the milk truck, a part of the scheme, and he doesn't know, he doesn't know. What could he know? You could tell him a life and a lifetime was depending on him shutting up, and he would go on talking. And it's not just today's children—thinking about all this, watching Sadie selling out her father, and the family, so that she could feel a little better for a few minutes in a run-down apartment in New Brunswick, you begin to see that it's not just today, it's yesterday, it's a long line of children going back to the first children, the little brats of Adam and Eve. They disobeyed—one of them, anyway, yes? And what kind of an example did they get from their parents? They, too, disobeyed their father—and did God Himself have a Father against whom He rebelled? And His Father, did He have a Father He fought with? I don't know where it all began— but I'm afraid I have a good idea how it ends.

So what do you think so far, darling? Manny asked her, meaning all of the land through which they had passed, these endless trees, the fruit, fruit, fruit, the barracks where the workers lived, the rail lines, the hospital—they took a tour—the mess halls, which were not such a mess, which were in fact very clean and the food very tasty, they were eating when he asked, What do you think? freshly fried fish from the nearby sea, fruit cocktail of mango and papaya and pineapple and, of course, the famous banana.

I can't believe that you own all this, Sarah said, touching a spoonful of pulpy fruit to her lips.

Own? Manny said, Nobody in this world owns, darling. But I have a good lease, a very good lease. He touched a hand to the back of his neck where the sweat was dripping from the roots of his silver hair. Are you hot? We can go to the guest house and turn on the air conditioning.

Do the workers have that too, Father?

He shook his silver head.

They are used to this, visitors are not.

They could get used to it, couldn't they?

He squinted at her, salt sweat biting at his eyes.

I'll look into it. It seems to be quite an exorbitant idea, but we'll look into it.

Thank you, Father.

But the food is delicious, don't you think? Fresh fish? Fruit?

Do they get fresh milk here, Father?

What makes you think of that? I'm not sure. I'll inquire.

Inquire, she said. Fresh milk.

Could a cow survive here without air conditioning? he said, hoping to make her laugh.

But she pretended not to hear.

Have you looked at the infant mortality figures for the company hospital? she asked.

(Right then and there he should have taken her by the shoulders and said, Where did you get that question? What made you think of that question. Are you my daughter or an investigating committee? Are you my daughter or some avenging angel? Where, where? If I had been there I would have said, Ask her that, Manny. Ask her where she thought of it. Ask her, Who prompts you? Some critic? Some reporter? Who? Who? And I would have taken my Manny by the shoulders and given *him* a shake—do you think you're dreaming all this? are you standing in front of your congregation lost in some daydream of a jungle company? are you making all this up? don't you feel the heat, you're sweating like a tapir, the jungle pig, the one with the dark brown body, the broad white stripes, there goes one, off into the brush, two small barefoot boys chasing after . . . Manny, my Manny, I would have said, if I had been there, if I had known, I would have said, Take off your white shirt, your dark trousers —he had already removed his dark coat, a big concession to the skin of heat that clung to everyone, everything in this jungle world—and strip off your underdrawers, and chase into the bush after those boys, that beast, and never return and you will be safe, alive and well and happy, too, probably, if a bit dirty and maybe even on some nights hungry too, unless you learn to eat the meat and fruit of these parts exclusively and like it—because he was lying about liking the food, he had become a snob about food, I'll admit that much negative about him, he had become a fiend for French cooking and merely tolerated all of the good things I put on the table before him—strip off, Manny, and run and hide and you'll be safe from all that otherwise will follow!

But, oh, he turned and looked again at her, his daughter, his—he was convinced—dutiful daughter, whose antagonism toward him—he was convinced—had burned away like the light morning fog that had dogged their heels on the train ride through the jungle, where palm fronds brushed against the windows of the plush car in which they rode sipping *limonada* from colorful pottery. He was convinced that she was learning about him, his new life, and that she could only but admire him for his vision and his values. Who did she know who had changed his life in this way? who had leaped from the mundane round of suburban Jersey to a deep-green jungle empire—yes, well, that was how he was thinking of it—who did she know like him? And could she be anything but worshipful? Couldn't she see what he had wrought? Only her opinion he cared about now. Mine, he knew he had in the palm of his hand. Maby's? She had none—she was lost in the world of her wayward mind. And yours? What did you know except that you wanted him for comfort in those hours when you were not painting? In those dark nightmare times when you awoke screaming of the awful past in the old country and needed someone to help fend off the ghosts. Whether he ruled a congregation or an empire, you didn't care. But as for Sarah-Sadie, he wanted her attention and her mind and her devotion and her admiration—and he was wooing her in a way he had never felt he needed to before.)

I want you to know, he said, that I have never put aside the values that I carried with me to my first meeting with the congregation.

Uh-huh, she said with a grunt, picking up a glass of iced tea and stirring endless spoonfuls of sugar into its swirling dark whorl of liquid and mint.

Never.

Never?

Never.

And furthermore, he said, I am showing all of these business people the way.

Is that right?

Don't doubt your own father. That is correct, I have the knack, and I do things well, but beyond that I show them how to impart certain values into their dealings. I show them how to make their operations humane and decent.

And you bring potassium to the tables all over America.

That, too.

You ship the fruit of the wise on the Great Seabird Fleet.

That I do. From your grandfather's barges to the Great Seabird Fleet—that is quite a distance I have come.

She stopped stirring her drink and looked him in the eye.

And what next?

(She really wants to know, he was thinking to himself. She cares, this offspring of mine, my only issue, and she cares about my plans.)

I was thinking perhaps politics.

Politics? She raised the glass to her lips and sipped the cool sweet mint-tinted liquid. Ahhh . . .

Politics. But before that, or possibly instead, maybe diplomacy.

Diplomacy?

An ambassadorship somewhere. After this, after I make clear how well I am going to handle this arrangement here . . . who knows?

Father, she said. (In her heart she felt a bit stunned by this confession of his. She hadn't been aware . . . she had never imagined . . . that he could think so big, so far, so high up, far ahead, so . . . grandly. Here she was just a college girl, trying to spy on him, taking notes and more notes. And at this moment she almost faltered in her loyalty to her plan, because she was sure as he said this last thing that there was a good possibility that he was not evil, but merely crazy. And yet she thought, he had come this far, and you don't come this far if you are crazy, but only if you have trampled on the hearts of others, kicked and flailed them and left them lying bloody and crushed in the dust of your passage—first your family and then the world.)

Father.

Yes?

Nothing.

What, my darling?

Nothing.

You had something on your mind. Tell me.

Nothing. It was nothing.

Nothing?

Nothing.

So, nothing. But now I'll tell *you* something.

What's that?

He got up from the table and motioned for her to follow. Several young men in white shirts and khaki trousers trailed after as they left the building for the thick world of heat and light as green as that beneath the ocean. A Landrover stood waiting, the brother-in-law in the back seat, the driver alert and attentive.

Hello, *Sa*rah, her uncle said to her, running a hand across his hairless sweat-beaded skull. Did you have a good lunch?

Hello, Uncle Mord. Yes, we did. Very good. And, oddly, she embraced him, as if she had only just now suddenly recognized their kinship.

Good, I'm glad, Mord said as they rolled off toward the gate.

You know where we're going, Mord said to my Manny in a quieter voice.

Of course.

Well, it's going to be one big happy family. He handed an envelope to my Manny and sat back to watch the green flow past. In a few minutes they reached the dockside, the place where workers loaded the fruit from the jungle into crates and loaded the crates onto the ships. A large white yacht lay at anchor in the deep harbor. From its mast flew, among other flags, one that showed the insignia of the curled and sleeping anaconda, a snake that grew more and more sharply defined as they roared closer and closer to the ship in a motor launch.

The national emblem, Mord said to his companions.

We can trust somebody who flies a snake? my Manny inquired, half in jest.

It's out in the open at least, Mord said, wiping sea spray from his broad bald forehead.

My Manny had one hand on, not so surprising, the shard in his pocket, with the other holding onto the rail.

You're all right? he asked Sarah.

Just fine, she said, licking salty lips with a dry tongue. She couldn't keep her legs still—they quivered as though her kneecaps were made of rubber. It had to be the sea, she decided, but here in the harbor there was no pitch and roll, only the steady thrumming as the prow of the launch split the water in a direct lunge toward the yacht. A girl shouldn't feel like wetting her pants over that, should she? *Oi*, she was nervous, and well she should have been. She knew only one thing that was about to happen—she didn't know it would be more than one.

(Could I have stopped all this if I had been there? Could I have asked for a wave from the east to roll the ship on its side? Could I have called up from the sleeping depths where it lay for a long time, thousands of years, coiled and waiting the green-scaled, red-eyed anaconda? Could I have forced it to wind itself around the yacht and crush the hull with its tangles? And if I could have done that, and I would have, would that have stopped the progress of this tragedy, my Manny's story, my Manny's end of life? There are some things the mamas cannot do—and one of them is stop a stone that's been rolling downhill when it's picked up the force of a subway train.)

Bienvenidos, welcome. A tall man with a crinkled brow and dark thin mustache says to father and daughter as they climb over the side of the yacht. Behind him on a chaise lounge a raven-haired girl with long thin legs lies stretched out sipping a drink through a straw. She blinks at the new arrivals. The sun behind her etches her into the deck.

My Mord makes some introductions. A boyish waiter appears with glasses on a tray.

Orange juice, please, says my Manny while Sarah agrees to something fixed with rum. Minutes go by. Sarah's wondering who they're all waiting for to appear before she realizes that this is the meeting that everything has pointed toward, and it is already almost over, a flurry of polite exchanges on the hot deck in fierce sunlight.

Swim? says the girl approaching her on coltish legs. The sun wings in and out of focus, like a photograph from positive to negative to positive. Sarah feels the light spinning out from her insides, singeing her thighs.

Who says these things can't happen the way they do? a shift of the ocean surface, the spinning sun like a pinwheel whirling, some strong chemical eating through thick cloth, seething, powdery smoke rising, acrid to the nostrils, thick as stone. Meeting the painter had showed her how to recognize such heart rumblings and squirts of gall, gush of sex-syrup into the main arteries, you know, you know, what you felt when my Manny first appeared before you, high on his dais, yes? a feeling in the veins, not an idea in the head—the news tingling at every joint and pore, saying, here it is, this is what you need. You might ask how a grandma knows this feeling, but don't inquire. Think instead to when you're old and nearly sightless, and how what you'll have left will be nothing but the ghosts of encounters you make for yourself each day when young. You'll wish that you'd done more when you have nothing but less. My darling, my daughter, granddaughter, she felt this power of the other standing before her, as though the general's daughter—this is who she is, isn't it? this is her father on the deck, isn't it?—had drawn the marrow from her bones. She follows the girl below. In a forward cabin, she undresses. The other girl undresses.

Collapse a year or more into a minute or ten—close the door to the state room—find the key to your sister's strengths and desires, the fusing of alternate organs, heart to heart becoming twin appendages of a single chest, breast to breast, double image of a passion now one, and deeper and deeper it goes, so that kidney and bladder and womb and liver, labia and eyebrow, toe and lip, nose and knee and tip of pelvis, apertures and roundings, breath and secretion, celebrate the occasion of the quest.

If I had been there would I have said What is this that you're doing? where are you putting your hands? your lips? your tongue? Ahoy, above on decks it passes between hands, the soon-to-be famous envelope, and later she'll learn of this, but now, smoking a doper, about to become the object in the arms of another, one sandal on, one sandal off, swimming in the perfumes of her own lust and the new friend's, she knows no father, mother, grandma, or even the children she might yet conceive if ever a man could educe in her the swinging wild wind of yes-I-want-it, that this dark and coltish sister inspires.

Let me tell you, these things don't happen every day. Such a locking, a joining, a what-do-the-goyim-call it? This girl and her Catholic family? communion? Slip off the other sandal and settle on the cushions upon the bed. She's undoing the – that's right – and now – see – put your – ahh, the way she . . .

And they talk, say many things important to each of them, say things that will change everything for their fathers – but only in passing, two girls of a particular persuasion, like two redheads or two left-handed girls, swimming in a sea of burning weed, disposing of empires . . .

A million is what he's giving him right now up on deck, the coltish girl said. Her voice had the most delicate Latin shading, something that her studies at Wellesley rubbed at but never rubbed off.

A million? Sadie sat up.

That's the agreement. So my father won't raise the tariff.

I see, Sadie said, and sank down again into the sea of pillows.

And all for this, said the coltish girl, giggling a little as she held up the slender curve of fruit. But watch!

If my closed eyes could close their eyes I could close them now. Here is what they're too shy to gaze upon: the general's daughter peels back the skin and holds up the wand of nourishment, and with a heavenly smile on her face crosses the small space between them and then sitting next to Sadie motions for her to spread herself somewhat, and with a gentle motion touches the tip to her bud and slips it further in, in, and then guides it out again, out, and Sadie, who has closed her eyes opens them, and yes her new found friend breaks the creamy fruit in two and with a slow and certain opening of the mouth and taking in of breath and touching of the tongue and working of the jaw they eat of this. Communion.

There is some way of telling time which even those of us who cannot see the hands on a clock can say. You feel the slight change of pressure on your face. There is a certain wind. It has a flavor all its own, a special weight and tone, a sound. Weather is the breath of seasons, the lingering reminder that some voice in the clouds has spoken. Time's teeth mark the rocks with ridges and gashes. A blind god could feel its presence by fingering the layers of soil and stone, sand, the dried up seas.

.   .   .

What? Did I say that? Or just think it, or remember it, or maybe dream it? Have I slept maybe for a few minutes? Taken a grandmother's catnap, made some grandmother's poetry, so never mind.

So good morning, though I know it's still not light.

Sarah, is that you?

Is it you and I'm not dreaming, Sarah come back from your evenings out—and where did you go? With friends? With enemies?—and back from hiding where you disappeared after the big trouble? Back back back from California? Too late—too late for the life but just in time for the story, and as the sun tries to rise, your grandmother salutes you.

And Florette, you're still here? Good. So Sarah, join the party, hand me a pill, a cup, braid my long white hair, make my bed—for all of such I am grateful—and in exchange I will tell you this, what you may have been wondering about, what you may have heard in newspaper and fable, what terrible information you do not have ears for to know.

On that last awful morning, back in the city, my Manny stuffed into his briefcase books he had not touched in twenty years—a volume of Graetz's *History of the Jews* (and where his history fits in we'll leave to the historians, yes? it's not for his mother to say, but it was a book that brought him together with Maby years before when they studied together), the *Encyclopedia Judaica* (a book that always came in handy when he was making his sermons), and the *Universal Jewish Encyclopedia* (the same use)—all of which had the effect of turning his usually slender leather case into a battering ram of knowledge. He could not, as hard as he tried, close the clasps. Neither could he fight off the anguish he was feeling, a sensation of the nerves that leaked from his heart like water from a broken tap. This day he was, you could say, hemorrhaging from pain, and the suffering seeped everywhere around his bones. The many questions he had had in his life, the whys, the whos, the hows, the whens, for these he had found a few answers. But, like always, nothing was good for him, finally. Nothing let him rest.

How did he get this way? From his father, a man he hardly knew (if you added up all the years he knew him and all the years he was alive)? From me, his mother? From both of us together? Sure, Mike, we had our questions—our lives *were* questions. If you could follow us with your eyes through time what would we look like, people running away from something, or people running toward something? Or both?

Now my Manny was running.

"RABBI GUATEMALA" PAYS LATIN GENERAL MILLIONS

So here it was, the news of the day, in the big black words in the newspaper (also it was on the radio, the early morning news). Can words make anything happen? If they can, then these were some of the words. Manny felt the shame, the disgrace like heat in an oven, and he was the dough, rising. Worse yet, he was the baker, he was the bread.

Mama? he said, stealing into my room earlier that morning. I had the extra good hearing as my eyes got worse and worse, as well as the seeing from the inside, the imagining from what they told me, and so I pushed off the switch on the radio as he got to the door.

Yes, Manny? I said. My Manny, I added in my mind.

I'm *tired*, Mama, he said.

Sit here, I motioned with my hand to the place next to me on the bed. It's morning. You shouldn't be tired.

It's early, he said, I'm tired.

But also late? I patted him on the hand, trying to think strong thoughts right into his heart and brain, supply him with strength so that he could go on with his day. You been up all night?

I haven't slept much, he said.

You been on the telephone. I heard you.

You heard me talking?

I heard you talking, not what you were saying, just the way you said it. You got trouble, Manny? I was asking, but I knew already, I knew.

I've got trouble, Mama.

And this tires you out?

I've been working for too many years, Mama. I'm suddenly very tired.

Like Maby got tired? So maybe you should try and take a rest like she did. Maybe you should call Sally Stellberg's Doctor Mickey, you could use a few words from him, a long time you haven't talked. Maybe you should stay home a little more.

I'd like to rest, Mama. But I have to go in to the office. There's going to be a big mess, there's going to be a lot of trouble. With the stockholders, with the reporters, the press.

Press, schmess. You're tired, you stay home. Let the brother-in-law clean up the mess.

My Manny shook his head and made a little laugh, unusual for him to laugh at all.

Press, schmess? That's what you say, Mama? In the middle of all this you're making jokes?

Did I make a joke?

Yes.

So I made a joke. I'm the mother. The mother can do what she wants.

I have to go now, he said, getting up from my bed.

You said you were tired, so stay a little bit. Go back to bed, take a nap.

I have to, he said. And . . .

And?

You know the and.

I know the and.

So if she calls.

Yes?

Ask where she is. Where I can see her.

You still want to see her?

You're a mother. Can't a father have the same feelings as a mother? She did a terrible thing but she didn't know how terrible. I forgive her. I don't know why but I do forgive her.

I'll ask her.

Tell her if she calls here that I forgive her and that I want to see her. Do you think I'm crazy, Mama?

You forgive her. That's not so crazy.

I forgive her.

I'll tell her.

Or maybe don't tell her anything. Just say I want to talk to her. Say I have some questions for her.

She's here in the city? And she's got answers for you?

I don't know. I don't know where she is. And I don't know
what she can say to me. But I want to ask.
Maybe she went to see her mother?
I called there yesterday. She hadn't been there.
Maybe she's hiding with her friend the painter?
How do you know about her?
How do I know? I know.
So you know. No. She found another friend. On our trip.
It could be she's back down there. Though how she got there,
with what money I don't know. And how she could show her
face there, either, I couldn't say.
Now you don't sound so tired, darling, now that you're get-
ting angry.
I'm not angry, Mama. I'm hurt.
She hurt you?
Maybe. She hurt me, and I also hurt her. And myself.
She did. But did you?
I have to go now, Mama.
You're tired. Stay home.
I have to go.
You're just like your father. Always up and on the go. He
never rested until the end.
Mama?
I was watching him with his hand in his pocket, the fingers
working around the edges of the little star.
Yes, Manny?
Are you . . .
What, darling?
Are you . . . disappointed in me?
No, no, no, darling. Never. Never. But – your eyes. Is there
something else?
Never mind.
Never mind? Like when you were a little boy you'd want
to say something and you'd say then never mind? Tell me, tell
your mother.
I've got to go.
One thing.
What, Mama?
Go take care of your hand.
What?
Your fingers. I can feel them like they were my own.

He took his hand from his pocket and I could see the blood on his fingers.

I'll take care of it.

You shouldn't do that, Manny.

I know I shouldn't, Mama.

Put a bandage on.

I will. Mama?

Yes, Manny?

Were you watching the TV when I came in?

How can I watch? With these eyes I could watch? No, I was listening to the radio—better than the TV, it makes more sense to the ear. And what are you so worried about, anyway? You're worried about what other people say? Worry only about what you think is right. I'm only your mother, but I want you to know that I've always been proud of you, and I'm still proud of you.

He nodded, but said nothing, and then he left the room. I could hear, very faintly far away on the other side of the hall in the long bedroom the sound of the water in the bathroom basin where he must have been cleaning his bloody fingers.

Mama, you take care, he said, as he passed my door.

Manny! I called to him.

What is it?

You come in here and give me a goodbye kiss.

In he came, leaned down, and kissed me.

Goodbye, Mama.

Manny, I said, you took a drink of whiskey?

To help calm me, Mama.

It's early in the morning.

I had a drink late last night, Mama.

I squeezed his good fingers in mine.

If it helps you, take another. Now. Before you go.

He kissed me again, and said no words. In a minute he had picked up his heavy satchel and was out the door. Our driver was waiting in the lobby, the nice Spanish boy, Daniel. He tried to take the satchel from my Manny but Manny said that he wanted to carry it himself. The ride through the streets to the office was nearly as smooth as the elevator ride down to the lobby—it was early, early, and there were very few cars, only some taxis speeding away toward the lower end of the Park as though they might be punished if they got caught with the sun full up over the buildings in the east. In his mind he had decided, my Manny, that if he was going to do what he was going to do he had to do it before too many people got out on the street. He didn't want to put people in danger—and I think, if I know him well enough, knew him, that he didn't want to become at the end a spectacle. He thought that he had become a spectacle enough in the day since the news had come out.

Let me, he heard my Jacob say as he climbed out of the car in front of his building and the books tumbled out onto the street. He started around and saw that it was the driver speaking, and he quickly went down on his knees in the gutter to retrieve the heavy tomes.

You're all right, sir? Daniel asked, because Manny had stood there for a minute now, listening to a ghost.

Give it to me, he said brusquely, out of character for this kind and gentle and thoughtful and generous person.

Daniel, averting his eyes, handed over the satchel.

Morning, the guard at the door said in greeting, opening the way for my Manny's entrance into the building he had just purchased a few months before. Gargoyles guarded its parapets—and the insignia our Sadie thought so funny, the slender half-moon fruit wearing the general's cap, it now crowned the entrance to the lobby. But what sign should he have endorsed? Any mark would by now have seemed as comical as it did serious—what should he have shown on his flag now, the star-shaped shard, perhaps? or the general's anaconda, or, maybe, the star in the center of the coiled and dreaming snake?

My child, conceived in a wheat field, borne across the ocean on a sturdy ship, nourished by adoring parents, only to lose one in an accident where cart and horse and wagon and truck and engine collided, student of the wisdom of his people, modern man ultimately rejecting this, pushing off from his past like a runner gaining added momentum in a race toward what? toward his own finished story, to the end he could not see because he closed his eyes before he saw it. This, all this, I know. But did I ever know him? He was an old man but a new man too, wanting a father from an early age and wanting to become one. Pointed star and anaconda became his new sign, a covenant with a future not even a blind see-er like his mama could picture and, if picture, understand. Even now his mother talks, talks, trying to define him finally and has to give up and say only what happened next, because life remains undefinable up until the very end when it becomes death and to know a definition is to know death, not the vital being that inspired it. So in a few minutes his personal chaos—his deep sense of fatigue after having tried for years to make love with his Maby and for years to make father love with you, his Sarah-Sadie, and for years to make more than love with you, his numbered mistress, and for years taking that power he never could find the way to exercise in his private life and creating the business he made in public—this man's, my Manny's maelstrom of a life, would become a pattern.

But Sarah—are you there? I want to feel your hand, darling! hand!—you were not so comical, and yet he wanted to see you.

Could he say at this moment, rising up and up in the smoothly geared elevator the doorman had commandeered for him at his approach, that he wanted nothing now but to see again, and speak with, the disapproving daughter who had betrayed him to the press? But who knows if that was what he really wanted? He could say, if I could get her back then I would have reason not to go any further with this, and we could become reconciled. She would no longer be such a fatherless child, and we could visit Maby in the green Jersey woods. He could say that, but who knows if that was his fondest wish? He told me, his own mother, how tired he was—and it could be as he ascended to his office that this was what he told himself to keep himself moving.

This picture (I imagined it while sitting at home) gave me a bad feeling—if they had been reading my blood pressure while I was thinking it you would have noticed on the doctors' face a frown of concern—as Manny was rising. Manny, I was thinking *go to the telephone and give your mother a call*. You said tired, you were tired, what does this mean? Oh, give me the power, Lord of the Universe, if you can give it, give me the power. You underwater people from Atlantis, if you exist, give me the words to say to Manny what he was doing on that morning. Step out of the elevator, say good morning to the security guard, smile a big smile, unusual for you, and the guard, he's no dummy, he knows this, but what else does he know, and enter the office, the reception part, and catch a whiff of expensive perfume and think, wait a minute, who's here? who's followed me here, or beat me here? and then you laugh, the last laugh, because you realize that it's the cleaning woman who's worked all night and splashed a little pleasure on her face and neck for home or wherever—or was it the brother-in-law wearing a ballgown and playing queen for the evening? *that* was the last laugh—and then you walk down the corridor and through the door to your own secretary's office—you use keys, of course, I forgot—and into your own place, and there, from the window, you catch the first glimpse of morning, the bright spear of light shooting up from behind the buildings far to the east in Queens, and you think, as the early light catches the airplane passing across the middle sky like a finger skimming along a page still blank but where some writing may one day appear, you think, I should fly, I should take the elevator right back down and take the car to the airport and leave at once.

(Or at least call your mother. Call her! Call!)

But the satchel weighs you down, like some idea you must work out completely before dismissing it—before it dismisses you—and so you lean against the wall of a window, take a deep breath, and your eyes light upon the telephone. I should call her, you think, meaning me, your mother, I think, but it could be Maby who's still, of course, in Owl Valley, asleep and dreaming, of what? sailboats on a river or pond, and stately swans, one black, a few white, soaring, then skimming across the top of the water and landing with a splash, or is she dreaming of wheat fields she's never seen, and men in masks, robbers who took her middle life from her, beasts who grew from seeds sown so early, Maby, Maby, he calls out to her in his thoughts, and toys with the notion of calling her right now this second to say that he is sorry for all but it got away from him.

Or will.

And then in one last call, or the call he thought would be his last, the call in his mind, he tries you, Florette, because you of all the others besides myself, the mother, gave him solace, perhaps because you were the person least real to him, the one he could imagine had a life apart from his own, nurturing and mysterious, you with your childhood in the death places, you with your numbers on the wrist, you with your art and your cigarettes and your desire for a friendship with the rabbi, the one man you thought might know something about what happened to you in your life, who turned out to be the last person. And he knew that, and he didn't call, and I can tell from the trembling hand you touch me with now, the way you touch my arm, that if he had called you you would have tried to have talked to him as I tried to talk to him, and that alone makes you an honorary grandmother, because you think like a grandmother, like this grandmother. So what if nothing ever came forth from your womb, because you held my good son in your arms and loved him hard, though you might have said to him that a mother can't be a lover and a lover can't be a mother, not in the flesh, but we can try to give that kind of tenderness that the other gives and that kind of instruction and that kind of heat and warmth, and a daughter can't either be a lover or a mother, but a woman who was once a daughter can show a lover how good a father he could become, and a mother once a daughter can do the same, as can a wife, if sane, and a lover, if you can call her, can try that too, but if you can make that call is a big if. He didn't call to say that he might be going. He was already almost gone. And he didn't call.

I have left you all, he is thinking.

And then he is thinking of Maby, and saying in his mind to her, if I never gave enough, and if I never gave, then, oh, well, I am sorry, sorrier than if I could see you now and say, because in the driveway that night, because in the street, I chased you, and if I held you too tight, it was love that impelled me, and if I turned to you and turned away, if I could never say, and if we never did, and if the verses I read, the *Song of Songs*, if it only in the words could be, and if I was not, and if your father, mother, brother, if they, if I, the feeling of it, my studies, my life, the family at home, I wanted you.

My darling.

That call to Maby he never made either. Because who would answer but a nurse?

And the other call, the last and final he thought about, he couldn't make because he didn't know the number. Where was *she*, the daughter, you, Sarah, Sadie, now Sarah again? As far as he knew you had skipped to the edge of the universe. Only later I found where you were—dancing, dancing in saffron robes, with a head shaved as close as a woman's cleft when first she's about to give birth. Could he have asked God for directory assistance? Lord, I would like my daughter's number, please?

(Now you step forward and tell me that that is the truth, and you take my hand and touch it to the back of your neck under your new thick length of hair, like a sheep's back it feels, curly and coiled, springy, full of health, and you tell me that all this is true, that you at the same time were with your own Indian lord and that he your own father would have had to have gotten through to God Himself in order to have gotten your number, because that was how far you had traveled after betraying him so that you could hide yourself from him—and I am glad that you have come to me here in this room in this country place late in the night, just before morning, I can smell it because the earth is turning, the light will soon arrive, and though I can't see it anymore I can feel it on my skin and taste it on my tongue and sniff it in my nostrils, oh, little girl, I could taste and smell you coming from the minute you said finally to yourself you wanted to leave that place of robes and dancing and come east again to see me, your grandmother, before the end, and here you are, standing in this room with *her*, she the childless one putting all her love and strength and caring into her paintings, like they were children, and grandchildren, making her a grandmother too, and you the girl who has been through so much but still can't imagine—can you?—one day reaching down into yourself and coming up through the stoppage of time with a child, but you will probably become a mother one day—oh, if I could live to see it—and then, like unseeing I, you will become a grandmother, one distant day from now, in another city, or country, perhaps, maybe even on another world, on the moon or undersea in the new discovered old city of Atlantis. Listen, girl, here, come into the circle, take my hand, take her hand! too, and listen, listen to the sorrows of men and women standing on the edge of time. Take it! take it! I want to hold your hands!)

Little did the father know at the time when he wanted to make this call that his daughter was dancing, dancing, and this only a week after she had gone to the Jews for Justice boy with copies of the documents showing the million, and a number where reporters could reach her, because, oh, this she needed to do, punish her father because he had and also had not punished her. He had, by keeping his distance over the years, by showing her the strictness when he never believed in it himself. He had not by not recognizing her pain, the mistakes she made, the wounds inflicted on her by others, and it was like mother, like daughter, and if you didn't know their stories separately you might think that it was one story, and you throw in my story and you've got all the tales you need and it's him against us, the universe—his life the counterpoint against our melodious and not so melodious music.

Hello? he said in his mind, leaning there against the window, that wall-high window, thick glass through which the brightening morning light now streamed, gushers of light, a torrent of light rushing down from the only slightly higher height (it seemed) of the eastern wall, the world's wall, the sky above the east.

Hello? I want to speak with you, I want to tell you how sorry I am, I want you to come home and I will take your hands and we will look into each other's eyes, and I will tell you, I am starting over, after all, this is America, the country of new lives, and haven't I started twice already? can't I start over again? and who can say I am finished before I begin?

Hello? The eastern wall is glowing with new-minted light.

And in his mind are you dancing? swirling, whirling in your saffron robes? your bald head like that of a newborn babe, glassy star in your look, your eye on the future, or past, whenever, all a swirling and a whirl, whorl, the eastern gate glowing with new whirl, and you cannot make the connection. Hello, he says, and you cannot make the connection. Hello? Hello? and where did you break the connection? Was it in the guitar? was it in the trip to New Brunswick? was it on the night you watched from your window the antics in the driveway? or did God Himself say before you came, Sorry, no connection.

Hello?

The last is never the last. He still doesn't give up. He's trying Maby again, Hello? hello? and she's sleeping, dreaming of a smooth sail on a glassy river, a human being, a nesting animal, all in one, and stirring now, a little before dawn, and turning now, in the last long step of a journey she's been dreaming through the night—or in the minutes before dawn—or who knows how long? the mother, the father, they stand holding hands at the water's edge, they drop hands, and then wave to her from the water's edge, and in her dream her heart leaps from her chest like a fish, and she weeps freely, wholesomely, tears of forgiveness and tears of conciliation, tears of homecoming, tears of remorse, tears of pleasure, tears of pain, and in the dream she steps out after her heart and she chases it as though it's a butterfly and her life is the net. Good morning.

Hello? hello? Is he calling—who?—the brother-in-law? Why does he need to call *him?* Long ago he decided how he would work with him—hello?—and he doesn't need to say anything more, let alone goodbye. And where is this man now? Waking in the arms of a slender young boy who inexplicably finds his baldness attractive, rubbing the boy's behind, a backside bald as the new-shaven head of his disappearing niece? But where else? And how else? and why else? And so we leave him. Almost where he began.

My Manny, and it's only early morning, drips sweat—his brow, just below the line of startling white hair, the sweat beads there, ready to roll down his creased and narrow forehead. Take off your jacket, I would have said to him if I had been there. Relax, you're in your own office, like a bear in his den, so take your coat off, why don't you?

Mama, he'd have said, Let me tell you something. I'll always be your boy, but I am a big man now.

A big Manny, I'd say.

And he'd laugh a little—I am the only one in the world I know who can make my Manny laugh.

Listen, I'd say, you're getting ready, you're a big man, you had many people very proud to work with you when you had the congregation and then you started buying up the companies, a carton place here, a bottle factory there, and pretty soon you had what you had. You had the power, you had the respect, so you had a little trouble with the family, so look down where you can see a few people, like ants, but smaller, just beginning to come out now, crossing here, there, on the way to work, early, and if you took any one of them up here, if you had the magical power, if you could play like a god, like God Himself, and if you could take off the wrapping on their lives and see what's in the package underneath, do you think you would find many people who had done better with their families than you? I don't think so, darling.

I'm old. I'm blind, and I'm your mother—but I don't think so.

Here, darling, look, the sweat, it's dripping, it's running, if you're not going to take off your jacket, at least, here, let me with a handkerchief wipe the brow.

And now you should call her, don't you think? *Her, her.* So many *hers* in your life. My Manny, such a lady's man, always with the ladies, with the *hers.* It makes you wonder what his life would have been like if there had been some *hims*, like his father, may he rest in peace, and a brother-in-law who was a better person.

The brother-in-law! Feh! you know what he's doing now even as my Manny has decided to take off his suit coat and set it on a chair? He's turning over in his bed, dreaming of little Israeli boys, of an oasis in the desert where he has just ridden on his donkey, and there's water, and the boys, almost children, and he's smoking a pipe with one of them, running his eyes over a little fellow's body.

And this is the world! All this goes on, in dreams and out, while my Manny is wondering to himself, should I call her? what for? or should I not? people waking, dressing, going to work, smoking cigarettes, patting the children on the head, women making breakfasts all over the country, millions of breakfasts, millions of stalks of fruit of the wise, while others lie in bed with their husbands, some men, some women mounted upon each other like riders heading west with messages of great importance, while other women in hospitals groan in labor, open their legs—excuse me, but that's how it's done—and push children out into the world of food and school, and others just in the next ward over, the floor below or above, groan in the lesser labor of dying, and out in the streets of cities, business as usual, newspapers, the radio news, television views, buses, trains, airplanes, frying eggs, fruit stands, electrical hum and factory smoke, firehouse (ah, fire engine, milk truck *oi, yoi!*), and teachers and bankers and sales clerks and do I have to name everyone? everything? the world is out there waking . . .

His wife of all those years is waking, alone in her madhouse bed.

His daughter turns in her sleep, you, Sarah, in saffron robe and saffron sheets, a cloud of incense descending upon you, still unconscious, in soon-to-be-sunny California.

And you, the woman called Florette, he's dialing your telephone number now, yes, he's going to do it, but you've become a jogger now, of all things and you're out for a run, you're in shorts and a T-shirt that says across the chest DRINK MILK and your skin is so tan you can scarcely see the line of numbers etched on your wrist, especially not when you jog past so swiftly. So goodbye Florette, no answer.

And up in Alaska — *Alaska? Alaska!* — the mad wife's teacher, the writer, one-time lover, he's asleep too, everybody in the West is still asleep, as always, dreaming their way through the East's bright morning, and in this artist's head he's running, too — he's running off the edge of the icy continent, pursued by a bear.

And in the mountains.

And on the plains, and in the deserts which are the old beds of ancient oceans, and on the Great Lakes, and in ten thousand ponds, in the sultry southern kudzu forests, something like the rain jungle down below the line my Manny crossed.

And here near the bare sidewalks of Jersey, and at the far rocky points where the country ends and oceans begin on both coasts, and the flat steps leading down into the blue-true Gulf.

And you say, this is his mother? this is what she's thinking? this is how she pictures it as he's about to — but it's happened so many times before, I've seen it and said it to myself so many times before, I've watched him, off with the suit coat now, and picking up the satchel, going to the window-wall, and out there, threading his vision like a needle between the buildings he remembers the pier where we all first arrived, and the ocean waves we rode upon, I've watched him, in my blindness, his story light upon my dark.

And I have thought, sometimes, that it *was* his fault, all of it, his flaw, so what if the death of the father, so what of the confusion of choices, so what if the woman bewitched him, so what if, what if, so what!

He wanted the power, he wanted the world, he got it, that's what I think sometimes.

And at other times I think that some great god of a bird or bird of a god, whichever, who knows, they never never let me pray, never gave me a place in the temple, so what do I know except what I imagine, this bird or godbird or birdgod sucks up into the path of its flight all such puny notions as human will and feeds on desire and sends it back, blows it back with the great powerful force of its wings as it flies past worlds and words.

And this bird fixed its eye upon my son, my only son, my Manny, and he could have turned, he could have not turned, but no matter which way he turned it would have ended all the same.

And lo the bird swoops back now into my vision.

Lights, lights!

Bursts of lights of suns!

My blotted vision returning.

And I can see Manny standing at the window of the great city, standing tall, powerful in his decision, looking out at the bird.

And I am with the bird too, I am in the bird's eye, thus the light, the returning after these years of loss of the light I once knew, and I am seeing with the eye of the bird.

And here it comes soaring out of nowhere – the place where all things are born, to which all things go, an America of the ether, all poles no poles, equator noquator, city country mountain ocean desert plain all one, up and down the same, sideways eastwest northsouth the same, I glance away and it becomes the bird.

And I'm riding in its eye, and next to me *my Jacob*, and I clasp his hand and he touches the place where my shoulder meets my neck, and we each say with our eyes I am with you again my love, my lovely, in the eye, on the wings of this bird of day, of night, and the sound of its wings fluttering makes the air tremble, and we swoop past the window and see our Manny standing, staring out, and we know it is time, time made of the years gone by, and my Jacob says to me, Mama, Minnie, my love, how are you? how have you been? and I say, Don't you know? you haven't been watching? and he says, Of course, I've been watching but I wanted to hear from you in your own words, and he touches me again at the breast, and I say in my own words, I have been happy and I have been lonely, I have been happy, I have been sad, I have raised our boy for the world to take, though he took a little of the world from itself himself, and he says, Do you think it would have been different if I had stayed here with you, with you and him? and I say to him, I say, Jacob, my darling Jacob, one way or another we weave a world, we make a pattern, and if it is not one design it is another, and in the end the light goes, and we ride here in the eye of this flying beast, and Yes, he says, it's all crazy, it's all sane, it's all up and down and the way to the past is the way to the future and to the future we . . .

No, I say, no, my darling, please don't give me speeches, here we are, and we are soaring, and there he is, the boy we made, and see him staring out into the blank air where the sunlight streaks up now, spears of light slicing the early morning sky? I see him, Jacob says, he's about to meet us, and I say, So who wants him? I want that he should live, but Jacob, he says, But we all want what we want, and what he wants this time he gets, because he has discovered how to get it, and I am about to ask him what this means when the bird soars into a steep turn and my throat locks up, and we're skimming now past the windows so close that I can see deep into my Manny's eyes, and what do I see? I see wheatfields, ocean, river, city, skullcap, velvet-covered Torahs, the inside of an office, handshake, daughter, jungle, Maby, forest, I see eyes, dishes, a closet full of dark suits, pieces of a guitar. I see purple and darkness and gold and metal, I smell onions and flowers, fruit, and feel the stone, the scrape of metal, the slick of blood on fingers as glass slits skin.

Tell him no, Jacob, I say, as we swoop past in our perch within the skull of the soaring bird and see our Manny who lifts the satchel back past his shoulder and prepares to lay into the window as if with a frontier axe. Tell him no, I urge him, he is our only son, and he's not only a son but a father and not only a father but a husband and a lover, and if he goes he'll take these people with him, in their grief their lives will come undone, and in that moment that seems like ice it was so frozen my Jacob says, Listen to you, you never were a liar, but listen, you don't care about the others, all you care about is what you'll feel if he does it? *nu*? and I shake my head, I'm shaking all over, it's not easy to ride within this throbbing bird in flight even when it's hovering quite still, and I say, No, if he dies, I'll die with him, and my Jacob says, No, no, that's not the worst part, the worst part is that you'll live.

Call him please.

All right, so I'll call him. But I'm warning you.

Me, you're warning? You never warned me before. So go 'head.

So here goes.

And he opens his mouth to speak, and the bird lets out a cry as terrifying as any I've ever heard, a voice of caves and murder and turds and tar, bones melted by radiation, wild and monstrous, devouring mutant cells, a people turned against their god, a god turned against a people.

This is how you call him, Jacob? My own body trembles yet with the noise of it.

Look, he heard me, Jacob says, and we notice that even as Manny stands poised, a man frozen for an instant, time-bound but timeless (and in that instant all his life passes before *my* eyes, baby, boy, student, father, pride-bound man with shock-white hair and white shirt, the trousers dark, dark), he opens his own mouth and moves his lips and through the as-yet-tranquil glass we see the words appear.

Pa-pa?

And I say to Jacob, or to the bird, whatever, I say, Tell him I'm here, too, that I'm with you, he didn't call me this morning, he said goodbye this morning but he didn't call when he got to the office. Tell him.

And the bird gives another of those fear-making shrieks, and I am sorry that I have asked, my skin is crawling, and even the old dried up parts of me inside they suddenly twitch and shrivel, and my fists are balled up into tinier fists, and those fists into even smaller balls of flesh.

Ma-ma, too?

We can read his lips.

Yes, Mama, too. I shout at him soundlessly. Both of us.

I'm coming, he makes with his lips.

And around and down he swings the satchel and makes a large bulge, then a crack, in the glass.

OOOsssh!

At this height the wind even on this seemingly calm morning comes whistling in around him, a stream of air he wades into deeper as he raises the satchel and makes another mighty smack. My Manny, my woodsman! Up and whack! once more, and the window gives outward, no star-shaped pattern now, because that design was another kind of accident, and it could have been a cross as well as a star or a half-moon, crescent and star, or in another life and time the anaconda and the star of David, or who knows but in some other world where birds are kings and gods are human beings, or so they imagine, where a feather and wing might be a sign of prayer, of devotion, or in the comical chance of a universe some crazy person could make up, in the book of a writer in Alaska or someone sitting in a madhouse rest home hospital dayroom, the sun streaming in like wine, and the wind a crescent-shaped fruit wearing an officer's cap, or in the daydream of a lover just returned from a run, a man with a broad young face beneath an ancient's shock of colorless hair, an emblem of someone no more than what he was, like the rest of us, lucky and an error, flesh and bones and mostly chance, the regard for a survivor, and now gone up or about to disappear like wind, smoke, water.

He was himself and all these things, or could have been or should have been, and all the while he was my Manny, I gave him birth but never knew him, and who can know except but we make up the motives and they are like feathers in the wind, twigs on a stream near the park near our house, this way that, falling leaves making erratic descent in an autumn thunderstorm — only the fanatic makes a pattern he believes in, and the mother is a fanatic of a kind we never see, except thank God, or bird, not like the killers in Europe, those who gave you your numbers, they were like lovers and mothers to a dream of murder, nursing it at all cost, or the dancers in the saffron robes where for a while you, my Sadie, made your life, you, thin, hair shorn, incense in your nose, bells on your toes.

Oh, to be a fanatic, oh to give yourself over to the force of another, to a pattern made by another! And that way to know what you mean!

Is this what he's thinking now as he stands with the wind on his face, the fear flowing out of him like blood from the wounds on his face and neck from the flash and splinter of the glass he's smashed? He could be thinking, I have made my own way, skimming, skipping through traditions and professions and families and lovers like a stone spit out of a hard man's swift-wristed fist, a stone he's spun upon the flashing dancing waters. He could be thinking, There is still room behind me (even as he hears the sound of the watchman approaching, because the breaking window has set off a fire alarm, a small blinking red light on a board many floors below, and he knows this), then changing again, thinking, I do not have much more time or any room at all, and I can't go back, make it up, go before a judge, seek a daughter, find shelter elsewhere, live my life, but there is this wind, and he cannot think anymore, all his life it has been go forward, go forward, a disease of motion, this is America, onward, upward, and he stares into the wind and into the light from the rising blood-gut ball of the new morning sun.

So.

His white hair streaming, his white shirt streaked with his own blood, he lets the satchel fall to the glass-littered carpet and steps forward one foot more and turning sideways inserts himself like a letter to his father into the jagged-edged opening.

Pushes against the wind, and looks up as he does so, searching for one split second the sky for the bird of passage.

And he pushes once more against the wind, this time as though he wants to climb back up into me,

his mother.

Prayer for the Living

All these years a million times I must have heard the words. But a woman doesn't say. I run my fingers around the jagged outline of this shattered star. On my lips, water. Ashes on my tongue. In my nostrils flecks of incense. In my ears, the tinkling of bells, the rustling of cloth. Could it be saffron? I see nothing dark or light so cannot say. What, anyway, is the feeling of saffron? Old woman, blind, sick with a swollen heart, bowels now clogged with growths like tubers of a tree, old woman shaking off a dream lying in bed in the green west hills of Jersey, in America, Western Hemisphere—so she doesn't know these things? so she hasn't been alive, a student of life for what feels like a million years?—on the planet earth. She moves her lips in prayer, though a woman musn't say it, and no one may be listening, a prayer for him, for me, for them, for you, for all of us poor creatures bound by stupid gravity to the mercies of a traveling sun.